DOCTOR MISTAKE

J. SAMAN

Cover design: Lori Jackson

Photographer: Rafa Catala

Model: Alex Badia

Editing: My Brother's Editor

Proofing: Danielle Leigh

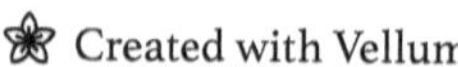 Created with Vellum

1

The second my pager goes off, I know it's going to be bad news. Nothing good is ever paged at the end of your shift. I stop in the middle of the hall—my back sore and my neck stiff after fourteen hours on my feet—to check the pager when a nurse comes barreling down the hall.

"Dr. Carter, they need you in the ED stat. They have a thirty-three-week pregnant woman with severe painless vaginal bleeding."

"Previa?" I question, reading through the page that says the exact same thing she's telling me.

"Don't know. She's not our patient."

"Tell them I'm on my way."

Without another word, or even so much as a complaint since my shift technically ends in ten minutes, I run for the elevator, hitting the button. Just as the doors open and I step on, Grace Hammond, my resident—and my younger brother Oliver's best friend—steps on beside me.

"You got paged too?" she asks, her voice soft and slightly melodic the way it always is even after a long day of delivering babies and performing surgeries. She leans back against the wall, folding her arms over her chest.

"Yep," I reply, shifting slightly so I'm not so close to her. So the scent of her floral, coconut shampoo doesn't infiltrate my senses. I hate being so aware of her. Still I can't help but surreptitiously take her in. Grace's blonde hair is wrapped up in a tight bun; her blue scrubs a shade darker than her luminous eyes that never seemed dulled by the grueling hours or the fluorescent lights.

I look away, chastising myself for the tenth time today.

"I thought you were off at seven."

"I am," I tell her. "But I got paged, so that's how it goes."

"Previa?" she guesses, clearly having the same thought I was. Heavy, painless vaginal bleeding in a pregnant woman in her third trimester can be signs of a lot of things, but a placenta previa—where the placenta covers the cervix—is usually at the top of my differential diagnosis.

"Probably, but we'll see once we get in there. She's not a patient on our service."

Just then, the doors to the emergency department open and we're immediately greeted by Margot, my sister Rina's best friend and a nurse here in the ED. She starts talking a mile a minute, setting off at a good pace as she updates us on the patient while we head toward the trauma room.

"Thirty-year-old thirty-three-week pregnant woman, G1P0 presented complaining of heavy, painless vaginal bleeding. Vitals so far are stable, but she's losing blood as quickly as we can give it to her, and her heart rate is tachy in the one thirties. Her blood pressure is a little low but holding at 96/62. Stat ultrasound confirms baby is not in any distress, but the placenta presents very low. Likely the cause of the bleeding, but since we can't do a transvaginal ultrasound, difficult to tell if it's a full previa. Patient reports no prior knowledge or diagnosis of a previa."

"Alright," I say, as we approach the trauma rooms. "Have you notified the OR yet?"

"Yes. They're already on standby and so are peds and the NICU. They're just waiting on you."

"You look a little flustered, Margot," I comment dryly, noting her flushed cheeks and messy dark curls. "All going smoothly down here?"

She flips me off without missing a step. "It's July, Carter. Do you know what that means?"

I laugh under my breath as does Grace. "New interns," Grace replies, because yeah, we have them too, though Grace seems to like her newbie, Dylan. I hate July. And August, for that matter.

"Yes," Margot expels dramatically. "New fucking interns who think they're God's gift to medicine and that nurses are placed on this earth to do their bidding. I had to literally smack one of their hands away because he was about to attempt a pelvic exam on this woman. Can you imagine?" She looks to each of us, horror in her brown eyes. "Did he not realize that sticking his hand into a bleeding vagina with a high likelihood of a previa could possibly cause a placental rupture?"

This is why Margot is a kick-ass nurse.

"Obviously not," I comment. "He'll quickly learn that nurses save lives that interns attempt to collect. Thank you for that." And I mean that genuinely. I can't count the number of times nurses have not only saved my ass, but the asses of fellow doctors.

"Any time. Though I highly doubt it will be the last today I have to stop one of them from doing something stupid. The patient is in here." She points to the door, and we stop in front of the trauma room. "Her name is Marissa, and she's scared shitless. Her husband was at a conference, and we were finally able to get through to him. He's on his way now."

"Thanks," Grace says, spinning around pushing open the

door of the trauma room with her back as she talks to Margot. "You still coming tomorrow night?"

"I think so. I have to see what time I get off. Rina will be there for sure though. Same with the other girls."

Grace gives Margot a wink and then we plow through the doors, straight into action. I nearly have to shove two interns out of the way—Margot wasn't kidding with how fucking inept they are—and then Grace and I get to work. We assess the mother's condition as well as the fetus's. Within minutes we determine that yes, she's losing too much blood from her previa to be stopped down here or even at all.

We have about ten minutes max to get this baby out of her before the mother goes into shock from blood loss and the baby goes into distress.

"Marissa," Grace soothes, coming right up to the patient's face, hovering over her and gently squeezing her shoulder. "We're taking you up to the OR now. You're going to deliver the baby."

"No," Marissa cries through her oxygen mask. "It's too soon."

"Unfortunately, we don't have a choice. We need to do what's best for both you and the baby, and that's delivering it. I know you're scared, but we'll be with you every step of the way. Don't worry, we're going to do everything we can for you both. You're in excellent hands."

Grace gives her that warm smile, the one that always gets through to patients, and then we're moving. Margot and another nurse are pushing the gurney as we all head for the elevator at a quick pace.

"You scrubbing in on this or is someone else taking over for you?" Grace asks me.

"I'll take it. I've come this far." We all step onto the elevator, the doors shutting. "What are you doing tomorrow night with my sister?" I question softly as my eyes cling to the glowing numbers as we ascend.

"Girls' night. We even managed to force Amelia to come."

Amelia is Oliver's girlfriend. Oliver and Grace have been best friends since infancy. And forever, people just assumed they'd be a thing, but it never happened. They view and treat each other as siblings.

You'd think that would have made Grace an unofficial part of the family and I guess in a way it has. But not for me. I went away to college and then medical school. Did my residency down in Virginia Beach, only returning to Boston last year as an attending.

So I wasn't expecting it. *Her.*

It had been years and years since I had seen Grace.

I wasn't expecting her to be... fuck, everything that she is. Smart. Beautiful. An insanely talented doctor. Funny. Sarcastic. Beautiful. I might have mentioned that once already, but hell does it bear repeating. As someone who has already been down the road of wanting someone you know you can never have, craving her the way I do is like a kick in the teeth.

On a daily basis.

"And Tony doesn't care that you're having this girls' night?" I try to keep all the bitterness from my voice. I try very hard, but Margot's head flies sharply in my direction, her gaze discerning as she cocks an eyebrow, so I'm not sure I quite hit my mark.

Tony is Grace's fiancé, so yeah, again, never gonna happen between me and her.

"He's got some work dinner thing he's going to."

"Right. Of course he does. Can't make partner without putting in all the hours."

Grace rolls her eyes at me, but it's true. The bastard is never around. At least not that I've noticed.

"Uh-huh. What time did your shift end this evening,

Doctor? Fifteen minutes ago, is it now? And you're, oh look, heading into surgery."

"Different. Medicine is a noble profession. Chasing ambulances, and then going after the doctors who saved the life of the injured, isn't."

Before she can lay into me for that, the elevator doors open and now we're back in game-on mode. We race down the hall while the OR nurses take the patient and prep her for surgery. By the time we walk into that OR, she'll be under anesthesia because we don't have time to wait for an epidural or spinal block to take effect.

Grace and I don scrub caps and boots before going about the process of scrubbing in.

"Do you feel you're ready to take point on this?" I ask, lathering my hands with antiseptic soap, washing every inch.

"Without a doubt," she answers confidently, scrubbing vigorously beside me and refusing to meet my eyes.

She's pissed at me for the Tony comment, but I don't care. I don't have to. I'm the attending and she's the resident and that's how our dynamic works. If we weren't in the hospital, she'd mouth off back to me until her face was red, but not here.

"I can have that baby out in under ninety seconds."

"I'm going to time you."

Now she meets my eyes, glaring blue fire into me. I smirk before I can stop it, thankfully she can't see it behind my mask.

"You do that, Carter." She presses her foot onto the pedal, rinsing off the soap.

"If you can do it safely in eighty seconds, I'll buy you something special for your birthday."

She shakes her head, her arms bent at the elbow, sterile hands held up and out in front of her. "You're such a condescending dick," she murmurs under her breath as she plows past me, headed for the OR.

"What was that? I'm not sure I heard you correctly."

"I said you're such a considerate doctor," she yells at me over her shoulder, and now I can't stop my laugh.

But the second we meet the OR floor, all humor is gone from my lips.

"Hi, Dr. Fritz," Angelica, one of the nurses, says to me, batting her long lashes at me flirtatiously as she goes about tying my gown and helping me with my sterile gloves. "I'm *so* glad you're in here performing this surgery. I know the patient is in the best of hands with you as her doctor."

"Actually, I'm the one doing the surgery, Angelica," Grace smoothly interjects. "Dr. Fritz is simply here to supervise me. So, if you're ready to get back to work, I'd like to start." With the patient fully prepped and ready, Grace gets into position, holding out her hand. "Ten blade, please."

The scrub nurse obliges, and all other commentary ceases as Grace sets to work while I watch on, here to jump in at any time if needed, but I already know I won't be. Grace, while only heading into her third year of residency, is as competent as any fourth year or attending. She's by far the best OB-GYN resident in the hospital.

Just as she makes the incision, the pediatrics and NICU teams roll in. The patient is holding her own, getting another unit of type-specific blood while Grace works diligently and methodically to get the baby out. That's actually the easy part. The fastest part. After that is where the real work for us begins.

Especially with a case like this. We have to remove the placenta without causing more damage or further bleeding.

"How's my patient doing, Larry?" Grace asks the anesthesiologist just as we get a couple of beeps on the monitor.

"Blood pressure dipped a little, but I'll get it back up."

"That would be greatly appreciated." Grace locates the fetus, working with skilled, precise movements. "If you're not too bored over there, Carter, maybe you could cauterize that bleeder for me?"

"I've got it," the nurse says, doing her job.

"I think *Dr. Fritz* is well beyond cauterizing bleeders," Angelica simpers. "I've seen him perform the most complex of surgeries with ease."

"Hey, Larry?" Grace cuts in once again, completely ignoring Angelica who has always been a flirty kiss ass. "Did *Dr. Fritz* ever tell you why he decided to become an OB-GYN when the field is predominantly female providers?"

"Here we go..." I mutter.

"Yes. Here we go." Grace extracts the baby, blue and wet, handing him directly to the waiting pediatric team. They immediately start working on him. "Time of delivery, nineteen-thirty-two." She glances up at me. "Seventy-eight seconds, Carter. I believe you owe me one hell of a birthday present."

"I'll let you use the robot in my next surgery."

She shakes her head. "No way. I want something better from you, Doctor. Something real I can sink my teeth into."

So do I, I think and then quickly shut that bitch up. "A steak then?" I offer. "Since we know Tony won't be around to take you to dinner."

I get a death glare for that.

"Wait, back up," Larry jumps in, before Grace can unleash more of her wrath. "Why *are* you an OB-GYN, Carter? You that into pregnant chicks and pussy?"

Grace, as well as every nurse in here, throws Larry a scathing look.

"I'm going to pretend you didn't just say that, because it makes you sound like a total misogynistic asshole," Grace barks while she goes about removing the placenta and tying off any active bleeding vessels. "But no. He actually walked in the room when his mother was in the throes of delivering Rina and after that decided birthing babies was his life's calling."

I hate that story.

It always makes me sound like such a pussy—pun intended.

Plus, Rina works in this hospital as an ICU nurse, so I know this will somehow funnel back to her, which never fails to make her laugh at my expense.

Speaking of... all the nurses, right on cue, start oohing and awing, humor dancing in their eyes. The NICU team who have an umbilical line placed and are giving the baby—who is pinking up and half crying—oxygen to help him along, are also joining in on the dig my resident just took at me.

She's not dumb either. Grace has to know I'll punish her for this. Professionally speaking, of course. I'm not actually allowed to punish her the way I'd like.

My comments about Tony must have really pissed her off this time.

Still, when you're engaged to a total dipshit, douchebag who takes you for granted and is never around, you should learn to get used to people making disparaging comments about him. Even Oliver can't stand the guy and Oliver generally likes everyone.

"That true, man?" Larry inquires, not bothering to hide his chuckle.

"Yes, it's true, and now I'm one of the top surgeons and OB-GYNs in Boston that you" —I point at Grace— "have the pleasure of learning from and watching in action. Just wait till you see what I have in store for you tomorrow, Dr. Hammond."

Grace peers up, likely to say something else that will boil my blood when pediatrics cuts us both off. "Five-minute APGAR is six. We're moving the baby up to the NICU. Have someone page us when mom is awake."

They roll out and we finish our surgery, everyone quiet as the team works, the tension in the room so thick you could cut it with a scalpel. Just as Grace finishes the last stitch, I turn and march out of the room, tearing off my surgical gear and going straight for the sink to scrub out.

Then I slink back, tucked in the corner along the shadows.

Two minutes later Grace comes out, glances around and when she doesn't spot me, she sighs. In relief or regret, I cannot tell, but she goes for the sink, rolling her neck until it pops as she begins to scrub out. And when her hands are lathered in soap, and she has nowhere else to go, I move in behind her, towering over her with my height. I take a deep inhale, marveling how she still manages to smell sweet and clean after a day spent in the hospital and my cock twitches in my scrubs.

She feels me behind her, not touching her but merely inches away, and she stiffens. "I thought you'd gone."

"Not quite yet," I whisper, my lips dipping down till they're hovering by her ear, watching as goose bumps dance across her neck. "Pull another stunt like that and I'll have you running scut along with the interns for the rest of your residency. As it is, tomorrow you're on postpartums. No surgeries."

"Carter—"

"The proper response is *yes, Dr. Fritz*. Anything else is completely unacceptable."

"Yes, Dr. Fritz," she grits out through clenched teeth, and I grin, making sure she feels it on my lips. That's how stupidly close I am to her right now. So stupidly close I feel her sharp intake of breath and quickly force myself to get control and step back.

I shouldn't have done that.

Each time I give in just an inch, I lose ground on forcing her into her neat and tidy role in my life. Brother's best friend. Resident. Engaged.

Off-motherfucking-limits.

"Good work in there, Doctor. Keep it up and I will take you out for that steak."

With that, I turn and leave the hospital, needing to clear my head. Clear it of her.

Because that's all I can ever do with her. Even when the desire for more is growing increasingly unbearable.

2

Pressing my back into the wall, I straighten my spine while adjusting the phone against my ear. My back is freaking killing me and if I don't take a moment to relax and realign myself, bad things can happen. I know that firsthand.

"What time do you think you'll be home?" I ask Tony, closing my eyes and doing my deep breathing exercises.

"I have no idea. You know how long these stupid dinners can go. Especially when they turn into drinks afterward. I'm just hoping before the bars close."

I grin at the way he says that. Like he hates it when he actually loves it. Tony is nothing if not the life of the party. He loves the dinners and drinks after. He loves schmoozing clients and networking. If he hadn't become a lawyer, he would have been a brilliant salesman.

"What about you?"

"Not late. You know me. It's just some drinks and dinner with the girls."

"Drinks?" he presses, concern in his voice.

I lean my head back against the wall and take another deep

breath. "Just one and I'll nurse it. It's been a long week and I don't want to push anything."

"That's why I worry about you having a drink.

Have you had any auras like the one you had last week?"

"No, but I've been doing my deep breathing and eating well and whenever I can sleep, I have been. I'm fine."

What Tony means by auras are actually focal awareness seizures and with me, they tend to be a precursor to a tonic-clonic seizure or what used to be referred to as grand mal seizures. Tony hasn't actually ever seen me have one. Hence why the man sounds nervous now. Then again, I haven't had one in four years, almost to the day. My last was on my birthday when I got wasted with friends in medical school. Oliver saved my ass that night and I woke up in the hospital with his stony face right in mine.

It was stupid. I knew better. Too much alcohol, too much caffeine, too little sleep, too much stress—whatever bad thing you can throw at your body—always triggers my epilepsy.

Since then I've put myself on a strict regimen. Very little alcohol. Regular—when I can get it—sleep. And when I can't, relaxation techniques, medication, yoga, stretches, exercise, whatever I have to do to keep my mind and body balanced. Managing my menstrual cycles—hormones were nasty fuckers during adolescence and I'm not talking about with my moods or my skin.

"Did that asshole, Carter, actually put you on scut all day?"

Yeah, there isn't a lot of love between Carter and Tony. Not a lot of love between Tony and any of my friends, for that matter. Tony likes to put off the alpha male, she's mine and no one else can have her vibe when he's around people. But with me, he's a sweet, loving teddy bear.

I snort out a laugh. "Of course, he did. I embarrassed him in the OR. There was no way he was going to let me get away with that. Today was my penance."

"I still don't understand your thing with him."

"He's my attending. My boss, for lack of a better term, but he's also Oliver's older brother and has known me since birth. It makes for a weird dynamic."

"As long as that's all it makes for."

I smirk, pushing away from the wall and checking my watch. "You have nothing to worry about. I gotta go shower if I'm going to meet up with the girls."

"Okay. I have to roll out too. Have fun tonight. I'll try not to wake you when I come in. Love you."

"Love you too."

I disconnect the call, slipping my phone back into my pocket, and glance down the hall toward the nurses' station. I can hear some of them laughing, Carter's voice present as the ringleader, and I roll my eyes. I bet he's not even saying anything funny. He's like all the Fritz men, and there are five of them.

Smart. Sexy. Charismatic. Gorgeous beyond all sin and reason. Those bastards can make a woman's panties wet with a simple glance or quirk of their lips.

Women swoon while swarming around them.

Men too for that matter.

But Carter, for all his cocky swagger and charming bravado, has this thing about him. This thing that makes every woman do a double-take and then stare whenever he enters a room. A commanding presence you can't help but acknowledge and admire. The very textbook definition of tall, dark, and irresistibly handsome.

Imposing. The kind of imposing that makes your nipples tighten and your skin buzz.

Maybe that comes naturally when you're born brilliant, gorgeous, famous, and a billionaire, but it doesn't do much for me. Well, at least not the latter two. Something about the first two on him always makes me want to ruffle his feathers. Chip away at that obnoxious arrogance and perfect façade.

Discover the man hidden beneath.

And look where it got you today.

Yeah. On scut. Not that I mind checking in on all our post-partum patients. I love seeing the new parents and babies. I love answering their questions and helping them through what is easily the hardest transition of their lives. But I live and breathe and die for the OR. For the rush I get every damn time I step foot in that room and Carter knows it.

I hear him start to make his escape and that's when I make mine, rushing down the hall to the locker room. I've been dodging my attending all day and so far, it's worked out well for me. With any luck, I won't have to see him again until Monday since I'm not working this weekend—a rarity for me.

The door to the locker room shuts behind me and I go for the showers, needing to wash a week of long hours and fatigue away. I wish I had time to go home before meeting the girls, but I don't, so this will have to do. After getting myself dressed in a red tube top with a shelf bra—because my girls have been crammed in a bra for the last thirteen hours, I just can't do it to them now—white ripped capri jeans and flats because heels can suck a dick, I blow out my long, blonde hair and apply whatever will cover my bags and make me shine pretty.

By the time I exit the locker room, I feel like a million bucks.

That is until I run into an asshole.

Carter is leaning casually against the wall on the opposite side of the entrance to the women's locker room, staring at his phone like he hasn't a care in the world and isn't waiting on me when we both know he is.

"Trolling the women's locker room, Fritz? That's kinda skeevie."

Dark chocolate eyes skip away from his phone, making a

slow trip, landing on my feet before gliding up, taking in every inch of my primped appearance until he meets my eyes, his just a touch darker and his cheeks suddenly flushed.

And before I know what the hell is happening, my stomach hiccups with a strange tingle.

He licks his lips and clears his throat. "You've been avoiding me all day."

I mirror his pose on the wall across from him, giving us a good ten feet of much-needed space.

"Yep."

"Things go smoothly with your patients or just pissed at your attending?"

"Yes."

He nods, pushing away from the wall, stalking like a lion in my direction until he's mere inches away. I straighten my position, meeting his eyes and trying to resist the urge to look away from their pounding intensity.

"Make sure my sister gets home okay tonight," he purrs, his warm, minty breath fanning across my face. "Brecken is with me, Oliver, Luca, and Kaplan at the Sox game."

Brecken is Rina's live-in boyfriend.

"No Landon?"

"Landon is home with Stella and Layla. My mom isn't up for watching them tonight and since Amelia is out with you, Landon offered to play babysitter."

The matriarch of the Fritz family, Octavia, is battling a recurrence of breast cancer. She had a double mastectomy a couple of months back and has been undergoing chemo since. Her five sons and daughter have been doing all they can to help, but Landon is very careful who he allows to watch his thirteen-year-old daughter, Stella. Amelia is the guardian of her younger sister Layla, who is fourteen and close friends with Stella, but I guess since Amelia is with us Landon is in charge of the teenagers.

"How is your mom? I was meaning to stop by, but this week got away from me." Octavia is also like a mother to me. More of a mother to me than my own.

"She's hanging in there. Two more rounds of chemo and then more scans."

I sigh, my gut twisting like someone punched it. "I'll keep my fingers crossed. She's always in my prayers."

Carter reaches out, taking an errant strand of hair that must be plastered to my forehead and tucks it behind my ear. And just like yesterday when he was standing behind me, I explode into chills, the rush of heat simmering beneath my skin doing nothing to warm them away.

His hand falls almost instantly, but it's too late. He spots my reaction to him. The self-satisfied grin on his face tells me so. He chuckles lightly, running a hand through his perfectly messed hair.

"I have a patient with stage IV endometriosis," he announces, his voice smooth as silk as it falls over me. "She has a large number of cysts and severe adhesions. She's thirty-two and looking to get pregnant."

"So uterine wall, cervical lining as well as fallopian tube and ovary preservation are key?"

"Exactly." He grins at my quick response, his head tilting in my direction as he folds his arms over his chest. "You interested? Seven a.m. Monday? Laparoscopic. I might use the robot if I can get it."

Is it weird that that just totally turned me on?

"I'm in."

Another step and now he's towering over me. My heart skips a beat as my back presses deeper into the wall. "I'll send you the patient file. I expect you to have memorized it as well as the procedure forwards and backward before stepping foot in my OR."

"Of course."

His head dips down, his face now inches from mine. "If you ever disrespect me in my OR again, I will make your last two years of residency a living hell. You're talented, Hammond, but don't confuse your relationship with my family as an easy pass with me."

Shit. I gulp down a breath. "Noted. It will never happen again."

"Doctor," he reprimands, his tone powerful, commanding.

"Doctor," I repeat.

His piercing gaze holds mine, my heart hammering faster than a hummingbird's until he's gone in an instant, heading straight for the stairs instead of the elevator. It's only now that I realize he's changed from his scrubs, dressed for the Red Sox game tonight.

Evidently, I couldn't look away from his face long enough to notice.

"Have fun tonight, Grace," he calls over his shoulder without bothering to look back. "You look beautiful in red." His voice rings out in the hall only to be snuffed out seconds later by the slamming of the stairwell door.

Cocky jerk.

~

"Jesus, your fucking brother," I bark at Rina though there is zero bite to my voice. It's not her fault I have the most complicated relationship on the planet with my attending.

"Which one?" she asks dryly, taking a seat in our booth at The Hill, our usual bar which just so happens to be a stone's throw from the hospital.

"Carter. Who else?"

"I have five brothers, Grace. Five *older* brothers. So when someone calls out to Jesus while dropping f-bombs about my brothers, I have to ask."

Touché.

"I thought Carter was supposed to be the nice one," I grouse, picking up the laminated menu on the table and pretending to peruse it when I actually know the damn thing by heart.

"He is, I guess." She shrugs. "I don't know."

"Well, you'd never know it. He's... intense."

"Ever since he came back from Virginia Beach last year, he's been kind of different. He was in love with his best friend and fellow resident down there and he never made his play for her. Then she met someone else. I think that did something weird to him. He was far more easy going before that happened. That or he's just a dick who enjoys the power trip of being an attending."

"I smarted off to him in the OR yesterday. I don't even know why. It's like my mouth got the best of me."

Rina laughs, flagging down the waitress. "Two cosmos, please."

"Rina—"

Her green eyes meet mine, her nose scrunching up. "Too much?"

Is it? I wouldn't mind, but yeah. I don't think hard alcohol after the week I've had is wise. I turn to the waitress. "I'll have a Sauvignon Blanc instead, and we'll have one of every appetizer. Thank you."

"Sorry, I didn't mean to just order for you like that."

I wave Rina away. "It's fine. I might have done it if I haven't had the longest week ever. I'm afraid of overdoing it. My new fellow third year, Janet Johnson, is like something out of *Heathers*. The bitchy rich girl who thinks she owns everything and everyone, and doesn't seem to know her stuff as well as she pretends. She's been here for a couple months and I bet she still can't decipher a vagina from an asshole without a map and a flashlight. I had to pick up her slack all week and her residents weren't much help either. Honestly, who transfers programs going into their third year?"

"Did you mention that to Carter?"

I shake my head. "Can't and you know it. Then I look like I'm complaining or can't handle the work. The worst thing a resident can ever do with her attending is show weakness."

Rina snorts, falling back in her chair as she appraises me. "Now you understand why I'm a nurse." She runs her hands through her long blonde hair, looking just as tired as I am. "Are you coming for Sunday dinner at my parents'?"

"I think so. Oliver mentioned it to me last night when he called to ask if it was too soon to actually make Amelia his real fiancée."

Rina cackles the way I did on the phone when he asked.

Oliver got himself involved in quite the scandal when he and Amelia pretended to be engaged at our ten-year high school reunion. Since it's Oliver, a guy who was photographed with a different woman on his arm every other day of the week, the media was all over one of their favorite Fritz bachelors suddenly being engaged. The two of them kept up the charade in order to keep the media and his mom happy, but they ended up falling in love. Amelia is still wearing the ring, but it's more of a placeholder Oliver is anxious to fill.

"He can't do that yet. They've only been together a few months."

"I know. That's exactly what I told him. Besides, I doubt... Amelia! Hey!" I throw Rina a quick *oh shit, I hope she didn't hear any of that* glance before jumping out of the booth to give the petite redhead a hug. "So glad you're here."

"Me too." She huffs. "I feel like it took forever to get out of the house. Oliver is like having a puppy, he needs constant love and attention and whines when you go out. He's probably chewing up my shoes as we speak." Amelia drops into her seat and despite her teasing words, there is no hiding the happy smile on her face.

"Didn't you just get a real puppy?"

"Yes, only Gulliver already weighs more than Layla, so calling that beast a puppy seems wrong. He's also better behaved than Oliver. Where are the others?"

"On their way," Rina explains. "They too have puppies that require love and attention before they can escape. I had to put mine on a leash and promise dirty sex when I come home before I could sneak out."

"Mine doesn't seem to have that problem," I let slip when I likely shouldn't have. Still, I can't help but feel the sting of jealousy at their words.

Both wince before quickly covering up their reactions. "How is Tony?" Amelia asks, staring down at the menu, unable to meet my eyes.

"Good. Out at a work thing tonight."

"Have you guys set a date yet?"

This time, instead of a sting, it's a straight-up sucker punch. The truth is, I can't remember the last time Tony and I talked about our wedding or even setting a date. He proposed, we got engaged, and that's how we've been ever since.

Generally, people have stopped asking me now that Tony and I have been engaged for over a year and a half and still aren't married nor have a date to be. But Amelia hasn't asked yet. Not once and I'm curious if this is Oliver or her. Oliver was riding me a little about it last night, but Oliver is my best friend and he can get away with it.

Octavia too has made all sorts of offers to me including the Fritz compound, their Vineyard home, or even their yacht for potential wedding venues. It's sweet and wonderful and since my family doesn't care if I marry him or anyone else or die miserable and alone, it's a comfort to know I have them in my corner.

But it doesn't make it hurt any less.

"He wants to make partner first and we think that will happen by the fall. Plus, this year of my residency will be insane. Maybe next spring or summer?" Yes, it comes out as a question because I'm completely pulling that out of my ass. And yes, I perpetually blame our busy schedules for our lack of planned nuptials, but deep down, part of me wonders if that's just the bullshit I've been feeding myself. If we'll continue like this, stalled and stuck in some relationship purgatory, resting on our excuses that don't always add up to a valid reason.

Her head pops up. "Oh, that's exciting. Not the insane residency part obviously. It would be hilarious to see Oliver as your maid of honor."

"It would be awesome," Rina chimes in. "Though I don't think I'd want him there for the bachelorette party."

I crinkle my nose at that, as does Amelia, grateful that our drinks and some of the food arrive just in time and Amelia orders herself a cosmo to match Rina's.

"Is Carter still running you crazy?" Amelia questions, popping some truffle fries into her mouth.

"That's one word for what that man does to me," I droll. "He pushes me harder than any other resident, including his fourth-years. Thank God I have a good intern this year or I'd really be screwed."

"Maybe Carter does that because he sees the most potential in you?" Amelia offers with a hopeful smile. "You did say he lets you fly solo a lot."

I take a sip of my wine, setting my glass down, but holding it in my hand. "He does and I'm grateful for that. He's an amazing doctor and attending and I learn so much from him. I just wish all of our interactions weren't as tense as they always are."

"You don't even get to escape him on your days off since you'll both be at Sunday dinner," Rina says, crunching on a chip loaded with guacamole.

Amelia snickers and just then the other girls arrive. Margot, Halle, and Aria, who are all Rina's friends but by extension have become mine—especially Margot—and Amelia's. After that, there is no more conversation about my engagement to Tony or what working with Carter is like.

But still... I can't help but think about Carter's words to me yesterday.

How deeply they stung. Why I lashed out so strongly. It's more than just Carter knowing exactly how to push my buttons to get a rise out of me.

Even Amelia's questions tonight hurt.

Tony and I have been engaged for so long and that's all it's been, a placeholder on my finger. Same as what Amelia has on hers, but Oliver can't wait to take the next steps, whereas Tony seems content to maintain our status quo. Add to that, between both of our schedules, I see him now less than I ever did before.

I want what Amelia and Oliver have. I want what Rina and Brecken have.

Now I just have to figure out how to get it.

Before it's too late.

I stir uncomfortably, my mind clinging to a troubling dream just as a hand on my face jolts me awake.

"Hey," Tony says softly, his face hovering above mine. "I'm sorry to wake you."

I blink, my head swiveling left and right only to refocus on Tony. "You're dressed? What time is it?"

"It's early. A little after eight, but I have to get into the office."

I frown, sliding up in bed and pressing my back against the fabric headboard, taking the sheet with me for comfort as I try to remember what I was dreaming about only to come up empty. Still, I can't keep the annoyance and hurt from my voice as I say, "It's Saturday."

It's also the first full weekend I've had off in I don't even know how long.

"I know, but we're working on a big case."

I sigh, rubbing my hands up and down my face, clearing my head of any residual fogginess. Tony sits on the edge of the bed, taking my hand and pulling it away from my face, linking our fingers together.

"You mad?"

"A little. I was hoping to spend the day with you. I didn't even hear you come in last night."

"That's because when I came home, you were already passed out. I'm all yours tonight and tomorrow," he promises, his blue eyes regretful, guilty. "I shouldn't be home too late. I'll try for four. How's that? You can take the day for yourself. Go to a yoga class or whatever. You need a break."

"So do you," I counter.

He smiles, leaning in and kissing the tip of my nose the way he always does. "Soon. I'm so close to this promotion and once I get it, we'll have more time for us."

More time for us. It's a promise I've been clinging to for years now. Both of us have been. My internship was hard on us. My residency is hard on us. His job is hard on us.

But if we can just make it through...

"Okay. But I want a date tonight. A real date."

He grins, kissing my lips. "You got it. Anywhere you want to go, I'll take you." His eyes track down to our joined hands where he gives me a squeeze. "I love you. I don't deserve you. I know that. But I love you so much."

Well, now I can't be mad that he's working today.

"I love you too."

He plants another kiss on my nose and then he's gone, up and out of the room with the sound of our front door shutting behind him seconds later.

I decide there's no sense moping around and now that I'm awake, I'm awake. Besides, that yoga class he mentioned sounds pretty good and if I move my ass, I can get there in time for the ten o'clock one.

～

THE CITY IS jam-packed with its typical weekend lunchtime rush. For once, I'm not in a hurry. My yoga class was exactly what I needed and after getting more than eight hours of sleep last night, I feel completely recharged.

The door to my favorite cafe swings open with vigor, practically smashing into someone about to exit. I make my apologies and head up to the counter to order my usual salad and soda and then snag an open table.

The sun shines in through the large picture window, creating a delicious warmth over me as I take a moment to people watch before I start to read over the patient file for Carter's surgery Monday morning. The robot. I could practically squeal with excitement. Not even having to face Carter—who has been doing wild, unfamiliar things to my insides lately—can even wipe the smile from my face.

"Thank you," I say to the waitress as she sets my food in front of me.

Just as I take the first bite of my salad, my seat is bumped from behind. "Oh, sorry," the woman apologizes with a warm smile that lights up her honey eyes.

I wave her away. "It's fine," I tell her, going back to my lunch and chart reading as she sits with her friend at the neighboring table. But once she and her friend start talking, I find it futile to focus on anything else. Partially because they're uncharacteristically loud for such a small café and partially because of the subject matter. Now, I'm not typically one to eavesdrop on a conversation that does not involve me, but the way they're speaking, my proximity, and the discussion make it impossible not to.

"Tell me about the guy you left the bar with last night," her friend demands with an obvious smile to her voice. "Did you get lucky with him?"

"Yes. Oh my God, Sheri," the girl who bumped my chair practically squeals in an overexaggerated cadence. "It was hands down the best sex of my life. I mean, you saw him, right?" I can't see her friend, but I'm assuming she's nodding. "He was so hot," she goes on. "Older, but hot. And even hotter in bed."

"Details." Her friend laughs. "I want every single detail now."

I do too, I think with an inward smirk as I take another bite of my salad.

"Well," the girl continues without missing a beat, like the words have been on the tip of her tongue just waiting to spill out. "We left the bar together, but at first, he said he was just going to make sure I got home okay. So when we pulled up in front of my building, I didn't expect anything to happen." She laughs. "I mean, I hoped it would, but I wasn't counting on it, you know?"

"Sure."

"Anyway, he leaned in and kissed me in the back of the Uber and after that, it didn't take much to get him upstairs with me. But once we did get upstairs, he was like a totally different man."

"What do you mean? How so?"

"He ripped off my dress, Sheri. Like into shreds. And then my panties, and before we even got back into my bedroom, his face was between my legs."

"Holy shit," her friend chokes. "I am so freaking jealous. I never get men to go down on me. I swear, it's like they have an aversion or something."

"Well not this guy," the girl says. "He got me off twice like that and then we did it three times. *Three*." She emphasizes the word. "And all kinds of crazy positions, too."

Damn. I'm jealous. I continue to stare at my phone, though by this point, I'm not even registering the words on my screen.

"Did he stay the night?"

"No. He said he had to work early today. He left around

three or so, but swore that if he could stay, he would have bought me breakfast. Then he kissed me goodbye and left."

I almost want to snicker at that. I guess I'm too far removed from the dating and one-night stand scene to relate. A guy saying he'd buy you breakfast doesn't really seem like it should be the big deal she's making it out to be. But maybe I'm wrong. That girl, from the quick glance I got of her, can't be any older than twenty-four. So maybe I'm just out of my depth here.

"Did he leave you his number at least?" her friend Sheri presses with interest.

"Yes, but I haven't used it yet. It's too soon and I don't want to seem desperate. I figure I'll text him tomorrow or something and see if he wants to meet up for a drink sometime this week."

"Good plan. What does he do that he's working on a Saturday?"

"He's a lawyer; like all the guys in the bar last night were. They work for some big firm in Back Bay. He's not a partner yet, but he said he was close. I teased him and said they'd have to add his name to the letterhead once that happens. Parker, Slade, Barker, and Marvelo."

Marvelo? My lungs empty.

No. It can't be. There's no way.

Before she can say anything else, I find myself on my feet, staring down at her. Her blonde head whips around at my sudden movement and she gives me that smile again. She's pretty. My mouth opens to speak, but no sound comes out. I don't even know what to say.

And young. Twenty-four might have been generous.

My mouth opens to speak, but no sound comes out.

"Are you okay?" she asks, but all I can hear is the sound of blood rushing through my ears. My heart is racing out of my chest and my legs feel weak, ready to give out on me any second.

All I can do is shake my head. "I'm sorry, did you just say Marvelo?"

She blinks up at me, surprised, and then blushes as she realizes I overheard her entire conversation. "Um. Yes." She shifts uncomfortably, glancing over to her friend and then back up to me. "I'm sorry, is there a problem?"

Yes. Yes, there's a big fucking problem.

I want to say something to her. I want to tell her that the man she had the best sex of her life with is my fiancé. I want to scream at her. Shake her. Pound my fists into her small body.

But I'm rendered helpless, my thoughts chaotic.

Everything blurs and somehow I'm racing from the café out onto the street, my hand pressed to my chest, my thundering heart beneath it. I can't breathe. Why can't I breathe?

Hot tears begin to rain down my face. I can't stop them. I can't do anything.

I begin to walk, the motion of the crowd forcing me along like the current in the ocean. But all I hear in my head, set on blaring repeat, are her explicit descriptions of their night together. He made her come twice with his mouth. They had sex three times. They did it in all kinds of positions. He kissed her goodbye before he left.

He gave her his number.

Last night. He did this last night when I was out with my friends. No wonder I didn't hear him come home. And then he kissed *me* goodbye this morning. He kissed me goodbye after he kissed her goodbye. He told me he loved me, that fucking son of a bitch.

We're supposed to go on a date tonight. Would we make love after all the things he did with her the night before?

Tony never gives me oral sex. Not anymore, at least. I think maybe in the three years we've been together, he's done it only a handful of times. And not since we got engaged. Every time I've asked him to do it, he says he's too tired. Or too stressed. Or has too much work to get back to. Or that his fucking neck hurts.

He's filled with a million bullshit excuses.

Same with the crazy positions thing. He doesn't do those anymore either. Missionary and occasionally me on top. But that's it.

Our sex life has become decidedly boring and lackluster. And that's when we can find time to fucking have sex.

Every time I've tried to mix things up for us, he's balked. I've tried toys, lingerie, anything I could think of to spice things up and it never worked. Never. The one time I attempted to talk to him about it, other than becoming angry, he said that couples at our stage just don't do the wild sex thing anymore.

And in truth, I let it slide.

I was afraid to rock our happy little boat. I figured it was a rut. We were both so busy and I dumbly assumed once we reached the top of our careers and things settled a bit, our sex life would fall back into place.

But now? Now I wonder how many women there have been. If his sexual indifference with me is a product of sex he's having elsewhere.

How did this happen?

How did I go from a relaxed, easy-going day off to this?

My mind swings back and forth, a runaway pendulum oscillating between completely devastated and inconsolably enraged.

For a fleeting moment, I consider going to his office to confront him. But then I think better of that. I've suffered enough humiliation for one day.

Home. I just want to go home.

So that's what I do. I walk the ten blocks home. This time with purpose. No more aimless wandering. When I get there, I immediately head for his closet. My hands ripping open drawers and rummaging through the contents before I can even comprehend what I'm doing or what I'm looking for.

Condoms. Maybe a note or a phone number of a woman. Clothes that smell like her and not me. Anything.

I need something that will tell me unequivocally, yes, my fiancé is a lying, two-timing piece of shit, cheater. That's what I need. Proof. But I come up empty after tearing apart his closet, his nightstand, and even his office. Nothing.

"Ahhhh!" I scream, pounding my fist on a shelf, somehow back in his closet. Reaching mindlessly, I tear every single piece of clothing down, throwing them in a blind rage. And when there is nothing left on the shelves or hanging from hangers, I drop down into the large pile I made and weep.

I weep so hard and for so long that eventually I must have fallen asleep, because in what seems like the next second, I'm startled awake by the sounds of my fiancé yelling at me. "What the hell is going on in here, Grace?"

His olive skin is ruddy with anger and confusion, and I take a second to look at him. Really trying to see the man beneath. The one he's been hiding from me.

I stand up slowly, my eyes trailing up to his and when I meet his blue eyes, I begin to cry again. Because somehow, just looking at him, I know everything she said was true. I can longer deny it. Write it off in my head. Pretend I misheard.

I know.

"You had an affair," I say, not even bothering to ask it like a question.

He blanches before quickly recovering, all that red-tinted anger disappears along with the blood in his face until he's an ashen white.

"Where did you hear something like that?"

He didn't even deny it.

"At lunch today," I tell him in a calm tone that surprises me, my tears drying instantly. All my anger is laying before me in the form of his clothes on the floor and I can't seem to resurrect it. "I was sitting in the café I like so much." I pause, tilting my head, still studying him. "A young woman with blonde hair and brown eyes sat down behind me. She proceeded to tell her friend in explicit detail all about her wild night last night with a lawyer who has the last name Marvelo and works at your firm. Not exactly the stuff of coincidence, is it?"

If I thought he was pale a moment ago, I was wrong. He looks like he's going to be sick, his forehead slick with sweat. His hand grapples for the frame of the closet door like he needs the support and then his head drops, his chin hitting his chest before it rises back up and he brokenly meets my eyes.

"Deny it," I challenge. "Go on. I dare you."

"It's not what you think," he states, his tone pleading as his eyes become wild. "It was one time. I swear to God, it was just—"

"How could you do it?" I whisper.

"—One time," he finishes because he didn't hear me. "It meant nothing. Absolutely nothing. I got drunk at the bar and then—"

"Bullshit," I rage, my anger rushing back through me with the force of an erupting volcano. "You're a goddamn liar!" I scream, pounding my fists on his chest. "I heard her, you son of a bitch. I heard all about the things you did with her. Things you never do with me. How could you do this? How could you throw us away like that?"

He grabs my fists, holding them against his chest with one hand as he tries to wrap his other around my waist to contain me. But I can't let him touch me. The thought of it makes me sick.

"I was drunk," he yells in my face. "I was stupid and drunk, and I wasn't thinking. It just happened. I stayed too long at the bar, and she came onto me, and we talked and then..." He growls. "I told her it wasn't going to happen again. I told her it was a mistake. I don't want her. I want *you*. I love *you*."

He says all of this, staring into my eyes, but he's lying.

Right to my face.

He didn't say any of that to her. He gave her his number. He told her he would have bought her breakfast if he could stay. He kissed her goodbye.

I push back off his chest and pry my hand away from his grip. Just the sight of him makes my stomach roil. I have to leave. I have to leave right this very second.

"I never want to see you again." And with that, I run as fast as I can; through our bedroom, down the hall, past the living room and kitchen until I get to the door.

"No, Grace." He rushes after me, trying to intercept me before I can leave. He positions his body between me and the door, his hands outstretched. "Wait. You don't mean that. You can't mean that. You're just upset. I made a mistake. I'll never ever do it again. I swear to fucking God, I won't. Please," he begs, desperately trying to wrap his arms around me again.

I shake my head. "I have to get out of here. I can't be around you anymore. I can't even look at you. You disgust me," I sneer; and with those words, I shove him out of my way. He lets me, his face crumpling, his eyes glossing over.

"We can figure this out," he murmurs dejectedly. Much of the fight knocked out of him with my harsh words. "I love you."

Liar.

I run through the door. I don't look over my shoulder. I don't look back. I just go. Knowing my life will never be the same again. That everything I thought I had is now gone.

4

The doorman calls, informing me that Grace is on her way up seconds before there is a knock on the door.

And when I see her, I practically drop my phone. "What the hell?" I snarl, walking over and grabbing her arm without a second thought. She's ice cold. Completely frozen through and soaking wet. "Your lips are blue for fuck's sake!"

It started pouring about twenty minutes ago, the warm summer temperatures plummeting along with it, and by the look of her, she was out walking in it. Her hair is matted down her face, her yoga clothes soaked and sticking to her like a second skin. She doesn't answer me, and I can't tell if it's because she's hypothermic or because something horrendous happened.

"Grace," I practically bark her name, drawing back to check her over. Her eyes meet mine, and even though I take that as a reassuring sign, they are utterly lifeless. Completely devoid of their usual sparkle. "You're scaring me. Talk."

"You're not Oliver," she finally manages, but it's quiet and her teeth are chattering so badly, it takes me a minute to figure out what she actually said.

"Huh?"

"Oliver. You're not Oliver. I came to find Oliver."

I stare blankly at her. Of course, she didn't come here to see me. "Oliver moved to Chestnut Hill with Amelia and Layla, remember? I bought his place from him and moved in last month."

"Right." She bobs her head. "I forgot that. My mistake. I'll go."

"The hell you will. Come with me."

I don't give her the choice. I drag her through my apartment, past my date who is sitting at my dining room table with her eyebrows at her hairline, and back into my master bathroom. I release her, steadying her with my hands because she looks like she's about to collapse at any second, and duck down until I meet her eyes again.

"Bath or shower?"

She blinks at me, seemingly lost in her own reverie, so I solve this for her. The bath will take too long to fill up. I walk into my shower, reach for the knob and turn it on, all five showerheads come on at once. I even add on a little steam to seal the deal. Shaking the water from my arm, I step out of the shower.

"The shower is running."

Nothing. It's like she's not even here in the room with me.

"Grace, you need to get undressed." *And I don't feel safe leaving until I see you move.*

But she doesn't move and now I'm scared. Like really fucking scared. What happened to her tonight? Wordlessly and with my eyes on the wall and not her body, I begin to lift her shirt up.

That must snap her out of her trance because she swats my hands away and mumbles something that sounds like, "I can do it."

"Can you really?" I ask, not even being a dick and she nods

once. My mind racing a mile a minute, my heart pounding just as fast. Something is seriously wrong. "Did someone hurt you?"

"No." But she laughs, the sound mirthless and chilling.

"Did you have a seizure?"

"No."

"Will you be okay if I leave you in here alone?"

"Yes."

One-word answers, but it's something. "Just get undressed and into the shower to warm up. Don't come out until I bring dry clothes for you. There are towels on the warmer right there." I point over her shoulder, but she doesn't so much as blink or shift in that direction.

I don't leave her until she moves toward the shower, and I can see that she's steady enough on her feet. Shutting the door behind me, I lean against it for a moment, blowing out a heavy breath.

What the motherfuck?

In all the years I've known Grace, I've never seen her like this. Not when her grandfather, who she was very close with, died. Not when her freaking beloved childhood dog was run over. Not even when she fell out of the tree in our yard and broke her wrist.

Grace is always in control. She's a picture of composure. Nothing rattles her. It's what makes her such a brilliant doctor and surgeon.

So again, what the motherfuck?

I listen for the sound of her entering the shower and when the pattern of water hitting the tile changes, I leave her and head back into the dining room to my date.

"What was that?" she asks, and I harden instantly at the way she crinkles her nose in disdain. "Why were you bringing a soaking wet woman into your bedroom?"

"Jamie, I'm sorry but I'm going to have to cut our date short."

Her eyes narrow and her back stiffens. "What?"

"My friend is going through a crisis, and I need to help her."

Jamie stands in a huff. "You've got to be kidding me?" Her hands go to her hips and it's like she's reading my mind because those are my exact thoughts. She has got to be kidding me. How can she not just say something like, *oh, I'm so sorry, of course I'll leave you to help your friend*?

"No. I'm not kidding you," I reply, my tone clipped as my patience run out with this woman. All I can think about is getting back to Grace. "Which is why you need to leave now."

She stomps off, back toward the kitchen, snatches her purse off the counter and continues to stomp like a five-year-old all the way to the door. I open it for her, making sure she walks through it and when she makes no move to do more, I press the button on the elevator.

Some kind of shrill sound escapes the back of her throat at that. "I am so not coming back," she threatens.

"I don't care," I tell her with zero emotion.

She lets out another small huff, but thankfully the doors to the elevator open and she steps on, flipping me off as the doors close. I roll my eyes, but quickly dial the doorman on my cell and ask him to make sure she gets into a cab or an Uber, and then I hang up and run back through my apartment and into my bedroom, practically at a sprint.

I hit up my closet, grab the first things I come across that will be way too big on her and then knock gently on the door to the bathroom. "Grace?"

"I'll be right out," she shouts, her voice sounding clear and strong.

"Okay. Take your time. I'm going to crack the door and place some clothes on the counter."

She doesn't respond, so I open the door, doing just as I said I would while avoiding the steamy mirror and the glass shower at all costs. I'm tempted to call Oliver, but I wait. Something had her taking to the dark rainy streets in search of him and I need to know what I'm dealing with first.

Sitting on the edge of my bed, I prop my elbows on my parted thighs and drop my head into my hands. But when I hear the door open, my head instinctively raises and what I'm hit with makes my breath stall in my chest.

Jesus Christ.

I swallow hard, doing my best to ignore the way she looks in my clothes with her long, wet hair cascading down the shirt making her nipples stand at attention. Blinking, I force my eyes up to hers as the scent of Grace wearing my shampoo and body wash assaults my nose.

"Are you hungry?" I ask as she stands before me.

I get a shrug for that, but again, I don't give her the option. Suddenly I need to get my brother's best friend who looks way too tempting out of my bedroom.

"I made food that you're going to eat." I stand, taking her by the arm once more and leading her down the hall to the kitchen.

"What happened to your date?"

I glance down at her, but she's not smiling and she's not teasing me.

"Gone."

She shakes her head slowly. "Sorry I ruined your night."

"You didn't. Now sit down." I guide her to one of the stools at the island. "Have a glass of wine." I pour her a very full glass of red. "And tell me why you showed up here looking like a drowned rat."

She stares down at the glass, clasping it in her hand before raising it to her lips and taking the daintiest of sips. When she sets it down, she lets out a weighty sigh. "I really want to drink this. I really want to get so drunk that I can't think or see or remember anything. But I shouldn't, right?" Her eyes meet mine for a flicker of a second before falling back to the wine. I can't tell if she's actually asking me or not. "Stress. Heartache. Too many emotions. If I drink, with the way my day has gone, I'll probably have a seizure and I didn't bring my meds with me. Nothing." She laughs then but there is no humor to the sound. "I left with nothing. Not even my phone."

"Grace..." I let her name trail.

With her eyes still on her glass, she says, "Tony slept with another woman."

"That stupid fuck!" slips out before I can stop it.

She doesn't react and I want to kill the bastard. I want to beat him to within an inch of his puny, pathetic life. I could do it too. He's a weakling, not to mention three inches shorter and about twenty pounds of muscle lighter.

Oliver would want in on that. Hell, all of my brothers would.

"How did you find out?" I lean against the island and place my hand on her shoulder because she looks like she needs the comfort and support. My other hand is balled up into a fist at my side. She leans into me, barely hanging on.

"I overheard the woman talking about her wild night of hot sex." She hiccups out a snort, shaking her head. "Can you freaking believe that? I mean, what are the odds of the woman who slept with my fiancé sitting behind me in the café I was eating lunch in?"

"One in a million?"

"At least. But she didn't just walk into the café and say I had sex with Tony Marvelo. No, she sat there behind me, gossiping all the juicy details to her friend."

"Shit," I mutter, briefly closing my eyes. Grace sits up, shifting away from me, and I release my hold on her shoulder. "I am so sorry, Grace."

I grip the counter when what I really want to do is hug her. Hold her. I want to wrap her up in my arms and kiss away all her pain. Erase that stupid piece of shit from her head and her heart because he never deserved either and I want them. Damn, I'm such a fool.

What the hell am I even thinking? These are not thoughts I can have. But seeing her like this? Every protective instinct I've ever possessed rages.

"What can I do?" I ask, feeling helpless. "Name it and it's yours. Do you want me to go kill him? Because I will. Happily, in fact."

"You'll go to jail."

"No, I won't. I'll just tell the jury I did womankind a service and they'll let me go. Besides, juries never convict attractive people. All I have to do is smile at them."

She lets out a small laugh, and I take that as a minor victory given the situation.

"Do you want me to call Oliver?" I offer.

"No. Don't bother him. He's with Amelia and, as you said, he lives out in the suburbs now. I can't believe I forgot about that."

"You had other things on your mind."

"I guess I did."

She gets up, walking through the great room over toward the large floor-ceiling windows that comprise that entire wall. For a second, I think she's going to open the slider and go out onto the balcony, back into the rain, but she just presses her fingers to the glass, staring at the glowing blurry buildings beyond.

"What am I going to do?" she asks only I get the feeling her question is for herself and not me.

"You're going to stay here."

She spins around at my voice, finding me still glued to the island, almost afraid to move. I shouldn't have offered that. The words tumbled past my lips without any restraint or bearing on repercussions. Having Grace stay here, even temporarily, is a mistake of epic proportions.

I want her, desperately in fact, and I can't have her. Ever.

Unrequited love seems to be my thing. It was with Alanna, a woman I was a resident with down in Virginia Beach. I was crazy about her for four years and then by the time I actually made a play for her, I was too late. She had met someone else.

I was stupid and arrogant, thinking I had all the time in the world to finish my residency and enjoy the last vestiges of being a bachelor before wanting to get serious and settle down.

Then I moved back here, a little heartsick, and found Grace. No longer the teenager I remembered, but the woman. The doctor. The spitfire. And during this past year, after spending eighty hours a week together...

Yes, I most certainly am a fool.

But what else can I do?

Her fiancé cheated on her. Oliver is living with his Amelia, and her little sister Layla, and they are starting a life together. They'd take Grace in in a second, but I know that's not what Grace desires. No one wants to be around a happy couple when you're miserable. All of her other friends are all in serious relationships.

And she's here.

"You're serious?" she questions. "I can't... Carter, how on earth?"

"You'll stay here," I tell her again, more certain of it now. "For as long as you need to."

A tear tracks down her face as her eyes continue to hold mine. "We'll kill each other."

I chuckle at that. "Possibly. But isn't that half the fun?"

"Carter—"

"It's done. I have three extra bedrooms and it's not like we're not used to being around each other. Even when we're not at work. You're always around, Grace. It'll be fine. Here," I say, walking over to the oven and pulling out the tray of chicken enchiladas I made for my date. "We are going to eat and then I'm going to run over to your place and pack up your stuff."

I plate the enchiladas, some beans and rice, and set the whole thing in front of her, complete with a napkin and silverware. I pour her a glass of water because she's right about the alcohol, and then I point to the seat.

She's eyeing the food like she's not sure if she wants to eat it or not, though I know for a fact she loves my enchiladas. It's one of three dishes I make exceptionally well and it's also Oliver's favorite, so I make it a lot when they're around.

"You're very controlling."

"Only when the situation fits."

"I like to fight back."

I grin. "I know. I like that about you. Keeps the game interesting. Now come eat so I can go get your things."

"You can't go to my place," she tells me, finally crossing the room to sit down. "I know you. If you see Tony, you'll hurt him, and while I might not care so much about him at the moment, I do care about your hands."

I hold up said hands in surrender. "I can control myself."

She raises an eyebrow, but I don't waver. I can. I won't actually kill her fiancé. I probably won't even rough him up too bad because he's a lawyer and who wants that headache.

"I'll just threaten him until he pisses his pants."

"I'll go over there tomorrow morning after he leaves for work."

"Tomorrow is Sunday, Grace. He'll be home and waiting for you."

"Shit," she mutters, picking at the food with her fork. "You're right. He will be and I... I can't see him, Carter. I can't. If I see him, *I* might kill him." She blinks up at me. "You really wouldn't mind going there to get some things for me?"

"I'm on it." Honestly, I'm looking forward to it.

"And you're truly okay with me staying here? Just until I can figure something else out?"

Her crystalline blue eyes, so guileless, hold mine, her expression impossibly sweet and hopeful. How could anyone ever cheat on her? She is so perfect. But if she's staying here, in my home, I need to get myself in better control. No more thinking about her beyond work. No more fantasizing. No more pushing the line, the line I love to push.

Can I do that?

It seems I don't have a choice.

"I'm positive."

I'm also fucked.

5

All through dinner, I'm forcing down bites when what I really want to do is go gangbusters into Grace's house and kick some serious ass. I've dreamed of this girl. Fantasized until my cock was sore and my mind restless. Unsatisfied.

I hated Tony when I thought he was a good guy.

Now I want to pulverize him for taking for granted what I should have had all along.

I wonder what Oliver would do.

In the year I've been her attending, I never allowed my thoughts to get this far. I brushed them off as sexual desire. A basic need never sated by other women. They weren't smart enough. Beautiful enough. Funny enough. Ball-busting enough. Whatever the fuck you want to throw at them, they weren't enough. They weren't *her*.

But now, Tony is a stupid motherfucker.

And Grace is staying at my place.

And I swore I wouldn't do this—not even fifteen minutes ago, I swore that.

But I don't know how to stop now that things are in motion.

I have to try though. These thoughts, they're going to torture me unless I can learn how to control them. *Lock it down, man. She's a no-go on every possible level.*

"He went down on her," Grace says out of nowhere and I freeze mid chew and mid thought and stare at her. Her blue eyes catch mine and I frown. "I know you're a man and I'm a woman. I know you're my attending and not my best friend. But you're all I've got right now, and I need to talk about it."

I swallow, practically choking it down, and manage, "I'm listening."

"The girl, the one he cheated with, was beautiful. Young." Grace leans back in her chair, staring out at the cabinets, her food forgotten. "My God, so young! Early twenties at best. She started talking about her hot one-nighter and ever the moron, I listened like a creep. She said he ripped off her dress and then went down on her for so long and did it so well that she came twice. *Twice.*" She repeats with emphasis. "Do you know the last time he went down on me?" Her head swivels in my direction and I can only shake my head. I can't believe I'm having this conversation with her. "My birthday, two years ago. I had to think about it. Not once since then."

I have no words for that. How can you be with a woman like Grace and not live inside her pussy?

"She also said that they had sex three times. And he would have spent the night with her had he not needed to work today. Or, well, come home to his fiancée, I suppose. We've never done it three times. Never, Carter. Not even when we were new and dating. We never had the, *I can't keep my hands off you*, stage." Her teeth sink into her bottom lip to try and hide its quivering.

I'm tempted to say something like then it must not have been right or you're better off without him, but that's not what she needs to hear from me now. Platitudes are bullshit and comfortless. No one wants to hear that when they're hurting. It's condescending.

"Maybe she's exaggerating?"

"Maybe," she says with a long sigh, her finger running around the rim of her untouched wine glass. "But I know it happened. He didn't deny it. He lied to me and told me he told her it was a drunken mistake, but that's not what happened. He left her with a kiss and his number. His goddamn number. Then he went and actually had the audacity to tell me screwing her meant nothing. That he wanted me and not her."

I open my mouth to speak, but she puts her hand up to stop me.

"He doesn't want me, Carter. If that were true, he'd want to have wild sex with me. He'd want to rip my clothes off because he couldn't stand them on me another second. He'd want to bury himself inside me over and over again. He went down on a stranger. A woman he had just met. We've been together three years and never once have we had that sort of passion. This girl said it was the best sex of her life and I can't even remember the last time I thought that with him, if ever."

"Then maybe this is the beginning of a fresh start for you," I whisper, clear my throat, and sit up straight so I appear convincing. "You deserve lust and passion. You deserve the best sex of your life every night. You deserve a man who thinks about only you when you're not there and when you are, won't be able to keep his hands off you."

A tear tracks down her cheek followed by another one. She wipes them away, but they keep coming. "I hate what this did to me. I hate my thoughts. I hate all of them."

"What are they?"

Her watery blue eyes cling hopelessly to mine. "What's wrong with me that he'd want to do that to her but not me?"

Shit. That fucking bastard.

And what do I say? What do I tell her? That I want to do all of those things to her times a million? That I want to explore every inch of her body, bring it to the height of pleasure over and over again? That I would spend hours with my face between her thighs and love every second of it?

I cup her face in my hand, whether I should be touching her or not. "It's not you, Grace. It's absolutely not you. You're..." I heave a breath, knowing I can't say all that I want to say, but still staring into her eyes with steadfast determination. "You're everything any man would kill to have. Just trust me on this. It's one hundred percent him and not you."

She sucks in a breath, another tear falling that I wipe away with my thumb. She shakes me off and I allow my hand to fall to my lap, frustrated and tormented and angry.

"That's what I want to believe," she says. "That's what the tough, no-bullshit woman in me is screaming. But the girl, the fragile, newly shattered girl? The one who wasn't even good enough for her parents to love? She says how can it be him if he did those things with her and not you?"

He will die. He will hurt and then he will die.

BY THE TIME we are done with dinner, it's late. Not late by Saturday night in Boston standards, but late all the same. It doesn't matter though. I tuck Grace in front of the television in my living room with a blanket and my remote because she says she doesn't want to go to bed until I get back, and then I leave.

I don't think I've ever been this furious before. As I drive the fifteen minutes over to the corner of Beacon and Mass Ave where Grace and Tony live, my anger only multiplies. How could he do that to her? How could he be stupid enough to cheat on *her*? To take all her sexy confidence and shatter it like that?

And what was all that about going down on the girl and crazy sex? Tony never struck me as the type of guy who was anything other than very vanilla in bed. So all of this is coming out of left field.

My instinct tells me that the girl was grossly exaggerating for the benefit of her friend. But does it really matter? No. And that's a big fat no because the damage to Grace has already been done. Her trust and confidence are crushed. Her sense of self-worth is in the toilet. I saw it. Plain as day in her beautiful eyes. That girl did more than just tell Grace her fiancé is a cheat. He made her feel undesirable and less than and as a man who deals with women on a daily basis, not just personally, but professionally, there is nothing worse than that.

But still, I have to tread carefully.

Grace isn't mine. She's Oliver's if anything, which is why I call him just as I pull up in front of the building. He picks up on the third ring, his voice groggy with sleep.

"Hey, what's wrong?"

He probably thinks it's about mom and now I kind of feel bad for calling him when it's nearly midnight. "Everyone is fine. Sorry to wake you, but there's a situation with Grace."

I hear him clear his throat and whisper something to Amelia. Then I hear blankets rustle as he moves. "Is she okay? What's going on?"

"Tony cheated on her. She overheard the woman he did it with in a café. It's bad, Oliver. She showed up at my condo in the pouring rain still thinking it was yours. She was a mess. I took care of her and now I'm about to grab some of her stuff from her place and possibly kill Tony, but she needs you, man."

Oliver breathes heavily into the phone. "Jesus. What a dumb bastard. I wish I could say I'm surprised, but I'm not. His ego was always too big and she was always too good for him. But wait, is she staying with you?"

"For now. Where else is she going to go?"

"Home with me."

"Oliver, think about that. You're in a very happy relationship with Amelia. You guys just moved in together. Bought that monster of a dog together. Is that something you want Grace to have to see on a daily basis while she's hurting like this? She won't want to intrude on that, and you know she will feel like she is."

He growls under his breath. "Fuck. Just fuck. Why do you get to kill him? I want the honors."

I chuckle. "I'll leave some of him left for you. Is there anything she needs that I should remember to grab other than the basics?"

"Her rescue meds. She keeps them out on the counter in her bathroom and in her purse. Just grab any bottles you see. She's been in good control with her seizures for a while now, but who knows what this could trigger."

"On it. Thanks for the heads up. You gonna come by tonight or see her tomorrow?"

"Yeah. I'm on my way. I don't want to wait until tomorrow."

"Alright. I'll see you in a bit."

"Thanks, brother. For everything. I hate that I wasn't there for her from the start."

"No problem."

"Break his nose for me." Oliver disconnects the call and I hop out of the car into the pouring rain. I suck in a deep breath, plaster an asshole scowl on my face and bounce up the steps. I hit the buzzer, hunching forward under the small overhang just as Tony answers within seconds with, "Grace?"

Stupid asshole. His fiancée left the house without anything on her, and he isn't out looking for her?

"No, dickwad. It's Carter."

"Carter?"

I shake my head. "Open up."

The door buzzes and I make my way up the stairs, taking them two at a time. They occupy the entire second floor. Tony bought this place right after he finished law school and got a high paying job. It's his place. No wonder Grace doesn't feel like she can live here anymore.

He opens the door for me before I can even knock and I hate to admit it, but he looks like shit. Then I catch the scent of expensive scotch on his breath and I want to beat the shit out of him all over again.

"You dumb fuck." The words leave my mouth again before I can stop them. "What the hell have you done?" I can't believe he sat here getting drunk without knowing where his fiancée was. A woman with a known medical condition out in weather like this without medication, money, or her phone.

Tony deflates before my eyes as he waves me in. "Where is she?"

"Where do you think? She's at my place. Why else would I be here? What were you thinking?" I step into him before I consciously make the decision to do so. He throws his hands up, warding me off. *Pansy-ass.*

"I fucked up," he admits defensively, scrambling back a step in the hall as I advance another. "I went to a work thing, got drunk, and went home with some twenty-two-year-old."

"Twenty-two?" I'm incredulous. That's twelve years his junior.

"She came onto me, man. I was a fool." He scrubs his hands up and down his face and then back through his hair.

"Was she the first?"

He looks away, guilt coating his features, and Jesus. This is bad. So bad.

"She was... yes. She was the only one."

"You're lying to me. I can see it all over your pathetic face."

"I... she... it's none of your business how many others there have been. Those women don't matter. Grace is who I want. Who I love."

"How. Many. Others?"

"I'm not answering that. How is Grace?" he has the nerve to ask, trying to redirect me.

"How do you think? She overheard your hookup admit to having you go down on her and then fucking her three times. She's a mess."

"Daisy said all that?"

"Daisy?" I practically growl the word. "You just throw her name around like that, huh? All familiar like?" I can only shake my head at him. But what I really want to do is wrap my large hands around his trachea and carotid arteries until he either passes out or dies. Whichever comes first. "And why the hell don't you do that with Grace? She told me all about what a boring fuck you are with her."

His beady eyes narrow. "She told you that?"

"Yeah, she told me that." I allow my grin to grow to evil proportions, stepping into him, using my height to overpower. "How do you do that with a stranger and not your fiancée?" It's really none of my business, but I am curious.

"Because Grace is going to be my wife," he says like that should explain everything, stumbling back until he bumps into the wall of the kitchen, rattling something in the fridge on the other side.

"I'm not following you, Tony. In fact, you're just pissing me off more, so you better make sense quickly or I'm going to bury your face in the floor and have you eat a different kind of carpet."

His head drops and he lets out a breath, his hands going to his hips. "I... I respect Grace, okay? I respect the hell out of her. And I..." Another big breath. "I never felt it was right to treat her like a whore."

I retreat a step, shocked by his words. Pressing my hand into the wall, I stare incredulously at the man. "You're messing with me, right?"

"Huh?" He raises his head, searching my face.

"Having crazy hot sex with your fiancée is not treating her like a whore, you dumbass. But you know what?" I pause here, wondering why the hell I'm bothering. "Never mind. You don't deserve my sage words of wisdom. You deserve whatever hurt and misery you're feeling. So I'm going to go and pack Grace a bag and then I'm gone."

I spin around and head to the back of the apartment where I know their master is. Tony is hot on my heels but wisely keeps his mouth shut. I step into her closet, locate a decent size suitcase up on a shelf, and then stare at her clothes.

I have no idea what to take. I grab jeans, blouses that I've seen her wear, a shit ton of scrubs that she has neatly folded and even a few nicer outfits including dresses, because why not. I grab nearly every pair of shoes I can. Then I go nuts in her underwear drawer, tossing in whatever my hands touch without thinking too deeply on any of it.

"She doesn't need that much stuff," Tony snaps, watching me intently. "She'll be home in a day or two."

I want to scoff at that, but I don't. I just keep quiet as I pack anything else I see. I have no idea if Grace will be back. If she'll forgive him or not. That's between them. But I'm packing enough so she doesn't have to come back for a while.

I brush past him into their bathroom and sigh. Women, right? They have a ton of crap.

But after opening a couple of drawers, I locate a large travel makeup bag and I just slide everything I see in there along with the pills Oliver mentioned, and I'm good to go. Tony steps back, a mournful expression on his face. But like I said, he deserves it. In fact, he deserves a hell of a lot worse for hurting the best woman I've ever known.

He's been screwing around on her for God only knows how long with God only knows how many women, all the while having boring sex with the one woman he should have been treating like a queen. I spot her purse on the entryway table and check it quickly, making sure her phone is in there.

But before I turn the knob on the door, I twist back to Tony who is still right up my ass, face him squarely, and then punch him right in the nose. It makes a delightful crunching sound, his nasal bones fracturing beneath my fist. It hurts my hand something fierce but it's totally worth it. Besides, I don't have surgery again until Monday.

Tony lets out a startled cry, his hand shooting up to his face as blood spurts from his nose, dripping down his mouth and chin and onto his white shirt. He staggers, reaches for the wall, misses, and falls to the ground in a heap.

"What the hell, man!" he barks, his hand still on his face.

That one was for Oliver. This one is for me. Bending forward, I rear back and clock him again, this time in the eye. I'm tempted to go at him again though he should have some pretty shiners from the broken nose and fist to the eye that is already swelling up nicely, a cut high on his cheekbone bleeding.

I guess my work here is done.

"You deserve a million times worse," I seethe at him, pointing my finger so he knows I let him off easy. "I should have kicked your ass until you begged for mercy. Put your stupid, waste of space, loser ass in the hospital but you're not worth the damage to my hands. You fuck other women because you're not man enough to fuck yours. Asshole."

I spit at him, hitting the floor between his parted legs.

And with that, I walk out of his apartment, down the stairs, carrying the suitcase in my hand, her purse in my other, and get back into my car. I let out a breath as I head back across town, flexing the hand I punched Tony with. It feels... good. It has a nice warm tingly sensation that's a cross between pain and satisfaction. I've never punched a guy before, not seriously anyway, not with any real animosity behind it, but I find myself smiling.

My brothers and I used to fight. Five boys will do that, but we never hit each other the way I just hit Tony.

But then I think of Grace waiting on me and my smile slips.

I should have hit him again. Harder. Kicked him in the ribs and cracked a few of those.

Pulling into the underground garage of my building, I hop out, grab the suitcase, her purse, and I'm inside the elevator in under a minute. And when the doors part on my floor and I enter my condo, I find myself sagging with a disappointment I have no right to.

Grace isn't waiting on me.

She is exactly where I left her on my couch, tucked under a blanket, but now Oliver is with her. His arms are wrapped around her, her face buried in his chest as she cries. His green eyes meet mine, noting the suitcase, and he mouths, *thank you.*

I walk the suitcase into one of the guest rooms and Oliver is behind me, Grace in his arms as he carries her. He gives me a grateful nod and I shut the door behind them. That's it.

And for the first time in my life, I'm jealous of my little brother.

He gets to hold her, comfort her all night. He'll take care of her because that's what they do for each other. She doesn't need me the way she needs him.

I'm just her new roommate. Her attending.

The idiot stuck on a woman who will never want him the way he wants her.

6

Bright sunlight streams across my face, warm and welcome on my skin as I slowly roll onto my side and scream at the top of my lungs. Oliver goes shooting off the bed, smashing his hip into the nightstand before tumbling back with an *oomph* against the wall.

"What the fuck?" he yells, rubbing his smarting side.

"Crap. You scared the hell out of me." My heart is racing a million miles an hour as I try to catch my breath. "I forgot you were here. I'm so sorry. I just didn't expect a head of dark hair to be on the pillow beside me."

He scrubs a hand over his face. "Yeah, I didn't mean to be. I fell asleep making sure you were asleep."

I sit up, bringing the blankets with me and laugh. "Do you remember the last time we had a sleepover together?"

He grins, running his fingers through his sleep-mussed hair. "We were twelve and my parents thought we were doing inappropriate things with each other."

I giggle. "After that, we weren't allowed any more sleepovers in the same room. I had to sleep in one of the guest rooms in another wing at your house whenever I stayed the night."

"Just as well, I think I would have been scarred for life if I had woken up beside you with morning wood."

I scrunch my nose. "Ew. Gross. I don't want to think about... that."

He laughs, coming back to sit on the bed beside me. His clothes are a mess, his white T-shirt wrinkled, his track shorts twisted. He's wearing what he showed up in last night. I must have changed because I'm in pajamas. My pajamas, no longer Carter's clothes. Carter. My suitcase. Tony.

"I don't remember much after you arrived."

"Once Carter came with your stuff, I gave you an Ativan. Remember?"

"Barely. Did you have me take it because I was an emotional wreck or because you thought I was going to have a seizure?"

"The first. You showed no signs of anything else. I wanted to make sure you'd get some sleep, and I didn't think you would without a little help."

"Probably right on that." I flop back against the pillow, staring up at the high, vaulted ceiling. "Tony isn't going to break my streak. If I can make it through the end of medical school and the first two years of my residency without having one, I can make it through a cheating fiancé."

"Wanna talk more about it?"

"No. I have a lot of questions. A lot of things to think through. But I'm not sure I have a whole lot left to say." I twist onto my side to face my friend. "Thank you for coming. For rushing out of your house in the middle of the night in a rainstorm for me."

He smiles softly, running his hand over my hair. "I'd do anything for you, babe. You're my no matter what. My ride or die. And you know, you're always welcome to come stay with us. We have plenty of space."

"I know and thank you." I sigh, twisting the sheet between my fingers. "It's weird, but this place still kind of feels like my second home even though you no longer live here. Something I still can't believe I forgot. I felt so stupid when Carter answered the door."

Oliver hitches up a shoulder. "He didn't mind. I think he's glad you came here."

I snort. "I doubt that highly. I ruined his date, cried about my boring sex life and cheating fiancé, and then imposed myself to move in."

"He invited you to move in. He wouldn't have done that if he wasn't cool with it."

I know he wouldn't have. Carter is a great guy. An amazing guy truly, but he would have never done that just to be that great guy. He's great because it's effortless for him and he doesn't even have to think about it. But me staying here puts him in a weird position. He's my supervisor. He evaluates my work. We were already playing a fine line with my relationship with his brother, but me living here?

I need to find a new place to live, but the thought of apartment hunting, of trying to move...

I just need some time to sort myself out. A couple of weeks at most. What harm can staying here for a couple of weeks do?

"Come to the compound today," Oliver suggests, cutting off my thoughts. "Bring your suit and we'll swim and eat. You'll be with family."

I smile at that. It's true, Oliver's my family. His parents and my parents were best friends until my parents decided I wasn't something they wanted to deal with any longer if they could avoid it. Then the Fritz clan sort of turned their back on that friendship. I haven't seen much of my parents since they moved to Australia to follow my younger brother, Scott's family. Scott got married straight out of college to an Australian woman, and now he has a daughter with another on the way.

The last time I spoke to my mother was when I called to

speak to my niece, and she accidentally picked up his phone. That conversation lasted all of three minutes.

I lift my hand, hovering it over my face, staring at the sparkling diamond. "Should I flush it?"

"You could sell it. Donate the money to a charity or use it to get yourself a new place."

I could do that, but knowing Tony, he'll make a stink and demand I return it. "I'll mail it to him." I don't want his money anyway.

"So you're done? Like, done, done? No second thoughts or waiting period?"

"Carter?!" I yell, making Oliver jar back, covering his ears.

"Damn. Warn a guy before you start screaming."

"Carter!" I try again, and a minute later, I hear him trudging down the hall.

The door opens and he pops his head in. "You bellowed?"

"Come in here, would ya?"

He grunts something under his breath but does as I ask.

"Was he there last night when you went over?"

He nods, hovering by the foot of the bed, visibly uncomfortable to be in here during my pajama party with his brother.

"He looked like shit if that helps."

"It doesn't. Did he say anything to you?"

He pauses, and I can see him mulling something over, debating his words and choosing them carefully when careful is the last thing I want him to be with me.

"Spit it out. I want all the details. Hold nothing back."

Carter sinks down onto the end of the bed, falling to his side and propping his head up with his hand. I sit up, scooting down the bed some and Oliver follows.

"He said he loves and respects you." I glare at that, but he holds his hand up in surrender. "Let me finish, okay? If you want the whole truth, I will give it to you, but it will hurt."

I snort out an incredulous laugh. "You think?"

"No sarcasm before I've had my coffee," Oliver quips.

I reach over and elbow him without removing my eyes from Carter. "If you're going to make an incision, do it without hesitation or second guessing."

Carter smirks. "I told you that."

"You did, now own it."

"Fine. The reason he doesn't get... wild in bed with you is because he loves and respects you and believes that if he does those things with you then he's treating you like a whore, which is not something he wants to do."

I let out a humorless laugh. "So he loves and respects me, but not enough to remain faithful to me or our relationship?"

"Yeah, I have nothing for that."

"You're telling me he thinks having sex with me, the way many, many couples do, is treating me like a whore?" I belt out another laugh and it actually sends a chill up my spine. That's how sardonic and bitter it is. "That's the stupidest thing I've ever heard."

Carter coughs out a laugh of his own.

"No," I continue, stretching my legs out in front of me, my feet nearly hitting Carter's chest as I absently rub my thighs under the blankets. "I'm totally serious. That makes zero sense."

"What can I say, you were engaged to an idiot."

I glare menacingly at my friend. "If you say I told you so, Oliver Fritz, I will hurt you. I'm not exactly sure how just yet, but I am a woman on the edge, not to be messed with." I turn back to Carter. "You're holding back. What else?"

He groans, falling onto his back, his hands behind his head, arms butterflied out. "You sure?"

"Positive."

"Fine. She wasn't the first, just the one you caught him with."

I had a feeling.

But it hits me so acutely, I have to suck in a breath, followed by another. I drop my head onto Oliver's shoulder, biting my lip, trying desperately to hold back the tears and make my chin stop quivering.

I open my mouth. Gulp. Try again and whisper, "Done, done."

Oliver kisses the top of my head, squeezing me closer into his side, and I close my eyes, shaking.

Never have I felt so betrayed. That's what hurts the most. The betrayal. The lying. The sneaking around right under my nose. I knew we had problems. I knew our relationship was struggling because we made more time for our work than for each other. But cheating on him never entered my mind.

Not once.

Yes, I've been attracted to other men. Hell, the man with the piercing brown eyes staring at me right now is highest on that list. But I wouldn't have acted on that attraction. Attraction to others is normal, cheating is not.

I slip the ring from my finger and chuck it across the room. It makes a *ping* when it hits the wall and falls to the floor. I wipe the few tears that escaped from my face. "Well, now he can fuck all those women all the ways he never did me without having to bother rushing home to me. My vibrator gave it to me better than he ever did."

Carter chokes on his breath, covering his face with his hands. Oliver makes a gagging noise in the back of his throat.

"Incidentally, did you pack it?" I ask.

"I have no idea," Carter grumbles between his fingers. "I grabbed from drawers and just threw whatever I touched into the suitcase."

"I kept it in my nightstand."

"Then no."

"Dammit. Good thing Prime has free two-day delivery."

"Christ," Carter wheezes. "I'll be sure to let you open any boxes that arrive here."

"Probably wise. I might go on a vibrator purchasing bender."

"And I just threw up in my mouth," Oliver declares.

All kidding—sorta—aside, I feel like I've been hit by a truck. Three years of a relationship. A year and a half of it being engaged. I thought Tony was my future. My forever. How do I go from that to this in the span of only a few short hours?

He would have married me all the while cheating on me the entire time.

Hell, how many times did he sleep with someone only to turn around and sleep with me?

The stupid ass and his overly traditional upbringing. Sex is a sin; marriage is sacred and holy. How easily this could have been avoided. We could have been having hot sex every night of the week. But no. He can tell Carter whatever bullshit he wants, but if he loved me the way he claims he does, he never would have done this. Any of this.

Maybe it's best that I found out now. Because even though it hurts like a son of a bitch, the thought of continuing on like this, of living a lie, of being made to look the fool, rips me apart.

Tomorrow, first chance I can grab someone to examine me —other than Carter—I'm going to get tested for every STI on the planet. Ugh.

"Coffee," I declare. "I need a lot of coffee. And a bath. With chocolate. And gummy worms. And Oreos with crunchy peanut butter slathered all over them. And a week on some Caribbean Island. Or surgeries. Lots and lots of surgeries. And delivering babies. All the babies."

Yes. Work. I'll throw myself into work and eventually my heartache will sort itself out.

And one day I won't wake up feeling this way.

Like my life is coming apart at the seams.

7

It's mornings like this, that I wish dawn came with amphetamines. I drag my lifeless body out of bed, peering out at the still navy-blue sky. I've slept in the guestroom here before countless times, but this is different. Suddenly this room is my new home away from home.

Home. What the hell is that anyway?

I can't go home.

I can't look at my former fiancé.

At least not without being arrested for murder one.

But it's Monday. Robot stage IV endometriosis day. I've studied this case inside and out. Learned all the techniques. My hands are itching to get going and I know, I fucking know, I'm going to slay this surgery. Because it's what I do best. Medicine.

Who needs love when you have passion in your careers?

I shower, slip into a pair of scrubs that Carter brought me, ignoring the fact that he packed dozens of matching bras and panties, and walk out into the kitchen. Carter is leaning against the island, his dark brown hair damp from the shower and he's wearing matching light blue scrubs to mine. He's drinking coffee out of a mug that says, *I like my coffee on the dark side,* while reading something on his tablet and munching on a piece of toast.

Carter Fritz does gimmicky mugs? Didn't see that one coming.

"Nice mug."

He takes a sip right on cue. "Ten guesses who got it for me."

I only need one. "Luca."

He shoots me with his finger. "You got it. He also got me one with baby Yoda on it that says Small But Mighty."

Luca is one of his older brothers. A twin but night and day from his counterpart, Landon. You'd never, and I mean ever, know that Luca was a closet Star Wars nerd if you weren't on the inside. Luca is the sexy bad boy player you read about in your romance novels. A total heartbreaker. Just ask the woman he left behind.

"Can I have that mug?"

Carter smirks. "You don't want the one where the handles are actually Princess Leia's buns?"

"Are we talking ass cheeks or hair?"

Carter chokes on his sip of coffee. "Hair. Fuck." He wipes his chin with a napkin. "Drink this." He pours coffee into a random, totally un-nerdy mug before sliding it in my direction. I'm insanely disappointed. "Are you ready for the case this morning?"

"No. I spent all night filing my nails before polishing them hot pink and sprinkling them with matching glitter. If I chip one during this surgery, I might go postal."

"Are you okay?"

I grin, taking a sip of my coffee, leaning casually against his island. I am *so* not okay. I'm living with Carter Fritz and my fiancé is a cheating swine of a man. "Perfect. Right as rain."

His dark eyes fly up to mine like he's calling bullshit, but then he gives me a smile that elicits butterflies in women the world over. Myself included. Not the best reaction to have to your new roommate especially when vulnerable is your new middle name and playboy is his.

"You look it." I can't tell if he's being sarcastic or not, but I don't get the chance to ask as he throws something at me that I instinctively catch. "It's an extra key fob to use with the code for my condo so you don't have to bother the doorman every time you want to come up."

I blink at him, at a loss for words. "Does this mean you'll allow me to have gummies in the cabinet instead of hiding them in my room?"

"No. Never." He cringes with an exaggerated shudder. "If I see anything resembling a gummy bear or worm in this kitchen, I'll kick your pretty ass out onto the streets."

Pretty? I wasn't even sure Carter Fritz knew I was female. And simply because I'm a wounded bird, I preen at that. Annoying flutter in my belly and all. That's all that is. Nothing more. The fact that he looks like a Roman god, all tall, muscular, and gorgeous, has no effect on me whatsoever.

"Thank you," I say softly with a smile I'm conflicted over. "You really came through for me, Carter. It's weird being here with you since ninety percent of the time we're together we're at work and you're yelling at me, but I'm so very grateful."

"You're welcome. I hope you'll treat this place as your home and use it for however long you need. Don't feel like you need to rush out on my account."

I resist the urge to hug him, but it's not easy. Knowing he's genuinely good with me staying for however long I need to clear some of the headache that's been plaguing me since I mistakenly showed up on his doorstep.

"Are you hungry?"

I shake my head. "I'll eat after surgery. My stomach is still a mess."

His eyes lock with mine. "You're going to be okay, Grace."

"I am," I agree, even if I'm not sure I mean it just yet. I'm hurting and raw and beaten down, but I'm not broken.

"You ready to get in then? We have a surgery waiting for us to kick its ass."

"I'm ready," I say, my smile spreading, probably to creepy decibels.

Carter takes the coffee I haven't finished and pours it into a to-go mug. He does the same with his and then we're out the door together, walking the blocks to the hospital in subdued darkness. We prattle on about work, our surgery, and I'm glad we can still be us after waking up and seeing him first thing, or sharing his space could be strained and awkward.

Typically, I run into work, but until I get myself into a new routine, I'll have to find a new way to exercise. I need exercise like I need air, coffee, and practicing medicine. But more than that, exercise is essential to keeping me neurologically balanced. I was diagnosed with epilepsy at the age of five. A condition that grew infinitely worse once I hit puberty.

I was having multiple seizures every month right before my period. It became like clockwork. Those improved dramatically when I started on Depo-Provera shots. But it took me until the age of nineteen to learn how to keep my seizures in good control and until twenty-four for me to fully get my ass in gear and make all the necessary lifestyle changes. Managing my epilepsy is something I'm fortunate to be able to do.

Many with epilepsy aren't as lucky and despite medications and lifestyle changes, continue to have uncontrolled and unpredictable seizures. Just because I'm epileptic doesn't mean I let it define me though. I live my life how I want, I just don't do it stupidly.

Carter sips his coffee, obnoxiously and uncharacteristically quiet as we enter the building. We make our way up to the surgical side of the labor and delivery floor and then without a word, Carter strolls off. Just any other morning. Me, his resident; him, my attending. I head for the locker room to get rid of my stuff. Carter has an office. I don't. Hashtag, job goals.

Once my stuff is stored, I walk over to the nurses' station in the back of the pre-surgical area to check the OR schedule when Dylan, my intern approaches me with a big beaming smile.

"You should have told me."

I blink at him. "Told you what? About the case this morning? I did. You're scrubbing in to watch."

He rolls his dark eyes at me. "No, girl. That it's your birthday. Or is it your anniversary?"

"Huh?" I reply with a small laugh. "My birthday is in two weeks."

"Then what's with the flowers?" He points over to the opposite end of the nurses' station and sure enough, there is the biggest bouquet of long stem red roses I've ever seen. "They just arrived for you like ten minutes ago. I assume they're from Tony, so it's your anniversary then? I had to bat fierce bitches away from grabbing the card like I was playing Whac-A-Mole."

I stare at them for a moment. They're beautiful. Stunning really, but also... generic.

Thoughtless while being thoughtful at the same time.

I had gone all morning not thinking about him. And with one stupid bouquet, everything comes flooding back. His texts, begging me to forgive him. To call him. To give him another chance. That woman's words to her friends. The things he did to her that he's never done to me. The other women I don't even know about.

"It's not my anniversary," I whisper as I push past Dylan over to the flowers. The fragrance of the roses hits me as I get closer, peppering the air with their sweetness. Flowers are not allowed in this part of the hospital. The scent can make people coming out of surgery and off anesthesia nauseated and since the pre-op area and the PACU are connected, I lift the heavy as sin glass vase and carry it back into the staff lounge—because again, no freaking office of my own.

As I set it down on the counter where the microwave and coffeemaker are, I take them in. Perfect. Each and every petal is perfect. He must have spent a small fortune on these. Especially, to have them delivered here at this time. And even though I don't want to feel anything about this, I do.

Enraged.

Grasping the card in my hand, I pry it free from the plastic fork that was holding it up proudly, and stare down at the white paper unable to open it. I have this big surgery and then a day of delivering babies. I will not allow myself to be distracted with this.

Instead, I slip it into my scrub pocket and do my best to forget about it. To pretend that it's not burning a hole in the fabric where it rests, anxious to get at me and ruin my artfully crafted composure. How dare he? Haven't I suffered enough at his hand? Does he truly feel a bouquet of roses will turn my heart back in his direction? Make me absolve him of his sins?

"Nice flowers," Janet Johnson, a fellow third-year resident and bitch supreme, sneers as she saunters behind me like the room belongs to her. It might. Her family is loaded. Not quite Fritz loaded, but I know for a fact her daddy paid her way here. "Did your loser fiancé pick those up at Walmart for you?"

God, she's such a condescending, entitled scag.

"Actually, the card says they're from your father to me."

"You're such a cheap, useless—"

"Don't you have a job to pretend you know how to do?" I cut her off, my back to her. I shouldn't have snapped at her like that, but I'd be lying if I said it didn't feel good. She seriously only got this job because her father has offered up millions to pay for a clinic, focusing on women's health.

"I heard Carter's giving you the robot. Does your fiancé

know you're sucking your attending's dick for favors you don't deserve and haven't earned?"

"Uh-huh. Who do you think taught me how to take it so deep?" I smart, rolling my eyes as I do. I spin to face her, trying to get past her when she dips to the side, blocking my exit. "Move, I need to get to surgery."

She steps into me again as I make another attempt at weaving around her, and seriously, this is not the time or the morning to start shit with me. "I saw you walk in here this morning with Dr. Fritz. You think you're his favorite because he knows you. But I'm better than you in every way. You're nothing now that I'm here. Know this" —she juts a finger in my direction— "your time with him is over. I'll make sure of it."

I make a show of rolling my eyes, this time so she can see. This chick is like a bad soap opera with her threats. I swear, every time she opens her mouth, it's a new rendition of the same song, ever since she started here a few months ago.

"Knock yourself out, Janet. And while you're at it, thank your daddy for the fun time and the roses for me, would ya? I have a patient to operate on."

I plow past her without a second thought or a look back. Maybe if she spent half her time learning how to be a good doctor instead of a hateful wench everyone would be happy. As it is Dylan and I, along with the second years, have to pick up the slack from her doing a shitty job.

But right now, I can't focus on her. Or her threats.

I have enough on my plate and Janet is the least of my problems.

8

***

Surgery begins in ten minutes, and I start scrubbing in, getting my mind in the game. Focusing my energy on my patient. Funneling everything external out of my head, I enter the OR like I own it, silent as the nurse gowns and gloves me up.

"Dr. Hammond, what is the goal of robotic-assisted laparoscopic excision of endometriosis?" Carter bellows and all eyes turn on me. Dammit, the cocky bastard is going to treat me like an intern.

"The goal is to treat and excise the endometriosis without harming the healthy tissue of the uterus around the abnormal growths."

"What are the benefits?"

"Faster recovery, less pain, smaller incisions, earlier return to normal activities, decreased risk of infection, and hopefully, better fertility outcomes."

He's smug, devilishly gorgeous, even with his mask covering half his face as he stands on the non-dominant side of the surgical table.

"Dr. Hammond, please conduct the time out and proceed with your surgery."

I gawk at him before quickly composing myself. When he offered this to me, I thought I was to assist. Not lead. A swell of nervous anticipation crests through me but I do just as he instructs. I run the hell out of this surgery. Knowing this is exactly what I was born to do.

It's complicated. There's a lot of scar tissue and adhesions. More than I was expecting from what was visible on the imaging in her file. Carter guides me through it with a sharp tone and strict instruction. I allow Dylan to come closer, allow him to view the surgical field so he can see what stage IV endometriosis looks like on the inside, and by the time the nurses wheel the patient out, her uterus is clean.

"Slayed it, girl," Dylan whispers to me with a wink as he goes along with the PACU nurse to help get the patient settled. I give him a wink in return; satisfaction bubbling up inside me like a well, flowing through my veins.

That's why I do this.

Because when she wakes up, Dylan and I can tell her that in six weeks, she can start trying to have children. I contain my squeal of delight but just barely. The scrub nurse gives me an elbow bump and a 'nice job', and I exit the OR like the rock star I am.

"Brilliant work," Carter commends, stepping in beside me as I start to scrub out.

"Thank you."

Understatement of the century. I can't name any other third years who have gotten to do what I just did entirely on their own.

"You didn't have to do that."

"I don't ever have to do anything. I did it because I wanted to, and you've earned it." His dark eyes meet mine and something about the way he's staring at me makes my skin tingle. "I'm in the office the rest of the day."

"I'm on the floor with deliveries."

"I'll see you at home then."

Dammit, now I'm buzzing. "I'll see you at home."

My smile as well as that strange kinetic energy flowing through me carries me down the floor, past antepartum and into labor and delivery until I find Tony there waiting for me.

He smiles when he sees me, having caught my smile and thinking it was for him. It's not. I have zero smiles for this man right now.

"Did you get my flowers?" he asks, that smile only growing as I walk toward an empty patient room and step inside. That card is still in my pocket. I never got to it and now doesn't seem like the time to fish it out and read it.

"I did."

Tony sighs when he realizes the way this is going. He drops onto a chair and then reaches for me, trying to stop me from hovering by the door. "Come here," he begs softly. "Sit next to me. Sit with me. Please, Grace. I can't talk to you when you're there and I'm here."

"I'm good over here."

He frowns, staring down at his hands in his lap and I take a minute to survey him. His eyes are black and blue, as is the bridge of his nose, and his right eye has a cut just below it and is decently swollen.

Carter. He didn't even say anything, but there is no one else it could have been.

"Carter did a nice job." I swirl a finger in the air, indicating his face.

"It was a sucker punch."

"Only one?"

"He got me twice. Happy now?"

Maybe a little.

The idea of Carter throwing punches in my honor does strange things to me. When I jested I was worried about his hand if he hit Tony, I wasn't fully serious. I never expected Carter would actually throw a punch, let alone two.

Is that why he had me perform the surgery this morning and not him? No. He used the robot, showing me a technique on how to hold and manipulate it to get a better angle.

Tony rises out of his chair, crossing the room to attempt and take my hand, but I fold them across my body to stop the contact. I don't want him to touch me. All I can think about is that woman. All I can see is that woman. All I hear are her words when she described the things my fiancé did to her. It makes the bile in my empty stomach churn, enthusiastically trying to climb up the back of my throat.

Tony frowns, dropping his head into his hands and running them through his sandy brown hair as he lets out an uneven breath. "I can't stand this, Grace. I can't. I miss you like crazy. I can't sleep. I can't eat. I can't think about anything other than getting you back. Getting our life back."

Tears threaten in the back of my eyes, my nose burning as I do everything I can to hold them in. I believe him for no other reason than I can see it. He does look like crap, bruised face aside. But is he sincere? A man who I know lies to me? Does it even matter if he is?

Then something occurs to me.

"Let me see your phone," I demand.

His eyebrows hit his hairline. "My phone?"

I nod my head. "Yes. Your phone." I hold my hand out expectantly.

He blanches and I know I'm onto something here. "What do you need with my phone? I'm trying to talk to you about us and you're trying to make a call?"

He knows I'm not trying to make a call. He's stalling.

"Just have dinner with me tonight," he continues. "Talk to me."

I shake my head. "Let. Me. See. Your. Phone."

"Why? There's nothing on there," he states firmly, but there is an undercurrent of panic too.

"If there is nothing on there, then you can let me see it."

He blows out a hot breath and then reaches into his pocket and retrieves his phone, handing it to me with so much reluctance my heart turns to stone. Why am I doing this? I don't want to see what they wrote to each other. But at the same time, I need to.

I unlock his phone and immediately go to his call log. Nothing from an unknown number or with a name I don't know.

"See," he says, trying to make a swipe for his phone. "Nothing."

I tug it away from his grasp and go to his texts. And sure enough, there are two names there that I do not recognize. Daisy and Bella. I close my eyes briefly and shake my head. Bastard. When I open them again, Tony is pacing around in a circle, his hands on his hips as he breathes heavily like he's been running sprints.

I open up the text messages from Daisy first and see a lot from her. And not a lot from him. They started yesterday, talking about the good time they had the night before. She's clearly the girl I heard in the café. A couple quick things about how much fun she had and wanting to get together. He says he can't and that he's busy.

Then I go to the other one. Her texts started three weeks ago and as I scroll through...

"You sexted with her?"

"No. That's not... I felt bad. I slept with her one time." His eyes beseech mine. "I swear, only once, and then she started texting me dirty stuff and I didn't know how to say no. I never planned on getting in touch and when she started messaging me, I kept telling her I was busy. I assumed she'd take the hint. She hasn't."

"But you texted them back. Both of them. You gave them your phone number to begin with. Them. As in multiple women and these are just the ones I'm seeing. You lied. You said it was one time. You said you told her it was a mistake. You told me she meant nothing. All of it lies."

He continues to pace. "I liked their attention. Not them. I love you. I never see you, Grace. You're this brilliant doctor. A woman who doesn't need me. These women did. They wanted me and I..."

"You cheated. I know." I can't stand the sight of him. "You need to leave. I'm at work and I can't be around you right now."

"Please, Grace. Just have dinner with me. Talk to me. We'll get counseling. You can't just throw away three years of a relationship. We're engaged. We'll go away on a trip together. Whatever it takes, we can fix this."

"The time to try and fix this was before you stuck your dick in another woman. I can't forgive you for what you've done. I can't. You can try and blame this on me, but I never cheated. We had problems, sure. We work long hours, both of us. But my legs stayed closed. I would have never betrayed you, but you betrayed me. You lied and betrayed me several times over. Now we're done."

With that, I leave him behind, heading out to find my next patient. Ready to tackle the rest of my day. A mistake. Being with him, trusting him, hoping things would change and settle down. All of it a mistake.

I should be shattered, but I'm not.

I'm sad, yet oddly relieved. I feel like I just escaped a death sentence. What would have happened to me if I had blindly married him? If I had never discovered his infidelity?

I shudder at that.

And even though I just said goodbye to my fiancé for good, all I can think about is how he looked. Carter punched the hell out of him. Something that seems so very un-Carter like to do. But maybe I'm wrong thinking that. Maybe there's so much more to Carter Fritz than I ever knew existed.

Whatever.

One thing I'm certain of, my old life is over and my new one starts now. I have no other choice but to hope my days of making mistakes are over.

9

For the first time since I bought the place from Oliver last month, I don't want to come home. I stayed at the hospital for an extra two hours after my shift, catching up on paperwork that didn't truly need catching up on. There weren't any patients for me to jump in on. Any surgeries to get lost in.

Tony sending Grace roses was all over the floor.

Him showing up was too.

All the nurses were talking about it. Janet Johnson was snarling to me non-stop both in text and in person about how inappropriate it is that she allowed that to happen—even going so far as to demand her immediate suspension since Grace knows flowers aren't allowed in the PACU. And when everyone realized Grace was no longer wearing her engagement ring, the rumors started spreading like wildfire.

Welcome to working in a hospital.

People need something to cover up all the sickness and death, the long, grueling, thankless hours and they use the drama of other's lives. A few even asked me about her situation, though I didn't say anything either way.

No one knows she's living with me now. If they did, well, it could cause problems.

I've already had to repel teasing comments from other attendings and residents that claim I favor Grace above all others. I'm essentially her boss. She is a senior resident, one who reports directly to me. I evaluate her work. I teach her.

Any sort of relationship beyond professional is frowned upon. Unethical given my position of authority over her. I can make or break her career with a simple word. Even worse, if something as deadly as dirty gossip spreads not just within these hospital walls, but throughout the country—trust me, gossip travels fast within our resident/doctor world—it'll limit where she'll receive worthy-of-her-talent attending position offers.

We're already toeing the line, but I assured my boss at the time that Grace's relationship with my family and my brother would not impact our work. That I could be fair and impartial.

Then I started to like her.

Then I started to *really* like her.

Now I'm living with her, and she's no longer engaged.

But all that means is I have to keep myself in closer check.

So yeah, I wasn't so anxious to come home today. I ate shitty hospital food for dinner instead of leftover enchiladas as I wanted. All I can hope for now as I unlock the door to my condo is that Grace is in her room.

Only the moment I swing the door open, all that unease flees from my body, completely overtaken by a surge of adrenaline. "Grace?" I yell, dropping my bag to the floor and rushing across the foyer to the edge of the great room where she's sprawled out on the floor. I fall to my knees, cupping her face in my hand and tilting it toward me. "Talk to me." She's not stiff, jerking, or twitching. No obvious signs she's seizing.

She blinks, her pretty blue eyes clear but a little distant. "I saw some flashes of light, so I sprawled myself out on your rug in case it was a focal aware seizure that wanted to turn into a tonic-clonic one."

"Is that how it happens for you?"

"Yes. Usually. I laid down and did my deep breathing exercises and it passed."

"Did you take anything? An Ativan?"

"No. They're in my purse and I was afraid of dropping in the kitchen."

Jesus Christ, I sit back on my haunches. "How long have you been on the ground?"

"I don't know. Ten minutes maybe? I was thinking mostly."

"Are you on any other medications?"

She shakes her head, slowly starting to sit up. I help her, moving her until her back is against the couch, nowhere near the coffee table, keeping a close watch on her eyes and body. I've never actually seen Grace have a seizure, but I know Oliver has, more than once, and I know it scared the shit out of him.

"I haven't had a seizure in four years and my neurologist weaned me off Keppra over a year ago. Now it's just rescue meds if I feel something coming on."

"Grace. Dammit." I should have been here. I was sitting at my desk avoiding her because I don't know how to be around her like this, but I should have been here. "Don't move. I'm going to get your Ativan."

"No," she snaps, reaching out and grabbing my arm to stop me. "I'm fine now. It was over before it even started. It might not have even been a FAS. I don't typically get flashes of light; I get more of a wave sensation followed by what sounds like a fan with people talking into it blowing in my head. Anyway, I didn't want to take any chances. I was just being overly cautious. I really am fine. It was... you know... a stressful day."

"Because of Tony?"

"That certainly kicked things off. Janet didn't help as the woman stalked me down all day just to make nasty comments, and then I had a delivery that didn't go well. Drug-addicted mom who was in the process of coming off her high, delivering a twenty-six-week preemie. Mom left AMA (against medical advice) not even two hours after delivering."

I grimace. "Sorry. Baby doing okay?"

"Up in the NICU with a Wonder Woman sticker beside her incubator. Her vitals were okay, but not stellar when I left." She tilts her head at me as I move to sit beside her. "You gave Tony quite the broken nose. He's sporting a pretty good shiner and a laceration under his eye."

I grin at her change of topic, rubbing my hand across my mouth to the back of my neck. "Oliver told me to break his nose. So, I did."

"And his eye?"

"That was a bonus."

"So you broke his nose because Oliver asked you to? Since when do you ever do what he requests?"

I look into her eyes, something in her tone as she asks that. "I didn't hit him only because Oliver asked me to."

"Then why did you?"

I reach out and cup her cheek in my hand, allowing myself to appreciate her soft, velvety skin for the first time. It sends a rush of heat through me, an electricity so potent all the hair on my arms stands up. She must feel it too because she sucks in a rushed breath, her eyes widening.

"I hit him because he had it coming. Because he deserved that and more. And when I walked out of there, I regretted not hitting him harder."

She stares at me for a moment, her eyes searching mine, my heart hammering in my chest. I can't do this with her. It's wrong. Us. The timing. All of it. I release her face and she quickly looks away.

"Did it feel good?" she questions, now staring down at her

hands. "I'm kind of jealous I didn't think to punch him this morning."

"It did feel good."

She takes my right hand from my lap and examines it. It's perfectly fine, but having her hold my hand, touch my skin, make sure I'm not hurt has me wanting to lean in and kiss her so badly I can hardly take a breath in from the crushing desire of it.

"Your hand appears to be okay. I would have been pissed at you if you had hurt yourself. Then again, maybe I would get more surgeries all to myself that way."

I chuckle, inching in before I can stop it. "I'm giving Janet a laparoscopic total hysterectomy tomorrow."

"What?" she gasps in outrage. "You can't. Janet isn't half the surgeon I am. Not even a quarter."

"Agreed. But she needs more OR time and people already talk about how you're my favorite resident."

"Am I your favorite, Dr. Fritz?" She bats her eyelashes playfully, tilting her head coquettishly.

I laugh, moving in even closer. So close I can see just how brilliantly blue her eyes are. The color pure and even like a cloudless summer sky. Even as her pupils dilate ever so slightly. The fragrance of her shampoo and the smell of her skin hit me hard on an inhale. I can feel the heat of her body, how it's starting to get warmer than it was even just a few moments ago.

"Not my favorite," I lie. "Just the best."

"I'll take that. I like being the best. It's all I've ever wanted to be."

"You seem less sad today than you were yesterday," I note and then hate myself for saying it even if the barrier it instantly puts up is an essential one. She stiffens, looking away again, but I don't move. I don't pull back. My arm is touching her arm and our knees are bent, our thighs side by side.

Kissing her would be easier than breathing right now. And

from this angle, I'd just have to turn a little—not even a lot—and I'd have full access to her lush bee-stung lips. I'd lower her to the ground in a second, my body on top of hers in even less time.

Which is why I'm glad when she says, "I opened the card he sent with the roses everyone was talking about. I hadn't read it all day. I was sort of avoiding it, especially after I told him I was done. But I read it when I came home tonight."

Home. My home. Now hers, I guess.

"What did it say?" I ask, my curiosity getting the better of me when she doesn't follow that up. Done. She told him she was done. That shouldn't make me as happy as it does.

"It said, *She meant nothing. You mean everything. I miss you.*" Then she laughs, dropping her head back onto the cushion of the sofa, her eyes closing.

"I'm confused."

"For all his whining that he misses me so much, he never came here yesterday. He never tried to find me until this morning at work. Maybe because of you and your mighty fists, but the man is a coward. A total coward who sends roses to my place of work, sends me texts, and confronts me there. A man who would rather fuck strangers—strangers he's still texting with, mind you—than his fiancée. He's not the man I thought he was all these years. The man I told myself I was in love with was a figment of my imagination." Her head pops up, her eyes finding mine. "So, no. I'm not sad anymore, Carter. I'm angry at so many, many things, but I'm also relieved. Think of the mistake marrying him would have been. All my friends, especially you and Oliver repeatedly pointed out all the ways he was wrong for me, and I never listened. Now it's like my eyes have been opened wide and I never want to shut them again."

"Then don't. You have so much freedom now, Grace. You can do anything. Be with anyone you want."

"There is a very good and distinct reason that smart, successful women tend to stay single longer and marry later."

"Why's that?"

She stares at me like I'm an idiot. "Because men are intimidated by us. Tony certainly was. That's what he said this morning. I'm a brilliant doctor and I didn't need him the way those girls did. Only I did need him, just not the way he wanted me to. I think that's what men don't understand. Just because we don't need them to take care of us financially or play the part of always minding what we do and how we do it, doesn't mean we don't need them on a different level."

"Men like Tony are weak. All ego. They fail to recognize that having an intelligent, confident, talented, successful woman as their counterpart will not only challenge them intellectually but is sexy as hell. Any man who feels emasculated by the woman he's with because she's all those things isn't worthy of her. It could be worse though."

"Worse?" She laughs the word. "How so?"

I point to my chest. "Try being an Abbot-Fritz."

She rolls her eyes derisively at me, straightening her legs out in front of her. "Yeah. My heart bleeds for you. Smart. Successful. Rich. Handsome."

"I knew you thought I was hot."

I get an elbow to the flank for that. "I forgot to mention arrogant, obnoxious—"

I pinch her hip and she squeals, smacking my hand away.

"For real though, you know the issues we have with dating."

"Yes. I do. Fame and money make you targets. Boston's billionaire bachelors. The Abbot-Fritzes. Only made worse by Oliver and Amelia hitting front-page news every other day. You boys make dating a sport the fans of Boston love to cheer for."

I smirk at the way she describes that if for no other reason than the truth behind it. Being a Fritz in this city is both a blessing and a curse. We're their favorite sons. Their royalty. Amelia calls us influencers and I hate to admit she's likely right.

"Now you know why I bring my dates here for dinner instead of taking them out."

"Oh," she remarks, an irresistible sparkle to her eyes. "I assumed it was easier to fuck them that way. You know, less work for you."

"Well, you've effectively cockblocked me by moving in, so it seems now I'll have to put in some effort."

"If you're as lazy in bed as you are with your dating habits, your dates will thank me. Besides, I don't fully live here yet. I have to get the rest of my stuff first."

"Trust me, Grace. I am the opposite of lazy in bed." I grin devilishly, loving how her cheeks tint up with just the slightest hint of a blush. "How about we move you in on Friday?" I offer, changing the subject back to safer territory. "Both of us have the day off."

"*We*? You're going to help me on your day off?"

"Sure. What's the big deal?"

"Saturday, we start a twenty-four-hour shift."

I shrug. "Exactly. It's not like I had big plans going into that anyway."

"No hot dates for Carter Fritz?"

"You sound jealous, Grace. You wanna be my hot date?"

She makes a scoffing sound, her voice dripping with sarcasm when she says, "Yeah. I'm all for being someone's hot date right now."

I stare at her, my eyebrows pinched. "Why wouldn't you be? Because you miss Tony?"

"No. Not because I miss Tony because I don't even know if I do, which sounds weird and bad to say since we were engaged, but it's a truth I can't deny either. Maybe because we hardly ever saw each other to begin with or because I'm as angry as I am, it's eclipsing any heartache, but I can't say it's that either."

"So why aren't you a hot date then?"

She bites into her bottom lip, trying to look away when I catch her face in my hand and drag it back to me. She doesn't want to say whatever is plaguing her mind and in reading her expression, I don't need her to. I know what she's thinking and it's so fucking wrong.

"You're hot, Grace."

"What?"

"Tony isn't a man worthy of stealing your confidence in that. You're my resident and my brother's friend and now my roommate. I shouldn't tell you this, but you're hot. Seriously fucking beautiful. Sexy and smart and funny. You've just been with the wrong guy. That's all."

Her eyes sparkle at me, glittering as they stare into mine, deeper than I think she's ever looked before. Deep enough that I feel her gaze like a fist, clenching my heart and squeezing my lungs. This would be the moment. I've thought of nothing but kissing her all night and if I lean in a few inches...

She smiles at me like I'm the sun after a rainstorm, her head falling onto my shoulder. "Thank you, Carter."

Disappointment slams into me with the force of a freight train. I open my mouth, needing to alleviate this strangling sensation by saying something stupid like no problem or a variation of it, but I'm stuck on what she just did. I've seen her do this move with Oliver hundreds of times, and I don't know how I feel about her doing it to me now.

I am her friend, I guess, but it's also the last thing I ever want to be to her.

Attending. Best friend's brother.

I could live with those.

They were tolerable—just barely—but tolerable all the same. I was fine when being near her was just at work, or when we were mixed into a group.

But being here alone with her is different.

I'm so acutely aware of all things Grace. I listen for her movements about the house. I think about what she's doing in her room. Hell, the place already smells like her, and it's only been a few days.

I can't escape the woman I'm crazy about and she just friend-zoned me with one simple move.

She fucking Olivered me.

And with that, any residual hope that had been impossible for me to kill just died.

Story of my life, right there. The guy always wanting what he can never get. Left in a permanent state of aching. The friend. The good guy. The one everyone turns to when they need something only to move on from just as quickly.

I've loved two women... The first, I took for granted though if we're speaking in truths, I always knew in my heart and the back of my mind that Alanna never felt the same way for me in return. It's why I never made a play until I was set to move back to Boston. I knew she'd reject me, and I didn't want that to ruin our friendship or residency together.

Still, it hurt. It hurt when she said we were just friends and it hurt when she found someone else.

Now there's Grace.

And I think my romantic woes with her are well established by this point.

I just wish... for once...

I sigh, sagging back against the couch and closing my eyes, my chest heavier than I think it's ever been as I let her take her comfort on my shoulder.

Maybe one day I'll meet the right woman at the right time. I'll act when I should act. She'll want me the way I want her. It'll be perfect. Maybe.

But that woman is obviously not Grace. No matter how much I had wrongfully, foolishly, desperately hoped it would be.

The moment we step over the threshold of her apartment Friday afternoon, Grace lets out a bitter snort. "Well, I see that missing me is going well. I wonder if whoever this belongs to was with him when he texted me that last night." She points to a woman's bra hanging haphazardly off the end of one of the chairs. "You realize that means she went home without it on. What woman leaves a place without her bra on?"

She rolls her eyes, stepping over an empty bottle of tequila.

The kitchen table is a mess of empty shot glasses, the saltshaker spilled over on its side, and sliced lime wedges sticking to the wood.

"That was my table set. I think he can keep it now."

My jaw locks up at the sight of this place. It's a fucking disaster and smells like a shitty strip club, complete with stale alcohol and cheap perfume. "Did you tell him we were coming today to move you out?"

"Um. No." She rolls her head over her shoulder and meets my eyes. "I was afraid he'd be here if I did. I'm not sure which scenario would have been better. This or him."

"Him," I grit out. "I could have hit him again then."

"Have I mentioned how much I like this feral alpha side of you?" she teases.

"Cute." I give her a small shove in the direction of her bedroom. "Let's get your stuff and get out of here."

"Agreed. I'm afraid to touch anything and that's including the floors. At least my STI screening came back negative."

I freeze mid-step. "What?"

She turns back around to face me, her eyebrows pinched, as her head tilts. "I can't tell if you're surprised it came back clean or you're surprised I got myself tested."

"You didn't mention anything."

"I didn't realize we were on that level of girl talk yet, Carter. If it helps, I didn't tell Oliver about it either. A woman's vagina, as I know you know, is a sacred vessel."

I shake my head. She's right. Nothing I'm saying right now makes any sense. "Sorry. I just hate that you had to go through that."

"That makes two of us, but I'm glad I did. By the look of this place, I dodged a bullet. If he had given me something, they never would have found his body." She glances around, staring at one piece of furniture, followed by the next. "Good thing all my textbooks are in boxes in the basement. Most everything else that's here we bought together, and I no longer want any of it. I thought I would want my table and chairs or maybe the couch I brought with me when I moved in with him, but I don't. They're just reminders of how far and how bad things have gone from what they once were." She points to the corner of the room by the big bay window. "He proposed to me there. Right in front of our first Christmas tree. He slid this ring" —she holds up her diamond between her fingers— "and I remember thinking how lucky I was. How happy. Now all I can think about is how stupid and blind I've been. How angry I am at all of this."

She drops the ring into one of the empty shot glasses with a resounding *clink* and then she's marching back into the bedroom.

"Jesus," she hisses at the condom wrappers strewn about and the sheets that are in total disarray before heading straight into her closet. She jumps up, grabbing a suitcase from a high shelf and drops it to the floor, unzipping it. "Just fill it with everything you see."

Then she marches out of the closet, and I set to work, doing the same thing I did a week ago when this all started. I have everything in the suitcase, zipping it up when I hear the sound of some twangy music and then what can only be glass shattering. Racing out of the closet, I search around the disheveled room only to come up empty. Another sound from the bathroom catches me and I go running in, only to discover Grace smiling as she slams a bottle of what looks to be expensive cologne onto the floor.

It explodes, shards of glass and liquid flying every which way, and then I realize what the twangy music is. "What the hell are you doing?"

She peeks up, smiling from ear to ear. Then shrugs before grabbing another bottle, this one some kind of face cream or something and doing the same.

"It's good enough for Carrie Underwood. Maybe next time he'll think before he cheats," she deadpans, and I crack, laughing so hard I'm nearly wheezing with it. "You wanna do one? He's got all kinds of expensive products. The man primps way more than I do. I mean, what self-respecting straight man has kelp facemasks and tinted moisturizers? He spends thousands of dollars on this crap."

I step further into the bathroom that now reeks horribly and survey what's left as Carrie Underwood sings her heart out about smashing a guy's car in. I spot a glass bottle of the face-mask she mentioned and pick it up, tossing it up and catching it in my hand to feel its weight.

"Give it a good throw. Let's see that pitcher's arm in action."

I grin. "How do you remember I was a pitcher in high school?" And college, but by that point, I never saw her anymore since I was gone and she was still in high school.

"I have a memory like a steel trap. Come on, Fritz. Impress me with that mighty arm of yours. Show me what all us girls used to swoon over."

"*All* you girls? Does that include you, Hammond?"

"I am neither confirming nor denying."

I chuckle, shaking my head at her, but do what she asks all the same. This is her party after all and whatever I can do to get that smile on her face instead of the frown that's been perched there since we stepped into this apartment, I will.

I push her behind me, so she doesn't catch any of the spray, get in position, go through the motion of my wind up, and then launch the bottle across the large bathroom through the open shower door and watch as it smashes against the tile wall, shards falling like rain all over the shower floor along with globby green stuff.

"Nice. Go again."

"Nope. Your turn, sweetheart. Let it fly." I hand her a large bottle of something that says toner, whatever that is.

"Show me how to throw a real pitch?" she asks.

"You serious?"

"If I'm doing it, I want to do it right."

Can't argue with that logic. I move in behind her, adjusting her so her back is against my chest, her ass to my thigh. My hand covers the one holding the bottle, adjusting her body until I have her the way I want her. Her breath hitches when she feels me flush against her, my face so close I know she can feel the warmth of my breath.

I shouldn't be doing this. I shouldn't be this close to her, but fuck it, she asked.

Her hair tickles my cheek as I speak into her ear. "Keep your hands up in front of you, take a short step back and then pivot to the side with your dominant foot." I use the hand not covering hers to adjust her hips, showing her how I want her to move. "Shift your weight to your pivot foot and then bring your other knee up. As you move forward, you're going to wind up your throwing arm and use the momentum of your leg coming down to hurl the glass as hard as you can." I keep her hand in mine, demonstrating the motion, and then I release her, stepping back.

"Like this?" she asks, glancing quickly to catch my eye before returning to her target.

"Perfect. Grip it and rip it."

She laughs, but does just that, throwing a somewhat sloppy pitch, not that it matters. It has the desired effect with more glass breaking. She lets out a small squeal of delight, clapping her hands. "Oh, yes. Felt more powerful that way."

"Anything else you want to break?"

She meets my eyes in the mirror, her expression growing contemplative before she shakes her head. "Nah, I don't need any bad luck coming my way. I never considered myself the crazy, vindictive type, but I have to admit, this felt good. Seriously good. Probably similar to when you punched him. I'm still jealous of that though knowing me I would have given myself a boxers fracture on his stupid, hard jaw."

"You know what you need?"

She spins around, her teeth meeting her bottom lip, almost as if she's trying to hide a smile. "Carter, there are so many things I need right now. I don't even know where to start. I'm hoping your idea is smarter than mine."

I give her a bemused look, hitching my hip into the side of the counter. "What's your idea?"

"Nothing that makes any sense at all and will only lead to trouble. Please, tell me yours instead."

I stare at her, trying to read her expression, but she shuts it down quickly, averting her gaze yet I'd swear there is a blush that wasn't there a few seconds ago. Carrie Underwood stops singing and the room falls quiet except for her slightly accelerated breathing.

Was she thinking about... no. Impossible. She wouldn't...

Before conscious thought can take over, I step into her, lifting her chin until her eyes meet mine. "What were you thinking?"

"Nothing. Just forget it."

My thumb brushes along the line of her jaw and I watch as her lips part and her pupils blow. Fuck. My cock jerks against the zipper of my jeans, and for a moment, I imagine hoisting her up on top of this counter, tilting her back, and eating her out until she comes on my face before flipping her around and taking her from behind while she watches us in the mirror.

But I can't do it.

I can't be her revenge. She's angry, she said so herself, and I won't be someone she fucks now and regrets later—because she will fucking regret it.

I want too much from her for that.

She doesn't actually want me. She just wants an act of rebellion, something to make her even with Tony. Something to make her feel better, more in control. Like breaking the bottles did.

I lean in, unable to stop the action and listen as her breath catches high in her throat. A small press in and somehow I'm right here. So close. So stupid, I am not who or what she wants. I clear my throat. Clear my thoughts.

"I was thinking about taking you to that ice cream place Drew and Margot always hit up," I offer, knowing Grace's crazy love for all things sweet will save us both.

A smirk quirks up the corner of her lips. "You mean the one where you can add alcohol to your shake?"

"That's the one."

"You trying to get me drunk?"

"Only on sugar. We can even pop into that candy store on Charles Street on our way home."

She moans and my cock jerks again, begging for attention I refuse to give. If Grace looked down, she'd find me hard and then I wouldn't be able to stop. She'd see how much I want her and that would be that, fate sealed. But not all my blood is in my dick. I still have enough in my brain to give me sense and keep me sane.

"Is that what you want to do?"

No. Not even close. "Yes."

"You're buying. You're a billionaire attending and I'm the homeless woman now trying to save up for a new place to live plus new furniture on a resident's salary."

"I'm buying, but you have to promise no gummies."

She laughs. "You and your weird thing with gummies."

"They're nasty, Grace. All gelatin-based products are. Jell-O is no better."

"All the chocolate I want?"

"All the chocolate you want."

"You've got a deal. Let's get out of here before we can never get this stink off our skin. Incidentally, your idea is a lot safer and a hell of a lot less messy than my idea was, though maybe not as fun if you know what I mean." She winks at me, skipping over the broken glass back into the bedroom and I groan.

"You're evil," I yell, following her into the bedroom that is like a sex crime scene.

"I know, but you're cute when you get all hot and bothered, Doctor. It's not a look I get to see on you very often. Nice to know I still have that affect on men." She glances indignantly about the room, and I was right not to act.

But still...

I grab her hand before she can grab her suitcase, giving it a tug until she spins to look back at me. "Don't let him take away that part of you. This is all Tony, Grace. Not you. What did I tell you the other night? You know me well enough to know I don't just throw out compliments to pad egos. I say something, I mean it. You are everything any man with half a brain and a pulse would want." *Myself included*, I don't add.

Hell, the woman gets me hard with a simple glance.

"I think it's lucky that Tony doesn't have half a brain," she whispers, swallowing hard.

"I think it's definitely lucky." I just wish it was lucky for me too.

Releasing her hand, I pick up her suitcase, and with one last look around the room, she leads the way out, dropping her key on the floor before shutting the door behind us.

"Done," I say. "You never have to go back."

"Now I'm stuck living with my cocky, oh-so-serious attending in a penthouse residence at The Ritz. How will I ever survive it?"

My thoughts exactly.

11

"I thought we said this was going to be a lowkey night?" Carter shouts in my ear as we enter the crowded restaurant that could easily double as a club of sorts. The place is packed. There is a DJ spinning a mix of Top 40 and indie rock—no complaints there—and the dance floor is filled to the brim with gyrating bodies.

"This wasn't my idea."

"Then why are we here? We start a twenty-four-hour shift tomorrow at seven a.m."

"Oliver said it was just dinner."

"Clearly he lied." Carter points to the table packed with all of our friends, his five brothers, and several women I don't know who are likely their dates. Adding to that, there are people openly taking pictures of them. "Jesus. Do the press have a tracking device on us or what?" he grouses, placing his hand on the small of my back as we try to maneuver through the room. "I'd rather not be photographed tonight."

"For once," I smart.

"Forever. I hate it. I come from a family of moncy. I date women. Who gives a fuck?"

He has a point in that.

"At least the music is good," I counter. "This is my favorite Wild Minds song."

"Which one is this?"

"Time Surrender. So good. Jasper Diamond's voice gives me chills every time I hear it."

"You just want to screw him."

I can't help but laugh at that. At the pinched scowl on his face as he says it. "You do know he's married with kids, right? Not to mention a celebrity." Then I laugh harder. "Sorta like you and your gang of hoodlums minus the married and kids part."

"Ha, ha." Carter isn't amused.

I spin around, walking backward, forcing Carter to take my hand. "Come on, old man. Fall into the role. Sexy. Billionaire. Bachelor playboy with a different woman on his arm every night. Smile for the cameras. Remember what it's like to be young. When was the last time you had any fun?"

He blinks at me, almost as if he's been stunned into a state of shock. Like my words hit a nerve and he's suddenly awakening from a coma, realizing that years of his life have past, and he has no idea what's happened while he was sleeping.

"You want to have some fun?"

"I think I deserve a night of fun, don't you?" I counter.

"Eat first and then dance or dance first and then eat?"

Only I never get the chance to answer that question as with my next breath, I'm swarmed like bees on a flower by a group of very determined women. They move me as a unit, prying me without challenge away from Carter and out onto the dance floor.

"We're so happy you came out to meet us," Amelia exclaims, a smile lighting her gray eyes to an almost smoky color as she moves and sways to the Wild Minds beat. "I've never been here before, but I think now that we've brought

Layla and Stella, it will be our new place." She points behind me, and I turn over my shoulder to find the two teenagers cutting loose and dancing with abandon.

I turn back to Amelia. "I wish I could dance like them. I'm like a baby giraffe. All arms and legs and no rhythm."

Two hands land on my hips. "I can help with that. Painting is all rhythm." Aria, one of Rina's BFFs shifts in behind me, dancing with me and getting me in tune with how I should move. "Perfect," she praises. "You've got it. You're just rusty. All that time in the hospital and not enough time living."

"No kidding," I deadpan. "Though I'm not usually a fan of clubs."

This place isn't bad, likely because it's not actually a club, but I've been to a few clubs that were all about strobe lights and while I've been okay at them if I close my eyes or avoid the light, I always worry about having a seizure from too much visual stimulation. There is a reason games like Space Invaders at the arcade have seizure warnings. It's not for regular folks, it's for folks like me, and they're warnings I heed.

If you've ever had a seizure in public, you quickly learn it's not something you ever want to repeat. I've had plenty. In elementary, middle, and high school. In college and med school as well. My last at a party one night after smoking a lot of weed and drinking too many shots.

I've been hospitalized. Put on so many drugs my mind was in a permanent fog. I've changed my entire diet, cutting out this thing and that. And for a while, as a child and teenager, I will admit, I was pissed off. Angry that my brain wouldn't listen, wouldn't react the way I wanted it to.

When you have a seizure, you feel powerless.

You have no control over anything. Not your movements, your breathing, your bowels and bladder—yep, as classy as it gets. You are a slave to your inner brain cell electrical activity and it's... well... it's fucking crushing to know that this is your reality. Much like any disease or disorder is. But with epilepsy, you're fine one second, going about your life, and then in the next, you're having a seizure.

I won't deny how lucky I am. How I've been able to mostly manage myself with a few crucial life adjustments. But I've seen the struggle others go through firsthand and simply put, it's a disorder that can shatter lives and break your heart.

"Well a fan of clubs or not, I know Oliver is glad you came," Amelia announces, dragging me from my thoughts. "He's been worried non-stop about you."

"Did he tell you how my apartment looked like a whorehouse?"

Amelia gnaws on her lips, glancing over to Rina, Halle, Margot, and Aria in turn. Oliver had texted asking for an update on getting my things and I told him all about it, sparing no detail. That's how Carter and I got roped into coming here. At least I managed to go candy shopping first.

"I'm going to take that as a yes."

"Are you okay? I realize that's such a dumb question, but I have to ask." Halle grasps my shoulder, slipping in front of me, mirroring the moves that Aria—and me, I guess—are doing. "I've had exes cheat and commit crimes and all sorts of wonderfulness, so I get it. When those assholes do that, they rob you of a piece of yourself you never even realized you gave them."

"Truth," Margot agrees. "How is it that the human psyche is so conditioned to giving ourselves away to those who are quick to harm us and so slow to believe and trust those who wish to covet us?"

Damn. I don't think truer words have ever been spoken.

Why is that? We can hear a million words of praise from a million people but then someone does something that rattles our inner core and it's like all those other things fall helplessly into the void. Tony made me feel unsexy. Undesirable. Too ambitious.

He made me feel like there was something wrong with me because he cheated.

As if it was my fault because I didn't 'need' him the way he wanted me to. I didn't fit into his preconceived mold of what a woman and wife should be. But he didn't just cheat. He was having sex with strangers in a way he never would with me.

The ultimate kick to the self-esteem.

And then Carter, with all those things he said. Why was I quicker to believe the negative of Tony's actions over the positive of Carter's words?

"I'm okay," I say to all the women who have eyes all over me. I throw my hands up in the air, allowing myself to have these women move and sway me as music flows around us. "I don't know. In truth, and maybe I'm just fucking up the stages of grief here, but I feel liberated. I mean, angry and hurt and shitty, sure, but just... I never want to be that Grace again. The one who never saw what was coming her way. The one who was with the guy she should have known wasn't right all along. I wish I had listened to everyone who told me he was trash before I found out they were right."

"No better time to be liberated than the present," Halle teases with a smirk I can't quite read.

"Huh?"

"You have this totally hot guy staring at you, so who cares if you didn't listen before, you get to do whatever you want now. Like him."

That's Margot and I can't help but stare at her only to laugh a second later as I catch some random man heading for our female circle of power. I blink twice, taking him in—he is pretty hot—and then back over to her.

"Maybe he's coming for you," I throw back at her.

"No way. I'm a nurse. We have instincts you doctors don't. He wants you."

"Oh right," Rina argues, dancing her heart out as the song

changes to some slower country ballad. "You mean the way you knew that Drew was in love with you all along?"

Margot shakes her head. "Different. Drew was in love with Aria."

"Until he kissed you," Aria counters.

"Whatever, I can read other people better than I can read myself and this guy wants Grace. She's all yours," she announces to him just as he reaches us, standing directly beside me with a smile that says he wants to do more than simply dance with me.

"I don't…"

"Hi," he says cutting me off, his tone pure seduction, his eyes drunk on lust. "Wanna dance?"

"I'm not sure that's such—"

Aria releases my hips and steps away, giving me a wink. Halle does the same and then off they fly like birds into the night sky. Suddenly, I feel abandoned, alone once again. Lost. But why? And how? I have the power here. He's just some random stranger in a restaurant.

"Sure, it is," he tells me, his hands coming for my body, resting on my hips, his eyes devouring me. "You're beautiful. I was watching you with your friends and I couldn't take my eyes off you."

"Um. Thank you. But I think I'm done dancing for the night."

"Fine by me. I just wanted to talk to you."

"I'm with some people."

"You can be with me tonight instead," he offers. "I'll buy you dinner. Unless you're here with a guy?" He glances up in the direction of the table all my friends are at. "The one you came in with?"

Jesus, how long has this man been watching me? "He's—"

"Because that guy is glaring at us. Is he your boyfriend?"

"Huh?"

He nods over my shoulder, urging me to look.

So, I do. I glance over my shoulder because instinct and curiosity are tricky fuckers. And when I do look, when I wade through the people getting their country on around us, I spot Carter, all the way over there, sitting at the huge table all of us are occupying, talking to his brothers... and staring directly at me.

His dark eyes are hooded, fierce, his sharp jaw lined in a stubble it's not typically known for is clenched tight. His eyes capture mine and once they do all that tension evaporates as a slow, easy, sexy as all sin grin glides suavely up his gorgeous face. He says something to someone and then he rises, stepping out of the booth and heading straight for the dance floor.

Straight for me.

"Is he your boyfriend?" the stranger repeats.

"No," I reply, but with the way he's staring at me...

My stomach tightens, coiling to uncomfortable levels as Carter saunters like a king lion across the room. People snap pictures, but he takes no notice of them. No, his eyes are solely on mine.

"I don't think he agrees."

"That's not how it is with us," I retort because it's not. Carter doesn't want me. He's just looking out for me. Trying to be helpful and protective. Caring for his resident and brother's friend the way anyone else in his position would. Right?

He brought me into his home and took care of me when I could hardly take care of myself. Even if I'd swear to baby Jesus he was hard today when he was teaching me how to throw a pitch. But wouldn't most men get hard if they were pressed up against a woman they claim they view as beautiful?

Yes, that's just biology. It means nothing.

I have no instincts right now. They're all blind, stumbling around in the dark, banging into walls and furniture, and messing everything up. I was engaged to a man who I swore faithfully loved and cherished me endlessly. A man who was actually doing the exact opposite behind my back and under my nose.

How does trust grow—with anyone—after that?

"Whether it is or it isn't, his glare is telling me something else."

Carter reaches us just as the guy's words hit the air. His eyes hover above mine. "Tell him to go," he demands and because he did, my instinct is to fight it. Is to demand in return that this random guy with a face I don't even remember stay. "Now."

"Hey man, I'm not looking for a—"

"Good. Then you can fuck off," Carter says coolly, no break in his veneer that is all control. All dominance.

The guy must be looking to me for an answer, but I haven't taken my eyes away from Carter. In the next second, the guy is gone, mumbling something under his breath, only to be replaced by Carter who is standing obstinately before me, commanding my full attention.

"You look a little lost out here, sweetheart."

God, how did he read that?

"Women like me are never lost. It's all a matter of read-justing."

A crooked smile curls up the corner of his lips. "That I believe. He wasn't the right one for you tonight."

"No?"

"No."

"I wasn't exactly interested." I stare up into his dark eyes, trying desperately to read between lines that are impossible to find. He's shuttered shut. A book locked up tight.

"Oliver ordered food for you," he continues. "It should be at the table soon. How about a dance until it comes?"

Without a word or a second's thought or hesitation, I raise my arms up to his shoulders, slipping them around his neck. "I'm not much of a dancer," I tell him.

"But I'm a hell of a teacher."

Don't I know it.

His hands find the crest of my lower back, just above my ass, clinging to the line between my lasered-on pants and crop top. His body enfolds against mine, a simple sway to an unfamiliar beat guiding us. My heart isn't listening to me when I tell it to relax. It's pounding along with the music, giddy and high with energy.

Carter clasps my hand, holding it firmly in his grasp before he shoots me out, twisting me around in some sort of crazy, convoluted spin of looping arms until he hauls me back, catching me, cradling me in his arm. My breath shakes, my laugh high in my throat. He starts to grind, to twist and dance like a man who absolutely knows how to move his body.

"Where did you learn to dance like this?" I ask, giggling uncontrollably.

"Fritz training program. It's like rich kid bootcamp. Dance, tennis—"

"Oh, fencing," I interrupt. "We should fence. I remember doing that with Oliver and Rina a couple of times when we were kids."

"Some other time, I think. I'd much prefer to dance than fight with you right now."

"Well, I'm certainly not complaining. Even if it is a first."

I give him a cheeky grin, cocking an eyebrow, the lights of the bar swirling red and green and blue all around us. Actually, the only place we do anything that could be considered fighting is at work. This past week in the condo has been easy and light.

"It's my job to be strict with you." His gaze holds mine. "And I'd be lying if I said I didn't love our fights. But there's more—"

"Hey," Oliver cuts in, his hand on my shoulder, squeezing me. "Your dinner is at the table. I know you guys have to get out early for your shifts tomorrow."

I meet his green eyes and smile appreciatively. And by the

time I look back to Carter, whose arms have dropped, and his body has created distance between us, I know that whatever this moment, this day, between us was is over. Tomorrow at work, we'll be back to us.

And for the first time, I can't help but be a little disappointed by that.

12

Dropping onto the couch, I turn on the game and take a sip of my scotch. I have to be at work tomorrow at seven, but I'm still too restless to attempt sleep. Especially after the day—after the night—I've had. I could go down the hall to the media room, but it seems a bit much just for catching the end of the Sox game, and for now, I'm relieved by the quiet.

I started to read a medical journal, but my mind wandered too far too fast, whereas baseball is the universal antidote to sex.

I couldn't stand it. Watching her with that guy. The way he stalked over to her, intent clear on his face. The way he touched her, talked to her. I was never like that with Alanna, never felt a tenth of that rage. I knew Alanna dated, I even saw her with some of the guys, and it never hit me like that. Not once.

But tonight, I was ready to rip that insignificant, nothing of a man apart. In that moment I knew. No one could have Grace but me.

But I can't even have her. What the fuck do I do with that?

I honestly don't know.

Sit and have a drink while watching the Sox. That's what I do.

She's so fresh out of a bad relationship I can't even attempt to try anything. It's far too soon for any of that. Her mind is a mess, her heart all over the place, and I will not be her rebound or revenge. She's here in my home because she trusts me, yet I can't stop the way I crave her.

So yeah...

Alcohol. Sox.

I need to decompress before I spend the next twenty-four hours with her on a shift. If I'm having this much trouble already, I shudder to think what the next, however long she's staying here, will bring. Maybe I should alter our schedules. Move things around so we spend less time together at work. Move her to another attending—the right thing to do considering she's now staying at my place.

Except I love seeing her at work.

I love watching her with patients. I love teaching her in the OR. That's become my drug. My fix. It's what I've thrived on for a year and now that I'm addicted, I have no idea how to quit without going through severe withdrawal. I sigh, leaning back and shifting my position, tossing one ankle onto the opposite knee.

I'm eternally screwed.

As if conjuring the woman directly from my thoughts, a flicker of movement catches my eye. Grace is ambling toward the dark kitchen, wearing my way beyond big T-shirt and sweatpants that I gave her last weekend when she mistakenly showed up on my doorstep.

That has me smiling stupidly big. She looks good in my clothes.

"Can't sleep?" I call out and she startles a little, clearly having been lost in her own introspection and didn't notice me sitting only twenty feet from her.

"Christmas carols you scared me," she mutters, as she brings a hand up to her chest, confirming my thoughts. She lets out a small, bemused laugh and then shakes her head. "No. I was just coming to get some water. What about you?"

I hitch up a shoulder, unwilling to tell her my reasoning for still being awake when I should be asleep.

She abandons her search for water, instead crossing the room and sliding onto the sofa directly beside me, her knees bend as she tucks herself into my side. I know this isn't anything. I know this is her just being comfortable with me. Like she is with Oliver. Like a brother. But having her pressed against me like this, feeling her close, smelling her skin, brotherly is the last thing I feel about her.

"Can I have a taste of that?" she asks, and I hand her my drink, watching as she brings the crystal to her lips and sips the liquid into her mouth. "Wooh," she exclaims, smacking her lips and handing it back to me. "That's good stuff for a quiet Friday night in front of the Red Sox."

"After a day and evening spent entirely with you, I needed it."

"Lord Jesus, yes. If I could drink, living with you would certainly drive me to it."

I chuckle, forcing my eyes to stay on the large television though I'm not watching any of it now.

She wiggles around beside me, stirring as if she's searching for a comfortable position, but I can tell that's not what this is. "What's on your mind, Grace?"

She stills and I can practically hear the smile in her voice when she says, "What makes you think there's something on my mind?"

Because I know you. "Wild guess. What is it?"

"What would you be doing tonight if you hadn't been forced to spend the day with me? If I weren't living here?"

I'm not sure what I thought she was going to say, but it's not that. My neck twists and I catch her eye. Hers are now laser focused on the screen like whatever the Sox are doing has life and death consequences for her.

I cup her jaw, forcing her eyes to mine. "What are you asking me?"

She works her bottom lip with her teeth. "I watched you tonight. I saw the way women stared. They took pictures of you. Of all of you, but I already found a picture of us dancing online. It was on Twitter and Instagram and there were already a ton of comments about it. They were all about you being seen dancing with a woman and the speculation around that. Thankfully my face wasn't in it, it was the back of my head, but I don't know. It just got me thinking."

It feels like there is something else she's not saying. Something she's holding back with that. I see it in her eyes, in their shift. In their reluctance to hold mine.

"You want to know if I would have brought the woman I was dancing with home if it had been a different woman and a different situation?"

"I guess. You're sitting here tonight, drinking expensive as hell scotch, and watching the Red Sox in your pajama pants because I'm here. You just seem… I don't know…"

"I would have brought her home," I tell her, staring into those goddamn blue eyes that never fail to rob me of my better sense. "If I were lucky enough for her to say yes. If I had gone up to the beautiful blonde and danced with her tonight, and she wasn't you and I didn't know her, and we didn't have all this other bullshit surrounding us. Yeah, I would have tried like hell to take her home with me."

Her breath catches and her cheeks flush. "But I was that woman."

"You were, so here I am, watching the Sox in my pajamas and drinking expensive scotch." *Because I can't bring you to my bed instead.*

She pulls her face out of my grasp, staring down at her hands and then up at the television. The Sox get a double play, and the inning ends, going to a commercial for pet food and who cares. I want her eyes back on me. I always want her eyes on me.

"You just seem lonely. Sad maybe. That's all I was asking."

Oh. Well... fuck me. My insides tumble, the perpetual ache in my chest flaring up to a slow burn. "I am sometimes. But isn't everyone?"

Because the reality is, I'm not sure what I have anymore.

I work and I come home, and I date random, meaningless women, and I hang out with my brothers and Rina, and I work some more. In truth, I loved that life. I love my brothers and Rina and I didn't mind the random women and I absolutely love what I do. But yeah, I could have more of a life.

I just haven't wanted to pursue it.

I choose to work more than I have to because for the last year, the woman I've been obsessed with has to work a crazy ton of hours and being with her is the goddamn highlight of my life.

I don't have hobbies because who has time for that. I don't have a lot of friends outside of my family and a few extended others because I learned a long time ago—all my family has— that people angle for you when you have money and are an Abbot-Fritz. It's why we choose our people carefully and keep things mostly just us. My mom is sick. Fighting for her life against recurrent cancer and until she's in remission that sad, and scared son will remain.

Things were different for me in Virginia Beach. I was more carefree. Less stiff. Alanna and our friend Billie were part of that, but there is also freedom for an Abbot-Fritz outside of Boston. Or maybe it was more the small, protective bubble my residency provided. Who knows?

I never thought about it as being lonely or sad until Grace

came around and showed me just what I've been missing... what my world could be like...

"Yes," she says after a contemplative moment. "I think we are all like that sometimes. I just worry my being here is doing that."

"It's not and I don't regret having you move in here, Grace. I'm glad you have a place you can come and go and make your own. A place you feel safe in. Oliver and Amelia would be all over you if you stayed with them and while it would come from a place of love, who wants all that attention on them all the time when they're trying to move past something?"

"I know they would be like that and as much as I love them with all my heart, it is a relief having my own space. My privacy. I just wonder what you're getting out of it."

You. I get you out of it even when I know better and most of the time I'm just torturing myself. "You worried about me, Hammond?" I quip, trying to lighten the heavy mood she set. "Worried I'm not living up to my Fritz bachelor status? I can change that you know. Pull out my phone and start dialing up some women. I could have a harem here within the next thirty minutes for an orgy if you'd like. I'll even let you watch."

"I was trying to look out for you, asshole."

She slaps my chest and I laugh, catching her hand and using her weakened position to tickle her. Grace lets out a squeal as I hit a particular spot and before I know what I'm doing, my glass is on the coffee table and I've got her pinned down on the couch, her hands over her head, my body hovering over hers.

I lock her wrists with one hand and continue to tickle her with the other, her body writhing, fighting mine. We're both laughing and smiling, our eyes bright with excitement. But in an instant, our playful vibe evaporates when we both simultaneously realize our position.

I look down at her just as she looks up at me, both of us

falling quiet as our laughter dies out, the soft sound of the television the only thing to break this new tense silence.

My eyes flicker to her lips. Linger there for a beat before they glide across the smooth skin of her creamy, now flushed cheeks back up to her eyes. Blue fire and... heated?

For me? I don't know. I don't trust my own eyes.

They've misled me before.

Our breathing morphs from lightly winded to heavy and rough. The urge to drop down, to cover her with my body, with my mouth, and obliterate this small space between us squeezes me like a vise. She blinks at me, but she doesn't move, and she doesn't speak. Her eyes stay fixed on mine and mine on hers because they can't go back to her lips.

If they do, I'll kiss her...

I'll kiss her and then I'll touch her. And then I'll do more than touch her. I'll pleasure her. I'll make her come. I'll show her over and over again that she's the most beautiful woman I've ever seen. And then...

Then I lose everything.

I'll lose her before I even get her because she's broken-hearted over Tony. Because she's sad and vulnerable and doesn't need me—her attending, the man she's staying with— taking advantage of her.

Fuck. What am I doing?

The only thing I can do. I climb off her, stand, and extend my hand to help her up. She takes it with a smile. A regular Grace smile that shows no indication that I had her body pinned beneath mine, ready to kiss her. To take her. To claim her.

But we both know the truth, right? She has to know. She had to have seen my desire for her. Hell, I did a shit job of hiding it all day. In the bathroom this afternoon and then again on the dance floor.

What the fuck is wrong with me? How could I betray her trust like this?

She came here when she had nowhere else to go. When she needed to feel safe. When she needed someone to take care of her.

I'm an asshole.

But I can fix it. I can give her the confidence she feels she's lost back without taking her into my bed. I can be the good guy in her story because right now, she needs one.

"Do you want to run into work tomorrow?" I ask, knowing that's what she used to do and hasn't all week while living here with me.

Her face lights up. "Yes. I'd love that. Thank you."

"Okay. We'll need to leave here early then."

"Right. Five-thirty?"

I swallow and nod, taking a step back and picking up my drink, suddenly so very done with baseball and alcohol. "Five-thirty works."

"We should get to bed then." She licks her lips. "You know. Get some sleep before our long shift and early morning."

I don't say anything, I just turn off the television, bathing us in a muted darkness, in a silence only made heavier by the beat of my heart and pulse of my semi-hard cock. I need to get control. I'm all fucking control, so why am I having so much trouble with her now?

"Good night, Carter."

"Good night, Grace."

She lingers, waits a beat, and when she realizes I'm not going to say anything more, she saunters off, back to her room.

I fall back onto the couch, scrubbing my face with my hand. She has to move out. She has to leave. But I can't stomach that either. I want her to stay, and I need her to go. Never in my life have I been this conflicted. This tied up in knots. She's wreaking havoc on my life, more so now than she ever has before.

The ultimate pleasure pain.

One that's hurting me, but I can't seem to stop poking at, needing it because without that sharp draw of pain, I think I'd feel more lost than ever. She was right with what she said tonight. All of it. I don't remember the last time I let loose. The last time I relaxed and had fun. Sure, I go out with friends and my brothers. We have a good time.

But it's different. It's simply me going through the motions.

It's a relic of the life I want. The life I should be living.

Standing, I walk into the kitchen, taking a final sip of my scotch and then pouring the rest down the drain, leaving the glass in the sink because I don't feel like washing it. Then I head for my room, brush my teeth, and get myself ready for bed. Ready to start another day.

Because I don't have a choice.

And pretty soon, she'll be gone. Just a few more weeks, tops.

One day it'll be easier than it is now. Eventually I'll get over her. I just hope I can make it until then before I snap.

13

"Night shift, oh night shift, I hate you, you suck," Rina sings as she scoops a large dollop of ice cream from her to-go cup from the cafeteria and plops it into her mouth.

"Patient die?"

The only thing Rina ever eats on a night shift is an ice cream sundae and only ever when a patient codes or dies.

"No," she marbles through her bite. "We pulled him through, but just barely and it's still rocky. It's going to be a long night with him, and I have a feeling come four am, he's going to try this on me again."

I grimace. This is why I like delivering babies. Not that we don't have our share of heartache and when we do, it's far more devastating than anything—we're talking either a new mom or a new baby—but still, our joy is infectious. It's why Rina is here, standing outside the nursery looking in at all the adorable new life.

"I'm here," Margot pants, briskly walking down the hall. "God, Drew was all up my ass with a patient tonight. Is it a full moon?" She blinks at Rina. "Shit. A sundae. Did they make it?"

"Barely," I answer for Rina who has her mouth full. I take a bite of my protein bar which is nowhere near as delicious as Rina's sundae appears to be.

"You know what's not so fun?" Margot questions rhetorically, I'm assuming since she goes on to answer her own question. "The fact that the hospital doesn't serve cocktails. I mean, think of how many people who come here could really use a drink."

I laugh before I can stop it. "That oddly makes some sense."

"Right? Then we could get Halle and Aria here too. It would be great instead of depressing."

"Except we all have to go back to work and that is definitely not something any of us can do after a cocktail."

Margot stares contemplatively at Rina for a moment. "I suppose that's true and that's why you go for the sundaes instead."

Rina points her spoon at her. "You got it, kid."

"Fine. But we need another girls' night out. Last night doesn't count because the guys were all there. This being engaged to Drew stuff is a lot to take in. I'm not good at it and he's all, *let's plan our wedding*." She mocks his deep voice. "Ugh. Doesn't he comprehend I'm damaged goods and damaged goods people cannot be rushed into things like marriage?" She blinks at me. "Shit. Sorry. Is this rude to talk about?"

I wave her away. "No, it's nice to hear. Not the damaged goods part, obviously. Drew is an amazing man and I'm so happy for the two of you. He's nothing like Tony. Drew would carry you barefoot over broken glass whereas Tony would have used me as his shoes if that makes any sense."

"It kind of does," Rina agrees, playing with the remains of her now soupy sundae. "But speaking of broken glass, I heard about your Carrie Underwood move."

"From Carter or Oliver?"

"Yes," she replies with a grin.

"God, those boys gossip, don't they?"

"You're deflecting."

"Wait? What is this?" Margot asks, her head ping-ponging back and forth between Rina and me. I lean against the wall, staring into the nursery through the large glass window, shrugging like it's no big deal. Then I think better of it and look over my shoulder, making sure we're alone. Janet isn't here tonight, thank God, but Dylan is, and that man will be all over it if he hears what I did.

I turn back to the babies.

"Carter helped me get the rest of my stuff from my now former apartment, which sadly wasn't a whole lot. Life of a resident, I guess. Anyway, I decided to go all Carrie Underwood on Tony's ridiculous assortment of beauty products and broke a bunch of bottles in the bathroom."

Margot cackles out a laugh. "Epic. I love it. Have you heard from him since?"

"Yes. He texted to say he was very sorry I had to see the place like that, and it was only like that because he misses me so much." I pause here to flagrantly roll my eyes. Twisting to put my back against the wall, I prop my foot up into it. "He blathered on about how he wished I had messaged him first to let him know I was coming by. I didn't reply. The apartment looked like a frat house complete with empty bottles and condom wrappers."

Both ladies scrunch up their noses in disgust. I'm with them on that. If I was rocking any sort of heartbreak from Tony's betrayal, seeing the apartment yesterday zapped any residual love or affection right out of me. Now I'm just appalled and remorseful and sick. Just thinking about Tony makes my skin itch and my stomach roll, ready to hurl.

"Well now you can get jiggy with someone else. That guy last night obviously didn't do it for you. How about Carter?" Margot suggests, and I choke to death right here in the hall, hacking and coughing, the bite of protein bar I had been chewing now lodged in the back of my throat. "Jesus, you okay?"

"Do you need us to Heimlich you or something?" Rina questions. "Crap. You totally do." Without waiting for my reply, she springs into action. You know, because I can't speak since I'm choking like a damn fool, hand on my throat and everything right here in the middle of the hospital. She rushes to my side and thrusts me forward while slamming the butt of her hand repeatedly into my back between my shoulder blades like you would a choking infant. Not quite the Heimlich, but it has the intended effect. The piece dislodges from my throat, and I gasp for air.

"Better now?"

I give her a weak thumbs up as I manage to finally swallow the sticky bite down the right pipe.

Wow, that was a super cool and classy move.

"Thank you."

"Any time," Rina answers with a frown. "But for real, one fucking code a night, Grace. There are only so many sundaes I can eat."

Heat crawls up my skin that has nothing to do with my near-death experience just now. I just hope the true reason for my choking and subsequent blushing isn't noticeable, or they'll never let me deny anything. I don't even know where that came from.

I mean, not entirely anyway.

"So now that you're not dying, you never answered me about boning Carter."

Is the woman trying to kill me?

"Carter is my attending," I explain to Margot because it's true and it's simple and it's easy. I wipe at a few tears from my eyes and straighten myself back up, resuming my position against the wall. "Nothing is happening there." Also true.

Though yesterday was all moments. A series of them, one after the other.

But I don't know how to read them or him for that matter. It's all so confusing. One second, I think there is some heat, a spark between us only to have it snuffed out just as quickly. Every time anything has been flirted with; he runs in the opposite direction. He couldn't get off me fast enough last night and the look in his eyes when he realized our position told me everything.

Horror.

He was horrified, and that's the last thing I ever want to see on a man's face when he's on top of me, pinning me down. Even when I teased him when we were in the bathroom, I could see there was no intent or interest to him.

It's just as well. Awesome really.

I live with him and I'm raw and sore from my breakup and the last thing I need is to jump into bed with another man. Especially a man as complicated as Carter Fritz. I need time for me. I need time to heal and get myself and my life back on track.

"Come on. The best way to get over someone is to get under them, and Carter is wicked hot. Plus, you know, he's not a serial killer or a random dude you have to vet before you spread."

"You're making the ice cream in my stomach curdle."

Margot waves Rina away.

I shake my head at Margot. "Work is my focus and nothing else." It's the safest way to be. "Dick complicates things I don't need complicating," I continue when neither of them feels the need to say anything, but exchange looks that say a whole lot. "I'm not in a place where I'm ready for anything with anyone, let alone someone like Carter."

"Why does it have to be something?" Margot persists. "Why can't it just be fun?"

"Because I've never done that before. I have no idea if my

stupid heart would be in on the casual fun my vagina needs or go and catch feelings like she's apt to do."

"Just because you've never done it before doesn't mean you can't. Dick can be just dick with the right guy. Especially if you know the score from the start."

"Can you stop saying the word dick when referencing my brother?"

"Sorry," Margot apologizes. "But isn't that what we're talking about here? Her getting jiggy with her hottie attending?"

"Well, yeah. Kind of, I guess." Rina pretends to shove her spoon down her throat, making a gagging sound as she does. "But it's against hospital policy for her to do that. And, you know, he's my fucking brother and Oliver's brother."

"Whatever." Margot waves her away, turning her focus back to me like she's ready to get down to business. "If Carter weren't your attending, Oliver's brother, and you weren't recently out of a nasty relationship, he'd be perfect for you."

I laugh at Margot and Rina grins, shaking her head, staring in at one of the babies who is starting to cry just as a nurse comes over and picks him up to soothe him.

"Oh, you mean if he weren't Carter, and she weren't Grace, they'd be perfect?" Rina smarts.

"Carter doesn't see me that way," I protest. "I don't see him that way either and it's how it should be."

Only, that feels like a lie. At least the second half of that does. Because I've always had a small thing for Carter. I wasn't lying when I said all the girls used to swoon over the hot pitcher because we did. Myself included though I would have never admitted to that as Oliver's BFF.

Carter was older, god-like, devilishly handsome, and untouchable. So serious and reserved unless you were part of his inner sanctum and then you saw him. The real Carter Fritz.

It was like discovering a rare gem among lumps of coal.

That's what this past week with him has been like. Glimpses, flirts, teases of the man beneath. He keeps so much of himself closed off and all it makes me want to do is dig deeper. Search harder. Uncover more.

But any attraction I've ever felt for him, I was quick to brush aside. I was engaged.

Now I'm not and though I'm trying still not to think about him in that way or confuse myself further, it's getting harder to do so.

"Still, he would be fun for an easy fling," Margot muses. "That's all Carter does, right? That might be exactly what you need to get over what Tony did once and for all."

"When is a fling ever easy?" Rina challenges, dropping her plastic spoon in her now empty cup before throwing it in a nearby trash bin. "It certainly didn't go that way for me and Brecken."

Margot laughs, leaning against the wall and playing with her hospital ID badge while throwing Rina a no-shit look. "That's because Brecken always had other ideas when it came to you. Carter doesn't strike me as that type. Just the kind who flings hot and fast and then moves on. He's a total workaholic and so is Grace. That's why it's perfect."

I shake my head, holding up my hand. "Stop. I'm not going to have a fling with Carter, hot, easy, fast, or otherwise."

"If not Carter then someone else," Margot persists. "You should definitely fling with someone. We'll set the whole thing up. I might even have the perfect guy for you. He's sex on legs and—"

"Evening ladies," Carter drawls, coming up behind me out of freaking nowhere, and my eyes bulge out of my head. *Oh shit!*

Rina looks like she just swallowed a bug and I think Margot is about to pass out since all the blood has officially left her face.

"What brings you two to our neck of the woods?" he continues, coming to stand beside me and I think I want to die. If he heard our conversation... But it's not like I said anything, right? Just that we're not going to fling. Totally true.

Rina holds up her hand. "Patient decided tonight should be his night."

"Was it?" Carter queries.

"No, thankfully, but I still felt life-affirming ice cream was in order along with seeing new life."

"I'm just here for the girl talk and babies," Margot states.

Carter turns to me, ever the stern attending. "No patients, Dr. Hammond?"

"My lady is only five centimeters and is still walking the halls with her wife. Dylan is on it. I was going to check on them after my lunch break."

"And this is your lunch break? At one in the morning?"

I hold up my half-eaten protein bar. "What would you call this?"

"Pathetic. Come with me, Doctor. I need to speak with you. Good night, ladies. Rina, you have whipped cream in your hair." He walks over to her, removing it with his fingers and kissing her forehead. "I'm sorry about your patient. Call me later if you want to talk."

"I'm good. That's what the ice cream is for." She throws me a wave and grabs Margot's hand. "Night."

Carter turns back to me and the second he's no longer able to see their faces, Margot mouths, *Oh my god, I'm so sorry* to me.

Yeah. No kidding.

"Later," I say, but it's cut off as Carter grasps my arm and drags me along after him, all the way down the mostly empty hall and then into the empty on-call room where he shuts the door behind us. "What are you—"

Only I'm cut off as Carter pins me to the wall, getting right up in my face, his expression feral. "Tell me you're not seriously contemplating having a random fling with a random guy," he seethes.

"What were you doing listening in on my private conversation with my friends?"

His eyes narrow. "You were in the middle of the hall. Not exactly a private place. Answer me."

"What business is it of yours what I do in my own personal, private time?"

His hand slams into the wall beside my head and I start. He inches in closer until we're practically nose to nose. "Because you live with me now."

"What does that even mean?"

He growls, his dark eyes turbulent, blazing as they penetrate mine. "Dammit, Grace." He slams his hand again. "You can't just jump into bed with some random guy simply because you're now single."

I shake my head, at a total loss. I've never seen Carter like this. Undone. Frantic almost. I doubt many have.

"I can do whatever the hell I want to, Carter. Last I checked, I'm a grown woman and temporary roommate or not, you're not my keeper."

"Grace. I fucking mean it. Tell me you're not going to do that."

Is he joking with me? "I'm not going to tell you anything of the sort. If I decide to sleep with someone that's my decision. It has no bearing or impact on you."

He lets out a mirthless, pained laugh.

"Why do you even care?"

His other hand comes up, bracketing me in and my heart starts to thrash in my chest. So violently I know he can see the pulse at the base of my neck.

"I care, okay? I care. I don't want to see you get hurt again. I can't watch as some loser who doesn't deserve you get his hands on you. Not when..." Frustrated, he runs his hand roughly over his face and back through his hair, panting out a heavy breath as he does. "Dammit!"

"Not when what?" I press.

His eyes bounce back and forth between mine; he opens his mouth to say something when his pager goes off, beeping loudly against his hip in the small room. He holds my gaze a second longer, takes a deep breath, and pushes off the wall, away from me. Without checking his pager, he storms out, slamming the door behind him and leaving me here reeling.

What the hell was all that?

14

You would never know that Carter and I had a mini blow out by the time we reach the end of our shift. It's like it never happened. Like he never lost the perfect control he's known for.

It's messing with my head.

I assisted him in a complicated crash C-section and after we're scrubbed out and the sun is rising and we hand off our patients to the next shift, we're walking out of the building together. It's silent and uncomfortable and tense. At least for me, it is. You'd have no clue by looking at him what the hell he's feeling.

Carter is an iceberg, I'm discovering. So much of his soul is submerged, held down deep beneath his cool exterior.

But after twenty-four hours awake and on my feet, I need rest. I need a real meal and then rest. Definitely a shower in there somewhere.

These shifts wreak havoc on my body, pushing it to its very limits, which in my case is a roll of the dice. I only have to do one of these a month with the way our rotations work and I'm grateful for that. But every time is like the first time. You never get used it. There is no adjusting.

It's Sunday morning now and Monday I'm in our outpatient setting, much easier to manage than being in the hospital or the OR.

"Want to grab some breakfast before we head home, or are you needing sleep?"

I'm going to take this as his weird form of an olive branch. I don't like it when things are strained between us. It makes for a fucked-up work and home dynamic. Challenging, sparing, fiery even, all that I can handle. But strained? Not so much.

"Sure. That sounds great."

"You like waffles, right? I know a good place."

My head whips in his direction. "How did you know I like waffles?"

"Staff breakfast. You ate like three of them."

"Staff breakfast?" I question, racking my brain. "But that was… last November?"

He shrugs indifferently, pointing for me to turn up Boylston, but I'm stuck on this waffle revelation. I wasn't even sitting with him. I was sitting in the back of the room with two other residents, and he was… I don't even remember where he was, but it wasn't near me.

His hand meets my lower back as he guides me into a posh restaurant that I am not at all dressed for overlooking The Public Gardens. I glance over to him and then down at myself. I changed sure—I hate wearing the scrubs I wore in the hospital out; it just feels nasty—but I'm also in ratty jeans and an old college T-shirt. Not to mention my hair is a mess, I have no makeup on, and you know, I've been awake for twenty-four hours straight.

"Carter?"

"It's Sunday," he says by way of an explanation. "They have an amazing brunch here. You'll love it."

I have no doubt I will, but I was expecting some greasy spoon place, not a five-star dining experience. Carter is a Fritz so maybe I should have known? My parents had plenty of money, but they weren't anywhere near Abbot-Fritz level. Then again, very few people are.

They're mega billionaires, for Christ's sake.

But ninety percent of the time, you don't get the billionaire vibe from them. They're a close-knit, family-oriented, down-to-earth crew. I mean, Rina is an ICU nurse. Oliver works in community health. Carter is an OB-GYN, Landon a cardiologist. Only Kaplan and Luca ride the masters of the universe gig with Luca being a neurosurgeon and Kaplan a pediatric cardio-thoracic surgeon.

I don't even know what I'm thinking right now.

I'm sleep deprived and a bit batty after the week I've had and now I'm being led to a table overlooking the beautiful gardens and getting sneers from women wearing Chanel.

"What are we doing here?" I hiss under my breath after we're left alone with our menus. The food does look amazing, I'll give him that.

"Having breakfast together," he says simply, his eyes all over his menu. I want to bring up what happened between us in the on-call room but I'm not that brave. Truth, I don't even know what I would say. He had no right telling me I can't sleep with someone whether I plan to or not. But why was he even doing it in the first place?

And why the hell was he that upset by it?

"Carter?"

He looks up at me, a soft smile warming his brown eyes. "I thought you'd like something nice. Something just for you."

Oh. That's... insanely sweet.

"Look at the menu, Grace."

I do now, reading it over. Mostly because once again, I have no idea what to say back to that. "Carter, you're giving me whiplash."

"And you're giving me heartburn. Did you pick out what you'd like to eat yet?"

There are all kinds of specialty waffles. Sweet ones, savory ones, all delicious sounding. And yes, waffles are my absolute favorite. He knows because he was... watching me? How does that make any sense?

"Next week is your birthday," he muses, accepting coffee from our waiter. I shake my head, covering my mug. I need sleep, not caffeine. "She'll have the mixed berry smoothie."

I will? It sounds good. Like something I'd order for myself if I had bothered to read the menu more carefully. For once, I don't argue.

"Very good, sir. Are you ready to order?"

"Grace?" Carter waves a hand in my direction.

Um. Jesus. Who knew breakfast with your boss could be this stressful? "I'll have the chicken and waffles, please." Because the spicy syrup with it sounds amazing and there are pieces of bacon cooked into the waffle itself though it was a close call between that and the Nutella and berry one.

"I'll have the lobster eggs benedict, please."

That sounds good too. I wonder if Carter is the type who shares or hordes all to himself. And is it weird if I take a bite of his breakfast? Why does this feel like a first date?

"Why does this feel like a first date?"

Carter grins, a twinkle of something in his eyes that I can't read. "As I said, your birthday is next week. We should do something special for it."

I take a sip of my water and sit back in my chair, studying the man across from me who just blatantly dodged my question. The one who doesn't look like he's been up for more than a day delivering babies and doing surgeries. The man who is becoming more and more unexpected and confusing as the days I'm spending with him tally up.

"What do you think we should do?" I throw back at him, curious if for no other reason than Carter seems to be the man with a plan. He brought me here this morning after all.

My smoothie arrives and I take a small sip, and wow, it's fucking fantastic. If my waffles are anything like this, I'm in for a real treat. And maybe that's why he did this? So I could have a treat? Something nice as he said.

Forget whiplash, he's giving me a migraine the more I try to figure him out.

Is he... is he *wooing* me?

Have I been reading the signs wrong all this time?

Or is this just Carter being a good guy, looking out for his resident and his brother's best friend? I legit can't tell. All I know is Carter isn't interested in dating me. If anything, he wants to fling with me. Sort of how Margot said. That's what he does. He doesn't do relationships, he flings.

I inwardly sigh at myself. I'm way overthinking something that does not require this level of insight... or oversight. This is what I mean. I can't do casual. Hell, I can't even have breakfast without dissecting every damn thing the man does.

"How's the smoothie?"

"Marvelous. Want some?" I stare as I hold my glass out to him, but all he does is shake his head no. Huh. "How can you drink coffee before sleeping?"

"I'm not going to sleep until this evening. If I sleep today, it will mess with my rhythm and then I won't sleep tonight, and I'll be a mess to start the week."

"I've tried doing that. I never make it past two without crashing hard."

"I usually make it to about five or six and then I crash for the night."

Ah. The life of a doctor.

"We keep skirting around your birthday," he says, and I can't fight my smile.

We do. We're skirting around a lot of things it seems. It feels like a game, one I'm not sure how to win or lose, especially when I don't know the rules or even the stakes.

"What would Tony have done for you?"

That's an interesting question for him to ask.

"Usually, Tony would have bought me a piece of jewelry and then taken me out for an expensive dinner. But maybe I'll do something with the girls this year? I don't know. I don't care all that much about it. Honestly, I never really did. All the jewelry he bought me I never wore because, well, life of a resident and most of it wasn't my style anyway. It was like he bought it for me because he read in a magazine somewhere that's what you're supposed to do. I don't mean to sound ungrateful, it's just..."

He never asked me what I wanted or gave any consideration to what he purchased. Every birthday and every Christmas, the same thing. Jewelry and dinner. Huge diamond drop earrings. An emerald necklace. A sapphire and ruby pin—who our age wears pins? If I were ever meeting the Queen of England, I would have had the right jewels, short of that...

It was always from the same jewelry store too and now I can't help but wonder if he was fucking the woman who helped him pick out whatever he bought for me. That's where my mind goes now whenever I think of him and the things he did for me. Right now, I only know about two women, but I know there were more. I just do and I... I hate him.

I've moved past disgust and now I've officially reached the hate stage of this.

"No jewelry or even fancy dinners for you then. How about a party?"

I stare blankly at Carter. A party? That could be—

"It could be just what you need."

I smirk at him. "Are you reading my mind now?"

He chuckles, taking another sip of his coffee without removing his eyes from me. The man is good at this. Getting my heart rate going just a little. Making my skin buzz with a gentle hum. Keeping me on the edge of my seat, anxious for what comes next. All with a look or a smile because let's be real here, his looks are damn intense. So intense you feel them in every cell of your body. And his smiles could melt butter in subfreezing temperatures.

"A party it is then."

"Carter, you don't have to—"

"I want to. But you have to promise me something."

I blink at him. "What's that?"

"You won't bring a date."

Now I nearly fall off my chair, but I don't get a chance to do that or even respond with *why do you care if I bring a date* because a massive plate of chicken and waffles is placed in front of me with a flourish and holy wow, it smells like the best thing I've ever smelled. Sweet and spicy, savory and salty.

Carter's benedict looks equally as scrumptious. The waiter leaves us, and Carter cuts a bite of food, layering it all up onto his fork and then holding it out for me. Without questioning him, I lean forward and take the proffered bite—the first bite, I might add—the flavors exploding in my mouth to the point where I inadvertently moan. Carter's eyes flare, his nostrils too as I lick my lips like the food hussy I am.

"Good?"

"I think I just came."

The woman at the table near ours gives me a scathing look and all I can do is shrug at her. Carter laughs, rubbing his finger along his bottom lip.

"Maybe that's what you've been missing with Tony all these years. An earth-shattering... meal."

Oh, hell in a handbasket.

"Definitely," I agree, going about making Carter a forkful of my breakfast, the way he did with his, and I offer him my fork. He takes the bite, humming appreciatively.

"Good?"

"Amazing. Now you try it. I want to watch."

And just like that, our breakfast has turned into some form of food foreplay. I can't tell if this is actually happening or if it's just sleep deprivation and I'm either dreaming or imagining everything.

"You're making me feel like a goldfish," I tell him as I make myself a bite. Carter chuckles, but he's undeterred. He watches with voyeuristic enjoyment as I shovel it into my mouth and sure as hell, I moan again. It's not even intentional, it's just that damn good.

Carter has a satisfied gleam to him as he takes a bite of his own breakfast and then it's just the two of us eating. Well, him eating like a human and me wolfing down my entire plate and smoothie.

"Do you want dessert?"

I glare at him, ready to explode. He knows it too because he can't keep the humor at my expense off his face or out of his voice.

"That a no then?"

"If I put anything else in my mouth right now, I'll die."

"Shame. I was hoping I'd get to see you put something else in there."

My jaw drops, my eyes a cartoon as they fly out of my head.

"Carter I-don't-know-your-middle-name Fritz!"

"It's James. But what's the look for?" he asks innocently.

"I. You..." I'm at a loss. I squint at him. "That was pervy."

"Only pervy, if that's where your mind went with it. For all you know, I was simply talking about dessert."

Standing up, he drops a ton of bills onto the table. His large hand extends for mine, smooth as ever. I stare up at him, allowing him to help me up. Is he being serious or not?

And why can't I tell with him?

It's maddening.

Am I just that far out of practice, or is Carter being sly?

"What are your plans for the rest of the day?" he asks as we step out into the bright Boston morning, heading up Boylston, crossing the street and turning left onto Tremont, strolling along the sidewalk.

"Likely taking it easy. That's what I have to do after long shifts. I'll do some laundry, some yoga maybe, and then fall asleep. What about you? I won't be in your way, will I?"

"No. I was going to shower and then ride out to the compound to see my parents before they leave for The Vineyard house."

Octavia finished her last dose of chemo the other day. "Has your mom had her scans yet?"

"Tuesday, but they plan to leave on Thursday regardless of if the results are back or not. They're hoping they can stay out there for the rest of the summer, but if she needs more chemo, that won't happen."

I know how terrifying it is having Octavia Fritz, the matriarch of their family, be so sick. I've seen it in Oliver and Rina. It's rattling all of them to the bone. Me too, if I'm being honest. I can't imagine losing her.

"Do you want me to come with you?" I offer.

Carter stops in the middle of the sidewalk and just stares at me for the longest of moments. Finally, he takes a step into me, towering over me until I have to crane my neck to meet his eyes.

"You'd do that?" he asks softly. "You'd come with me even after you've worked all night and have laundry and yoga to do?"

"Of course. I love your parents. I'd love to visit with them before they leave town."

"How are you feeling though? I know disruption in sleep can cause—"

"I'm fine, Carter. If I was at all concerned about having a seizure, I wouldn't have offered. I'll bring my rescue meds with me just in case."

"We'll only stay a little while. I'll make sure you're home by two. That sound okay?"

He's worried about me. Similar to how Oliver worries about me, but yet... not the same at all. Especially with how I feel about Carter doing it.

"Sounds perfect."

"We're going to take my Ducati..." He leaves that hanging and I smirk.

"God, I totally forgot you ride that thing. What kind of doctor rides a motorcycle? Especially one like that? I'm shocked your neurosurgeon brother hasn't killed you already."

"I'm an organ donor, Luca's thrilled."

I roll my eyes but smile all the same.

"It's faster to get out to the compound. You think potholes and traffic are a deterrent? Nope." Now he's grinning. "You'll have to hold on real tight to me and prepare to fly."

I hesitate, the thrill of adventure lighting his eyes quickens my pulse and heats my blood. I've never been on a motorcycle before. Truth, it scares the crap out of me. But with him driving it...

"Is that a warning? That I have to hold on tight while you take me for a fast ride?"

His grin turns impish. Like the devil.

"Absolutely. Come on, Grace. When was the last time you had something that powerful between your thighs?" He dips in, his mouth gliding along my cheek until his lips hover by my ear. "Trust me to show you how good it can be?"

Oh hell.

"I trust you," I tell him, and he smiles that Carter dazzling smile. The one that never fails to make me flutter in the most girlish of ways. Taking a strand of hair that's blowing across my face, he tucks it behind my ear, his fingers lingering for just a second longer than they should. I like that too.

Especially with how I feel about Carter doing it. I like Carter taking me out for breakfast because he knows I like waffles. I like him offering to throw me a party for my birthday because he knows I want one. I like him wanting me to come with him to see his parents but makes concessions for me to ensure I'm safe and looked after. I even like his slamming me against the wall and getting all up in my face, boiling with fire and passion over a man who doesn't even exist.

Hell, I think I just like Carter.

But more than that, I want to rip his clothes from his body and suck him blind for dessert. Hell, he dropped the idea in my head in the first place. Then there's all that fast ride and something powerful between my thighs. Wooh. I'm totally sweating, and my panties are absolutely wet. I wonder if he's as talented in bed as he is in the OR.

Is it rebound from Tony? I don't know.

Is it too soon after my relationship just ended? Probably to most definitely.

But as I stare up into his oh-so chocolaty eyes, it's a truth I can no longer fight or ignore.

Yep. It's official. I want to fling with Carter. And I'm thinking he might want that too. But how could that ever happen when it feels like everything is stacked against us?

15

The ride out to the compound took forever, but for once, I didn't mind the drive. Even if we didn't get to take my bike. The idea of having Grace behind me, holding on tight... fuck. I would have been hard the entire time. Then it decided to start spitting rain and while that might not have been a deterrent for me, I wouldn't take the risk of slick roads with Grace.

There was an accident on I-90 West, and Grace ended up falling asleep while we sat in traffic.

But the second the tires hit the gravel of the long drive that leads to the compound, she jerks awake, swiping at the moisture on her cheek before she anxiously checks the door where her head was plastered.

There's drool there too and I fight my chuckle as she furiously wipes it away with the sleeve of her shirt. "Wow, that's super classy."

Now I can't stop the small laugh as it flees my lungs.

"Hey, don't judge," she snaps when she hears it. "You loaded me with sugary carbs after a night of no sleep. What did you think would happen?"

I throw a hand up in surrender, trying to rein in my amusement. "I didn't say anything. You're cute when you sleep."

She rolls her eyes at me as I pull the car to a stop, throwing my Mercedes S-Class convertible in park.

"You talk in your sleep too."

Her jaw unhinges as she stares indignantly into the side of my face. "I do not."

I shrug with an *if you say so* expression.

"Jerk, I do not talk in my sleep. I would have known by now. Tony never said anything to me. Neither has Oliver. Or my college roommate." She points at me as if that last one seals the deal on it, only to retract it equally as fast. "But wait. There was that one time she said I had an entire conversation with her when she came home late from a party one night that I don't remember at all. And now that I think on it, Tony has mentioned me whimpering or mumbling, but that's not the same as talking in my sleep."

"Agree to disagree."

She shakes her head wildly, her still damp hair from the shower she took before we left flying all over the place. "No, now you have to tell me what I supposedly said, or I'll presume you a liar."

"Presume away, I know the truth and if you weren't worried about it, you wouldn't be freaking out the way you are. Concerned you said something you shouldn't have?" I bounce my eyebrows suggestively at her and then hop out of the car before my little minx can lash back at me.

In a second, I'm opening her door for her, offering my hand and showing off my permanently ingrained Fritz manners. She smacks it away, making me laugh.

"Just tell me what I said," she demands, stalling beside my car.

"Come on." I beckon her, walking backward toward the house while crooking my fingers at her. "My parents are waiting and it's still raining. I'd rather not get wet right this second."

"I hate you."

"That's not what you said in your sleep."

"Ugh!"

She doesn't actually talk in her sleep, but as she said, she does mumble and some of the mumbling does sound like words. I turned the music all the way down in the car so I could try to catch a few, but there wasn't much. Still, messing with her like this is impossible to resist.

The front door opens, and my dad steps out onto the porch to greet us with a smile and a wave. "What a wonderful surprise you brought with you, Carter. Your mother will be delighted beyond words."

"That's the point."

I ascend the few steps up but before I can even make it to the landing, he has Grace wrapped up in a hug. "Hi Dr. F. How's Mrs. F?" she whispers into him.

"She's having a good day," he replies, releasing her to hug me. "It'll be an even better day now that you're both here. Oliver and Amelia, or your other siblings coming too or just you two?"

"Just us as far as I know," I tell him, slapping his shoulder. My father is tall and broad and dark, like me. But my mom's illness is weighing on him, streaking his hair with a few more grays than it used to have and staining the skin beneath his eyes purple. He looks older, tired, and it's gutting to see.

"Stella was here riding this morning," he explains. "Your mom spent over two hours with her in the stables, so she's exhausted. Just fair warning. I have Mr. Fairchild and Raven packing everything up for us to leave tomorrow."

"Raven is here?" My eyebrows hit my hairline.

My father glances around as if he's expecting Luca to jump out of a bush. "You can't say anything to Luca. She made me promise not to mention a thing to him though knowing him, he already knows."

"Jesus. How long is she home for?"

"Just until your mother and I leave on Thursday, because she has to fly back to London to perform with the London Symphony Orchestra. First chair cello," he finishes with pride because Raven Fairchild, daughter of Morgan Fairchild, our house manager and chief of security, is like yet another daughter to him. A daughter who had her heart shattered by his son. "After that, she's moving back home having accepted a position with The Boston Symphony Orchestra as well as The Pops, also first chair. Luca does not know about that either, nor can he. She starts her contract with them this fall."

"This could get interesting," I quip, following after him as we head into the house.

"Let's hope not. For both their sakes," Grace says warily.

Except Luca has never gotten over Raven or the way he hurt her. I have no doubt he'll be all over her moving back to Boston now that she's finished studying at The Conservatory.

We follow my father all the way back through the house to the solarium, my mother's favorite room, and find her on her chaise reading a book. If my father looks older, my mother looks frailer. Bone-thin she sits with a blanket over her lower half. Her hair is gone, has been for several weeks, and she has an Hermes scarf wrapped around her bald head. Still, she's as immaculately put together as she always is.

Ever the Abbot-Fritz.

Her eyes lift, locking on Grace first, and a smile blooms across her lips.

"My girl," she says, holding her arms out wide. Grace doesn't hesitate, she practically sprints over to her, cocooning herself in my mother's embrace. I'm thunderstruck by the moment. Electrocuted from within.

The two of them immediately start whispering and within

seconds, both are in tears. What the hell? Then they're laughing and crying some more and Jesus. I knew they were close, but clearly it's been a while since I saw my mother with Grace one on one. It stirs something unexpected in me. Something soul quenching.

Something that whispers, *home*, directly into my ear.

I lost my cool with Grace last night. But fuck, can you blame me? Margot was mouthing off about flings and other men and Grace went and said nothing was ever going to happen between us. I went mad. If another man so much as touches her, I will not be responsible for my actions.

No one can touch her.

No one else can have her.

But seeing her with my mother, the way my family embraces her as one of their own, loves her as theirs? It fills the sweetest spot in my heart, not just for her, but for me.

"Hi Mom," I call out. Nothing. "Good to see you, Mom." Nada. "Love you too, Mom."

She throws her hand up and waves at me. That's it.

"I'm thinking maybe it's best if we leave them?" my father asks in a low tone so as not to disturb them, also lost in a state of confused bliss as he watches them.

Grace is holding my mother's hands now, nodding her head that is angled, nearly touching my mother's. "Yeah. I'm thinking we're superfluous at the moment."

"But look at that," he whispers and all I can do is nod because I am looking.

"I haven't seen her this happy in so long. I think she needed this more than I realized."

"Any time she's with her family, she's like this. She lights up. It's what keeps her going. Keeps her strong and motivated to beat it."

My father is talking about my mother. I was talking about Grace.

"Come on." He throws his arm over my shoulder. "Let's go open a bottle of something we shouldn't and drink it on the patio."

By patio, he means the stone structure off his office. There are three patios and those are just the ones attached to the back of the main house. This one is his own sanctuary, cut away from the main gardens and outdoor space, my father hides here frequently. His office is in the farthest reaches of the compound, and he uses it wisely.

We claim chairs, tucked away, hidden behind evergreens, arborvitae, and flowering hydrangea while protected from the misting rain by the overhang.

"L'Chaim," he says, lifting his glass to mine, and I nearly choke on a sputtered laugh.

"When did we convert to Judaism?"

"We didn't, but the sentiment is powerful. To life. Can you think of anything better to toast to? With your mother being sick, I've been searching through many religions, taking in the pieces that mean something to me."

"L'Chaim," I repeat, clicking my crystal with his and taking a sip of the insanely smooth bourbon. It's like butter down my throat and I lick my lips, immediately taking another drag.

"You must be wrecked after your shifts last night. Still, we're so happy you came."

"Unfortunately, we won't stay long. I promised Grace an early departure so she could get some rest and maintain her balance or whatever she calls it that keeps her neurologically in line."

"Are Grace's seizures becoming a problem again?"

"No. And that's how we're trying to keep it."

"*We're*?"

"I'm her boss."

"You're more than that, Carter," my father states with assurance, his eyes on his glass as he swirls the liquid around. "Or at least, she's more than that to you. It's written all over you. The way you look at her. The way you've looked at her over the last year, even when we're all together and you think no one notices you watching her. Your mother and I have both noticed it."

Great.

"She's single now, correct? And temporarily staying with you? Seems the perfect ingredients for something more to happen."

"Nothing more can happen between us, Dad. She can't be anything to me other than what she currently is."

"Except she already is, so you can quit lying to your old man. But if you'd rather not discuss this with me yet, I understand. Timing is everything. I was in love with another woman, the wrong woman, before I married your mother. I know Oliver told you of this." His eyes meet mine and I incline my head that yes, Oliver has told me with our father's permission. "I thought that woman was right for me, my one, when she was anything but. Sort of like Grace with Tony?"

He cocks an eyebrow at me and I just chuckle, sipping my drink, and throwing my ankle up on my opposite knee. "Tony was definitely wrong for Grace, but that doesn't mean I'm right for her." Though as the words tumble from my lips, they feel like a lie, and I know he sees that in me. "In any event, she's been single a little over a week. Besides, it's... complicated. For too many reasons."

"But you love her."

It's not a question and I freeze. I haven't allowed myself to think that way. To use that word as directly as he did. "I..." I lick my lips. Do I love her? Does it matter? "Grace is not someone I should be in love with."

He stares at his glass as he speaks. "Sometimes love comes from places you least expect it. Places you shouldn't even go searching for it. But the funny thing about love is that it doesn't care. About your plans. Your expectations. Your wants or desires. You can scheme. You can pretend. You can imagine and think and maybe even believe. But love, it knows better. And in the end, it always wins out."

I gulp down my drink in two hard swallows, holding the glass out for a refill. He lifts the bottle from between us and obliges, hitting me up with another two fingers.

"She's not there with me, Dad."

"No," he agrees. "Maybe not yet. But that's where patience and persistence come into play."

When I said I wanted to throw a party for Grace's birthday, I didn't expect Oliver to take over and rally the troops so the gang's all here. All five of my brothers, Rina and Brecken, plus Margot, Halle, Aria and their guys, Drew, Jonah, and Wes, as well as a smattering of other friends of Grace's.

We didn't invite any of Grace's friends from the hospital except for the trusted few here because we haven't told anyone else there she's living with me. She said the last thing she wanted was for Janet Johnson to find out about that and I am, for once, in one hundred percent agreement with her on that.

It could be bad news for both of us if that secret got out. Especially with that conniving snake.

But this party...

Food. There is so much food spread across my counters and let me tell you, these are big ass counters. Barbeque, because that's what Oliver wanted. Tapas from this amazing place in the South End because that's what Rina wanted. Mexican and sushi—don't ask—because that's what Margot wanted. Grace didn't have an opinion either way, she was just excited for anything.

All with a lot of alcohol.

Margaritas. Martinis. Beer. Wine. My condo has become a Fourth of July backwoods fest and everyone is partying accordingly. My big mouth started this party, and it appears everyone else is finishing it off for me. I haven't moved from my perch in the kitchen, keeping my distance and pretending to play host all the while watching from afar as Grace has an amazing time.

She's been laughing and drinking with her friends. I've been trying not to stare at her since the moment she left her room earlier and I saw what she's wearing. A flowy coral-pink dress with a deep V-neck and straps that tie around her neck. Her smooth, creamy back is partially exposed as are her legs since the dress ends a couple inches above the knee.

I nearly passed out from all the blood in my body rushing to my dick.

Oliver bought her a weekly organic food box subscription which is so brilliant for Grace, I'm pissed I didn't come up with it myself. For all the sugar that woman packs away, she also tries to cook and eat extremely healthy for herself during the week. Lots of fruits and veggies as well as lean meats and protein.

She was so excited when he showed her that she squealed and threw her arms around his neck and kissed his cheek. Being jealous of your baby brother sucks and now it makes me question my gifts for her. The ones I have yet to show her.

I'm working this harder than I've ever worked anything with any woman. My father's words a lead blanket covering me with their weight and potency.

I don't just want Grace for a fling—the way Margot said we should—but for real. All week Margot has continued to spew nonsense about hooking Grace up with this guy or that. I've nearly lost my fucking mind each and every time.

I can't let that happen. I just fucking can't.

Grace has to be mine. There is no other option.

I will make her fall in love with me. I will erase that douchebag Tony from her mind and her heart. I let the woman I was desperate for go once and I won't do it again. I won't.

Because Grace is it for me.

I knew it the moment I saw her standing before me in her scrubs with that wry smirk and those glimmering blue eyes and that I won't take your shit mouth. I just had never considered it an option. She was engaged after all, but now, here, this... it's my moment.

Even as my father's words ring through my head with annoying clarity. Patience and persistence.

Which is why I've been sipping my margarita, picking at some of the pulled pork, and pretending to ignore her.

"Does Oliver know you're overtly lusting after his best friend?"

Shit. I wasn't staring at Grace. Was I? Of course, I was. I ignore Luca, who slides in beside me, leaning against the counter and staring out at the group in the great room.

"Go eat a chicken wing." I point to a large platter of them.

"You know what this party is missing?" he continues without missing a beat. "Dessert. I'm thinking we need some pies to counterbalance the brownies, cookies, and cakes. Apple. Pecan. Lemon... what's that white topping on it called?"

"Meringue."

"Right. That. I'm thinking we need pies. Because you're obviously lusting after a pie you cannot have."

"I'm throwing that bullshit back at you."

I turn to glare, only to find his green eyes loaded with so much amusement he could fill a park. He brings his drink up to his lips, smiling through his sip. "My romantic woes are well documented. Yours, not so much. You were digging on that

Alanna chick, right? The one with the fucked up past who ended up with the dude who saved her life?"

"I hate you."

"Everyone does. You're missing the point."

"And what's the point?" I snap.

"You're coo-coo for Cocoa Puffs over Oliver's BFF. Why else would you allow her to move in and throw her a party? You hate parties."

"I don't hate parties."

"You do," he tells me, picking over some of the food on the counter without eating any of it. "Especially ones in your place. You're as fucked as a man can get short of bringing your mistress to your daughter's sweet sixteen party."

My eyebrows scrunch. "Huh? What the hell does that even mean?"

He shrugs, taking a bite of an empanada and talking through a mouthful of spicy beef. "I'm drunk. Deal with it. It made sense in my head since my neuro partner just did that and is now getting a divorce. Whatever. This is your moment to act."

Didn't I just think those very same words?

"It's not." At least not yet. It's too soon. She was with Tony for three years. She's only been single for two weeks.

"Explain."

Grace is sitting on my sofa between Rina and Aria. They're all munching on who knows what while drinking who cares what. Actually, I think they're doing shots and I don't think I've ever seen Grace do shots because typically Grace doesn't drink.

"She's my resident," I start, throwing all my own personal arguments that I don't exactly care about any longer at him.

"Not the first time such a thing has occurred. It simply requires a conversation with the residency board and your supervisor. What else you got?"

"She's Oliver's best friend."

"Do you intend to use her like a high-class hooker?"

I glare daggers into my brother, who only smirks in return, wiping his mouth with a napkin.

"Didn't think so. Next."

"She just got out of a long-term relationship where she was *engaged.*"

"Do you plan on cheating?" I flip him off and he laughs, tossing the now balled-up napkin in the direction of the trash and making the basket. He turns back to me. "Again, didn't think so. You're not selling me on anything that's pushing this as a hard no. Especially when I've seen the way you've been watching her all night. Landon has too by the way. The broody bastard is the one who told me to dig into it."

"You can leave now. All of you."

"Actually, I'm thinking that's wise. You know, give the two of you some alone time. You should put on a rom-com and cozy up with popcorn and champagne. Help spark your fledging love and maybe even learn a few pointers along the way."

Jesus. I can't even with this right now.

"What did you buy her?" he asks, not relenting even an inch.

"Shut up."

He laughs, leaning against the counter beside me, folding his arms over his chest as he cocks an eyebrow at me. So perfectly coiffed because that's Luca. He doesn't even try, it's just natural. Asshole.

"Leave him alone," Landon demands, coming up and standing on the other side of me, mirroring his twin's pose, but not expression. For how much Luca and Landon are identical, their personalities could not be more different.

"But messing with him is fun," Luca whines like a toddler.

"Should I tell him you've been stalking Raven again?" Landon quips, a rare smirk replacing the perpetual frown on his face. "He's still pissed no one informed him she was in town for those few days before Mom and Dad left."

I burst out into a laugh, elbowing Luca in the side. "I thought you had kicked that habit, man? You need to be careful. If she presses charges, none of us will bail you out. She looks good, by the way. You know, for a teenager. Where did you stalk her to this time?"

Luca glares at us both. "She played Carnegie Hall last night before flying back to London. Carnegie Fucking Hall. I wanted to see it, that's all. She didn't know I was there. She never knows when I watch her perform."

Landon and I exchange quick glances, both of us smiling like bastards at Luca. "Congratulations to her. What is your pretty, *young* cellist doing next?" I tease, already knowing she's moving back to Boston in a couple of months.

Luca flips us off and my mood just improved exponentially. Even Landon is now smiling. Like a full, real smile. The kind he only ever gives to Stella.

"She hasn't posted anything else on her social media. Whatever," Luca grouses, twisting around and picking up a random drink and finishing it off. I scrunch up my nose, as does Landon.

"That's nasty. You have no idea who that belongs to."

Luca shrugs. "We're all family here. Besides, tease me all you want about Raven, but at least I have a goal unlike you." He points at me. "Better man-up soon before it's too late."

"Before what's too late?" Kaplan asks, dropping his hand onto my shoulder and pushing me to the side.

"Nothing," all three of us respond at once because Kaplan has the biggest mouth of all of us.

"Whatever," he gripes, surveying the bottles of alcohol. "We're doing shots."

"No," Landon and I clip out while both Kaplan and Luca respond with a resounding, "Yes!"

"Two each," Kaplan demands. "Landon has no Stella tonight since she's staying at a friend's house and none of us are driving. You have a cleaning crew coming in the morning to take care of this disaster, so there is no sensible reason why you can't."

"What's your excuse for drinking like a college kid, Baby Face Nelson?" I throw back.

Kaplan rolls his eyes at me, having heard every nickname under the sun for his baby-faced appearance. The eldest of us most definitely looks the like the youngest with his clean-shaven face, lighter hair, and bright green eyes. I'm the only one in my family to have gotten our father's darker features.

"I don't have any of the love woes you poor bastards do, and I intend to keep it that way."

"Goodie on you," Landon snaps at Kaplan. "What are we drinking?"

As fucked up as Oliver's past with love is, Landon's is worse. Worse than all of ours combined times ten. It's why he is the cantankerous, miserable bastard he is. Except when it comes to the gooey, soft heart he has for Stella. Well, and the rest of his family of course.

Kaplan pours all of us a round of tequila shots because that seems to be what everyone here tonight is drinking the most of.

"Oliver!" Kaplan shouts in my ear. "Shots, baby brother. Get your pussy-whipped ass over here."

"Dick," I hear Oliver mutter, but he crosses the room and joins us anyway, perched against the island on the opposite side. "Love what you've done to the place since I moved out, Carter. It looks like a frat house in here."

"Smells better though."

"Can't argue that."

"Rina, you too," Kaplan yells right beside my ear. Again. This time I punch him in the shoulder. "Sibling shots, princess."

Rina groans but drags herself up and off the couch. "Shots? Aren't you a little old for that?"

"No," we all say in unison, and she laughs, resting her forearms on the counter and managing to shove some of the food aside to make room beside Oliver. He straightens, tossing his arm over her shoulder.

"Damn, I think we overdid it with the food," she muses, surveying the massive buffet.

"Yes," I agree. "You're all taking stuff home. I have no room for all of this."

"We're keeping my cake," Grace announces as she skips over, wiggling herself in between Luca and me, her soft, full breasts rubbing against my arm as she does. "I have to keep my cake and eat it slowly all week."

Luca smirks smugly at me, bouncing his eyebrows up and down suggestively, and I narrow my eyes in return. "Carter likes to eat it slowly too, I've been told. If you like it that way."

Grace turns quickly, her eyebrows pinched in at him in confusion.

"No one is taking your cake," I promise her.

"But I know someone who might want to eat your pie. Slowly, of course."

Jesus. Fucking Luca. I reach behind Grace and punch him in the shoulder. Hard. He grunts, shutting his mouth for once and taking the shot Kaplan hands him.

"Don't be a crude fuck," Kaplan snaps at him. "You want one of these too, birthday girl?"

I watch as Grace deliberates having a shot, but she nods after a half-second, a smile erupting across her face. "Sure. Let's do it. Only one for me though. I'm officially approaching my limit."

In the next second, we all have glasses in hand filled with tequila. "Happy birthday, my beautiful Grace," Oliver toasts.

"May twenty-nine be better than twenty-eight and all the years before it."

"Yes," Rina agrees. "To an amazing last year in your twenties."

"I'll drink to that," Grace asserts, bringing the glass to her lips, but just before she swallows it down, our eyes meet, along with a simmering heat that rolls through me like a wave. I take my shot, she does the same, our eyes holding.

And when she's done, she smiles up at me.

"Thank you," she whispers and now I know what that look was. It wasn't heat; it was gratitude. Bliss. She's a little drunk and we're making a fuss over her and yeah. That's all that is. Fuck.

"You're welcome."

A second later, Oliver calls her attention back to him and the moment is over.

But still, I meant it.

I'm not giving up. Not this time.

It just means I'm willing to bide my time. She has to be ready. Her eyes have to be opened to the possibility. The possibility of us. Even if she's not there yet, I know how to be patient. I'm an OB-GYN for Christ's sake. We invented the damn term. Babies don't come on our schedules, they come on theirs.

And Grace, it seems, is no different for me.

But she's here. And she gives me looks.

Looks that tell me not pursuing her would be the mistake of a lifetime.

17

Grace

I'm a little drunk. One margarita. One of Rina's crazy martinis—though she swore it was a weak one—and two shots and I'm rocking a buzz like a college freshman pledging for a sorority. Tonight was everything I hadn't realized I truly needed.

I will admit, I was not looking forward to this birthday. Tony, being a lying, cheating swine of a man sort of put the damper on that. He sent me a ring for my birthday. A diamond eternity band that looks damn similar to a wedding band. Especially when my engagement ring was nestled in the same box.

The card and texts and phone messages were nothing short of adoring and forlorn.

But the party tonight turned it all around.

It's somewhere close to 1 a.m. when the crowd finally leaves, many with a Tupperware of food in their hands. Everyone went all out. For me. Drinks and more food and desserts than I could consume in twenty lifetimes. Presents and fun. So much fun.

Now it's just me and Carter staring around at the mess that is his kitchen and great room.

"Leave it," he says just as I go to pick up a random glass. "I have people coming to clean this all up tomorrow. It was more the food and that's either all put away or sent off with others."

"Carter—"

"Did you have a good night?"

I beam at him. "I had the best night. Thank you."

"Did you have enough dessert?"

"I had too much dessert."

He smiles at that, walking around the island until he's directly before me. "Perfect. Then you can come and see your presents."

"You didn't have to get me anything. This party was already more than enough."

"I know I didn't have to. I never *have* to. I *wanted* to."

Oh. Okay then.

Without another word or objection on my part, he takes my hand, intertwining our fingers like it's the most natural thing in the world for us to do—hold hands—and then leads me down the hall in the direction of my room. My heart starts to thunder in my chest. Is he... is he taking me to bed? Is that his present to me? I know he teased me that I needed a good meal or whatever euphemism he used for orgasm, but this feels a bit... I don't know, out of left field? Unexpected? Strange? Exciting?

Before I can get carried away with myself, we continue past my bedroom, past the media room, past the extra office— goddamn, this place is huge—past two more bedrooms until we reach the large, open exercise room at the end of the hall.

So... that's a no to the orgasms? Probably better that way, right?

"I didn't know what to get you, so I sincerely hope you do not take this the wrong way. I realize I am teetering on a line between thoughtful and pig, but please know, it was only meant as thoughtful."

"What?" comes out as a bemused laugh.

"I heard you mention to Amelia on the phone the other

night that you were getting bored with your yoga class but didn't know what else to do. I also heard you tell Rina that you wanted one of these. Both of these, actually. But if for whatever reason, you don't like either or you think I'm telling you something that I'm not, I'll return them and get you something else."

My eyebrows crease. "Carter, what the hell are you talking about?"

He steps to the side and that's when I see the large rectangular mirror against the wall. It takes me a moment to realize just what exactly it is, but when I do, I gasp. "Carter."

"It has this whole catalog of fitness things including yoga, Pilates, cross-fit, whatever. You get to customize what you want and inside the mirror are weights and mats and bands and a whole bunch of other things."

"Carter." I have no other words than his name on my lips. I amble toward it, wanting to touch it but afraid of messing with its prettiness. He bought me a fully stocked, interactive fitness mirror? Jesus Harold Christ.

"I also got you this to go with it."

More? There's more? I turn back to him, and he hands me a large rectangular black box. I open it to find a thick silver band tucked inside. "Carter!"

He chuckles. "You keep saying my name, sweetheart, but is any of this a swear?"

"This is too much."

He shakes his head adamantly. "It's not."

I remove the decently weighted ring from its holder and place it on my pointer finger. It fits perfectly.

"You need to set it all up with your phone."

I know I do. Because this ring is no ordinary ring. It monitors my heart rate. My sleep patterns. My respiratory rate. My fitness levels. I deliver babies for a living and wearing a watch when you're wrist deep in a woman's vagina isn't happening. But this ring I can wear under my gloves because it's thin and smooth. It won't tell me when I'm going to have a seizure—nothing can—but it will help me monitor how my body is actively doing and what corrections I need to make.

"Do you like it?"

"Do I like it?" I parrot, staring down at the ring before meeting his boyishly hopeful face. "This is everything. The best birthday I've ever had. I'm not even kidding with that. You've turned what could have been an awful day into something extraordinary. Thank you. Thank you so goddamn much."

And with that, I launch myself at him. My attending. My best friend's brother. My roommate. The man I'm starting to want more and more with each passing second.

My arms around his neck, my body hugging his, I give him no room to breathe. He just spent thousands of dollars on me and his only thought with all of that was that he wanted to make me happy. Nothing about this gift was obligatory. It wasn't some fancy piece of jewelry he knew I'd never wear but wasn't thoughtful enough to consider something else.

This was all thought. All consideration. All perfect.

Which is why I can't stop myself from inhaling his cologne as my face dives into his neck. Why my fingers swirl into the back of his hair, gripping the strands. Why my body is now completely flush with his until I pull back and find his lips. Right. There.

Lips I want to kiss. Lips I want to indulge in.

It's been so long since I've felt desirable. Sexy. Tony stripped me of all that with his cheating but it's not like I was getting much of it anyway before I found out. No, he was giving that to every other woman *but* me. If I were a lesser woman, I would have noticed it sooner. The things he was attempting to rob me of. The pieces of me he almost got away with stealing.

But Carter is staring at me like he wants me more than his next breath, the fire in his liquid molten eyes an inferno I'm desperate to be consumed in.

"Grace?" He whispers it as a lust-coated question. One I'm all too eager to answer.

Staying with Tony for as long as I did was a mistake. Knocking on Carter's door when I thought it was still Oliver's was too. But this. Now. Here. Tonight. There is no mistake. Carter is the break of dawn after waking from a nightmare. I can do this with him. I can just have a fling with him. A night or two of passion where I know strings won't be attached.

Carter doesn't do those and even if he did, I doubt he'd do them with me.

I'm a fucking mess. Untrusting and love hating, and sex starved.

He knows I'm not looking for something real beyond this and I know he isn't either.

Screw it, it's my birthday. What harm can one night do?

The alcohol is making me bold in ways I likely wouldn't otherwise be with him as I clutch the back of his head and drag his lips down to mine. He responds immediately, a throaty groan searing past his lips directly into mine, his hands coming up and framing my face in his steel grip. Before I know what's happening, Carter spins me around, pinning me against the wall and then his mouth really takes over.

Head tilting, tongue plundering into the depths of my mouth, seeking, exploring, tasting, claiming. His chest rumbles with pleasure as he presses deeper against me, the hard planes of his body molding to my soft ones.

And all I can think is, *yes*. Yes! This is exactly what I've been missing. Exactly what I needed. "Don't stop," I plead because I feel it, his brain kicking in where his brain has no business being.

"Grace. We shouldn't—"

"We should. We absolutely should. If you want me, Carter, take me tonight. I'm yours."

"Fuck," he hisses sharply, his hand slamming into the wall beside my head. "It's too soon."

Probably. But I don't care. If he stops, I'll die. If he rejects me, it's game over. "Please." I pull back, meeting his obsidian eyes. "I need this."

His thumb roughly pulls along my lower lip, dragging the skin along with the pad of his flesh. "I can't say no," he speaks gruffly against me. "I know I should. I know it's likely wrong and I'm taking advantage, but I can't say no."

I hike my leg up to his hip, grinding shamelessly against him. "It's not wrong. You're an adult and so am I. You're not taking advantage because I am saying yes. I am begging, pleading, without shame for this. I need a man to take control of my body and give me the pleasure I need. And I am woman enough to admit that."

"Oh, Grace," he hums against my lips, his eyes locked on mine. "You knocked on the right door that night if that's what you need."

In my next breath, he's hoisting me up by the backs of my thighs, lifting me until my body is crushed against his, thighs strangling his hips. Then we're moving. Out of the exercise room, down the longest hallway in the history of hallways until we reach my room. I'm guessing because it's closer but not once has Carter Fritz removed his lips from mine. They've been ravaging, taking no prisoners, and showing no mercy.

They eat at my lips, taste at my tongue, bite at my jaw, lick down my neck. They're voracious and devouring and absolutely, unequivocally, everything I forgot I needed all this time. Years and years wasted with boring, lifeless, unimpassioned kisses. Kisses that were dull. Flat.

But not with Carter.

Kissing Carter is an explosion. The ticking time bomb I never knew existed inside me detonating. Waiting on him to light the match and strike the fuse.

I hit the bed hard, a thud of a bounce at my back, my dress flying high with it.

But before I can comprehend any of that, he has me by the calves, dragging me along until I reach the edge, my legs spread wide, knees bent high.

"Carter!" I screech just as I feel his hot breath on my panties, over the thin satin that I have no doubt is already visibly soaked.

Carter is on the floor, on his knees, directly between my legs. His eyes meet mine, dark and intoxicating. "If we're doing this, Grace... If you tell me, it's just tonight... I'm doing everything I want to do to you. I promise you'll love every single second of it."

I have nothing to say to that.

"Good. No more arguments. You said, yes, remember?"

"I said yes."

"Do you still mean it?"

Do I?

"Yes."

A wildly sexy grin tilts up the corner of his lips. With his eyes still on mine, he leans in between my spread thighs, his hot breath all over my most sensitive region. I shudder and shake, suddenly embarrassed I clued him in on how long it's been since a man has done this to me yet oddly grateful I did all the same.

The look in his eye tells me he's not thinking about that at all. That whatever he's about to do is purely based on what he *wants* to do. His nose dips in, finding my clit, rubbing it back and forth through my panties as he inhales deeply. My eyes instantly roll back, a moan fleeing my lungs.

"You smell like heaven, but I bet you taste like sin."

Jesus fuck.

Closing my eyes, I lean back into the bed as he slips my panties to the side, kissing gently at first. I let out a soft sigh only to immediately follow it up with a sharp inhale as his tongue plunges inside me. My hips shoot off the bed when I feel his thumb circling my clit, the pressure a tease in comparison with the deep thrusts of his tongue.

"Mmmm," he hums into me, the vibrations dragging a whimper from my lips. "I was right. Heaven and sin. Delicious."

His mouth ravages me, a hot, messy whirl of lips and tongue. I cry out, my insides unraveling as he strokes and toys with every nerve ending I'm comprised of. Deft fingers play with my opening as his tongue switches up, flicking my clit before sucking it between his lips, working me up into a frenzy, his pace building, growing strong and faster.

All I can do is hold on. To his hair. To the blanket. My body is arched, my neck stretched, my eyes clenched tight until I feel a smack on my inner thigh. My head whips up, eyes wild, finding his, wicked and dirty and dripping with lust.

"Eyes on me, sweetheart. Watch me lick your sweet cunt."

"Fucking hell," I cry, as his fingers slip inside me, his tongue and mouth eating me in a way that has sounds I've never made before spilling past my lips. I can't do it. I can't look into his eyes as he does this to me. It's too intense. Too intimate. Tonight isn't meant to be like that.

Only I can't look away either.

His eyes are giving me a twisted voyeuristic thrill. It's almost as if I can read every salacious thought and dirty idea as it crosses his mind. And once he realizes this, sees that it's only turning me on more, building me up higher, he grins like the devil, the darkness in his eyes from Satan himself.

Cool air hits me as he blows on my wet flesh. I whimper, my body shaking with tremors as long fingers drag, crook, and find that incredible spot inside me over and over. His eyes dance between his fingers and my eyes like he can't decide which show he'd rather watch. The sound is lewd and erotic and I'm so fucking close my mind is spinning.

"You're so close," he says, an awed whisper, reading me perfectly. "Look at you. Dripping wet and clenching around me. All for me, Grace."

God. I can't with that. I just... "Please, Carter. I need to come." I need to get lost. To not think. To forget everything other than the pleasure he's giving me.

"Then come, sweetheart. I'm not stopping you." His lips wrap around my clit, sucking it hard, his fingers picking up their pace, and I don't just come, I erupt on a piercing scream. My body locked in overdrive, the sensations plow through me, swirling over me, consuming me thoroughly.

I wrench at the bed, arching deeper and finally closing my eyes as wave after wave hits me harder than the one before it.

He continues to work me through it until I'm too sensitive, my hands pushing his head away, and then he's standing, removing his shirt and pants, leaving his charcoal briefs on. Panting for my life, I take him in, my gaze dragging all over. Carter is tall, all broad shoulders and defined pecs trailing down into tight stacks of abdominal muscles before they reach the V of his trim waist. He is the definition of masculine.

Sexy as all fuck.

Blazingly gorgeous, my body heats up just from the sight of him.

"Are you on anything?" he asks, taking my hand and forcing me to sit up, undoing the ties of my dress behind my neck with skill and patience.

"Depo."

"I have no condoms in here unless you brought some."

I stare up into his eyes, black as midnight. "I don't have any, but I was just tested, remember?"

"I haven't been with anyone in a few months, and I was tested after the last time."

My lips quirk as he slides my dress off me, leaving me in nothing but my strapless bra and skewed panties.

"Now that we've gotten the sexy pregnancy and STI talk out of the way, Doctor, are we doing this?" I lick my lips and swallow hard. "Just us? No protection?"

He smirks in response, angling toward me, forcing me back as his hands press into the mattress, bracketing me in until his face is mere inches away. "You need protection from me, Grace?"

"Yes. Yeah, I think I do." I think he knows it too. We're playing a dangerous game. One I started. But now that the alcohol is starting to burn off, realization is sinking in. This is Carter. And I just crossed an irreversible line with him. Even if tonight truly is just tonight, we'll always know this happened. It will always be a thing between us, something we remember with every glance.

He kisses me passionately, his tongue invading my mouth once more, staking its claim, only to end the kiss just as quickly as he started it.

"Too fucking bad. We're doing this, Grace. Just us. But only if you tell me you want me. No games. No fear. No more teasing. I want you more than my next breath, but I won't touch you again until you tell me you want that too. So what will it be? The choice is yours."

18

Grace's pretty blue eyes flutter as she digests my words. I don't know what I'm doing. Why I'm agreeing to this other than I wasn't lying when I told her I want her more than my next breath and I can't say no. But the problem is, I don't want her just for tonight even if that's all she's after.

I told myself I didn't want to be a fling to her and yet here I am, ready to be just that if it means I can have her. Even just this once. Because having Grace once is better than never having her at all.

At least that's what I'm telling myself.

I know full well I might never get this chance again. Tomorrow she could wake up and create a world of distance and space between us. Laugh it off as a drunken birthday thing.

That's likely what will happen, given all the constraints we face.

It'll suck and I'll have to deal with the weight of my disappointment, but it would be nothing compared to the disappointment and regret I'd feel by saying no to this.

"I want to do this with you," she breathes the words.

In a flash, I cover her, my mouth back on hers, my hands on her hips, my chest pressing hers down. Never in my life have I been with a woman I've wanted this much and if I'm not careful, I'll embarrass myself by saying too much. Reaching around, I unhook her bra, tossing it over my shoulder. My mouth drops down as my hand swipes up, cupping her full breast, squeezing it and sucking on her nipple.

She's so beautiful. And her skin tastes so sweet. And she fills up my hands perfectly. Like she was made for me. Meant for me. Grace's fingers run through my hair, dragging her nails along my scalp as I consume her breasts, one and then the other. I take my time with them. Savor each second, study every breathy moan she makes.

One hand slides down her stomach, looping into the thin string of her panties, dragging them down her legs and off. And once she's completely naked before me, I pull back and stare at her. Every dip and curve. She's exquisite, almost too stunning to look at, and judging by the sparkle in her eye, I said that aloud.

"Now I want to see you," she says, sitting up and going for my briefs. Her hand squeezes my cock over the cotton, ripping a hiss from the back of my throat. "Wow. Never in all my high school fantasies did I ever imagine I'd actually get my hands on your dick."

With my hands on the waistband of my briefs, I freeze, tilting my head and staring right into her eyes. "I'm sorry, what did you just say?"

"What?" She shrugs as if it's no big deal. "All the girls thought you were hot. You rocked the mysterious bad boy mystique. We couldn't get enough. Oliver's oh-so-serious and sexy older brother. Well, one of four that is, but you were a junior and senior when we were freshmen and sophomores, so we saw you more. Not to mention heard all about how good you were in bed from the girls lucky enough to find out."

Did she just call me sexy? And admit to wanting me in high

school? Not just wanting but having fucking fantasies? Oh, hell yes. And oh, hell no this is not only tonight. If she wanted me once, she'll want me again. I'll make it my life's fucking mission.

"Tell me more about these fantasies," I demand as I stand, removing my boxers as I go.

Her eyes widen when she sees all of me. She stares and stares hard—pun intended—for a few moments before slowly skating up my body until she meets my eyes.

"This," she says, her voice a shaky whisper. "I pictured this. Me naked before you, you staring at me with fervor in your eyes, us about to have sex." Her already flushed face heats further with teenage embarrassment though she doesn't divert her gaze or cover her naked body.

My hands cup her cheeks, sliding back into her hair seconds before my lips crash down on hers once more. I groan the second my tongue tastes her, feels the heat of her mouth. I need her. This second. With my mouth still against hers, I press her back down into the mattress, lift her thigh until one knee is resting on my shoulder, her other bent, and then I slide inside her in one swift, hot move.

She sucks in a breath, her teeth clamping down on my bottom lip. Nails dig into the flesh of my shoulders while her back bows, her body tense as she tries to acclimate to my size.

My lungs empty at the tight feel of her, the way her body clenches mine, a vise-like grip.

I open my eye, wanting to tell her to relax. To take a breath. To ask if she's okay only to lock on her beautiful face. Her eyes are closed, her brows creased, but her lips are soft and supple, the crest of her cheekbones so delicate.

"Grace." I whisper her name.

And the second her eyes open and meet mine, everything inside me changes. It's as if I've spent years of my life in hibernation only to be awoken in this moment. Hungry. Desperate. *Alive*. Never have I been more alive than I am inside her.

Roughly cupping her jaw, my thumb scrapes sharply along her bottom lip, needing her to experience this with me even when deep down, I know she's not. She wants the fling. The hot, dirty sex of it. I do too, but it's obvious this moment means a hell of a lot more to me than it ever will to her.

"Can I move now?" I ask as her body starts to relax around me.

She gives me a jerky nod. "Yes."

I slide back, my eyes trained on hers as I practically slip from her body only to thrust back in, deeper, harder, all the way to the hilt. Her neck arches, her lips parting on a moan. My hand clasps her neck before I can stop it, holding on tight without squeezing as I start to pound into her.

Her tits jiggle, bouncing with the force of my thrusts, my other hand grasping her hip, compelling her body to take every inch of me. She meets me thrust for thrust, pound for pound, our bodies working in tandem as I unleash everything I've worked so hard to keep buried. Everything I've kept pent-up all these months.

All my wicked desires. Every ounce of want.

And that other thing. The one I refuse to give a name or a voice to. Not now. Not in this moment, it'll ruin me completely.

"Grace," I rasp, grunting and groaning with each push and pull.

I've never gone bareback in a woman before. Never. Not once. Not even with girls I dated for a few months here or there. Always with condoms. I was in college, and medical school, and residency. I knew the dangers of not using protection. I saw first-hand what happened to Landon. That was enough to scare a dude into a lifetime of condoms.

"Fuck," I growl. "You feel so fucking good."

"Carter, harder. I want it harder."

I give her neck a squeeze before releasing it, pulling completely out of her, groaning from the loss of her hot, wet pussy around me. In a flash, I clutch her hips and haul her off the bed, forcing her across the room. Her feet trip over themselves, her movements clumsy.

"What are you doing?" she asks, her voice startled as I slam her against the dresser on the opposite side of the room.

"Open your eyes, beautiful."

Blue eyes snap wide, only to strike immediately on her reflection in the mirror. She gasps, her body flushing over instantly just as her gaze snags on mine.

"Hold on," I warn her. "And don't close your eyes. I want you to watch."

I kick her legs apart, line up my still wet cock with her tight pussy, and ram into her. She jerks forward, having to use her hands to catch herself, but her eyes nearly roll back in her head.

"Yes," she hisses.

"That hard enough for you, sweetheart?"

"Yes. So good. Just like that. Don't stop."

There is nothing fucking sexier in this world than a woman who is not only comfortable and confident in her body and what she wants but isn't afraid to tell you. One arm wraps around her waist, pulling her hips back, holding her there. My other grabs her breast, squeezing it as I start to fuck her, never removing my eyes from her reflection. It's exactly what I pictured that day in the bathroom. Only better. So much better.

Being with her like this surpasses all of my filthiest fantasies.

We're not even close to done and I already know this once will never be enough for me.

Sweat glistens on my forehead as I set a punishing rhythm, the sound of skin slapping against skin over and over, the back of the dresser banging into the wall. It's loud and messy and sweet. She's so sweet. Her sounds. Her breathy fucking moans that fill my head and swell my chest. The cries of pleasure as she gets closer and closer. The feel of her body, against mine, in my hands, all over me.

My teeth capture the lobe of her ear before I suck into my mouth. "After this, I'm going to eat your pussy in the shower," I tell her, our eyes locked, her blue to my brown. "Then I'm going to fuck you again, Grace. You might have thought this was a one-and-done thing, sweetheart, but I plan to go all night."

A moan flees her lips, her body starting to tremble against mine, her legs buckling. My fingers find her clit, slick and throbbing. I rub her, never slowing my pace. My hips piston into her as pleasure and pressure build within me. Never has anything felt better. More right.

Her hands slide along the dresser, the mirror swaying dangerously with our movements. I slip out of her again, flipping her around once more and then hoisting her on top of the dresser. She wraps her legs around my waist, her arms around my neck.

But that's not what I want.

Not yet at least.

With my hand on her chest, I push her back until her head and shoulders are pressed against the cool glass of the mirror, then I grab both of her legs and throw them over my shoulders. I dive back into her pussy, licking her out, tasting how aroused and close to coming she is. She screams, her hands ripping at my hair.

"Carter. I can't..."

"You can," I growl. Because she can. "Fuck, you taste good. I could eat you all night."

We're not doing this the gentle way. This is dirty and raw and uninhibited. The shower is where I'll take her gentle and slow. It's where I'll feel her, stare into her eyes, and coax her pleasure from her body. But right now, she needs to let go. She needs me to fix the wounds her previous fuckface gave her even if she doesn't realize that's what I'm doing.

She needs to know how sexy and desirable she is.

How much I want her.

And maybe, just fucking maybe, I can trick her into staying with me just a bit longer.

I make out with her pussy until she's a quivering, dripping mess all over my face. Until she shatters before my eyes, writhing, undulating against my lips, crying out her release. Then and only then do I shift her, move her legs around my waist once more, and unleash myself inside her. So deep I can't tell where she ends, and I begin.

I fuck her. I fuck her so hard and so good all she can do is hold on. Is bite into my shoulder. Is dig her nails into my back.

"Fuck!" she screams it this time and that's it.

That's all it takes.

Her clenching around me, so quickly after her last orgasm, and I lose my mind. My balls draw up, pleasure shooting up my spine and through every nerve ending in my body. A rough, feral growl is ripped from the back of my throat as I lose my absolute mind in this woman. My pace slows, my hips lagging as I come inside her, shooting my load for the first time without protection.

Breathing ragged, we're both clinging to each other, sweaty and spent, but so goddamn sated I've never felt this euphoric before. This whole. This complete.

Her head falls against my chest along with a strangled, breathy laugh.

My hand trails down her hair, cupping the back of her head, my lips pressing into her crown.

"I think we broke your dresser," she muses, humor in her voice.

"I don't care. Your clothes are in it, not mine."

She laughs, the sound shaky.

"I wasn't expecting that though maybe I should have."

"What?" I ask, cupping her jaw and pulling her back enough so I can see her face, her eyes.

"For that to be the best sex of my life."

Warmth swarms through me like a flashflood, flowing into my chest and sticking there, drowning me in her. My hand brushes back the dampened strands of her hair. "It was for me too. No question."

Her eyes sparkle, a hesitant smile on her lips.

I lift her up in my arms, heading into the bathroom. Her bottom hits the counter and I go about turning on the shower, making sure it's hot and then lifting her again and walking us both in. This shower isn't as big as mine, but it's big enough for two.

I press her against the tiled wall and kiss her lips. My hands in her wet hair, framing her face, and I kiss her like a man possessed. Like a man obsessed. Because that's exactly what I am. If I thought I was obsessed with this woman before, that has nothing on me now. I'm consumed.

Owned.

Our tongues meet, dancing, tangling yet soft and coaxing. Neither of us are hurried, yet we can't deny the resurging lust mounting between us. She rolls her body against my already hardening cock and I emit a grunt.

"More?"

She smiles against my lips. "Definitely more. I was promised all night."

"You're inviting the beast, you know. Once you take him out of his cage, there is no going back."

Her fingers dive into my hair, her forehead pressing into mine.

"Maybe the beast is exactly what I needed. Besides, I already know that hidden beneath your beast is the heart of a prince. You can growl at me all you want, Carter Fritz, but I'm on to you."

I hoist her up, her legs around my waist, feet digging into my ass, and I enter her.

And this time I do take it slow. I worship her body until we've both exceeded exhaustion. Until our limbs are weak and our minds spent. Then and only then do I tuck her into bed, my arms around her, holding her close. She passes out almost instantly, leaving me awake to watch her.

Sated. Happy. Terrified.

Tonight was everything I've dreamed of for a year and in a few short hours, I'll lose it all. Time is already running out. Even now I feel her pulling away, her body twisting out of my arms in her sleep. And worse yet, I have no idea how to stop her.

19

Morning comes with a headache and a realization. I slept with Carter Fritz last night. And he's still in bed with me.

Blinking my eyes open slowly, I stare straight ahead, listening to Carter's slow, even breaths. I kissed Carter. I told him I wanted him. We had sex. A lot of sex. A lot of insanely good, mind-bending sex. To the point where I'm a little sore this morning. My muscles aching in that wonderfully used way.

But... I slept with Carter Fritz last night.

Did I already mention that?

A weird, twisted smile curls up my lips that I bite into, trying desperately to stop it.

I can't get carried away with this. I have to tuck all thoughts of last night away or I'll never be able to look at him—or fucking Oliver, for that matter—again. Now I have to figure out what to do. He's in my bed—I still can't believe he fell asleep in here with me.

I want to get up and shower and hide and run and scream and freak out and laugh and cry. But I can't do any of that with him here and I can't exactly kick him out of my bed in his apartment. Can I?

I don't pretend for a second that last night meant anything to him beyond what it was. And for me, well, I think it's pretty damn obvious I'm a mess. I ruefully admit Margot was right. I think I needed that to hurdle myself over the Tony hump, so to speak, and Carter was a very safe person to do that with all things considered.

But can people truly go back to being just—I have no idea what Carter and I actually are—again after experiencing something like that? When there is so much heat and chemistry? I hope so. God, I hope so. I need Carter right now. I need him as my attending. As my roommate. As my quasi friend. The last thing I could ever tolerate between us is losing him.

And that's what would happen if we kept this going.

I'd develop feelings. He wouldn't. It would be a disaster.

We're too intricately connected.

Maybe this was just our way of getting it out of our systems? Of burning off all our excess heat that seemed to be simmering between us over the last couple of weeks? Definitely. Now that we've done that, I'm sure we can—

"You're thinking awfully hard over there," he mumbles, and I inwardly shake my head. I should have known he was awake.

"I am," I admit. "It's what I do best."

"I don't know about that. I can think of a lot of other things that you do best."

He shifts in my direction, his morning wood hitting me in places that instantly make me wet, soreness be damned.

I must tense up because he pulls back, shifting until he's propping himself up behind me, his head in his hand. He rolls me onto my back, so I'm forced to look up at him. Worry creases his forehead, but otherwise he's not giving me anything to go by.

"Talk to me," he commands. Just like that. As if it's that simple when it's anything but.

"I had a good time last night."

"So did I," he hedges. "But..." he trails off, waiting for me to fill in the blank.

"I can't lose you," I tell him.

"Why would you think you'd ever lose me?" He's genuinely perplexed and that relaxes some of my unease. His brown eyes are dancing about my face trying to read me as I sort through what I want to say.

"I don't know, Carter. Because we had sex."

"And?"

"And sex does things to people."

"And you're worried it's going to do something bad to us?"

"I pushed you into it."

He smiles the most beautiful, soul-stealing smile. "Sweetheart, I'm pretty sure you didn't push me into anything I didn't already want to do."

A swarm of intoxicating and clearly hateful butterflies takes residence in my belly. Statements like that and the resulting way they make me feel should be illegal.

"So we're okay then?"

"Of course."

"Good. But now what? We just move on and pretend like it never happened?"

"No. I didn't say that. That's certainly not what I want, and I could never pretend last night didn't happen."

"I'm not a casual fling girl."

He studies my expression intently. "And you're not interested in anything more than that," he surmises.

Now it's my turn to be confused because I can't tell if he's disappointed by that or not. To the best of my knowledge, that's all Carter Fritz does. I've never heard him speak of anything else other than the woman he was in love with during his residency. But even then, he never did anything about it, so how in love could he have been? If he wasn't willing to settle down and be a one-woman man for her, then he sure as hell isn't willing to try that with me.

And is that something I'd even want? So soon after ending my engagement?

The only reason last night happened was because it was Carter. Yes, I'm attracted to him, but it's more than that. I trust him when trusting a man right now feels nothing short of impossible.

I mean, if it were anyone other than Carter, would I even be—

"You're doing it again," he admonishes, interrupting my thoughts, pressing his finger into the groove between my brows and flattening it out. "Stop overthinking this, Grace, and tell me what you want and what you don't want."

"I..." I blink at him. "I don't want to get hurt again." *And being only a fling to you is a recipe for just that very thing.* "And I think, in truth, it's still much too soon after everything that happened with Tony to even entertain getting involved with anyone."

A frown marks his lips before it just as quickly disappears. "That's what I figured you'd say. I knew it was too soon last night."

Now it's my turn to frown because I feel like I'm missing something in nearly everything Carter says. It's impossible to read him when his face is this stoic, and his words could be taken a lot of different ways.

"I don't regret last night," I explain. "I just don't want it to change us. I don't want it to change our work."

"I'd never ever let that happen. I'm glad you don't regret it, because I sure as hell don't either, and if you're not ready for anything real yet, I understand. You've been through a lot in the last couple of weeks and I'd never want you to do something you weren't ready for."

"Thank you, Carter. You have no idea how much I needed to hear that."

He leans in like he's going to kiss me only his lips find my forehead instead and I'm hit with something strange. I can't even discern what it is exactly. I just know it's settling in my bones all wrong.

Without another word, Carter pulls away from me, grabbing his boxer briefs off the floor and getting up. With his back to me, he says, "I'll give you your privacy to get yourself ready, but the cleaning crew will be here soon, so we likely should get out of their way."

And with that, he's gone. Door shut behind him on a soft click.

I blow out a breath, rattled and simultaneously relieved by that entire encounter. By everything we did last night. I still feel like I'm missing something, but it's impossible to pinpoint what exactly. All I know is that even though neither of us regret what happened, what I started, I just hope I didn't make a mistake by crossing a line we can never uncross.

Getting myself up and out of bed, I debate showering, but then decide a run might be just the thing I need to help me clear my head and sort out of my thoughts. I don my running gear, throwing my hair up into a high ponytail just as I hear the doorbell ring shortly followed by the sound of women's voices.

A pang of guilt hits me at all the extremes Carter went to just to ensure I had a wonderful birthday. That fitness mirror. The ring that's still on my finger that I have yet to set up. The party. He spared no expense. He's been surprising me in ways I never expected.

Last night included.

Exiting my room, I head down the hall in the direction of the front door. Carter is dressed casually in jeans and a T-shirt, speaking with the cleaning crew when I catch his eye. He gives me a long once over, a slight scowl marring his handsome face just as one of the ladies catches his attention, diverting it away from me. I throw him a wave, not wanting to be in the way as he said, and leave the house, assuming space is the best course of action.

Only the moment I step outside, the warm sunshine raining down on my face, I regret fleeing so hastily.

"I called the hospital and they told me it was your day off," Tony says, stepping out from the side of the building and marching determinedly in my direction. He's dressed in a blue button-down and khaki slacks, a bouquet of roses in his hand. Him with those fucking roses. How did I spend the last three years with a man who doesn't even know that roses aren't my favorite flower? How did I allow myself to sacrifice so much while receiving so little in return?

"What are you doing here, Tony?"

"It was your birthday yesterday. I came by to see you. Only Carter threatened to perform a total hysterectomy on me, anatomy be damned."

I shouldn't be grinning at that, but I am. Carter never even mentioned it and I'm grateful for that. It likely would have ruined my birthday.

"I hand-delivered my present to you. I wanted to see your face when you opened them. You did get them, right? He didn't throw the rings down the disposal or anything?"

"No. Carter gave me the rings." Though I thought they were delivered by courier, not by Tony. "They're still sitting in the box they came in."

"And yet you have a new one on your finger," he snarls. "Who gave you that?"

I glance down, staring at the ring Carter gave me, one meant for health and fitness but still a ring. Something that is often associated with possession even if it's on the wrong finger.

Is that why he gave this to me? No. Carter wouldn't have even considered that angle.

Funny how this simple ring—purchased with thought and purpose—means more to me than the engagement ring and wedding band combined. Tony doesn't know me, I realize. I'm not sure he ever did. He has no clue what makes me tick. What I love and what I don't. What makes me smile and what makes me frown.

Somehow Carter seems to. A man who, by all accounts, shouldn't. He's figured me out because he pays attention. Because he... cares?

"Grace?" Tony snaps, dragging me out of my thoughts.

I look back up at him, seeing him with a clarity I wish I had had years ago. "You should go. In fact, you should have never come."

"Grace," he starts, softening his tone and approach, taking another step, his eyes all over me. "I got rid of those women. I told them I was in love with my fiancée. That I was ready to set a date and marry her. That losing her because I was reckless and egotistical and stupid was the worst mistake I've ever made. Please. Please, don't give up on me. I swear, you're it for me. I'll do whatever it takes. I'll never look at another woman again. You're all I want. All I'll ever want."

"Tony, I—"

"She's not interested," Carter says, cutting me off.

My eyes expand to the size of Fenway Park when I feel his hand slip along my waist. Tony's are the opposite, the thinnest of narrow slits he's practically Voldemort hissing parseltongue at us and cursing Carter's life. If Tony had a wand in his hand, Carter would be dead for sure.

"In fact," Carter continues nonchalantly. "You should know Grace belongs to me now."

What in the actual fuck does Carter Fritz think he's doing? My first instinct is to go all She-Ra Princess of Power on his ass and say I belong to no man, but the look on Tony's face is holding my tongue.

"No," Tony declares assertively, shaking his head. "She can't stand you. All she's done for a year is shit talk you."

Well that's certainly not something I want my attending to hear. Especially when it's not *entirely* true. Sure, I shit talked Carter—some of it to his face even. But it wasn't him exactly as much as the whole low on the totem pole attending making their resident's life hell dynamic thing.

Carter chuckles but it's the sort of chuckle that promises I'll pay for that at a later time. Awesome. Because my nightmare isn't quite complete yet. This is what I get for throwing myself at my boss. Lines that shouldn't get blurred get blurred.

"Be that as it may," Carter replies coolly. "It doesn't change the reality of our new situation. Grace is with me and you're a cheating piece of shit who lost out because he couldn't keep his stupid dick in his pants." Tony opens his mouth, but Carter advances a step, raising his hand and cutting Tony off. "I'm going to make this insanely simple for you. Grace has already told you to fuck off and now I'm doing the same. But if you continue to deliver a ring she's already returned to you, a ring she wants no part of, or even show up at our place of residence or business again, I will have no choice but to lodge a formal complaint. As an attorney, I'm sure you're fully aware of the ramifications of what any sort of public registry of harassment could do to your chances of making partner."

Tony looks like he was just sideswiped by a car.

"Grace?" he questions and really? How can he actually question me right now? Because Carter might be talking out of his ass about us, but he's right that I've told Tony—more than once or twice now—that I'm done.

"It's over, Tony."

"You're actually with him?" Tony points to Carter. "Already? How could you? We were engaged for a year and a half!"

Yep. That right there was part of our problem, but routine and comfort lead to complacency. That part is on me, I guess.

"Take care of yourself, Tony," I say instead of anything else because I'm not all that great of a liar and he'd likely see through it. "Soon you'll agree this was always the way it was supposed to be."

With Carter's hand still on my waist, he turns us around and we start walking away, up toward the main street. We're silent and I can't decide if I'm pissed at him or not. At the very least, I think it's safe to say Tony is finally out of my life for good. Of course, I have to get the damn rings back to him, but that's the easy part.

"Are you pissed?" Carter finally asks as we turn the corner by the movie theater, the sidewalk busy with Sunday Boston hustle.

"I'm trying to figure that out."

"Want me to take you out for brunch while you decide?"

A wry smirk unerringly fixes itself to my lips as I look up at him. "I was going to go for a run."

"But you're hungry. We'll run into work tomorrow."

"Just like that?"

He smiles, his brown eyes lightening. "Just like that. You didn't want last night to change us. So we're not letting it. You can pick a fight with me tomorrow when you see your assignment."

"My assignment?"

"You didn't think I'd let that whole talking shit about me for a year thing go did you?" He winks at me, setting off in the direction of that breakfast place I liked so much. Knowing full well I'll follow him—especially if he's buying. But damn him. He won this round, and the smug bastard knows it.

20

"I hate Carter in the springtime," I grumble-sing under my breath as I leave a patient room, heading down the hall toward the nurses' station. "I hate Carter in the fall."

All fucking week, I've hated Carter and his goddamn bullshit. Here he's the boss from hell—one I can't challenge. At home, I hardly see him because I mostly hide out in my room—something I'm considering a blessing in this moment since I'd likely want to chop him up into small pieces and serve him as dinner to the feral cats that chill in the alley nearby. All Tony said was that I shit-talked him and didn't like him. And for truth, that's my damn right as a resident. But does that mean I deserve to be treated like an intern? No. No it does not!

"Fuck, I just hate Carter every fucking season there is."

"That's a lie. You just don't like the way I punish you," he says from behind me, and I growl.

I can't even lament my jerk attending without him finding out. I feel him shift in behind me, the corner of his mouth kicks up against my ear and my heart—that should freaking know better by this point—trips over itself in my chest.

"You've been avoiding me."

I swallow hard and sink my teeth into my bottom lip. I have been. Because in the week since we had our wild night of hot, dirty sex, I've been reliving it. Every night. In my fucking dreams. I wake up sweaty and turned on. My panties soaked. How am I supposed to live with a man, look at him day in and day out as both a roommate and a boss after dreams like that? Dreams that I know are based on reality.

"I haven't been," I lie, and he knows I'm lying because I suck at it. "I've just been busy. You're the one who's been changing the board to move my name off your service." That and I haven't been able to stop picturing you naked, so until that happens...

"I was thinking we could have dinner together tonight."

I'm thinking that's a horrible idea because I'm liable to jump him for dessert. Ugh!

"Maybe another night, Doctor," I bit out acerbically. "I have a lot of scut that needs finishing."

"Where's your intern?"

"Running damn labs and swabs since you're making us do them for all of the residents in the department."

"Don't you want to know why I'm punishing you so relentlessly, Doctor?"

Yes! But I'm too stubborn, so I'll never ask.

"Because you're an evil sadist?"

He chuckles. Bastard. Inching in closer until his chest nearly presses against my back, the scent of his bodywash and heat of his proximity does funny things to my insides.

"I didn't say you could touch me, Dr. Fritz."

"I'm not touching you, Dr. Hammond. I'm speaking directly to my insubordinate, smart-mouthed resident."

"Dick."

"What was that?"

Before I can tell him exactly what that was, Dylan yells to us from ten feet away. "Dr. Johnson has a patient hemorrhaging. She needs extra hands."

Carter and I take off at a sprint, following Dylan down the hall and straight into the patient room. Straight into absolute pandemonium. Dr. Johnson is on the ground, her face ashen white, her scrubs saturated in blood, her arm visibly broken, being attended to by a nurse.

Meanwhile, Seliene, another nurse, has her hands on the patient's abdomen, massaging. "Her uterus is obtunded. I've opened up her Pitocin IV and given both buccal (in the inner lining of the mouth) and IM (intramuscular) Misoprostol. Nothing is helping."

Jesus.

Carter and I immediately gown and glove up. Dad is sitting in a chair up by his wife's head, holding his newborn baby, a look of pure abject horror on his face. Meanwhile the patient is lying there, calm and quiet, but visibly shaken.

"She needs the OR," Carter states, as I maneuver myself in between the patient's legs, inserting my gloved hand up into her uterus.

"I'm able to appreciate retained placental parts," I state.

"What happened?" Carter asks Janet.

"I slipped," she snaps, throwing me a scathing look like it's my fault she fell, and her patient is bleeding everywhere. "I had to pick up extra slack since Grace hasn't been pulling her weight with patients."

First, that's a fucking lie if ever there was one. Second, every time I check the board, my name is missing from it and hers is everywhere. Why would Carter do that to me in favor of her? Clearly she wasn't capable of handling all he was giving her.

"That's not what I asked," Carter barks. "I meant with the patient."

"The placenta was retained," Seliene answers for her. "Dr.

Johnson attempted a manual extraction, but in doing so, it came out missing a piece and then the patient's uterus began hemorrhaging. This is Courtney and her husband Brandon." She points to the patient and her husband.

"I'm Dr. Fritz and the woman whose hand is inside you now is Dr. Hammond. We're going to take excellent care of you."

Courtney licks her dry lips and nods her head, her skin tacky and pale, likely with blood loss.

"I've ordered some type-specific," Dylan says. "I've arranged for it to be waiting for us in the OR."

I throw him a grateful look. "Good thinking Dr. Williams."

"What about me?" Janet barks from the floor.

Carter twists his neck to stare at her, stunned she's even brazened enough to ask that. "Take her down to the ED," he tells the nurse helping her. "You need your wrist x-rayed and casted. And get yourself cleaned up too then go home and rest. Come in first thing tomorrow to my office so we can talk."

"Yes, Doctor," she says, embarrassment and discomfort staining her features, but I can't focus on her because even internal massage is doing nothing to slow this bleeding. Nothing is helping.

"Dr. Fritz, we need to move now. Has the OR been prepped?"

"Yes," Dylan answers. "She's also already been consented by Dr. Johnson."

Well at least Janet did that right.

"Okay, let's move," Carter orders.

"We're going to take you to the OR now to stop the bleeding," I inform the patient. "Don't worry, you're in excellent hands and we'll do everything we can for you. Seliene, will you take Dad and baby…"

"Simone," Dad supplies, his voice thick with emotion.

"Simone down to the nursery? There's a rocking chair in

there that might be more comfortable, and the nurses can help you feed her."

Dad stands up, cradling his baby in his arms while the nurses unplug the IV pump and raise the bedrails, ready to move her. I have my hand still inside the patient because I might have found the source of the bleeding and I'm not moving until we're in that OR.

Brandon kisses Courtney on the lips before shifting the baby so she can kiss her too.

Then we move, me climbing up onto the base of the bed so I can stay in position, us being wheeled down the hall and straight into the prepped OR. There is a scrub nurse already in there waiting as well as an anesthesiologist.

"Grace, don't move your hand until I'm scrubbed in and ready," Carter growls at me before turning on the anesthesiologist. "Give the patient a bolus of Fentanyl into her epidural line."

With that, Carter flies out of the room only to return two minutes later, gowned and gloved up, he gets into position and immediately takes over, working at lightspeed. I step back, ready to go scrub in when Carter stops me.

"I've got this. You can either watch or go check on your intern."

I blink rapidly at him, trying to make sense of what he just said. "You don't want my help?"

"That's what I just said."

Heat crawls up my face. What the fuck is going on? This goes way beyond punishment. This is exactly what I was afraid of. Every bit of it. We had sex and now we're this. Angry and avoiding each other and fucking with my career.

There are four other people—including the patient who is not fully sedated—in this room, so I can't exactly start the fight I'm itching to start in here. Not only that, everyone is now staring at me. He just completely humiliated me in front of everyone.

Without another word, I spin on my heels and march out of the room, fuming.

I snap off my bloody gloves, throwing them into the biohazard waste bin and slamming the lid shut. Then I start vigorously washing my hands at the scrub sink, banging around and stomping onto the pedal.

Once I'm all cleaned off, I wait. Only, I don't want to wait here and face everyone else who already saw our little performance, so I sign out all my patients before heading toward his office, knowing that his shift ends in ten minutes, and he'll come here next.

"Grace?" Dylan comes running up beside me. "Holy shit, that was intense. Why aren't you in the OR?"

"Dr. Fritz kicked me out."

"Wow. Okay. You'll have to fill me in, but I'm guessing Janet's career is over. She didn't just slip. She ripped at that woman's damn placenta without injecting Pitocin straight into it or anything and then when the poor patient started bleeding out, Janet got woozy and collapsed, breaking her fall with her hand. I'd feel bad about it if she wasn't such a backstabbing cunt. Whatever magic she's been using on Dr. Fritz is working. Her name has been everywhere on that board and yours nowhere. It's such bullshit. Anyway, I finished off all the labs. Is there anything else... girl, what's wrong? You look like someone just bitch slapped your mama and now you're out for blood."

He's right about that last part. "Go home, Dylan. We're done for the day but be ready to scrub in tomorrow for surgery. After today we're going to officially be off scut."

"Oh shit," he gasps when he realizes the direction I'm headed, walking briskly beside me, trying to keep up. "You're about to kill a Fritz, aren't you?"

"That's the plan."

"I'm going to run away now for fear of my career, but if you need help hiding the body after he's already dead, I'm your man so just text."

I'd smirk at that if I wasn't so fired up. "Will do."

Dylan scurries off just as I reach Carter's door testing the handle. Locked. I inwardly roll my eyes. Like he has anything in here that anyone would want to steal. So arrogant.

I spin around, pressing my back into the wall beside the door, crossing my feet at the ankles and my arms over my chest. I hate standing here waiting for him. I'm playing into him. Giving him what he's after. But he just upped the ante in that OR and I can't let that stand.

But as the minutes tick by, I start to grow restless. I could just ambush him at home, but something that's this important, something that's work-related, feels like it needs to be hashed out here. Not there.

And for real, I seriously need to start searching for a new place to live.

Just as I'm about to say screw it and leave, he strolls in my direction. He's showered. The bastard showered and changed his clothes.

"I was wondering if you'd still be here waiting for me," he drawls.

And wow, he seriously has no idea what's coming for him. I don't appreciate being made to feel trivial. Like my time and my words and my feelings aren't important. Like my work isn't valued.

"In fact, I'm shocked it's taken you this long to seek me out."

"You arrogant motherfuck—"

"I'd watch your mouth, Dr. Hammond," he cuts me off sharply. "You're speaking to your attending in the halls of the hospital you work in."

I push off the wall, standing up tall, fury leaking from every pore. "Dr. Fritz, with all due respect, you're a real asshole of a boss. And the crap you've pulled this week is not only uncalled for, it's unprofessional. As much as I've valued the experience and training you've provided me in this last year, you should know that tomorrow morning first thing I will be going to my residency adviser to request a transfer to another attending."

"Good," he says, calm. Cool. But beneath that façade, his eyes are burning embers on the brink of igniting.

"Good," I parrot in utter disbelief.

"Was I unclear? I said good. As much as I will miss being your primary attending and instructing you in the OR, I am not sorry to lose you as someone I teach and evaluate."

I'm stunned. And hurt. So hurt my body reacts physically to the assault of his words.

I open my mouth, wanting to spew a thousand nasty things at him, but the sting of his brutal rejection cuts me out at the knees. In my entire professional career, I've never been reduced to tears—and let me tell you, doctors eat their young without remorse. It's life and death and coddling and holding your feelings in their palm is not something that happens. It's The Hunger Games meets medicine when you're an intern and young resident.

But *Carter* looking at me this way—utterly apathetically—telling me these things—without a hint of remorse or regret—it absolutely guts me. And I have no one to blame but myself.

"Sleeping with you was the worst mistake I've ever made."

With that, I plow past him, slamming my shoulder into his arm as hard as I can so I don't sob.

I can't go home tonight. I can never go back there again. What do I do now? I have nothing. Everything around me is tearing apart at the seams, inch by inch, my life is unraveling. I don't even know if my residency adviser can switch me. I was pulling that out of my ass, hoping Carter would crack and soften and I'm so stupid.

Carter Fritz doesn't crack or soften.

He's a—

A scream wrenches from my mouth as I'm suddenly lifted off my feet, swung wildly through the air, and dropped unceremoniously with a hard *oomph* onto Carter's shoulder. Right here in the middle of the damn hallway in the middle of the goddamn hospital.

"What the hell do you think you're doing?" I cry out, slapping at his back since that's all I've got to work with. Who the hell throws their resident over their shoulder fireman style in the middle of an argument?

He doesn't answer. He just unlocks the door to his office and storms me inside, flipping on the lights as he goes, and shutting the door behind us with a swift shove of his foot. Papers go flying across the room as he clears his desk of them, slamming me down on my ass with an unforgiving thud.

"You total asshole!" I fume. "I cannot believe—"

Getting right up in my face, he booms, "You stubborn, prideful, *beautiful* woman. What the fuck is wrong with you?"

"Me?" I yell, shoving at his muscled, unrelenting chest.

"Yes. You. Why the fuck did it take you a week to get here?"

"What?" squawks past my stunned lips.

Carter practically rolls his eyes at me. "I've been torturing you for a week. A *week*, Grace. And it isn't until you're cut out of a surgery that you literally had your hands in that you finally approach me?"

"I-I..." I stutter over my thoughts. "I thought this was all punishment because of what Tony said."

Carter half laughs-half groans. "You've been avoiding me. Every time I try to talk to you, you run. I never see you at home because you hide from me. I put you on scut, that didn't do it. I put you on scut for every other resident, that didn't do it. I had to cast you out of surgery to get you to finally acknowledge me."

"Carter..."

I'm so confused.

"Tell me why you've been avoiding me," he demands, baiting me. "You didn't want it to change us and you're the one who's changed. Tell me why."

Only I can't tell him why. Not the truth anyway. And I have no idea what to do about it now that I'm cornered.

"Tell me," Carter snaps when I remain silent.

All I can do is shake my head. What do I say? That every time I'm near him, look at him, I'm pulled back to that night? That I still fantasize and get myself off to it? To him? That I'm an emotional mess and I have no idea if I'm thinking about him in this way because I never realized how lonely and bored and emotionally unstimulated I was even when I was with Tony until I slept with him?

He stares into my eyes, his face inching in closer and I hate that he's doing this. Trying to read me. Trying to weed out every hidden thought from my head the way only he seems to know how to do.

"Tell me you haven't been thinking about it," he goes on. "Tell me you haven't been replaying and reliving every second of last Saturday night in your head." His hands meet the desk on either side of my thighs, his face so close I can see every fleck of gold and brown in his beautiful irises. "Tell me," he demands sharply, making me jump. "Tell me you're not here for me."

"I..." I lick my lips. "I'm here because of the way you've been treating me all week."

"Bullshit. You've been running and hiding because you don't trust yourself around me. Because all you can think about is how good my cock felt inside of you. Is how hard you came when I ate your sweet-as-fuck pussy." He takes my legs, spreading them open and stepping in between them, caging me in completely. "Admit it."

My heart rate kicks up from a jog to a gallop as nervous adrenaline shoots through my veins.

"Carter—"

Only my words die as his hands capture my face a half-second before his lips crash down on mine. His tongue instantly dives into my mouth, taking possession of mine as a hungry growl is rent from the back of his throat. Our kiss is messy, urgent, his mouth and teeth all over me, marking my skin and bruising my lips. My breath gets tangled up in my lungs as he trails down my neck, the very tip of his tongue skating down before sucking his way back up my flesh.

I shiver against him, my belly trembling as his rough hands slide up my scrub top, ripping it up and over my head before his mouth comes back down against mine. He licks the space between my lips, sliding his tongue back inside. Deft fingers loop into the elastic holding my ponytail up before ripping it from my hair, only to massage away the sting immediately after as my hair tumbles down around me.

"I don't give a fuck if you think it's too soon," he growls into my mouth. "It's not too soon. None of this is." His fingers go for the drawstring on my scrub pants, tearing at the knot. "I'm done being patient. I'm done waiting for my turn. No more messing around, Grace. This is happening between us. I'm going to fuck you so good on my desk you won't be able to walk straight. Then I'm going to take you home and do it all over again."

My body blazes with heat. Burning.

Carter is going to fuck me in ways I've never been fucked before. I can feel it. See it in the raw, unbridled desire in his wild gaze. And I'm here for it. My body craving that more than it craves oxygen for my next breath. I know why this is a bad idea. I know all the ways this could—and likely will—go wrong.

But in this moment, I can't mount any form of defense.

I'm held hostage by a lust so powerful all rational thought is eclipsed by it. Still...

"If you fuck anyone else while you're fucking me—"

His hands grasp my face, holding me firmly, his eyes right before mine, so powerful and intense I see nothing else. "Never, Grace. I am fucking you because I can't stand not fucking you another second. Haven't you figured it out yet? I'm yours."

Before I can ask him exactly what that means, his mouth is back on mine, his kiss so passionate my head spins. His lips are punishing, unforgivingly fierce as they take from me. My hands grasp the strands of his hair, yanking hard as my tongue savagely rakes along his; hungry, tireless, desperate for more. I have no limit with him. My trust is boundless. My desire uncontrollable.

I scoot to the edge of the desk, wrapping my legs around his waist and rolling my hips against the hard ridge in his jeans. My hands grow greedy as they attack his shirt—this thing needed to go like ten minutes ago—and I make quick work of it, still pissed the bastard showered when I haven't.

It hits the floor and then I explore him, nails raking over every inch of flesh they can reach. His skin is hot to the touch, electric as it pulses a current straight through me. My scrub pants get tugged off my body and then I'm being pushed back, more papers flying about the room as Carter shoves them off the desk.

"Those could be important."

"Not as important as punishing you while eating your pussy is."

"What—"

Only I get cut off as Carter flips me over, shoving my chest down onto his desk, my cheek against the hard wood grain.

My thong slides down my legs and now my ass is on full display to him. My pussy too since he's widening my stance. He kneels behind me, his face now level with me, and I shut my eyes, biting down hard into my lip. I'm so exposed. So open to him. At his total mercy.

And yet, I've never felt sexier. More desirable than I do in this moment with his face inches from my pussy.

He grasps my ass cheeks, rubbing and squeezing the globes, spreading them wide and ripping a gasp from my throat. His tongue juts out, licking the seam of my lips, toying all around my clit without giving me the pressure I need. That's when the first smack happens. A hard *clap* against my ass quickly followed by another on the opposite cheek.

I jolt forward, the desk cutting into my upper thighs, my eyes shooting open in shock.

Carter is spanking me on his desk while eating me out from behind. Jesus Henry Christ, how is this even happening right now? We're at work!

He goes back to rubbing me, still playing with me with his tongue.

I whimper, feeling wetness leaking out of me which he licks, groaning into me as he does. Holy shit. I can't... My eyes roll circles in my head as he does it again, thrusting his tongue up into me as his hand comes down on my ass again. Harder this time. The pain is sharp and exquisite, my blood thrumming, rising up to meet my smarting skin. My body is so absorbed in the pleasure he's giving me that every smack spirals me higher to a state of erotic bliss I've never come close to reaching before.

Six more smacks and just as the last one finishes, his lips close around my clit before sucking it in.

"Fuck!" My cry rends the air, my orgasm building, making my needy, empty core convulse.

"Next time you get it into your pretty head that avoiding me is the way to go, I will not make it feel this good. I will make it hurt, make you beg before I ever grant you pleasure." I moan. Something like that shouldn't sound as hot as it does, but my body clearly has other ideas. "No more of that shit, Grace." He blows on me, and I grind against the desk, needing the relief he's teasing me with. "I've waited so long for you. You have no idea."

I moan again, louder this time. "How long?" How long has Carter Fritz wanted me and I had no clue? How long have I denied myself this when I was with the wrong guy the entire time?

I get another smack for my question and then he's going at me. Licking me, flicking me with this tongue. His hands on my ass, holding me against his mouth as he eats at me like a man starved. I come on a whirlwind, a chaotic explosion that rips through my body, taking my mind with it.

I have no clue what I say. If I scream or not. All I know is that I can't stop it or control it.

My body has been taken over, with Carter Fritz as the master puppeteer.

Before I can even catch my breath or adjust my position, he's inside of me with a long, deep thrust. My lungs empty, my hands clutching desperately onto the edge of his desk for fear that I'll fly off the other side.

One hand grasps my hip, the other my hair as he tugs my head up and off the desk, arching my back. Bending himself in half, he starts fucking me, his lips capturing mine as he pounds into me from behind.

Harder and harder he takes me, the desk rustling, inching

along the worn carpet, more and more papers and things tumble off it all the while Carter's mouth devours my cries of pleasure.

"You're gonna get us caught," he accuses, his voice coarse and untamed as his hips drive, hitting that spot inside me that lights everything up in euphoria.

"Afraid someone will see you drilling your resident, Dr. Fritz?"

He grins against me. "I couldn't care less other than I don't want anyone seeing your perfect tits and sweet pussy but me."

"You should know after last time I'm not very good at being quiet when you do this to me."

That grin spreads into a smile. "Tomorrow you're finding a new attending. I'll tell your adviser your pussy is mine so she knows and then I can fuck you whenever and however I want."

"No. You're not telling anyone that. What about me? What about what I want?"

"You want this." He thrusts harder into me, all the way to the hilt, ripping a shuddered gasp out of me as if proving his point. "And I can't deny you what you want."

Shit. I'm in so much trouble.

"No one can know, Carter. No one."

His grip in my hair tightens as he raises up from my back, clutching my hip in a bruising grip as he fucks me relentlessly. It's loud and messy and this is not how I saw tonight going but I'm certainly not complaining. The sex is too good to pretend otherwise and if this is all we are to each other, I guess I can handle that.

At least until I can't anymore.

Until my heart decides it doesn't do flings and grows attached.

Another smack to my ass pulls me out of my thoughts and before I know what the hell is happening, his fingers are rubbing my clit, and I explode. All over him. Crying out his name while multicolored stars rain like confetti behind my eyelids.

For a moment I panic at that, my heart tripling its speed only for me to quickly realize it's not a seizure. Just one hell of an orgasm. One that seems to go on and on and on, especially as he grasps my body, folding his over mine, and roughly grunting out his release in my ear. Making Carter Fritz come undone is without a doubt the sexiest thing I've ever witnessed.

It's a high unlike any other.

This man, always so in control, losing it completely with me.

His ragged breathing pants across my ear, mine across his desk, leaving a ring of condensation with every exhale. Brushing back some of the wayward strands of hair from my face, he kisses my temple, dropping his forehead to the side of mine.

What does this mean for me going forward? Am I doing this? Flinging with my hot roommate? With my boss?

"We should never have gone a week without that."

I close my eyes, trying to settle my turbulent thoughts. "This is going to get complicated."

"Only if we let it," he says simply, pulling himself up and off me, helping me to stand and making sure my legs are steady before he goes over to a cabinet in his built-in bookshelf and pulls out a towel for me. He wipes me up—which feels weird, yet tender, so I don't say anything—and then he's pulling up my thong and scrub pants that I evidently never took off. My shoes either.

This was the definition of a quick, dirty fuck, and I hate that we're still here, in the hospital. I hate that I now have to find a new attending. I hate that I'm already such a slave to Carter with his magic dick, stern alpha-ness, and his soul-crushing sweetness—the latter something that feels like a secret only I'm in on.

"I should move out."

He shakes his head, cupping my jaw and tilting my face up from the floor. "You should stay. You'll never find anything affordable close to the hospital and you left all of your furniture at Tony's. You can stay in your bedroom if that makes you feel more comfortable."

"I'm scared, Carter," I admit and hate that I feel weak doing so, but never in my life have I felt less in control or more out of sorts.

"What can I do to fix that?"

"You can't tell anyone. I mean it. If word around the hospital got out that we're sleeping together, my career, the respect of my fellow colleagues, all of it would be gone. I've worked too hard for too long for that."

"Alright."

The earnest intensity in his gaze relaxes me. Carter isn't out to hurt or ruin me. He wants to help and take care of me—while having seriously hot sex. And when our flame burns out—an inevitability—we'll go back to being the way things were before we ever did this. That's what these guys do. I've witnessed Oliver do it so many times and it never affected his work. It was fun and nothing more. If I realign my preconceived notions of what sex and love and fun, for that matter, are supposed to be, can I do this?

"One more thing?"

"What's that?" he asks.

"Don't mess with my heart."

His eyes bounce back and forth between mine as his lips dip down. "I'd never mess with something I wa—" He cuts himself off sharply. Clears his throat. "I'd never do that. Promise."

I nod, but all I can think is, I hope we're not making promises we can't keep.

22

Trying to win Grace's heart over feels like I'm climbing Everest in the middle of a blizzard without a coat on or an oxygen mask. I'm un-fucking-prepared, but I've already come this far, so there's no turning back now. Even if I end up dead on the side of the mountain.

She thinks I'm a player out for a hot fling.

And if she were any other woman, that would likely be true.

But she's not any other woman. She's the woman I've been obsessed with—unrequitedly in love with—for a year. All I can think is, this is your shot, so don't fuck it up. But now everything I do is a balancing act. A game of chess and I have to perpetually think three steps ahead or I'll lose.

I can't tell her how I truly feel—she's nowhere near ready for that yet.

Still, once the woman sets her mind to something, she's fiercely determined.

I seriously made her life hell for a week—the only move I had left—until she sought me out. She thought she could avoid me. She thinks she can avoid what's happening between us. There is no switch to turn off wanting someone. You can't force your feelings back into a jar once you've already set them free, allowed them to breathe.

Grace is scared. She wasn't lying about that. She believes I'm going to mess her around the way Tony did. But she's only afraid because deep down, she knows how good we are together.

I don't need any more friends in my life. I have plenty. If she thinks this is some casual friends with benefits nonsense, she's got another thing coming. I have no intentions of being her buddy.

I am not Oliver.

I will not be Oliver to her.

This would be easier if she weren't my roommate and subordinate. If she weren't so recently out of a bad relationship. I hate having to tread carefully. It's boring and feels counterproductive.

Maybe I should be giving her space, but I can't do it. I want her too badly.

"Dr. Fritz?" Janet Johnson is waiting outside my office, and I completely forgot all about her. Her right wrist is casted up, but she's wearing scrubs and a determined smile. "You wanted to see me this morning?"

"Come inside," I say, opening my office door for her and allowing her in.

The room is cleaned up, but just barely. My desk is still a ridiculous mess and I smirk at it before I can stop it as I picture Grace's gorgeous ass turning red beneath my palm.

I take a seat behind my desk and Janet does the same on the other side. "It's a distal radial fracture," she launches immediately. "No surgery required."

"You'll be out of the OR and direct patient care for a minimum of four weeks."

She blanches, tucking her dark hair behind her ear. "Yes, but—"

"I'll rearrange schedules to pick up the slack your absence creates." Though there isn't much slack. Janet is a mediocre doctor at best. Grace told me what Dylan told her about what she did with the patient, and we'll be lucky if the family doesn't sue us all. She's also been messing with the patient assignment board, erasing Grace's name and adding hers instead. "You'll need to write up an incident report on what happened in that room. All of it."

"I don't know what you mean. I slipped."

"After unnecessarily ripping that woman's placenta from her body and causing her to hemorrhage."

"No. That's not what..." Her eyes narrow. "Did Grace or Dylan tell you that?"

I shake my head. "It doesn't matter who told me what. The facts are the facts. Write it up."

She puffs out a breath, but nods. "Yes, sir."

"How do you feel you should fill the extra hours? Teaching or—"

"Actually, I was hoping that now that I have this extra time, I could help you out."

"Pardon?" My eyebrows draw together as I lean back in my seat, appraising her. The extra makeup on her face. The low angle she has her scrub top arranged so it reveals a hint of cleavage. The attempting to be sexy upturn of her lips. I know what women look like when they're trying to be seductive. When they're trying to seduce me.

I know what Janet Johnson looks like when she's playing this game as well, since she's been doing it since she started here two months ago. I've just been ignoring it and her as much as possible. Now it seems she wants to up the ante.

"You don't have a personal assistant. Just one you share with two other attendings. I could be your own *personal* assistant, Dr. Fritz." Her good hand plays with the line of her scrub top. I don't take the bait.

"I'm all set, thanks."

She's undeterred. "But you have so much on your plate. So much stress. I could help you relieve some of that. It would be my pleasure."

I shake my head no.

She's still undeterred. "If you change your mind, I'd be more than happy to accommodate you." She licks her lips. "In any way you need."

"I will not be changing my mind, now or ever. And you can stop with the crappy attempts at sexual innuendo. I'm not interested. You may go now."

"But. No," she gasps incredulously, flying out of her chair, her good hand landing on my desk with a hard smack. "I see the way you look at me. I know you want me too. This is how it's supposed to go." She pounds her fist.

Jesus. I don't have time for this right now. And how in the hell could she have spun this so out of control in her head? I've heard the rumors about her. I know the way she treats her fellow residents, especially Grace. But this? This is next-level shit.

I stand too, hoping this finally gets through to her. "Dr. Johnson, I can assure you any thoughts or desire I have for you are strictly related to your work as a doctor in this hospital. And nothing more."

"It's because of her, isn't it? *Grace*," she sneers her name, venom dripping from her lips. "I know about your relationship," she accuses, "your family connections with her. She's trying to poison you against me, and I won't let that happen. You're why I chose this program. You." She points again. "My father could have gotten me in anywhere, but it's you who I wanted, Dr. Carter Fritz. Don't you see how perfect it is? Johnson and Fritz."

Ah, so that's where this is going. Money. Power. My family name.

Her family has some of that. Her father is a multimillion-aire who obviously overindulges his daughter. But their family isn't mine.

"This conversation is over, Dr. Johnson. You may take the rest of the week off to heal after you give me the report I requested. And if I ever discover you've been messing around with the patient board again, removing fellow doctors' names from it, you will never touch another patient on my service or anyone else's again. What you did is dangerous and stupid and you're lucky that patient didn't suffer a worse outcome."

I brush past her, opening the door to my office and holding it wide for her to leave. She huffs out, stomping loudly like a two-year-old down the hall. I close my eyes, rubbing at my temples to try and stave off the headache that woman just gave me.

But something is niggling with me about that whole inter-action. About her. Something doesn't quite feel—

"Good morning, Dr. Fritz," Dylan greets, interrupting my thoughts with a polite smile that fails to hide the smirk beneath. "Nice to see you're still alive and well."

"Where's your resident?" I ask instead of addressing any of that. I can only imagine what Grace said to him last night before our fight and subsequent make-up session in my office.

"Speaking with Charlotte, her resident adviser."

No wonder she snuck out so early this morning. After we left the hospital last night, I grabbed us Chinese takeout and we ate in front of the television before I took her to bed. My bed. And when I finally fell asleep in my tangled sheets, she was right beside me, in my arms.

Waking up alone was not how I wanted this morning to go.

"I see." As much as I want Grace to stay my resident, it's likely for the best if she transfers.

I start to march off in the direction of her adviser's office when Dylan's words pull me up short. "If I were into women and wanted to catch the attention of one woman in particular, a woman who has recently been hurt and now has some trust issues, I'd forgo the torture and plan something special instead. You know. Just for me and her."

I spin back around, eyeing him. I take a step in his direction, looking him up and down. Dylan is tall. Lanky, but tall. Just about my height. He gives me a cautious smile, knowing he crossed a line but not backing down from it either. I haven't given Dylan much thought other than he's a new intern until this moment.

He reads people well, it seems, and clearly has some balls. My respect for him is growing.

I stare into his golden eyes, a stark contrast with his black skin. I cock an unamused eyebrow. "And you think that's what I'm trying to do? Catch the attention of one woman in particular?"

"She's stressed out right now. Confused and scared. She needs to remember what fun feels like and learn without being told that you won't hurt her the way he did. I'd go slow and be patient."

Not exactly my strong suit, but in Grace's case, I know he's right. About all of it. It's only been a few weeks since she and Tony ended and while she seems okay with it now, I have to remind myself of the way she showed up at my apartment that first night. She might very well be licking her wounds in private without my curious eyes catching on.

I've been pushing her hard, my impatience to finally be with her getting the best of me.

"Psychiatry is in the other building on the eighth floor."

"She won't be happy with another resident," he goes on, ignoring my barb. "The only other options with openings are Hopkins, who only performs simple D&Cs and Laverty, who can't tell a vagina from an asshole, and she has a set of her own."

I choke on my own saliva. "There's no one else?"

"Nope. Everyone else worth having is full or doesn't take on new teaching, and despite your good looks and incredible talent after the week of hell you put Grace through, I doubt any other resident will be willing to switch. Plus, now you're down a resident."

Well, fuck me.

"Do you know the steps for a laparoscopic salpingectomy?"

He squares his shoulders. "Not fully, but I can learn them in an hour."

"You do that because we scrub in in two. And Dylan, if you ever try to pull the stunt you just did with me again, you won't see the inside of an OR for the rest of your residency."

"Understood, sir."

I give him a curt nod and with that, I turn on my heel and march down the hall. Grace's adviser is little more than a pencil pusher at this point, having quit seeing patients two years ago. But pictures of all the babies Charlie Higgins delivered over the years line her office walls.

She's a legend.

And she'll eat me for breakfast without skipping a beat if I don't handle this the correct way.

I reach her door and with a knock, open it up, unwilling to wait to be invited in. Grace's eyes go comically wide when she spots me, before straightening her spine to face Charlie again, effectively dismissing me. Charlie stares at me as if she was expecting me, her gray hair tied neatly back, and a no-bullshit expression firmly affixed on her round face.

"Ah, Dr. Fritz. The man of the hour. Please, come in and sit down." She waves for me to enter before returning her hand to her desk.

"That won't be necessary. Grace, if you're finished here, we have surgery to prep for."

Grace blinks at me. "But. Um. I was actually in the process

of switching attendings. You know, since we don't seem to have the best working relationship."

I nearly roll my eyes.

Moving my attention to Charlie, I say, "Grace will continue as my resident since I am her best option for learning. Especially now that Janet Johnson will be on medical restriction for a minimum of four weeks. No other attending will be able to provide her with the education I can. I'm sure she agrees with me on that."

"And what about your harsh treatment of her this past week?" Charlie cuts me off and touché.

"I've already discussed that with Dr. Hammond and made the proper apologies." I hold in my grin as I meet Grace's eyes and watch as color stains her cheeks. "She and I are in mutual agreement that patient care and her education are our priorities and there will be no further problems." I smile at Grace. "Is there anything else you'd like to add to that?"

She sits up straighter, not pleased with me at all. "It seems you've said everything there is to say."

"Perfect." I clap my hands together, still hovering in the doorway. "Then if we're all in agreement, we can get moving."

"Grace?" Charlie questions without skipping a beat. "Is this an acceptable arrangement for you? I want to ensure you're comfortable working so closely with Dr. Fritz. You clearly came to my office this morning with specific concerns. I agree that as of right now, Dr. Fritz is your best option for learning, but if you feel Dr. Fritz has not provided a positive learning environment, we will make the necessary arrangements to transfer you to someone else."

"No. It's fine. I want to continue to learn from Dr. Fritz."

"If you change your mind at any point, please come back and talk to me. My door is always open."

Grace rises to her feet, her hands intertwined in front of her, the ring I gave her still on. "Thank you. I understand."

Charlie glares at me. "Dr. Fritz. A word before you leave?"

Grace exits the room and I enter, not bothering to sit down after I shut the door. Before she can start, I launch with, "Dr. Hammond and I have entered into a romantic relationship. I will be discussing this with Dr. Westerfield, Dr. Smart, and Dr. Rohrs, as I am no longer able to evaluate her work without a conflict of interest. Dr. Hammond has asked that we keep our relationship a secret and separate from the walls of the hospital as she does not want it to reflect negatively on her work. I have agreed to this as I am unwilling to risk her current or future career. But in order for my position as her supervisor to remain ethical, I will be transferring that aspect of her residency to my supervisor, Dr. Westerfield."

Charlie analyzes me for a very long, hard few minutes of silence. Not much makes my skin itch, but this woman has a way. Finally, she bobs her head, purses her lips off to the side and then glares. "Alright. This conversation will remain between us as long as you keep up your end of the bargain. If I catch on that you're playing favorites, I will speak with your supervisor and alert the residency committee."

"Absolutely. My fourth years are not complaining at all with the demanding workload I'm giving them. Most are running things on their own, with very little oversight on my part. My other primary third-year resident broke her wrist yesterday and as of this morning, all of my first and second-year residents will now report to Dr. Hammond."

Charlie gives me a satisfied stare and I turn around to leave, knowing Grace is waiting for me just outside the door. Knowing she's a little pissed at me. A point she proves when we get into the hall and she grabs hold of my scrub top, dragging me along the hall until we reach an empty patient room.

She shuts the door and paces across to the far window before turning back and storming toward me, getting right up in my face. I wrap my arms around her waist, hauling her against my chest as I lean against the closed door. This, this right here. Having her in my arms willingly, even when she's pissed, is the best feeling in the world.

I'd fight dragons barehanded for this shot with her.

"What are you doing?" she challenges, her palms pressing into my chest though she's not trying to escape me. "You had no right to barge in on my private meeting with my adviser. What did she say to you after I left?"

"That I better not show favorites and I better keep up my end of the bargain."

Not even close to a lie.

"Carter, you're playing with fire. We don't even know how long this thing between us will—"

I cut her off with a kiss because I know what she's about to say and I don't want to hear it. She might not be ready for us to go prime time, but I am. And it's like I told Charlie, I won't risk her career. Or mine, for that matter, but I'm more worried about her. She's a resident. It's her reputation on the line if this thing isn't done on the up and up from the start.

And this *is* the start.

I can be patient and I can prove to her I'm a man worthy of her, but that doesn't come without taking risks and that's precisely what I did this morning with Charlie. Even if Grace doesn't know I told Charlie yet.

"I want to take you to a concert next week," I hum against her lips, taking a play from Dylan because I think the kid was on to something.

She shakes her head, confused at my total change of topic. "A concert?"

"Wild Minds is playing at Gillette. I got us tickets. Floor seats." I didn't, but I will have by the end of the day so it's as good as done. Kaplan quasi knows Jasper Diamond because Wild Minds played a charity event that Kaplan headed through the Abbot Foundation for children on the autism spectrum, so I wonder if I can even arrange a meet and greet.

I know Grace loves him.

"You got us tickets to Wild Minds? When? It's been sold out for months."

I shrug. I don't care if it's sold out—I'll get them.

"It's too much, Carter. You've already gotten me so much."

"No. It's not too much." I run my fingers through her hair, stare into her pretty eyes. "I want to take you."

"How did you know I like Wild Minds?"

A grin splices my lips as I nibble on her bottom one. "Other than you mentioning them the night we went out to the club-restaurant thing? You're always rocking out to music during your in-between time. I hear it when you sing along, Grace. I listen."

"You mean you watch me."

My nose brushes against hers, my tongue swiping out, licking her lips. "I watch you. I've watched you for a year."

"Because you're my attending?"

"Not because I'm your attending."

I study her reaction, hoping she'll ask the next inevitable question. Knowing it's too soon to tell her I'm hopelessly in love with her. Only she doesn't get the chance to say anything. My pager goes off, alerting us that our patient is in pre-op and waiting for us.

It's just as well.

She's not ready to face the truth yet. Even if I am. But it's only a matter of time until I convince her.

23

My body sags with exhaustion as I lean against the glass of the nursery, staring at all the adorable new life. I delivered two of those babies today. Well, I guess it was technically last night into today but today never ended with me going home because I still had a full shift to do. I'm picking up the slack for Janet since she's not only recovering from a broken wrist but has decided that I should be her resident—pun intended—Sherpa of work since she can't do anything.

That means I had to take her twenty-four-hour shift in addition to my regular shift and take on all of her patients since she was Carter's only other third-year resident beside me. That and Dr. Westerfield has randomly been asking me to follow along on some of her cases.

This week has been nothing short of sheer hell and a total nightmarish heaven.

I should have known it would be like this. We're talking about Carter Fritz. Billionaire bachelor and playboy. Brilliant doctor. The sexy seductor who has spent the last week making me feel like we're so much more than a fling.

Like we're... dating.

Not just fooling around and enjoying a physical connection and nothing more.

It's freaking me the fuck out, and that's on top of everything else going on.

I know I sound like a broken record, but this is Carter Fritz. And yet, he's not. He's like a totally different man with me. My head is an absolute disaster with it. My heart on a damn roller coaster, up and down and side to side and all over the place. I don't know what I want. I don't know what or how to think.

I've had no breather between Tony and this.

A recipe for disaster if ever there was one.

It has me questioning what's real and what's not. And that's just myself I'm talking about there. I can't even contemplate Carter's angle in all of this. That's just too terrifying to even begin and who has the time for it anyway. Certainly not me.

We're going on hour thirty of being awake—it's a wonder I'm still upright and conscious.

In the hospital, he's my teacher. My attending. I absorb his skill and talent like the needy doctor sponge I am. We've had no further incidents—no more scut or punishments. I have freedom with my cases. I've been teaching the younger residents in our outpatient office, in the delivery room, and even in the OR.

I come home exhausted. Together, most nights, he's there with me, staying later when I have to or having dinner ready and waiting for me on the nights he doesn't. We eat and watch TV. Read books or journals and talk.

Not just talk. Open up to each other. He tells me things I'd bet his inheritance he's never told anyone, not even his brothers. Like how even though he always knew he wanted to be an OB-GYN, he also wanted to play professional baseball and even had an offer from an AAA team in Oakland.

When I asked why he didn't pursue it, his response was, "That's not the Fritz way."

How awful and yet how beautiful.

I don't think he regrets his decision to go into medicine, but it also makes me want to push him to join a league or something.

At night I'm in his bed. And it's not always sex. Some nights it's just sleeping together. I mean, hell, we're OB-GYNs. We work long, grueling hours and most days don't get off when we're scheduled to and that's without me picking up the slack.

But being with Carter in this way, it's... it's...

"Here," he says, coming up from behind me like the ghost of men I can't stop thinking about. Damn, I need sleep. I'm not even making sense anymore. "Eat this."

I open my eyes, not even realizing I had shut them, and straighten up. I stare down at the protein bar he's holding at me. "What is that?"

"Food. When was the last time you ate?"

That's a seriously good question. I have to think for a minute. And another minute. And when I can't remember, I grab the proffered protein bar and open it. "I hate this kind."

"I know," he replies with a smirk, running his hand over my cheek and managing to catch a few strands that fell from my bun, tucking them behind my ear. "That's all that was left in the vending machine though. I'll buy a box of the chocolate and egg-white ones you like and store them in my office."

I stare at him, my eyebrows likely creased and giving me premature wrinkles as I take a bite. It's like eating shoe leather. No chocolate on this one, which is a total crime when it comes to protein bars, if you ask me.

"Are you this nice to your other residents, or is it just because I put out for you?"

He raises an unamused eyebrow. "Go home. You need sleep. Especially if we're going to the concert tomorrow night."

Right. The concert. That's another thing.

"I can't go home. I have patients. A surgery later with Dr. Westerfield."

"Let someone else take them. You need sleep. Let me see your phone."

"My phone? For what?" I know what he wants and he's not getting it. I've already turned off the notifications from my ring because it was annoying, so I have no idea what my body is up to. I just know it's likely not so great given what the last thirty hours has brought.

"Pull up the app for your ring. I want to see your numbers for oxygen, heart rate, and sleep."

"And what if I don't? Are you going to make me?"

He rolls his eyes at my childish antics, but I can't bend. If I bend and he sees I'm not taking the best care of myself that I should be, he'll go all alpha attending on me, and I can't let that happen. I'm a doctor. A resident. I constantly have to be on my A-game and the moment I show weakness, my career suffers for it.

Sound dramatic?

Yeah, it's also true.

"Sign out at three during nursing change of shift and go home. That's a fucking order."

I stick my tongue out at him and blow a raspberry.

I'd flip him off too, but there are babies present.

"I see you two haven't improved your working relationship," Oliver drawls, walking through the swinging doors and heading our way. Ah, my best friend. I forgot he works in the hospital as a family medicine attending—bastard just finished his residency and is now living the sweet life—on Fridays.

I might have also been avoiding him.

"My attending is a dick," I tell Oliver, only to have Carter growl beside me.

"So you like to say. Wanna go grab some lunch and tell me about it?"

Lunch? It's lunchtime?

I stare balefully down at my horrid protein bar.

"I have a patient at seven centimeters."

The thought makes me want to cry. Seven centimeters. It might as well be two for how long this could take.

"They can page you, can't they?"

"They can." But that means I have to leave the comfort of this window. Have to walk somewhere to eat. So much work.

"What about you, Dr. Evil?" Oliver asks Carter. "I've secured Rina from the ICU. Want to join your youngest siblings for a meal?"

"Grace, go catch a nap," Carter snaps, ignoring Oliver. "I'll have the nurses page you when your patient hits nine. And yes, Oliver, I'd love to go to lunch with you and Rina."

"I hate you," I seethe.

"Yeah, I'm kinda thinking Carter is right on this whole nap thing though. You look exhausted, babe. Go rest. I'll bring you back a warm cookie from the cafeteria. The ones you like."

Love glimmers through my body as I stare at my best friend. "You'd do that?"

"I'll even make sure they're the ones with Reese's Pieces on the top."

I could cry. Actually, I think I am. Shit.

"Wow, okay, yeah. Go sleep. You're a fucking mess."

I sniffle, wiping at my stupid nose and eyes. "They're happy tears."

Carter takes my forearm, giving me a good tug and lurching me away from the comfort of the glass. "Save me a seat. I'll meet you down there. I have to make sure my resident does what she's told."

"I love you, Oliver," I call out to him, only to hear him

chuckle as I'm unceremoniously herded like cattle down the hall. "Hey, ease up there, Hulk."

Carter doesn't speak, he just finds the nearest on-call room, ensures it's empty and then transports me inside like I'm an unruly child. "On the bed, Grace."

"Kinky, but you know there's no lock on that door."

He growls at me, forcing me down onto one of the cots. Carter kneels before me, removing my clogs one at a time and setting them against the wall. He pulls back the itchy white blanket and presses my shoulders back until I'm supine, his body now sitting beside me.

"I would have brought you cookies." His hand runs across my face, his pinched up in annoyance. "I saw you and I went and grabbed the first thing I could find that wasn't total garbage, but I should have gone to the cafeteria and gotten you something better. A sandwich or something."

"It's not your job to make sure I'm eating," I tell him. In truth, I should have done a better job of it today. I knew this was going to be the never-ending shift from hell and I didn't plan accordingly.

"It is though. I like taking care of you. I hate that Oliver does what I should be."

My eyes glitter with more tears that I will never allow to fall. I have no words for that. All I know is a girl could fall in love with it. If she were stupid enough to allow herself to think along those lines.

I run my hand up through his hair, catching the back of his head. I pull him down to me and kiss him. Because I have to kiss him. "Carter. I—"

His nose brushes mine so tenderly my heart skips a beat. "Just get some rest, okay? You need sleep, sweetheart. You're pushing yourself too hard." With that, he kisses my forehead. The tip of my nose. My lips. And then he's gone, shutting the door behind him with a soft click that feels more like a thud.

Except it's not the door that just made that noise.

It's my heart.

Both the click and the thud.

Pushing all the madness and questions and emotions away, I close my eyes, settling in on the bed, my body drifting almost instantly. But just as the first glimpses of a dream hit the backs of my eyelids, my pager goes off. Not even ten seconds later, my phone rings.

With a weakened groan, I sit up slowly, my head spinning as a round of dizziness takes hold. "Yeah?" I answer blindly, not able to open my eyes just yet.

"Sorry, Dr. Hammond. Dr. Carter told us you were resting but your patient, Natalie Southers, is telling us she's getting the urge to push. When I checked her, she's at a ten and the baby's engaged at a plus one station."

Hesitantly, I open my eyes into the dimly lit room. No more spins. "I'll be right there."

I hang up and do a series of deep breathing exercises. Then I drag myself up and off the bed and back out into the hospital. Passing by the vending machine, I spot an energy shot and give it some thought. I don't typically drink a lot of caffeine. Just one cup of regular coffee in the morning and maybe half a soda in the afternoon.

Too much caffeine has never agreed with me, but today I think I need the boost to make it through. I can sleep tonight. I'll go home at seven and go straight to bed. I'll sleep through the night and tomorrow morning I don't have to get up early because I'm not working and then Carter and I have the show tomorrow night.

So, one little energy drink won't do me any harm.

I haven't had a seizure in years.

Mind made up, I grab the shot from the machine and down it all in one long gulp. Then I toss it in the trash and make my way to my patient's room, ready to deliver a baby.

24

With Grace's hand in mine, I help her out of the limousine beside the VIP entrance. I don't even care if I'm playing the Fritz card. I want this to be a night Grace never forgets. A night of just her and just me and just us, not in my apartment hanging out, but a date. A real fucking date even if she's pretending it's not.

"What did you do, Carter Fritz?" she asks with a gleam to her eye and an incredulous shake to her head as she looks around us. The concert doesn't start for another hour or so, but you'd never know it by the mass of cars and people already here tailgating.

I give her a wink, gripping her hand a little tighter. "Come on and I'll show you." I look to our driver, "We should be ready around midnight."

"Very good, sir."

And with that, I pull Grace along to the door, manned with security. Our family has a luxury box on the fifty-yard line at this stadium, and I could have used that for tonight—Kaplan and Luca will be up there with their dates and a few of their friends. But that's not how I want my girl to watch one of her favorite bands perform. For a concert like this, you have to be in it, down on the floor, feeling the pulse of the audience and the thrum of the music.

"Carter," she hisses and then squeals when she sees just what I'm up to. "Oh my God. You didn't. Tell me you freaking didn't!"

I turn back to her, wrapping my arms around her back, the late summer sun steadily heading west, casting a golden glow on everything it touches. "Sweetheart, sometimes it's like you don't even know me. Of course, I did. It didn't even take much of a favor. Oh, and when you see Kaplan and Luca, just be nice and smile."

I laugh at her stricken expression. "Kaplan and Luca are here? But... do they... they know you're here with me?"

"Yes. I told them," I explain, pulling out the VIP badges from the back pocket of my jeans, handing one to her.

"And they know we're..."

I shrug up a shoulder. "I didn't tell them the details. Just that you're a big fan and would like to meet the band. They didn't ask because I'm positive they already know or at least assume."

"What about Oliver? Rina?"

"Not worried about Landon?" I quip as we reach the security guard and display our badges. He looks them over and opens the door for us, waving us through. Inside, we're greeted by another guard and then ushered along the bowels of Gillette stadium toward what I'm assuming is a green room of sorts for the band.

"Carter?" She tugs on my hand, pulling me to a stop. "Does Oliver know we're..."

"A couple?" I supply for her when she fails to come up with a definition for us.

"A couple?" Her eyes widen and she takes a step back, her

fingers clutching to mine. Maybe I shouldn't have thrown that word out there so fast?

"I was going to say sleeping together. I didn't think... You know, we were..."

"What would you call us then?"

"I don't know." Her eyes blink in rapid succession, her free hand coming up to her mouth as she grapples with the implications of my question. "I was trying not to think about definitions of things. I was afraid of being... I didn't want to get..."

"Okay. Let me start then since you're having trouble." I grasp her shoulder and slide us to the right, so we don't take up the walkway that's loaded with roadies trying to do their jobs. My eyes lock with hers. "I consider us a couple. To me, that means I'm not sleeping with anyone else. I'm not dating anyone else. I'm not looking at anyone else. It also means I have you in my bed or against the wall or in my office or any other place I can manage as often as I can. It doesn't have to be serious, and it doesn't have to be something that requires a whole lot of mental energy if you'd rather not go there yet. But for now, this is where I'm at and I'd like you to be there with me."

"I've been lying to Oliver. And avoiding him."

"I know."

"I hate it. It breaks me in two."

"I know."

"What if I'm not ready for a full relationship yet?"

Rejection stings through my blood like a toxin, but it's no less than what I was expecting from her. It's why I never bothered or tried to have this conversation with her until now. Grace isn't ready. Or maybe it's just with me but I refuse to think on those terms. If it was just me, she wouldn't be here at all. So we'll go with not ready *yet*, since that's the word she used and I'll keep playing the system until she is.

"Then you're not ready yet, but I'm still not sleeping or dating or looking at anyone else."

She licks her lips nervously. "I'm not either."

"Then we're good. You good?" I check.

"I think so."

"Then quit all your worrying and relax. Tonight is about fun." I cup her face in my hand, drawing her back to me. "I know you feel that because Janet is suddenly gone that you have to pick up everything from her since she was a fellow third year, but there are other residents, Grace. It doesn't have to be you that takes everything on."

I tried to have this conversation with her earlier in the week and she wouldn't hear of it. That is until her twenty-four-hour shift plus her regular shift after. I think that did her in. She fell asleep last night at eight—in her bed but we won't go there now —and woke up at nine. She's pushing herself like she has something to prove to everyone, including herself when she has nothing to prove to anyone.

She's a rock star.

A future leader of our field.

Her work already far outshines doctors with twice her experience. She just hasn't learned balance yet. No resident does. Their world is one big challenge where it's win big or go home. I get it. I lived it. You want to learn as much as you can, garner as much experience as you can, obtain the best fellowship or attending position as you can.

But all of that comes at a cost and in Grace's case, this week spread her thin.

"I don't want to talk about work. I want to talk about tonight."

"Fine, we'll talk about it tomorrow morning over breakfast."

She shakes her head. "No. I have to go in. No one picked up Janet's shift, including any of her residents."

Fuck. They didn't because they knew Grace would. That means she has to be back there at seven am tomorrow. Another night of limited sleep.

"Do you want to go home? Get more rest?"

She glares at me, ready to rip my eyes out for even suggesting something so ludicrous. "Not on your life. Now take me to meet the band."

So that's what I do. I hold her hand and we're guided by yet another mammoth security guard to a room that houses four rock stars. Jasper Diamond. Gus Diamond. Keith Dawson. Henry Gauthier.

Kaplan and Luca are already here, shooting the shit.

But Grace hasn't moved past the threshold. She stares at these guys, one by one, her grip on my hand becoming ninja-like.

Jasper notices us first, standing and giving us a look. He runs his hand through his reddish-brown hair, his tattooed arms on full display under a white T-shirt. "Hey," he says with a hint of a smile. "You must be Grace. Welcome."

And that's when she loses it. "Oh my god. I'm not hallucinating."

Gus laughs, standing too. "Come here, little darlin'. Your guys here were telling us all about you. My wife Naomi and I are expecting twins and I think I need to know what to expect when we're expecting directly from the source and not a book, if you know what I mean."

"Naomi Kent is pregnant?" Grace squeals, entering the room and marching over to him. "I haven't heard this."

Keith chuckles, taking a swig directly from his bottle of Jack Daniels before pointing the end of the bottle at her. "Nor will you, since Gus here wasn't supposed to make that public for another six weeks or so. But since you're all doctors, we'll invoke some HIPPA shit."

"My lips are sealed, but wow, congratulations," Grace gushes, practically bouncing on the balls of her feet with her excitement. "That's amazing. I'm sorry if I look like a psycho right now, but I don't think I can blink for fear that this will all be a dream."

The guys all laugh good-naturedly—I'm positive this isn't the first time they've met a big fan—and then Henry tosses his arm over her shoulder. "We're happy to have you. Any friend of Kaplan's is a friend of ours. He hosted a charity for one of our favorite causes and raised a lot of money that went to help kids on the autism spectrum. Anyone who cares about that is good people in our book."

"Without a doubt," Jasper agrees, picking up a bottle of Grey Goose and handing it to me. "Join us for a drink before the show?"

I take the bottle from him but notice it's completely full and unopened. Jasper isn't drinking and I'm assuming that's because he takes his duties as front man seriously.

"Ignore the boring guy over there," Keith says, pointing to Jasper as if reading my thoughts. "He won't party with us until after the show."

"Someone has to keep you assholes in line," Jasper shoots back.

"Well, I'm all for a little pre-game," Luca announces, swiping a bottle of Patron from off the counter and taking a swig before handing it to Kaplan, who does the same. "Grace?"

"Um. Well. A little, I guess."

She takes the bottle from Kaplan and drinks some of it down, grimacing immediately after and wiping her mouth with the back of her hand.

"Alright." Henry laughs. "Now we're getting serious."

BY THE TIME Grace and I stagger out of the green room and down in the direction of the floor, I think we're both rocking a good buzz. The band was more than hospitable. We took shots

—well, swigs from bottles—and picked at some food on the platters they had set up and each of the guys took selfies with Grace who was so over the moon she was practically floating.

We missed the opening act completely, but none of us care. Kaplan and Luca divert from our path, heading up to the booth to meet up with their friends who they had not invited for the meet and greet with the band. Grace and I meander down to the floor, only five rows back from the main stage.

By the time we reach our seats, there is a heavy bass drum thumping through the air and Grace screams out, jumping up and down and clapping her hands, the thrill of the night coursing through her blood.

"Happy?" I whisper into her ear.

"The happiest." She spins around to face me, her face dark since the stage hasn't lit up yet. "I can't believe you did all of this for me. Got us tickets and arranged for me to meet them."

"Like I said, it wasn't that difficult."

"Sometimes I forget you're all Fritzes. I forget what comes with that. I grew up with Oliver and our parents were close friends, but... thank you, Carter."

Before I can respond, the crowd goes wild, roaring out their cheers and excitement as the rest of the band runs onto the stage that illuminates with multicolored lights flashing, swirling all around. They immediately launch into a song, Wildfire, I think it is, but Grace hasn't looked away and neither have I.

Our eyes hold, my arms snaking around her waist, hers around my neck. I start to move us, swaying to the music, my forehead now against hers. I could spend forever like this, trapped in this moment with her, seeing the stars twinkle in her eyes and the swirl of pure delight dance across her face.

She is a vision that stops my breath. That holds my heart.

Never in a million years will I tire of her.

She's it. My one.

She's been promised forever, love and devotion before only to have it fall way short. I can't tell her with words, not yet, so instead I lean in those few tiny inches and place my lips to hers. I kiss her, hold her, dance with her, smile with her. We have the time of our lives listening to her favorite band, sipping on beers, and laughing our asses off. But more than that, I haven't stopped touching her. Not once all night. I hold her, her back to my chest as we watch the show. We make out like two teenagers during some of the slower ballads.

And by the time the concert is over, and we make it back to the limo, we're both riding a high like none other. The door shuts behind her and she sinks into my side, letting out a contented, tired sigh.

I raise the partition, settling in for a long drive home through post-concert traffic.

"Close your eyes," I say to her, shifting her head so it's on my lap, running my fingers through her silky blonde hair. "Get some sleep."

"What if I don't want to?" she rasps, angling her face until her mouth hovers over my thickening cock hidden behind my jeans. "What if I want to play for a bit first?"

"Grace," I growl, grasping the strands of her hair. "You need sleep."

"I need to suck you off first."

Jesus.

She clasps the zipper of my jeans in her teeth and drags it down, breathing hot air on me as she goes. Her fingers undo the button and before I know what's happening, my dick slides between her sweet full lips, all the way down to the back of her throat.

A groan rips past my lungs, shredding the air as my hand dives into her hair, holding the back of her head. She hums in response, gripping my thigh as if to say, hit me with your best shot. Something I fully intend to do.

She starts bobbing on me, slurping me up and licking the head with her tongue only to dive back down and deep throat me in her next breath. I just about lose my mind, the need to thrust up, to take control, to fuck her perfect mouth nearly suffocating me. My hand grips tighter, my groans louder.

"That's it," I tell her as she reaches in and cups my balls, squeezing them as she flattens her tongue and glides up along the underside of my dick. "Fuck, that's perfect."

The desire to blow down her throat, to watch her swallow me down is almost too much, but I want to see her on top of me too. I want her to straddle me here in the back of this limo and ride me until we're both spent.

I tell her exactly that, forcing her mouth off me just as I get to the point of hovering between control and oblivion. In the next motion, I have her pants off, her panties pulled to the side, and her sweet cunt sliding down on me.

Both of us hiss out strangled sounds, the sensation so over the top there is no way to make sense of it. Having her on me, me being inside her, us touching and kissing and holding... This. I could live in this world with her forever. She is euphoria. Paradise. Happiness. She is a happiness I never knew was possible.

She is euphoria.

My mouth covers hers, unable to pull away as she rides me in the back of this limo. Up and down and forward and back. We're laughing, teasing, toying. Silly and sloppy and so good. She sinks down deeper, more of my cock filling her up. Her hands rake through my hair, clutching my shoulders.

I drive up into her, over and over, taking control when her body is no longer able to keep up. I fuck her while she fucks me and holy shit. Just holy shit, this woman. Our eyes hold on, staring deep as we experience this together. The pleasure mounting to the point of combustion.

"Come, Grace. Come all over me. I want to feel you, sweetheart. I want your wetness to coat my cock. I want to smell your pussy all over me."

She loses it then. My dirty words and my hips that refuse to slow down, taking her over the edge. Taking us both over. My forehead hits hers as we ride out this high, our breaths mingling, our bodies one.

My love for her infinite.

And once we're done, once we're both dressed and sleepy, cuddled up in the back of the limo, I smile. A true smile. One I haven't felt the need to have escape my lips in I don't even know how long. Years? I can't remember. Probably because I've never felt like this before. Not with anyone.

No way I can let her go. Not now. Not ever. Come what may.

25

"**Y**ou don't have to walk me in," I tell Carter as he holds my hand, walking us from the garage into the main building of MGH. Truth is, I'm wiped. Past the point of exhaustion and I'd rather not have an audience for it. I had the time of my life last night but today, today I need a little space to get through.

And coffee. I need that too.

"I'm not walking you in. I'm coming in to catch up on paperwork."

"Liar."

He is. Carter has no paperwork. He doesn't want me here covering Janet's shift. He wants me home, in his bed, tucked under his covers. Truthfully, I want to be there too, but this is life, right? Life of a resident and I have no choice but to be here. Someone has to cover her shifts and that someone is me whether I like it or not.

"It's not a big deal. I'll do my thing and you do yours and if you need me along the way, I'm already here."

"I don't need a babysitter."

"Never said you did, sweetheart. Like I said, I'll do my own thing."

"Fine."

Whatever. I'm too tired to care. We didn't get home until close to two, only to have to wake up at five thirty. I'm on my second cup of coffee but only because the first did absolutely nothing to rouse me to the point of consciousness.

"How about we take a week off in August or September?" Carter proposes. "We can go to The Vineyard house or to Italy or Hawaii. What do you say?"

Only a fucking Fritz would propose something like that and actually mean it.

I've been to their Vineyard house plenty and Oliver's house that he co-owns with Luca in Italy a few times. When you travel Fritz, you travel on private jets or yachts and stay in five-star luxury. I never cared all that much about it. I still don't.

But doing something like that with Carter feels different because it is different. Vacationing with someone is relationship-y. And while the thought of that with Carter makes my heart beat faster, I'm just not sure I'm quite ready for such a big and bold move. He's doing all the right things. It's me who's having difficulty adapting.

I just need a little more time. That's all this is.

These past weeks have been amazing, and last night almost felt like a turning point—in a good way. We're not in a full relationship, but we are together. And I think I like it. I think I like it a lot.

"How about you ask me that question again in a few weeks?"

"How about I just plan something and kidnap you?"

"You think that would work for you with me? Subterfuge?"

"Seems to have so far, yeah."

I can't argue that. I have to keep reminding myself that I started this party train with him. And it's not like I want to hop off it. I just want it to chug down the tracks instead of racing. Carter seems to want the opposite. He's full steam ahead.

Something that's surprising me more and more about him.

Or maybe I'm reading more into this than is actually there.

What did he say to me last night? *It doesn't have to be serious, and it doesn't have to be something that requires a whole lot of mental energy if you'd rather not go there yet. But for now, this is where I'm at and I'd like you to be there with me.*

He's asking me for fun. He's asking me to relax and just enjoy whatever it is we have going on. I'm the one busy over-thinking everything.

With that thought in my head, I reach up and kiss his cheek. He twists to me with a smile that lights up his eyes and my insides quicken. "Thank you again for last night," I tell him. "And for coming in with me this morning on your day off. I know what you're doing, and I appreciate it. Even if I'm too much of a stubborn, tired grump to admit it."

Seriously, who does that? Comes in on their day off? He's doing it for me.

"It's my pleasure, sweetheart. All of it is. I just like being with you, even if that means I have to come into the hospital to do it."

Damn him. So perfect. I even like it how he calls me sweetheart.

But once we reach the floor, we're all business. Carter walks off to his office, telling me to page him if I need him just as Dylan comes scurrying over to me, holding up a to-go cup of something for me like an offering.

"Oh my god. You're going to need this." Dylan thrusts the cup into my hand. "I want to hear all about the show last night, but there is zero time. Dr. Johnson's residents are not picking up the slack at all. Her intern confided in me that she's learned nothing under Janet because she wouldn't let anyone do anything and threatened their careers if they ever said anything."

"What?" pops out of my mouth. "Are you joking?"

"Nope. We are so fucked, girl. They said Janet had no clue what she was doing and anything that didn't go wrong, was pure luck."

"Shit." I had been wondering all week why her residents held back in the OR and watched my every move like hawks, but I just assumed it was a lack of familiarity and comfort with me. Not that they weren't learning. Hell, some of them are second-year residents. "I'm going to have to talk to Carter about this."

"Yes. Just not now. We have two laboring women and with the way one of their contractions are stalling, I'm thinking she'll end up having a section."

Awesome.

I take a sip from the cup in my hand. Espresso. Strong espresso. I take another sip, this one bigger than the previous one, and then throw the now mostly empty cup in the trash.

"That should perk me up. Thanks. Let's go."

With Dylan on my heels, we find our way to the nurses' station and sure enough, there are two other residents, one a first-year and one a second-year, just standing around like fish out of water.

"You. Astrid." I point at the second year. "Who is your patient?"

She shrugs. "I don't know. Usually we just followed Dr. Johnson around."

Are you flipping kidding me?

"Okay. As of today, that changes. There are four of us, which means we'll go in teams of two for backup and support. Dylan, you're with Astrid. Georgia, you're with me. We'll take the patient with the stalled labor, but if she does end up needing the OR, all of you will come in and watch and assist. Understood?"

"Yes." And judging by the excited and relieved expressions on their faces, they're ready to work.

"Alright. Let's go. Georgia, bring me up to speed on our patient."

That's how the morning goes. It flies by with me running the show between what ends up being three patients and three residents. There are no fourth years on the floor today—just a fellow who is stuck in the OR. And other than one other attending—and Carter who doesn't count since it's his day off —we're managing the floor.

We deliver Dylan and Astrid's baby like champs. I watch as Astrid takes point, guiding her along and encouraging her. She has the basics. Whatever she did as a first-year wasn't for naught, but she should be farther along with her training. I have no idea what Janet was doing with these two, but by the looks of it, it wasn't much of anything.

That's something we're going to have to remedy and remedy quickly.

My stalled labor—going on hour thirty, poor woman—does end up in the OR having a section. I perform it with the fellow sitting up in the observation area charting. I throw questions at the residents, to which they all eagerly and immediately respond. And once the baby is out, I allow them to close, working together as a team.

And me, I take a step back, exhaustion hitting me like a truck. My eyes are straining to see the field. My back tight and tense. My limbs heavy and sluggish.

It seriously becomes all I can do to finish up this surgery and get out of the OR.

The moment we're scrubbed out, I send everyone to lunch. There are only three other women on the L&D floor right now and they're all less than six centimeters dilated. Which means it's the perfect time for a nap.

"You sure you're good with all of us going?" Dylan asks as I pull out my phone, about to text Carter.

"Yes," I tell him, pulling up the message window. "I'm going to text Dr. Fritz to have him keep an eye on the floor. I'll let the nurses know to page him if anything comes up. I'm going to try to catch a half an hour of sleep."

"Please. You look like you need it. Your bags are growing bags and they ain't Prada."

I smirk, flipping him off as I text Carter who replies immediately.

Carter: Despite how much I'd love to join you, I'm glad you're taking a break. Don't worry about the floor. I've got it.

I smile at that, so grateful he decided to come with me this morning even if it is ruining his day. "Bring me back a sandwich or something," I call out to Dylan.

"Will do."

The three of them head for the elevators, talking rapidly about all we accomplished this morning while I head over to the nurses' station. "Hey," I say to one of the nurses who is at the counter typing on the computer. "I'm going to the on-call room for a quick nap. Dr. Fritz is here in his office and can be paged if you need anything. I think Dr. Schwartz is finally almost done in the OR, so she'll be around as well." Thank God. The other attending was in the OR for most of the morning.

"Okay. I'll make a note of that. Do you want us to wake you at any specific time or just if there is an emergency?"

I open my mouth to respond when my right hand stiffens painfully to the point where I'm unable to move it. I glance down at it, confused until I feel a wave sensation going through my head. I blink, panic swimming inside me as the sensation grows more and more intense. I take a deep breath, followed by another, closing my eyes, and begging to all that is holy that I can stop this.

It's a feeling I dread from the depth of my soul to the marrow of my bones. My breathing quickens despite my best efforts, and I know it's too late. I know what's coming. Having a focal aware seizure wouldn't be the worst thing in the world if I wasn't positive what was to follow.

Mine start in my frontal lobe on my left side—hence why the right side of my body is affected. But that's not where they stay. They go from localized to generalized, typically within seconds in my case.

"I need Ativan. I'm having a seizure."

The nurse is staring at me like nothing I'm saying makes sense; alarm crawling up her features as she stands, asking if I'm okay.

Only I can't respond.

I'm aware of everything.

Fully conscious for at least the next few seconds, only I'm trapped in my body. Unable to move or speak as my seizure progresses. They call these types of seizures auras. As in you know what's about to come next and there isn't a damn thing you can do about it.

Nothing.

It's too late.

Terror and helplessness swim through me, tearing a gasp from my lungs. A rising pulls at my insides, like the downslope of a roller coaster, growing more intense as my head fills with a sound similar to a fan blowing at full blast inside my skull.

Thank God I'm in the hospital.

That's the last thought I have before everything goes black.

26

I've been sitting in my office all morning, dealing with the Janet Johnson nightmare. After our meeting last week, something wasn't sitting right with me. I've looked over her files and after getting a few texts from Grace this morning stating that Janet did absolutely zero teaching and that her not fucking up sooner was an act of God, I know it's going to be a very long few weeks going forward as we get this all teased out and settled.

But that hasn't been my real issue.

My real issue has been resisting the urge to be on the floor because that's where Grace is. I've been hoping she'd seek me out. Come to my office just to see me or kiss me or anything really. She hasn't, I didn't expect her to, I know she's busy—I just hoped. But that hope, my inability to get her off my mind, it's consuming. I don't know how much longer I can play this game.

The one where I pretend to be casual when I'm anything but.

All I know is that I'd be insane not to fight tooth and nail for her. To prove to her just how perfect, how meant to be, we are. It's words I never thought I'd say, but now can't seem to stop. I don't want another woman because she's not her. I think when you realize that, you know it's the real deal, so yeah.

Now the fuck what do I do?

My phone starts ringing at the exact second my beeper goes off, startling me out of my reverie. I grab my phone first, answering it as I read my beeper.

"Fritz," I answer, but whoever is calling me gets drowned out by the loud overhead announcement of *rapid response team to labor and delivery nurses' station. Rapid response team to labor and delivery nurses' station.*

I'm out of my chair and sprinting down the hall before my brain can even catch up with what I'm doing. I have no idea what happened because I don't have time to read my page or talk on the phone. All I know is that it's something and whatever it is, it's not fucking good.

But the moment I turn the corner and take in the scene, it's like someone is strangling me to the point of cutting off the blood and air to my head. I've never seen Grace have a seizure and it isn't until this moment that I understand what true, violent, soul-gripping fear feels like. Dread spirals through me, a vise shredding me from within as I sprint down the hall, shoving people out of the way and not caring one bit.

"Grace." My voice isn't my own. My body either as I drop down to the ground near her head. They managed to slide something under her to protect her head and position her on her left side as she seizes, her body jerking in a rhythmic motion. Her eyes are open, fixed, and unfocused. Blood drips to the mat from the corner of her blue lips.

I can't look away. I can barely move.

My breaths are sharp, short, ragged.

I'm scrambling to make sense of this. Of Grace having a tonic-clonic seizure. Knowing it's my fault. I pushed her too hard. Allowed her to work too many hours. Encouraged her to have a drink last night. Took her to a concert where the strobe lights might have overloaded her system and then brought her home so late knowing she was getting up so early today.

The need to grab her, hold her, help her consumes me, but I know better than to touch her.

"Ativan, 4mg IM on board," someone announces.

"Come on, Grace," I rasp but medications administered intramuscularly can take minutes to take effect, not seconds. She's still going. Her body rigid, her limbs spastic. "How long has she been seizing?"

"A little more than a minute. We need to move her to the ED."

"While she's seizing?" I bark at whoever just said that.

"We don't have stronger benzos or other anticonvulsants up here, doctor," the nurse informs me. "She needs an IV and to have her airway secured. We typically give mag sulfate for seizures and that's not what she needs."

Fuck. They're right. This is labor and delivery. Not the ICU or the ED or even a med/surg floor. Typically our patients are healthy and if they're not, there are only certain medications we can give them for fear of hurting the fetus or having it pass through breast milk.

Just then the rapid response team—also known as the code team—come hurtling down the floor, practically tossing me aside. Drew and Margot are on the team today, their eyes briefly touching mine before they get to work on Grace.

Margot starts a line in no-time flat even with Grace's seizure still going strong. The respiratory therapist manages her airway and just as Margot slowly pushes IV Dilantin Grace stops seizing. Relief rattles my bones as her body sags down onto the mat they have her on. She's still unconscious, not even yet in a postictal state.

"She's epileptic, right?" Margot questions as they work to

get Grace strapped onto a board and then up onto a gurney, an oxygen mask now over her mouth and nose.

"Yes. But she hasn't had a seizure in years. She's only on PRN (as needed) rescue meds."

"Okay. Let's move," Drew commands once she's secured and everyone starts toward the elevator at quick-pace, including me. "Do we know what caused this? Any drug or alcohol use I should be aware of?"

I shake my head. "Some alcohol last night. No drugs." We step onto the elevator, pressing the button for the emergency department. "She's been working a lot of hours. Not sleeping as much as she should have. We went to a concert last night and she's here today on only a few hours of rest—"

My sentence abruptly cuts off as Grace starts seizing again, her face crashing into the railing of the gurney, creating a gash on her temple. "Dammit," Drew hisses. "Roll her now."

The team rolls her back onto her side to protect her body and airway.

My hands dive into my hair, gripping the roots while my heart and stomach plummet into my feet. I can't watch this. I can't watch her like this and stand here and do nothing. My vision blurs as the monitor alarm blares loudly, her heart rate shoots up along with her blood pressure.

Margot curses under her breath. "One minute fifty-two seconds between seizures. We need to start a Dilantin drip. IV push might not have been enough. She already got four of Ativan IM. I'm switching over and pushing five of Diazepam IV now."

"Is that enough?" I snap. "Why doesn't she already have a drip going? Why is she seizing again?"

Everyone ignores me and I'm going out of my fucking mind right now.

It's like all medical knowledge I've ever accrued is gone.

Right out of my head. All I can see is Grace. Is her body jerking. Is her complete loss of basic functions. She has no control and I feel just as powerless.

Out of control and fucking powerless.

It's not who I am. I'm always composed. Never one to panic, even in the diciest of situations or the scariest of surgeries or the most complicated of deliveries. Never. But this is Grace. *My* Grace.

"We need stat labs," Drew interjects just as the doors to the ED open and we race out. "I need to know what I'm working with."

"On it," Margot replies. "You want the standard panel? Anything else with it?"

"A blood gas. Let's also add some glucose to her bag when we get it up. First labs though, Margot. I want someone to sprint them down to the lab themselves and wait while they run them. We're not missing anything."

"You hear that, Bonnie?" Margot questions the nurse on her side. "That's you. You're on point for labs."

"Got it," Bonnie, who has been documenting the event, says.

"Oxygen levels are holding steady," the respiratory therapist states. "Her heart rate and BP are leveling out too."

They push Grace through the doors of the trauma room just as she stops seizing for a second time. "Alright, seizure stopped," Drew announces, noting the time. "Let's make sure it's her last. Is there anyone we should call?"

"I'll do it," I tell them. "I'm her attending."

And her roommate and her best friend's brother and her lover, but no one really knows that last part. Few know she's living with me, though Drew and Margot do. I run my fingers through her hair, staring down at her sweet face, pale as a sheet, her lips caked in blood and saliva. Her eyes now closed, her body limp and lifeless.

Not even caring about who's in the room or people talking, I lean down and press my lips to her forehead. It's in this moment that I realize the true destructive power of love. The crushing, brutalizing agony of loving someone more than you love yourself. The fear and ache and torment that you'll lose them far before you're ready to. I'd give my life for this woman and here she lies, unconscious and bleeding, and I can't save her from this.

It's an affliction, a disorder, a condition of the human body. One she's lived with nearly her entire life. One that acts like an earthquake. Unpredictable. Devastating. Soul-rattling for those who survive it with her.

It just goes to show you how no one is ever safe. How love isn't enough protection when we need it to be.

"I'm sorry," I whisper into her sweaty flesh. "I'm so sorry, sweetheart."

I kiss her, press my forehead to hers, and then leave the trauma room, ambling out into the hallway just beyond, letting them continue to work to make sure my girl is okay. On shaky legs with trembling hands—my hands never fucking tremble—I first call upstairs and tell them we need the floor covered by any resident, attending, fellow, or even med student. Then I call Oliver because I don't know her parents' number and they're in Australia.

"Hey," he answers, picking up on the second ring. My body vibrates with relief at the sound of my brother's voice. Not just for Grace. But for me too and suddenly I hate that I've been holding back telling him how I feel about her. I fall against the wall, pressing my entire weight into it.

"I'm in the ED with Grace. She had two seizures back-to-back. They seem to have her stabilized now, but I—" I choke, emotion taking over in ways it never has before with me. Not even when my mom was diagnosed with breast cancer. Not even when it came back. "Fuck, Oliver. I don't know how to reach her parents. I don't know who to call. I just know I won't make it if she's not okay."

He clears his throat. Then he's silent. Finally, he says, "We're on our way." And he hangs up. I tipped my hand. I let it out there for him because he needs to know.

But Grace doesn't want to be in a relationship with me. She told me as much last night. She also asked that I keep this thing between us a secret.

Do I care? I'm not so sure anymore. Today was a game-changer for me.

My love for her is overpowering but I wouldn't risk changing it for the easy route.

Tucking my phone back into my pocket, I march back into the trauma room. Grace's position hasn't moved, but her eyes are now open.

"She's postictal," Margot informs me, checking Grace's lines. "She opened her eyes about a minute ago, which is a fantastic sign. She's still non-responsive, and TMI the reason I changed her to a gown is because she peed her scrub pants and underwear, but that's sorta how it goes with seizures. She'll likely be out of it for a while and we're going to keep her on the Dilantin and Diazepam drips, but I expect she'll be up and bitching you out in no time."

I blink, blowing out a breath. "How long will she have to stay in here?"

Margot shakes her head. Her dark curls all over the place as they spring out of her bun. "I have a room for her down the hall. Drew wants to keep her here in the ED for a while, just in case. I don't think he trusts the floor to do its due diligence with her. That or he's afraid of dealing with Oliver and Rina. And you, it seems." She winks at me. "Want to help me move her?"

I shift to the left side of the bed, staring down at Grace. The bed unlocks with a loud click and then Margot is walking, pushing the large gurney with her. I help, adjusting some of the weight for myself.

"How long have you been a thing?"

I smirk. "Not that long."

"But you love her."

My smirk grows at the self-assured way Margot said that.

"I have for a while, yeah."

"I didn't trust a lot or well until Drew came along. Sometimes it just takes the right person to realign your thinking. Think about Rina with Brecken. She and I were hard set on the anti-love train. Clearly that didn't work out so well for us."

We walk down the hall, passing room after room until we reach the end. It's quiet back here, almost secluded for such a busy part of the hospital. We enter the room and lock the gurney into place. In a flash, Margot is gone only to return just as quickly with a warm blanket that she places over Grace.

"I don't think Grace sees it quite that way between us yet."

Margot stares at me, a contemplative tilt to her head. "I saw the way you looked at her from almost day one. You fell, and you fell hard. It's why I've been pushing her to hook up with you, which it seems like she has. She might just need some extra time to catch up to where you've already been. For her, this is new. For you, it's not. Remember that. Take good care of her, Doctor. Page me if she doesn't come around within the next thirty minutes."

And with that Margot leaves, going to take care of her other patients. I lower the bedside rail on the side facing me, drop into a chair, and scoot it until I'm pressed against the gurney. My head finds the miserably hard mattress beside where her head is resting, my hand in her hair as I cup the back of her head.

In addition to changing Grace into a gown and cleaning her up, she also dressed the wound on her head that she got from smacking it on the gurney. I kiss it gently; grateful it didn't require stitches. Then I close my eyes.

I stay like this for I don't even know how long. Silent. Grace still. My only reassurance coming from the monitor sprouting her vitals and the steady rhythm of her breathing.

That is until Oliver walks in.

27

My head pops up at the sound of footsteps entering the room, and I immediately lock eyes with my brother. He's staring at me, almost in disbelief whereas Amelia and Rina, who are by his side, don't look surprised at all. Despite the inauspicious reasons for them being dragged here on a Sunday, the ladies are grinning with a self-satisfied gleam to their eyes that suggests they were on to me for as long as Margot evidently was.

"So, we're going to get coffee," Rina announces, tugging on Amelia's arm.

"Right. Coffee," Amelia agrees. "And cookies. Grace loves the cookies from the cafeteria. She'll definitely want those when she's feeling better."

And then my sister and one day soon to be my sister-in-law leave me here with my brother who does not look happy.

He grabs a chair from the corner, dragging it along until he's on the other side of Grace's gurney, his gaze never wavering from mine. "I texted her parents," he starts, the edge to his voice unmistakable. "It's the middle of the night in Australia and they're not the closest with her anyway. Actually, they're straight-up assholes who don't give a shit about her, so I doubt they'll even reply."

I sit up straighter. "Oliver—"

"How long?" he interrupts.

"A few weeks. Since her birthday."

"And is it just fun or something else?"

"I suppose that would depend on which of us you ask."

He practically snarls at that. "I'm asking you, asshole. Grace is like Rina to me, except Rina has five brothers and two parents who would lay in traffic for her. Grace has me. I'm it."

"Not anymore."

Oliver shakes his head in dismay, running his hand over her hair and checking her over. "Grace? You waking up yet, honey?"

She doesn't respond.

"How long does it typically take for her to come out of her postictal phase?"

"Depends. I haven't seen her have a seizure since we were in medical school. That was a bad one. A night of too much drinking. After that, she sort of found her stride with them. Got herself into a routine and a regimen. What's happened that that all changed?"

The accusation in his tone isn't unfounded. My guilt has been riding me since the second I saw her on the floor.

"That's my fault. She's been working too many hours with not enough sleep to pick up the slack of another resident who was injured. That and I took her to see Wild Minds last night and we had a few drinks."

"With Kap and Luca?"

Now he looks pissed and I'm not about to throw my brothers under the bus. Especially when they kept our secret, not something any of us enjoys doing. "No. We had floor seats." Not a lie, but not the full truth either.

Oliver runs his hands over his face, blowing out a harsh breath through his fingers. "She's living with you."

"Oliver, grow the fuck up and get over it. Jesus Christ. Grace was in a shitty relationship with a shitty guy, and you hardly had a goddamn word to say about it. I am not a shitty guy. I know you know this. Hurting her isn't an option for me."

"Except she hasn't had a seizure in four years and within weeks of moving in and hooking up with you, she has not one but two."

It's true and I have nothing to say. I'd rather die than let her go, but maybe being with me isn't the healthiest or the safest option for her.

"It wasn't Carter's fault. It was mine," Grace grumbles, her voice coarse like she's been eating sand.

Oliver's face drops to the gurney, resting on his side so he can stare straight into her eyes. "Hey beautiful. How's your head?"

"Awesome. I forgot how much fun having a seizure can be."

"You had two."

"Even better. No wonder I feel like I was just hit by a truck." Ever so slowly, she shifts on the gurney, trying to roll onto her back. Immediately I stand, helping her, staring into her eyes as they adjust to the overhead lights.

"Pupils are equal and reactive," I say, running my hand along her cheek. "Welcome back. You scared the shit out of me."

She doesn't say anything to that, raising her arm in the air and surveying her IV before arching up to take a look at the pole, spotting the two bags of meds and fluids they're giving her. With a huff, she sinks back down.

"It wasn't your fault," she repeats. "It was mine. I wasn't taking care of myself the way I should have. The way I know I need to. I drank a lot of caffeine in the last few days. Didn't get a lot of sleep. Drank some alcohol on top of that. I was stupid. And careless. And this is the result."

"You got lucky."

She frowns at Oliver's words. "I got lucky. The last thoughts to flow through my head were that I was grateful I was already in the hospital. Who's covering my patients?"

My heart pinches at that. Status epilepticus is terrifying. Grace was here and the nurses were able to call for help immediately and respond with medications within seconds of her initial onset. If a person is home when it hits, sometimes they're not so lucky.

"Dylan, the other residents, and Dr. Schwartz as well as a fellow," I answer, but she doesn't react beyond one simple nod of her head.

"Amelia and I have a big house, Grace. Come live with us."

"Fuck you, Oliver," I growl, ready to kill my brother where he sits.

"Fuck you back. If you had taken care of her the way—"

"Shut up!" Grace yells and then flinches, licking her cracked lips and lowering her tone. "Both of you. Just shut up. Damn. Why are boys so dumb? God. Do you think because I have vagina, I'm weak and incapable of making rational decisions about my life? What happened is because I didn't do what I needed to do. I was arrogant. Something you two pricks should relate to. I drank too much caffeine. I got too little sleep. I had more alcohol than I should have. I knew better and I did it anyway. But as of this moment, I'm not moving out and I'm not living with you, Oliver. I will make my own choices and decide my own path and both of you will have to learn to adapt to it."

I sink back down onto my chair, taking her hand and forcing her gaze to hit mine. "I don't want you to move out. I want you to stay. With me."

There. Heart on the line. Feelings served up in a Petri dish.

Grace sputters out a breath. "Get me discharged. Get this line out of my arm. The drugs are making me feel like I'm walking through sludge." I nod absently. Everything inside of me hurting until her hand squeezes mine and she finishes that off with, "I want to go home."

"Grace?"

She turns back to Oliver. "What do you want me to say? I need you. You're my best friend. But I lied to you for weeks because I wasn't sure how you'd take it."

"Not well."

"Obviously. I'm sorry." She frowns, letting go of my hand and reaching for his. "I'm so sorry. But it's new and we're not... I just got out of my engagement to Tony... and I..."

"He seems to care about you."

"I'm right here," I groan only to be ignored.

"I'm not sure I'm ready to discuss that," she continues. "Mostly I'm scared about doing everything wrong the way I did with Tony. But for now, I'm okay."

"If you're ever not, you'll come and stay with us?"

"Promise."

"Shit, Grace." Oliver crumples, his expression breaking. "You can't do this to me again. I can't handle you avoiding me. You're my best fucking friend. I can stand anything you can throw at me, including your motherfucking seizures and you screwing around with my brother, but I can't handle that."

"I'll never withhold from you again."

Oliver stands up, adjusting his T-shirt that somehow is misaligned. He wipes at the emotion on his face, and I watch as my brother grapples with letting go of being the man in Grace's life. Even when she had Tony, Oliver was still it. And likely, Oliver will always be her go-to person.

But it's Oliver. And I'm okay with that.

"Carter, let it be known now that I will fucking destroy you if ever hurt my girl. She's the B side to my A side, brother."

"And she's the A side to my B side."

Oliver glares at me for forever and then he kisses Grace's forehead and walks out.

"Your family is so dramatic."

I chuckle, grasping Grace's body in both my arms, my face right beside hers. "I like you."

She laughs. "I like you too."

"Don't move out, okay?"

"I won't. At least not yet. But when you get all fancy and decide breaking hearts is what all the cool kids are doing, I might."

"And if I decide to be lame and never do that?"

"Then you better not ever make me overhear how you're a sex god with another woman in my favorite café."

"But the local diner?"

"Carter?!" I get a smack to my head which makes me laugh harder.

"I'm your sex god. Your body is my temple. Your pussy my house of worship." I raise up, dropping my chin onto the gurney and smirking at my girl. "Sweetheart, there is no getting away from me because wherever you go, I follow. I will always follow."

"You mean that?"

I don't get a chance to answer because just then Drew returns, his gray eyes on us as he approaches the other side of her gurney. "Oliver just informed me I'm to release you. But since this is my ED and you're my patient and not his, I thought I'd come speak to you first."

"I'd like to go home," Grace tells him.

"And I'd like Margot to finally marry me. We don't always get what we want. Is there any way I can convince you to stay the night? Get an EEG? A neuro consult?"

"None of this is new for me, but I promise I'll follow up with my neurologist."

"Do you need a refill on your meds until then?"

She shakes her head. "No. I have plenty of Ativan at home and I'll likely start taking it for a few days just to be certain."

"Damn, doctors make the worst patients. How about you *will* start taking it for a few days and if you need anything else, well, Carter can write it for you or I can. Margot or Rina will be here in a second with some—"

"I'm already here," Rina announces. "I have a clean pair of scrubs for you, but unfortunately the only underwear I could scrounge up are the lovely full coverage hospital mesh ones."

"Awesome," Grace deadpans. "Super sexy but very appreciated. I'm not going to ask how many people I work with saw me seize, lose control of God knows what, and get naked because I don't want to know."

"Only I saw you naked," Margot replies, coming in to join us. "I cleaned you up and changed you into a gown after the room was cleared."

"Thank you," Grace says, her voice cracking with gratitude. "All of you."

"Rest up and take it easy," Drew tells her. "I don't want to see you back down here unless you're here as a doctor and not a patient."

"Agreed."

"I'll take out her IV," I offer.

I take the scrubs and mesh underwear from Rina and the room empties after Drew does a quick exam and Rina and Margot hug Grace. Shutting off the pumps, I wash my hands, put on some gloves, and go about removing the IV from Grace's elbow crease. Then I untie the string in the back of the gown, helping her get changed.

"Why are you still here, Carter?"

I blink at that, shifting to catch her eye. "What do you mean? Did you want me to step out while you change?"

"No. I mean, why are you still here with me, telling me you want me to stay?" She shakes her head, staring down at her hands. "You can't be for real."

"I don't understand what you're asking me," I admit.

She blows out a breath and for the longest of moments, just sits there, lost in her thoughts. Finally she says, "When I was first diagnosed, my parents didn't know what to do with me. It scared them, sure, but I think it also embarrassed them. I had a seizure in public once and I remember when I came to and was feeling better, my mother told me I wasn't allowed to do that again—like I had a choice in the matter—because two people from their country club saw. After that, they pretty much kept me in the house or parked me at your house with Oliver. I think they assumed because your father is a doctor that he'd be able to handle me better than they would."

"Grace."

I sit back down, taking her hand in mine. I never knew about this. Oliver never mentioned it. He said her parents weren't part of her life. That they don't give a shit about her. I had no clue it was like this though.

"I took my meds. I did everything I could not to have any more seizures. I went on Depo-Provera when we discovered my periods were making them worse. I was desperate for my parents to want me and love me back, but they never did after that episode. Once I realized that was the case, I used my epilepsy as a weapon against them. I wanted to be normal. Just like every other teenager and college kid. I wanted to drink and party and not think of the consequences. It took me a very long time to understand how doing that was not hurting them the way I intended. I was only hurting myself in that game. I got straight with my seizures—lucky I was even able to do that when so many can't—and in my entire relationship with Tony, I never had one. Only a few FAS symptoms that never went beyond that. In fact, I think he mostly forgot about it. He'd mention things occasionally, but he never saw me seize. I used to be so afraid he'd leave me the way my parents did if he ever saw it happen. And then he cheated on me and I guess…"

She puffs out a breath, staring up at the ceiling so she

doesn't cry and God, my chest aches just watching her wrestle with this.

"My head is a mess, Carter, but it's not you. You're the one thing that feels like it's going right in my life. And because of that, I'm scared you'll be the next thing I lose because that's how it always seems to go for me."

I thread my fingers with hers, both hands, giving hers a squeeze so she'll look at me. It takes her a long beat to do so. "I saw you seize. And I'm still here with no plans on going anywhere else. It takes an awful lot more than a couple of seizures to scare me away from something I want as badly as I want you. I haven't done this before, Grace, but that's not going to stop me. If you need time, I'll be patient. But no matter what, you're not losing me. I promise, sweetheart."

Tears line her eyes, holding on tight, refusing to fall.

"I just hope you know what you're getting into."

28

In the four weeks since my seizure, time has moved at warp speed. And not necessarily in a good way. Janet came back after her time off, meaner than a snake and more ruthless than one at a mouse-eating competition. Carter had to readjust everyone's schedules, including mine.

Now, I work mostly with Dr. Westerfield and Janet works primarily with Carter. Even if he moved me so our schedules align. It doesn't take a genius to figure out it's because he's worried about me.

But still, I can't stand how closely he's working with Janet and not with me—something she's insanely smug about and loves to rub in my face. He's pushing me out of the OR and making it, so I have more oversight than I did before. Dr. Westerfield is amazing and I'm learning a lot, but she's not my attending. Carter is. So why the hell does he think I need a second attending all over my ass? I was handling my patients without error before.

Any time I bring up the subject to him, he blows me off. All I can think about is that he's lost confidence in me. That having a seizure in front of him like that has him rethinking everything including my ability as a doctor.

He says I'm reading too much into it. Possibly so. But still... the proof is in his actions. He's all over me and not in a hot or sexy way. In a way that demands management and limits my work. Especially my OR time.

It requires me to take matters into my own hands and fight about it later. Which we do. He gets pissy when I go behind his back and schedule surgeries or don't consult him every time I go into one. In return, I fight back, and we end up having hot, sweaty sex somewhere in the condo. Or in his office.

That was yet another thing that took time to come back.

I practically had to force him into having sex with me and the first time we did, he was terrified that when I orgasmed, I'd seize. Nope. Thankfully that's never been a trigger for me.

But still, the man needs to learn that just because I'm epileptic doesn't mean I'm going to cower and wilt at a little stress and extra work. I never wanted this disorder to define me. Yet, I still see some of it in the eyes of the people I work with. The people who either saw me seize or heard about it. They look at you like you have cancer. A plague.

Something terrifying and catching.

Fighting with people to force them to view you as you are is the ultimate uphill battle. For anyone. But I can't change people's perceptions with words, I can only do it with actions, and letting my epilepsy win isn't an option for me.

Even if I did feel a little dizzy when I woke up yesterday morning.

Something I'd rather die than tell Carter about because I know how he'll react.

I get it. I scared him. I had a seizure, but I'm epileptic.

It's unfortunately what we do and as much as I'd like to imagine that was the last seizure I'll ever have, I know it's not. But in the month since I had that seizure, I haven't had so much as a twitch. So him treating me like I'm a porcelain doll is grating. And sweet. I know it's sweet. I'm lucky with him. He's the mystical prince from my dreams I never imagined real. I'm crazy about him. But I need his trust too and I don't feel as though I have it.

Most of the time.

"Dr. Hammond, can I have a word with you?" Carter barks into the open OR, mask held up over his mouth, causing every head other than mine to swivel in his direction.

"I'm busy at the moment, Dr. Fritz."

"Surely Dr. Westerfield can set aside scrolling through her phone to take over for you. This is your third surgery today. That seems like at least one too many." Damn him, it is not too many!

Dr. Westerfield with how much I've been working with her lately will let me in the OR. I didn't even have to offer up favors of the non-sexual variety to get this surgery behind Carter's back. No way in hell am I giving it up now.

"I'm sorry, Dr. Fritz. This really isn't the best time. I'll be sure to come find you when I'm done."

Carter snarls out a slew of unkind words before storming out of the OR. And God, is he hot when he does that or what? I think it's safe to say holding off from falling for my attending has been a futile attempt at best. But I'd rather be on scut for a month than admit that.

"Cauterize here, Dylan."

"Wooh girl. You have ice in your veins," he comments as he does as instructed.

"I second that," Dr. Westerfield mutters without removing her eyes from her screen—her typical MO while letting me do her work. Absolutely no complaints there. "Let's just say I'm glad I'm his boss and not the other way around. I get the pleasure of ignoring him, you don't have that luxury."

"The man treats women delivering babies. Surely he's more

than aware of just what our bodies and minds are capable of. My attending needs to relax."

"I don't think that's the issue," Sally, the scrub nurse on this case, says to me. "Dr. Johnson broke her wrist and Dr. Fritz has been unrelenting with her. With you, he's careful and worried."

I shake my head dismissively and make a show of rolling my eyes. "He barely works with me anymore. He's always too busy teaching Dr. Johnson." I try to keep all bitterness and contempt from my voice, but I'm positive it leaks through anyway. But fuck, it hurts!

"You landed a Fritz," she continues, effectively dismissing my point. "That's like mining for diamonds or diving for pearls and coming up with a jewelry store full."

I snicker at that. "I've landed no one. I've known Carter since I was born. That's all this is. Besides, who cares if he's a Fritz? Their money is the least interesting or special part of any of them. I'd rather he spend more time teaching me than worrying I'll have another seizure." The way he's doing with Janet.

"Honey, I'm not even talking about his wealth or even his celebrity," Sally continues. "Though neither of those are anything to sneeze at. I'm talking about the man. He's gloriously gorgeous, deliciously arrogant, brilliant with a scalpel, and absolutely batshit crazy in love with you."

"Totally," Dylan exclaims. "If he pitched for my squad, I'd be his batter anytime."

"Blah. You've all been watching too much nighttime drama TV," I grumble. "He's not my Mc-anything." *No, he's my Mc-everything.* "Working for him makes me want to drink tequila all day long and smoke copious amounts of weed, only I can't because I'll have another public seizure and then they'd revoke my license before shipping me off to Betty Ford. The man stresses my last nerve in the name of being my attending and it doesn't look pretty on me."

"Such a hardship," Dylan quips. "A billionaire doctor looking after you. Remind me to send you a condolence card while shedding a tear. I'll be sure to discuss your tragedy at my next Gays Take Boston night out."

I blink at him. "That's a thing? And why am I not in on that? It sounds fabulous."

"It's a thing, but only if you're LGBTQ+, which we know you're not."

"Yeah, yeah, blah, blah. Whatever. I'm officially hurt I can't party with you like that. Can we finish this surgery and not talk about Dr. Fritz?"

"Fine," Dr. Westerfield jumps in, finally putting her phone away. I kinda forgot she was here. Oops. "But in the interim, while you're complaining about your attending, I like having someone else do the brunt of my work, so I won't complain about Carter putting you with me."

Well, now I feel bad. I probably shouldn't have opened my mouth like that in front of her. A fellow attending to Carter and his boss. Something I frequently forget with how chill she is. "You're right. I shouldn't have said all that about Dr. Fritz. I'm beyond grateful for the opportunity to work with you, Dr. Westerfield."

"A point you've proven, which is why I let you operate behind Carter's back. I'm his boss, so I can get away with it. Just as long as I get an invite to the wedding. Or that Gays Take Boston thing because I agree, it sounds fabulous."

"For real," I snicker. "Not the wedding thing."

I want to remark that there will be no wedding, but there is no point. This room is obviously team Carter-Grace and there is no dissuading them. Despite their teasing and speculation, no one knows what's actually going on with us. That we're a couple. Having crazy hot sex. Living together. Whatever. He likes me and I like him. There has been no mention of the L-word and certainly nothing about marriage.

It's only been a couple of months and we're taking it slow and steady for now.

Even if things are going well, that doesn't mean they always will. I know that firsthand.

I'd say shows like *Grey's Anatomy* are purely based in fantasy, but gossip is the eternal driving force of this place. Patients and gossip. It's what we do. Especially about others' love lives. So arguing is futile and will only provide more fodder for their gossip mill.

By the time we get out of the OR, and I'm officially scrubbed out—a brilliantly done job, if I do say so myself—it's more than an hour later and I know Carter isn't going to be happy with me. My shift ended twenty minutes ago. His too.

But just as I turn the corner for his office, a fresh wave of dizziness hits me so hard I have to stop and grab on to the wall for fear that I'm going to either fall over or pass out. Nausea comes along for the carnival ride and for a few moments, I just stand here, pressed against the wall, eyes closed and breathing slowly.

What the fuck is going on?

This is not how my seizures feel. I don't typically get dizziness or nausea with them, but I do know that's not uncommon for a FAS depending on where it originates. Only, I don't feel like I'm having a seizure. Maybe I needed to eat more lunch? Take more breaks? Drink more fluids?

The dizziness and nausea pass after a few minutes, but the confusion and questions don't.

Before I can think twice about it, I pull out my phone and text Margot.

Me: Hey, you on?

Thankfully she responds right away. **Margot: Just got on. Night shift. What's up?**

Me: I'm coming down for a quick exam. Keep it between us unless we need Drew.

Margot: Done. I'll be waiting.

I'll have her run some blood work under a fake name. Check my vitals. Maybe another EEG. First, I have to blow off Carter.

"You look like shit," Janet hisses, startling me away from the wall. She's standing in the middle of the hall, staring at me like she's one of the twin girls from The Shining. Scary and creepy as all hell. "I heard you not only have to sneak in surgeries with other attendings but got called out for it in the middle of your surgery. That has to be so embarrassing. Especially after you had a seizure in the middle of the floor in front of everyone."

"You mean embarrassing like nearly blacking out and breaking your wrist after your patient practically bleeds out because you have no clue what you're doing?"

Ugh. I likely shouldn't have gone there. Why, oh why, can't she just go away? In fact... "Go away."

"I'm back now. My PT is going great, and Carter is beyond impressed with my work. He tells me so all the time. Or haven't you noticed the board and how my name is always with his. Yours, sadly, is hardly anywhere to be found."

"Honestly, I haven't noticed," I lie and it's not even a good lie at that. Obviously, I've noticed. It's what I was just bitching about in the OR.

She reads this flawlessly. A self-satisfied gleam covering her face, her chin lifting arrogantly as she proudly folds her arms. Such a damn peacock. "I overheard him say he's removed you from surgeries because he thinks you'll seize during one and kill either the patient or yourself."

No he didn't. He'd never say that. Would he?

"Now you have to beg other attendings to take you on. So sad. So pathetic."

Uneasiness grips my chest along with a healthy dose of insecurity. Something I don't wear all that well.

Steadying my features, I meet her dark eyes head-on. "Janet,

I don't know what your play is, but we both know that when you were here before your injury, you did nothing. Your residents knew nothing. You're a hoax. A hologram of a doctor. So how about we stop playing games and maybe I can help you."

She scoffs shrilly, squaring her shoulders above her slight frame while pushing her hair back and trying for imposing, falling so short it's almost comical. "I don't need your help. I've got Carter all over me. You're nothing. Some poor joke of a woman who thinks if she puts out for her attending, she'll get ahead. Clearly, that didn't work out so well for you. I mean, seizing like that in front of the whole floor? No wonder he doesn't want to teach you anymore. You're a liability if ever there was one. A point he's proving by taking me under his wing while casting you out."

She stares at me, waiting, hoping I'll crack at that. I'm kind of tempted, though I keep that to myself. She's the cat and I'm the ball of yarn. She pinpointed my greatest fear and is playing it against me perfectly.

"You're a liar."

She grins so smugly I can't help but jolt with her certainty. "You're ancient history, Grace. You'll be done in this hospital in no time. As it is, you're no longer number one, and we both know it."

I shake my head. I can't deal with this, with her, right now. "Maybe. But you're still a miserable, hateful bitch." I leave her behind, my mind spinning, sick, my heart tumbling like an empty dryer. Her words tonight have a particular lash to them. A knowledge almost. Tentacles of doubt wrap around my most tender, vulnerable parts, squeezing them until they nearly burst.

She can't be telling the truth, can she? But if she's not, then why *is* Carter working so closely with her while pushing me out? Another surge of dizziness consumes me just as I reach Carter's office. Luckily, this time, no one is around to see me fold against his door, my forehead pressing into it as I breathe. I need to figure this out first. Everything else can wait.

I rap my knuckles on his door as he grumbles out a, "Come in."

"Hey," I say with a smile I don't feel.

He sighs. "I hate that you snuck that surgery."

I shrug unapologetically. "Then you need to give me more OR time. Or, you know, work with me." Instead of always being with Janet.

He stares at me for a very long moment and I'm trying so hard to read him, but I get nothing more than the usual Carter in return.

"Okay," he finally relents. "You're right," he agrees, running a hand over his head. "I've been scared of pushing you too hard, but you know your body and you know what you're doing."

I nearly collapse in relief. "Thank you. That means so much to me. What happened is not your fault, Carter. I've told you this a thousand times, but I don't think you believe me."

He smiles cheekily. "That's because I don't. Are you ready to go?"

I shift my weight in the doorway, watching him as I say, "Janet has been working very closely with you since she returned."

"I know. She's on tonight." He tilts his head curiously, like he's waiting for me to follow that up.

"She thinks you're pushing me out and she's taking my place."

He scoffs dismissively.

"Okay. Good for her. You ready?"

That's really not the response I was hoping for.

"Um. I'm meeting up with Margot for a bit. I'll just see you at home?" Damn, I suck at this.

"Sure. I didn't realize you had plans, or I wouldn't have waited around."

"Sorry. I should have said something sooner. It slipped my mind." I hate lying to him. I hate it so damn much.

He stands, rounding his desk. He's still in his scrubs, his dark hair messy like he was either running his hands through it or he ripped a scrub cap off in frustration. His arms wrap around my waist, and he pulls me into his office, shutting the door behind me so no one can see us.

His mouth drops to my neck and for a moment, he just breathes me in.

Like I'm his air.

I cannot explain the sensations that flow through me at that.

My eyes close and I succumb to the feel of him holding me. It's beyond glorious and yet pragmatically alarming. Carter has become something I'm starting to believe I don't want to live without. And that terrifies me. I had put so much of myself into my relationship with Tony. Held so much of myself back out of fear he'd stop loving me. I blame my parents for most of that. Myself too. It was a lack of confidence or sense of self-worth in so many ways.

I watched as my parents' love for me dwindled until it died out completely, shifting everything they ever gave me entirely onto my brother. He became their focus, and I was just the girl with the embarrassing disorder. I carried the pain and trepidation of that with me because I knew how afraid Tony was of that side of me.

The unpredictable side. The sick side.

Then he went and cheated on me in the most gruesome, self-esteem destroying ways, and it was like... I was right.

Forever the only person I knew I could unequivocally rely on was Oliver.

Then Carter came along.

Saw me at my worst.

And not only is he still here with me, but he's stealing my

heart. Something I've been so reluctant to give him. Knowing there must be a breaking point for a man like him—one I won't be able to handle when it comes. Why else has he stayed single this long? Why else did he not make a move with that woman he claimed to love?

I've been trying to have faith. In him. In us. Sometimes that's easier than others.

"Maybe I'll go out and grab a beer or two with Kaplan and Luca or something," he muses, pulling back and grabbing his phone off his desk, likely texting them. "I haven't been out in so long."

No, because you've been home babysitting me. "That's my fault."

"I like being with you any chance I can get. But it might be fun to see what trouble we can get ourselves into."

"I can only imagine," I deadpan with a wry grin on my face. I don't want to think about it. There will be women all over them—throwing themselves at them. Photographs taken and published on the internet.

"Have you seen Janet? I want to make sure she's good for the night before I take off."

Jealousy flares through me. Has he really been pushing me out in favor of working with her because he views me as a liability? No. That doesn't even make sense. Carter wouldn't. I need to get my head on straight with him. He's just worried about me.

Then why is he only working with her and not you?

"Right before I came in here. That's when she me told you're pushing me out in favor of her."

He chuckles derisively, and again, not what I was fully hoping for. It's almost as if he's dodging this completely, refusing to meet my eyes when he never does that.

"Is something going on with you and Janet?" I ask point blank.

Another chuckle. But still no direct answer. And still not meeting my eyes.

"Have fun with Margot and I'll see you later." I get a chaste kiss on the cheek, but his mind is already elsewhere, and I'm hit with a pinch of not only guilt, but of resentment and nerves.

Thanks, Tony, for instilling trust issues and doubt. Thanks, Janet, for striking the perfect nerve at the perfect moment. Ugh.

Five minutes later, I'm walking through the back part of the emergency department, searching for Margot. A hand grabs my arm out of nowhere and suddenly I'm being hauled in the direction of the exam room I woke up in after my seizure.

"I told Drew I had menstrual cramps and needed a few minutes, but I think he's on to me since he went down on me earlier today and knows I don't have my period."

"Then I'll cut right to the chase before he discovers our clandestine meeting. I've had three episodes of dizziness in the last couple of days. The last one the worst and it came with a wave of nausea."

Fluorescent lights flicker on as she slides the plexiglass door closed and pulls the curtain, giving us total privacy. "Was it a focal aware seizure?"

I shake my head. Then I shrug. "I don't think so. I've never had one that way before."

"And this just started today?"

"Yesterday."

"Do I need to ask all the routine questions?"

"I've been getting plenty of sleep, eating regular meals, no new medications, no upper respiratory infection symptoms. I'm vaccinated against Hep A. Could be food poisoning, but legit, I've been living off of PB and Fluff because it's all I've wanted to eat, so I doubt it."

"When was your last period?"

"I don't get them. I've been on Depo for over a decade to help with my seizures that were hormonally induced."

"So, you want me to what? Just check some blood work? Your blood sugar? Vitals? We can do an EE—" She freezes mid-word. "Wait. You're on Depo?"

"Yeah. Why?"

"Do you and Carter use condoms?"

"Um. No. We don't. We never did. We're both clean and again I'm on Depo."

Her face goes ashen, and she takes a step back until she smacks into the wall, covering her mouth with her hand. "Fuddruckers."

"What?"

"We gave you Dilantin when you had your seizure."

I shake my head. "No. You gave me Diazepam."

"Grace, we gave you both. I gave you an IV push of Dilantin and then we had you on a drip."

I fall into a chair, my forearms to my parted thighs, my face hanging between them. "I didn't see that. I didn't notice it. You don't think..."

"That you're pregnant? You could be."

Because some anticonvulsants interfere with hormonal contraception, rendering them ineffective. Dilantin being one of them.

"But... did Carter know you gave me Dilantin? He knows I'm on Depo."

She shrugs. "He might not have thought about it. You were actively seizing and then postictal and he had just come clean to Oliver about your relationship. The man had other things on his mind and likely didn't think about it after."

"Fuck."

My face hits my hands, my body trembling. I can't be pregnant. That's not what this is. No way. This has to be... something else.

"Before you go off the deep end, let's check a dipstick. It might be a hundred other things."

Right.

Except it's not a hundred other things. Not when you're staring down at a stick with two pink lines. And three others that match it.

"Have you taken any anticonvulsants in the last forty-eight hours?" Margot questions, standing over my shoulder and eyeing the sticks we have lined up on the gurney, sitting atop of a disposable pad.

For the first time in my life, I wish the answer was yes. "No."

"So at least it won't be a false-positive."

I can't stop glaring at them. Four tests. All positive. How the hell did this happen?

I look over my shoulder at her. "You realize the irony of this, right? I'm an OB-GYN. Accidentally getting pregnant is like the most ridiculous thing we can do."

"Not just accidentally pregnant, babe. Accidentally pregnant with your OB-GYN attending man-lover. This is like a Top 40 solid platinum album here. You're a country ballad waiting to happen."

"Thanks." I can't even manage proper sarcasm at the moment. I turn back to the tests. My heart in my throat suffocating the breath from my lungs. "Just because they're positive doesn't mean—"

"Vaginal ultrasound?"

"You gonna do it? Shove something that looks like a lubricated dildo up my vag?"

She laughs. "See one, do one, teach one." I give her another look. "I can assist. You'll walk me through it."

No. I can't do it. Not yet. I'm just... "I'm not ready yet." I'm hard and fast in denial town. I mean, how many women have I treated who had positive pregnancy tests and then ended up not being pregnant? Or the pregnancy wasn't viable?

Or... fuck.

I'm pregnant with Carter's baby.

How could I have made such a mistake?

And what about my career?

That! My career!!

It's already shaky with Carter pushing me off his service, keeping me out of the OR. What will this do to it?

I have another almost two years left of my residency. You can't have a baby during residency. Shit gets all kinds of fucked up. People view you differently. You lose credibility and surgeries, and everyone thinks if you're assertive, you're just a hormonal bitch—fucking misogynists. And then you get into breastfeeding and diaper changing and burp cloths and lack of sleep and...

"I can't do it," I reiterate.

"Alright," Margot barks, her voice growing stern. "Cut your drama off here at the bitch. For now, let's do some blood work. You know we should. I'll put it under the name Bellatrix Lestrange. No one will know it's you."

"No, they'll think I'm a pregnant psychopathic death eater instead."

She shifts in beside me. "If you were Amelia, I'd go with Ginny Potter. You know, 'cause she's a redhead. You're blonde." She tilts her head, studying me before she snaps her fingers in an ah-ha way. "Luna Longbottom. I was always secretly team Luna-Neville. It's perfect."

"I can't believe this is what my night, my life, has turned into. Maybe we should do more tests? Just to be sure I'm consistently getting two pink lines."

"Only if I can bill your insurance for it, Doctor. Do you have any idea how perpetually strapped the emergency department is for funds?"

"Fine. Blood work it is."

"And who should I put as the supervising physician to receive the results of all your—"

"Margot?" Drew opens the sliding door and then the

curtain and Margot and I both spin around at light speed, closing our ranks so that Drew can't see what's on the gurney behind us. He stares at both of us, a suspiciously bemused expression on his face. "What's going on in here?"

"Nothing," Margot snaps. "I told you I had menstrual cramps, so I called in a professional."

Drew's eyes cast over to me and then back to her. "Uh-huh. What's really going on in here, Freckles?"

"I'm pregnant," Margot states, and I choke on my own spit. *The fuck?!*

Except he must know his girl perfectly because he just rolls his eyes like he doesn't buy it for a second. "Whatever. If you're done with your nonexistent menstrual cramps and fake pregnancies, are you available to come out here and do your job? I have like five patients who need a nurse."

"I'm hurt, Drew. Totally hurt. I could be pregnant. Or heavily menstruating."

"Not at the same time, you can't. And we both know you're not either. You called Grace in here tonight to freak out over the fact that I'm pressing you to set a date for our wedding. I'm shocked you didn't drag Halle, Aria, and Rina here as well."

"They were busy."

"I'm sorry to hear that, but we do have patients to see."

"Fine," she groans, sagging almost exaggeratedly. "Give me five more minutes. But if you mention a wedding date again, I won't give you after-work morning sex."

"Liar. It's your favorite sex."

She turns to me. "It totally is. Okay, I'm back to work, but thank you, Dr. Hammond for coming down and discussing my cramps with me. I feel much better about them now that I know they're normal. I just have a couple more very quick questions I'd like you to answer for me if you have a second."

Drew makes some sort of dismissive sound in the back of

this throat before he turns and saunters out of the room, throwing me a wave as he goes.

"Saved your ass, Doctor," Margot says to me once the door is shut. "Let's get going on this blood work before he comes back and figures out what we're really up to. HIPAA or not, your baby news will spread faster than an STI at a fraternity pledge party. I don't think that's how you want Carter to find out you're carrying his spawn."

Yep. I'm officially screwed.

29

I make it home in a daze. My mind set on an endless loop, rolling from incredulous to bone-shivering petrified to slightly excited to ready to curl up in a ball and never move again. But amidst all that, one universal question remains unchanged. How could this have happened?

To me.

I'm a doctor. An OB-GYN. I am the champion of safe sex and birth control.

If it were any other circumstances, it would be an insufferable embarrassment.

Icy fear lingers on my skin, the heat of the Boston night doing nothing to warm me. My thoughts are frazzled. My body no longer feeling like it's my own.

But as I enter the condo, Carter's condo, I'm hit with something else. A deep pang in my gut, twisting uneasily as it seems to burrow into my marrow. There is something bigger, scarier than having a baby at a completely inopportune time in your life. Telling the guy you've only been dating a couple of months that you're knocked up with his kid.

I'm a Lifetime movie cliché without the benefit of this being fiction.

Nerves assault me as I shut and lock the door behind me. The condo is dark and completely silent. "Carter?"

No response and it's just now that I remember he's out with his brothers.

I head straight for my room, strip out of my scrubs, and immediately get in the shower. For a few minutes, I manage. I wash and condition my hair. I wash my body. But when my hand hits my lower abdomen, that's when the tears start.

I don't even know what kind of tears these are.

The last few months of my life have been one thing after another.

No break.

Just one major life changing event quickly followed by the next. Tony. Knocking on the wrong door and then moving in with Carter. Sleeping with Carter. Having a seizure at work and now this. Never in my life have I felt so unsettled and just plain old scared about what my life and my future are going to look like.

What happens to my residency?

I don't even have a real place to call home.

I'm squatting at my boss-turned-lover's house.

Being pregnant only adds confusion to everything.

Christ, I haven't even told my parents Tony and I are no longer engaged because I haven't talked to them in months. Never have I needed a mother's advice more than I do now, but I can't go to mine and I sure as hell can't go to Octavia Fritz.

Carter and I are too new for this. If we were ever going to work before, I don't see how that can happen now. What if he doesn't want this baby? What if he doesn't want me the way I hope he does? What if I fucked us up? I've been so afraid of jumping into this thing with him and now here we are and... What if in my attempt to pump the breaks I wounded his pride, and all he'll ever want from me is sex until he grows bored and moves on?

No. Carter wouldn't abandon a baby. His baby.

But where does that leave us?

I sit on the shower floor, knees drawn up, head in hands, crying until the water runs cold. Until I'm shivering and wrecked and exhausted and done. Just so fucking done with everything.

I can't even call Oliver because he's Carter's freaking brother. Oliver will be an uncle to this child. I take comfort in that. In knowing this baby will have a clan. A Fritz clan who are fiercely loyal and endlessly loving. Regardless of what happens or doesn't happen between Carter and me, this baby will have a dad who loves it, uncles and aunts and cousins and grandparents too.

And no matter what, I'll be okay because I have no choice but to be.

I throw on an old tank top and a pair of boy shorts and crawl in bed, tucking myself deep under the covers. Tears continue to fall like my body doesn't know how to stop them. And I toss and turn. No position is comfortable, and I can't just lay here.

I have to do something to stop these thoughts.

Clamoring out of bed, I throw the blankets off and storm down the long hallway into the kitchen. I flip on the lights and then slam open cabinet after cabinet. Crunchy peanut butter. Oreos. Fluff for sure. Popcorn. Definitely need popcorn. And where the fuck are the gummy worms I've been hiding?

If Carter threw them out, I will... found them. Crisis averted.

I pop the bag of popcorn in the microwave and while that's popping up to crunchy buttery perfection, I head for the fridge. Leftover sesame noodles with spicy chicken. Absolutely. Oh, and lemonade. That's for sure.

Once the popcorn is done, I dump it into a bowl and then survey everything I have littered on the countertops. No way I can carry all that all the way down to the media room. Especially when there is a huge TV in his family room that is right there.

It takes me four trips plus one to the bathroom before I'm able to start up the movie.

Knocked Up isn't an option. I mean, let's face it, they make my entire profession look like bumbling, stupid idiots. And What to Expect When You're Expecting can go fuck itself sideways. No one wants to be mocked by a stupid romcom when their life is in so much upheaval. So Juno truly is my only option. If a sixteen-year-old girl can figure her shit out when she's pregnant and the adoptive mother decides to raise the baby alone then surely I'll be fine.

I'm halfway through the movie, gummy worm a half beat from my lips when the door opens and Carter comes strolling in. He glances around until he spots me, sitting on the sofa with an orgy sized pity-party of food.

"Hey," he says, a smirk dancing on his lips. "Rough night with Margot?"

A mirthless laugh bursts from my chest, but I can't form words, any words.

He saunters over to me, his eyes slightly glazed, and I know he's had a few drinks tonight. I can't tell Carter he's going to be a father when he's drunk. That's a sober conversation if ever there was one and suddenly my stay of execution is granted.

I look down at the candy in my hand and then back up to the television. Juno is meeting with the prospective adopting couple, and guilt swarms through me. I can't meet Carter's gaze, though I can feel him desperately trying to get me to look at him.

He removes the empty bowl of popcorn from my lap, setting it down on the table. His body slides in beside mine on the couch and before I know what the hell is happening, he's slapping the gummy worm from my hand.

"Hey," I snap but then he's on me, his lips all over mine as he pushes me onto my back.

"I can't kiss you if you're going to eat that disgusting crap and right now Grace, I have to kiss you."

His tongue slides in my mouth, the taste of whiskey and something spicy heating my blood to desperate degrees. My stomach dips as he shifts my leg to wrap around his waist, his thumb brushing my inner thigh. He grinds into me and goose bumps bloom across my skin, flushing my cheeks from the inside out. I shouldn't do this. I mean, I need to tell him what's going on.

But in this moment, I can't.

Tomorrow, everything for us is going to change.

I'm so afraid this will be gone, never to return. He's a little drunk and I'm a big coward and I need to feel him. Know he's real, here, with me. Whether it stays that way or not.

My tank top meets the floor and Carter's gaze drags heatedly up my body. Eyes clouded by such surprising emotion, it makes me nervous. Does he already know?

He rips his shirt over his head and then he's back on me, chest to chest, skin to skin. He leans forward and kisses me again. Hungrier. Dirtier. His lips are unforgivably fierce as they punish mine only to switch things up as he lifts me off my back, sits up, and forces me to straddle his hips.

Strong hands dive into my hair, holding me, caressing down my back, but his eyes are steadfast on the place where our bodies meet. His hard length, trapped behind his dark slacks. My boy shorts, nothing but a terrible nuisance that needs to be eliminated. But to remove either of them, we'd have to stand up. Shift. Adjust.

Instead, Carter unbuttons and then unzips his pants,

freeing himself. Cotton is shoved aside, cool air hitting my wet heat, and then he's inside me.

"Don't move," he rasps, his jaw clenched tight. "I want to look at you like this."

And look, he does. He stares at my face. My swollen lips. The blue of my eyes. Down the column of my neck to my breasts, swollen and achy for his touch. Past my still flat stomach and when they reach the spot just below my navel, I bite my lip, quivering.

He sticks his thumb in his mouth and then rubs the moistened digit along my exposed clit, watching with rapt attention at what that does to me. The feel of his large cock inside of me. The spike of pure pleasure he's supplying externally.

It's the most earth-shattering moment of my life when he starts to move his hips, a gentle thrust up, never slowing the motion of his thumb. My head tumbles back, a low, throaty moan catching the air. He rocks into me, and I clench my eyes shut, an attempt to stop the threatening tears from escaping down my cheeks.

My heart is splitting in half.

My body silently sobbing as he takes me, holds me, whispers dirty and sweet words into my ear and mouth.

There is no more me without him, and why did it take me this long to realize I had the perfect man all along? I've been so afraid of making a mistake, but that's all I've done. One after the other.

His hands cup my face, trying to force my eyes to his, but I can't. If I look at him right now, when he's being this tender with me, I'll lose it completely. As it is, I'm already trembling, barely hanging on. His thumbs brush my cheeks and I know they're stained with tears again.

"Shhh," he breathes against them. Warm lips kissing the wetness away as he speeds up his thrusts. "I've got you, sweetheart."

I clutch him tighter, my forehead falling to his. *Don't let go. Don't ever let me go.*

I could love this man. I could love him forever and never grow tired of it. Eternity isn't nearly long enough to spend with Carter Fritz.

I used to believe in that. In forever.

I used to have faith.

But how many times can someone lose faith and trust and love before it's rattled, its foundation cracked? I just know I can't let go of him now.

Carter tells me I'm beautiful. How sexy I am. How he's thought about nothing else all night but being buried inside of me. My eyes flash open and he's right there, right in front of me, watching me as if he was waiting for this very moment all along.

I cry out, overwhelmed and overpowered by him, my orgasm unexpectedly rushing over me. A guttural groan erupts from his chest, his arms encircling my back, crushing me into the hard grip of his body. The muscular planes of his chest. His face hits the groove of my neck, and he lets go, coming right here along with me.

Inhaling, I catch the heavenly scent of his skin and cologne. *Home.* They'll imprint themselves on my brain along with this moment, locked in my memories, never to escape.

Being with him... it's everything.

I blink my eyes open at the feel of his hands across my forehead and through my hair. I could tell him now. I should have told him before. But the breathtaking smile that lights up his face steals my breath along with my nerve and then in the next second, he's lifting me up, carrying me down the hall to his bedroom, wrapping me up in his arms.

Tomorrow, I think.

I'll tell him tomorrow.

I just need one more night like this with him before I ruin it all.

30

I don't even have to open my eyes to immediately recognize two things. One, it's not even dawn yet. Two, Grace is not in the bed beside me. I frown in disappointment, more than just a little tired of the patience game she's forcing us to play.

On the one hand, I get it. On the other, I'm ready to scream in her face, I love you, so get the fuck over it and accept it already.

Rolling out of bed, I check the bathroom before padding down the hallway into the darkness of the kitchen and then over to the family room. The mess of junk food from last night is gone and I wonder how long she's been awake or if she ever went to sleep when I did. I had fun last night with Kaplan and Luca, but much of my evening was spent nursing a couple of drinks while they either hit on women or women hit on us.

I don't want women.

I want one woman.

But something was different with her when I came home. For as much as the woman loves to pack away food and sugar, she doesn't typically binge out like that unless she's stressed or upset about something. Then there were the tears while we were making love. And yes, I know I just used that term and it's kinda corny and I hate the way it sounds, but whatever.

That's what it was.

I was inside her and I love her, so yeah.

But why was she crying and why isn't she in my bed this morning? Is she planning on leaving me? Ending this?

With a sudden surge of rising panic, I quicken my steps, heading down the hall to her bedroom. The door is closed, and I knock softly. When there is no response, I open it to find the blankets in disarray, but no Grace.

The exercise room, office, media room, all empty. It isn't until I reach one of the empty bedrooms that I find her, standing in the dark, pressed against the window, staring out at the muted sky, still thick with night. She's dressed in a T-shirt and yoga pants, her blonde hair hanging loosely down her back.

"Grace?"

She doesn't even stir, but I know she hears me. I cross the room, wanting to take her into my arms but holding myself back. If she's going to eviscerate me, I'd rather not be touching her while she does it.

"What are you doing in here?" I continue when she doesn't so much as acknowledge me. Her eyes are lost, unfocused, and for a beat, a different surge of panic hits me, jacking my heart rate up. "Sweetheart, can you respond? Are you having a seizure?"

Honestly, I have no idea if she is able to respond when she's having a FAS. I know she explained to me that she's completely conscious during them, but that doesn't necessarily mean she's able to tell me what's happening either.

I reach out, going to touch her face when she shifts to me, her eyes falling to my bare chest. She holds there for a beat and then meeting my eyes whispers, "Carter, I'm pregnant."

It takes me entirely five seconds longer than it should to comprehend the meaning of those words. And even when I think I understand them, I don't. She couldn't have said what I think she just said.

"What?" That's how brilliant I am. "You said…"

"Yes."

"No. You said you're—"

"Pregnant. Yes."

Tremors overtake my limbs, and suddenly I need to sit down. Only there is no furniture in this room. Nothing. My heartbeats turn hysterical and my hand flies out, clutching the window frame.

"How?" Another winner.

Blue eyes still locked on mine immediately grow glassy with tears. One. Two. Three. They start coming. My mind is yelling at me to do something. To grab her. To hold her. To kiss her. To wipe away her pain and promise her the world. But I can't turn those thoughts into action.

All I can do is stare at her, utterly mystified.

"Are you sure?"

She shakes her head. "I got dizzy yesterday and I didn't want to tell you about it."

"You got dizzy? Why wouldn't you want me to know?"

"Carter. You have to stop throwing my words back at me in the form of a question and let me talk or I'll never be able to get this out."

"Fine. You're right. Talk."

"I got dizzy, and I was worried something was going on. I don't typically get dizzy. Not even before a seizure. I texted Margot and we did some tests, and did you know they gave me Dilantin when I was seizing?"

I blink at her like I'm staring into the sun. It's like she's speaking to me in Urdu and I'm using Google to translate.

Nothing right now is making sense to me and I'm still five seconds behind before I can catch up.

I press my hand deeper into the window frame, praying it holds up upright when I feel like I'm about to pass out.

"Dilantin? Um. I don't know. I mean, maybe I remember hearing them say something about that, but..." Realization smashes into me with the force of a sledgehammer. "You're on Depo. They gave you Dilantin."

And I didn't think about it because why the fuck would I think about it? Grace was having a seizure and my heart was splintering inside my chest watching it happen. I didn't care what they gave her as long as they made it stop.

Fury pounds through me. I should have known. I should have thought about it. Anticonvulsants interfere with birth control. That's second year of med school. That's my job. To know what to prescribe to my patients and what to warn them about taking.

That's why she was watching Juno when I came home.

That's why she was eating the entire kitchen's worth of food.

That's why she was crying and that's why I woke up alone.

I don't know how to respond to this. As a doctor, we learn to temper our reactions when informing someone they're pregnant. That news is not always a happy one and I can't tell where she lands with it.

I feel like I let her down. "I let you down."

"No. It wasn't your fault. It wasn't my fault. It was a mistake. We both made a mistake."

A mistake.

No.

Pain flares in my chest and my thoughts stutter to a halt. A mistake? Fuck that. Nothing we create could ever be a mistake.

"We should have caught the Dilantin and we didn't," she continues, and I blow out a relieved breath. That's what she meant was a mistake. Not catching the Dilantin. Not the baby. Right?

It suddenly hits me that I'm elated.

Grace is pregnant with my baby. Unexpected as hell? Absolutely. A little scary? No doubt. But I love her, and I want her, and the idea of her growing something we made together inside of her is just...

"Did you do an ultrasound?"

She falls exhaustedly against the window. "Just blood work. So, you know, that might come out differently than the sticks. Those aren't always accurate. Especially with the medications I take."

It's insane. This feeling in my chest right now. It's insane.

"But it could be," I say, taking a step because I have to be closer. I have to touch her, and I do, taking her hand in mine and knotting our fingers together. "It could come back showing we're having a baby."

A tear hits her cheek, and she licks her lips. "I think it will." Her watery gaze meets mine, but in a flash, her expression grows resolute before my eyes. "I don't want you to think that I expect anything from you. I'm prepared to do whatever I have to do, but I'm not trying to trap you or force you into anything you don't want or aren't ready for. Just because I'm likely pregnant doesn't mean that you have to be involved or we have to be involved or—"

"I'm going to assume you're saying this bullshit because you're still processing this," I interrupt, irritated that she's even doing it in the first place. "You don't have to try to let me off the hook. I am the father of this baby. That means I'm as involved as a father can be. End of story. As for the you and I being involved, well, I think I've made it pretty damn clear that's what I want. What I've wanted all along, regardless of you carrying our child."

She blows out a breath, her features crumpling. She nods, mumbling, "How can you say it like that? So casually?"

I laugh. "Shock, maybe? I don't know. But I'm not freaking out about this the way maybe I should be. I was more upset over thinking you believed the baby was a mistake."

"Mistake? No. Unplanned? Most definitely."

"Not all surprises are bad. Maybe because it's you and it's me and it's us."

"Carter, I've completely dismantled your world since I stepped foot inside this condo."

"No truer words have ever been spoken." And I wouldn't change any of it.

"But that's what I mean. I don't want you to do this with me out of—"

I shut her up with a kiss. First on her lips then on her neck because it's right here and it smells good. Her pulse is thrumming a mile a minute. "Be quiet. Stop arguing with me. Turn off that crazy brain of yours that has a penchant for overthinking and sending your thoughts in the wrong direction."

A tired laugh escapes her lips. "It's a chronic problem with me."

"I know. So listen and listen close. I want to be part of this with you. I will tell you that every damn day until you believe me, but it's true."

Her forehead meets my chest and I clutch the back of her head, holding her to me. My lips meet the top of her head, resting there.

"I want that too," she whispers, sighs. "Okay. After the blood work comes back, I need to make an appointment with my neurologist. Find a doctor or midwife. Christ, there is so much to think about. So much to consider."

"Do we have a lot to figure out? Yes. Are we going to do that together? Also yes. I want you to have an ultrasound. I want to see what your blood work shows. I want you to start taking prenatal vitamins and—"

"And you are not my doctor or this baby's," she smarts, righting herself, arching an eyebrow at me like she's not about to take any of my shit. Only she's too fucking stubborn to listen. She already hid her dizziness from me, what else will she hide in the coming months?

"No, but I am your attending. Once we know for sure you're pregnant and things are going the way they should, we're going to have to discuss your schedule. You'll likely have to cut back some hours or some surgeries so that we know you're taking care of yourself the way you should."

With that, she shoves at my chest, forcing me back a step. "Don't you dare fuck with my career, Carter Fritz. I have worked too hard for too long to allow you to do that. You've already cut me back after the seizure, pushed me onto another attending while you took on Janet as your number fucking one. I know you'll only try harder to push me out now that I'm pregnant. Do you have any idea what that could do to me? To my career? How weak and inferior that will make me look? Do you not have a clue how much I love what I do?"

I can only stare at her, eyes squinting.

My silence incenses her further. "If you so much as attempt it, I will fight back with everything I am to the highest authority possible. I am a resident with two years left in my residency. It's the most crucial part of my education. Being pregnant and having a baby will not detract from that. I won't let you do it."

And then she's gone. Flying out of the room and out of the apartment with a slam of the front door. Shit. I seriously fucked up.

31

Sprinting down the hall, I throw on the first clothes I come across, grab my keys and phone, and I'm racing out the door after her.

What the hell did I just do?

I told a scared, vulnerable Grace, who just found out last night that she's accidentally pregnant, that I was going to cut back her work. Her. Work. The one thing she loves above all else. The one constant in her life. The one thing she's worked tirelessly for.

Everything she's accomplished, she did it herself.

She had no parental support or financial backing from them.

She got herself a full scholarship to college. Paid for medical school with student loans—loans I know she's still paying. Got herself a coveted residency position.

And I just made her believe it's all at risk because I'm a stupid fucking caveman.

Dammit, Grace. Where are you?

"Did you see which way Grace went?" I ask the doorman as I fly out onto the street, frantically searching both ways.

"She went up toward the park, sir. I asked her if she needed any assistance and she declined."

Of course she did. My girl likes to do it all herself because that's what she's used to. But she has me now. God, she's had me for so long, even when she didn't know it. Other than giving her a place to stay, what have I done to prove that to her though? To prove that she can trust me? Open up to me?

I dictate and demand and alter behind her back. Where I thought I was being protective, she thought I was being controlling. I was so afraid to tell her how I felt because I didn't think she was ready, and she ended up doubting me instead.

Everything I've done is wrong.

Except be with her.

Nothing has ever felt more right than being with her.

I have to apologize. I have to reassure her that I'll be her partner in this.

My feet carry me through the empty park, save for a few homeless people sacked out under a random tree. It's dangerous out here at this time of night and I hate the idea that she ran out into this darkness. I hate that I can't find her.

I call her phone only for it to immediately go to voice mail.

It's off, and that forces a feral growl from my throat.

I have no idea where to go and I'm not getting anywhere by searching on foot.

But after over an hour of searching by car and still coming up empty, I have no idea what to do. Everywhere I could think to go, I went. Oliver's house was pitch black, no movement or life beyond the curtains. I tried calling her a dozen times, all with the same result.

It doesn't take a genius to realize I said the wrong thing. I wouldn't cut her out of her career. I just don't want her to stress herself. Who knows what this pregnancy will do to her body and knowing Grace, she'll just push through because she feels that's what she has to do in order to prove herself.

But I handled it wrong.

Grace doesn't need any man saving her, but hell if I don't want to be the one she depends on.

Dawn takes over the sky, filling the passing landscape with hues of pink and gold, and I still can't find her. She hasn't called or returned my texts, so I drive west, out into the suburbs, knocking on the one person's door I can think of who might have the answers I need. Landon opens for me, his green eyes tired with sleep, his hair all over the place.

"What's going on?" he asks, worry now creasing his features when he sees it's me and I likely look like hell rolled over me.

"I need to talk."

He steps back, waving for me to enter and I head straight for the kitchen, because it's far from Stella's room and I don't want to wake my niece. I practically collapse onto a stool at the island, staring down at the smooth stone and running my fingers along the gray pattern.

Landon quietly goes about brewing coffee, never one to demand but always one to listen. I'm grateful he's giving me these few moments. I hadn't realized I needed them.

Folding my hands on the counter, I slowly raise my eyes to his. "What I'm going to tell you stays between us."

"Okay."

He turns his back to me and the sound and smell of fresh coffee filling a pot fills the air.

"Grace is pregnant." The words slide from my tongue, the admission easier than I thought it would be. "She just told me this morning after she found out last night. She was visibly shaken and upset to start with. Panicky, I think. She kept saying she didn't expect anything from me and shit like that. She thought I was going to cast her away because she accidentally got pregnant."

"Which you would never do. Whether it was Grace or another woman."

A smile attempts to flicker up the corners of my lips at his complete confidence in me, but I don't feel prideful. I feel guilt and remorse and agony that I made her run off like that.

"Don't go singing my praises yet, brother. I ruined everything. We were talking and it was going well. She was listening to me, and then I started to worry about her. She had already hidden the fact that she had felt dizzy. That's what led her to discover she was pregnant in the first place. But by her hiding it, I..."

"Turned into a macho dick?"

I nod. "Something like that. I mentioned how we were going to have to adjust her work schedule. Pull back hours and surgeries."

Landon slides a cup of black coffee in my direction, not even caring to ask if I want cream or sugar because Landon doesn't do that. You take what you get with him most of the time and are grateful for it. It sounds fucked up, but believe me, right now, I am grateful. He sits beside me, holding a cup of his own, blowing on it before taking a sip and then setting it back down again with a soft clink.

Finally, he exhales. "Alright. Let's start with the basics. How do you feel about her being pregnant?"

"Surprised. Thrown off balance. Scared. Happy. The idea of her having my children feels like a gift I never considered dreaming of. I love her. I love her like mad. But she's not on the same page with me on that. She hasn't been this entire time."

"You know that for sure?"

Do I? I don't know. Sometimes I think she's right there with me. Sometimes I look into her eyes, and I know she feels something for me. I know it's not anything insignificant either. Last night on the couch, we were tethered together, body, heart, soul.

Then she was gone when I woke.

"She hasn't wanted to be in a relationship yet," I go with

instead. "After what she went through with Tony, I think she felt it was too much too soon to try to tackle. Too many obstacles for us to overcome. Sometimes I think she feels her career is all she has. The only thing that matters."

"You remember what it was like to be a third-year resident. That *is* how it feels. Your career is your life. The thing that defines you most of all."

I know. And I just threatened to mess with it, having the power to do just that.

"How did you react when Reese told you she was pregnant?"

I wait with bated breath for his response to my question. We don't talk about Reese with him because he doesn't talk about her with us. Not anymore. Only with Stella and then only in the capacity of how much Reese loved Stella and how much he loved Reese. Landon's pain and guilt thrives inside him and nothing we've done has been able to help that.

"I was twenty and in college," he says with a hint of uncharacteristic humor in his voice. "I freaked out. Thought our lives were over before they even began. There was only one thing I was certain of and that was that I was madly in love with her. That only she could ever be the future mother of my children, so why not start popping them out young."

My heart hurts so much at the way he says that. A crushing vise we all feel whenever we think about all that Landon has been through.

"And now you have Stella."

He takes another sip of his coffee. Clears his throat. "Now I have Stella. And with her, the only remaining piece of Reese. It was definitely not what we planned, but I would never change how it happened or that I have Stella now. She's my world. The best part of my life."

"You made it through college. Through medical school and residency and a demanding fellowship with a baby, and then a toddler and then child. How did you do it? I mean, I know, but I wasn't around much. I wasn't here, so I didn't see it."

"I had help, Carter. I had a lot of help. I had Mom and Dad and I hired nannies and put Stella in hospital daycares. Having money helps and I knew that was the one thing I'd never have to worry about. Stella would never want for anything other than the mother she lost."

My head bows and I feel him grow tense beside me. Landon hates talking about this, but he's doing it for me. The love my brothers feel for me and the love I feel in return still surprises me sometimes.

He sighs, sliding the mug in his hand back and forth. "Truth, it was awful. I had just lost the love of my life and suddenly I was a single dad trying to get through medical school. I never slept. I hardly ate. But I did what I had to do, and I made it through. I thought about giving up, going into an easier specialty or leaving medicine altogether, but that's not the father I wanted to be for Stella."

"I don't want Grace to have to worry. But I worry about the extra strain and stress she'll put on herself and her body. She's epileptic. I'm terrified of what all those hours in the hospital and being pregnant will do to her and the baby."

"Is that what you told her?"

"No. I told her we were going to cut back her hours and surgeries. Now she's gone and I don't know where she is or how to fix this."

"By shutting your mouth and trusting the woman you love. By listening when she talks and considering her and not yourself. By showing her with your actions that she can trust you and open up to you. She's been epileptic nearly her whole life and knows what she's doing. She doesn't want to have seizures any more than you want her to have them."

He's right. I know he's right. The problem is, I'm not

thinking like a doctor. I'm thinking like a man worried about his woman. About his baby.

"A hundred says she's with Oliver. You came to me. She goes to him. She's smart and knows how to take care of herself. So put that part out of your head. My advice is to listen and talk, not dictate. Carter, you're the middle child in a family of six kids. You always had to assert yourself louder than the rest of us to be heard. Had to demand things in order to get us to listen—which we still rarely did. If you were Grace, would you want someone to sweep in and command how you should not only do your job, but live your life?"

I sit back on the stool, thinking about Grace. About how stubborn and headstrong she is. Persistent.

We're both alike in that.

Control is what we thrive on.

If I want to keep her, I must learn to trust her and vice versa. Something she won't do if I continue to stomp around, throwing my weight and position. If I had trusted Grace, she wouldn't have hidden anything from me because she would have trusted me in return. I told her I want her to be partners, and so far, we haven't done a great job in that.

We're still so new with each other.

Clearly, we have a lot to figure out.

But first, I have to convince her that things are about to change. No more bullshit. No more messing around. No more running. It's time she learned... she's *mine*.

I've successfully dodged Carter all day. After the tenthousandth call, I texted him back, stating that I was at Oliver's and that I needed space and time to think. I felt bad for ignoring him for as long as I did. I wasn't trying to hurt him—I'd never want to do that. It's just that everything feels like it's been parachuted on top of me, and I need a minute to breathe. A moment to regroup and get control over the situation that has zero chance of being controlled.

Him telling me that we were going to have to cut back my work schedule was my breaking point. I hadn't realized how close I was to hitting it until he dropped that on me, and I lost it completely.

I took an Uber down to Oliver's house in Chestnut Hill—thankful I was smart enough to leave with my phone and purse this time. At my call, he turned off the alarm and unlocked the front door for me. He didn't ask me why I was running to him in the middle of the night. He didn't ask me what had happened with his brother. He just gave me a hug and showed me to the guest room, knowing I wasn't ready to talk.

I spent the rest of that morning thinking things over.

Deciding what I want and how I want it and how I'll make it happen.

The bright side is my blood work came back. Everything is normal with the exception of my HCG (the hormone your body produces when it's pregnant) level that came back over 7500.

Pregnant for sure.

I went to the hospital this morning and repeated the test to make sure those numbers increase—hopefully double—from my initial test. Now I'm here, sitting in front of my neurologist.

I still have to find an OB or midwife. I have to think about what genetic testing I want done. If I want to learn the sex. But this appointment needed to come first. I need to come up with a safe plan for this pregnancy that takes my epilepsy into consideration. I also want to know if it's safe for me to work. If he tells me it's not, I'll listen.

It'll break my heart, but the baby comes first.

"I appreciate you squeezing me in," I tell Dr. Bates, sitting up straight in his office chair that feels more like what they electrocute people in.

"It's my pleasure. Tell me what brought you here today. Have you had another seizure?"

"No. I'm pregnant. About six weeks along."

"I see." He sits back in his cushy office chair, rocking gently. "And you're concerned about how your epilepsy will affect the pregnancy?"

"Yes. I want to know from a neuro standpoint what precautions I should take. What things I'm still safe to do."

"Proper seizure control is the primary goal in treating pregnant women with epilepsy. That said, many of the medications we prescribe are dangerous for the growing fetus. Some interact with essential vitamins like folic acid. Psychological, hormonal, and pharmacokinetic changes in pregnancy may escalate seizure activity. But other than that break through seizure you had and taking as needed benzos, you haven't been on regular medication in about a year."

"I'd rather not start on anything new unless I absolutely have to."

"No. I don't advise it. The loading doses of those medications alone aren't safe. Your third trimester is another issue, as I'm sure you know, but we can address that when it gets closer and see how your body is responding to the pregnancy. Honestly, your best course of treatment right now is to continue exactly what you've been doing these last four years. Exercise. Eat well. No alcohol or drugs, but that's a given with your pregnancy anyway. Sleep when your body tells you it needs it and then get some extra whenever you can. Be warned, if you have any concerning symptoms, mild or severe alike, we will have to readdress this plan. I'd like to get regular EEGs. Say once a month just to confirm we're on the right track."

I blow out a breath only to suck one immediately back in. My hands clasp onto the wooden arms of the chair, white knuckling the ancient timber that creaks beneath my grasp. "What about work?"

He grins knowingly, reading my trepidation for precisely what it is. "I don't see why you can't continue your residency as you've been doing. I wouldn't sign up for extra shifts and you will require extra breaks, rest, and snacks, as I mentioned. But you've been doing this for two years already, Grace and medical school prior to that. Your body is used to the rigors of your practice. I think you should be just fine."

I walk out of his office feeling exalted. Vindicated. There's no turning back now. Passion and love. Both of which I desperately hope Carter is still on board with.

Still, I can't find it in me to call him. I'm angry. I'm hurt. His words, his previous actions after my last seizure, none evoke a great deal of trust. I know I need to communicate more, I own that, but he has to stop trying to control and take over everything I do. Trust is a two-way street and neither of us has breached that divide yet.

It's as if everything Janet said to me about Carter was dead on right and I cannot let that stand. I won't. If he wants to keep me, he's going to have to work with me, not against me.

First, I need to tell him it looks like Luna Longbottom is definitely pregnant, likely six weeks along. I need to tell him a lot of things. And while every fiber of my being aches for him... I'm lost in fear. Fear that he will continue what he's already been doing—pushing me out. Fear that by doing that he'll make me choose—my career or him.

What if falling so hopelessly for Carter, giving him everything that I am, turns out to be my biggest mistake of all?

It might be.

It truly might.

But I refuse to choose one or the other. I want them both.

I have to take a leap of faith. He says he's wanted me all along—deep down I know he has. I've been the hold-up. Not anymore. I'm ready. Even before I found out about this baby, I think I was there. It took me a while, battle wounds take longer to heal and even after they do, they leave scars.

But I can't let the scars of my past dictate my future.

I'll miss too much by doing that.

I'll miss out on Carter and that would be the biggest mistake of all.

I meander my way through the farmer's market, lost in my introspection. About this baby. About Carter. About what the next chapter of my life will look like. It's a lot to take in. Nearly too much to process. Especially with so much uncertainty looming. By the time I decide I'm ready to go home and face Carter, it's well past late.

I stop at a Dunkin Donuts since I'm looking for quick and easy and grab a muffin, eating it on my way home. Not exactly the best or healthiest of dinners, but starting tomorrow, that will all change. I'm going to eat regular meals. Healthy meals—no more junk unfortunately. I'm going to do whatever I have to do for me and this baby.

For all of us.

My thoughts battle, my nerves war as I finally open the door to the condo. I have no illusions. He's supremely pissed off that I ran out on him and then didn't pick up when he called. I was too fired up and anything that would have come out of my mouth in that moment, would have only hurt us more.

No. This distance was essential.

It got my head and my heart straightened out. Allowed me to think on my own without anyone else's thoughts or opinions weighing me down.

I step inside, locking the door behind me and dropping my keys in the small bowl on the foyer table. My heart thrums out an uneven beat as I slip off my shoes and quietly pad toward the kitchen and great room. Carter is standing there, his hair in disarray, wearing nothing but a pair of flannel pajama pants.

The look in his eyes pulls me up short. They're breathing fire and thunder, loud and explosive without him even having to say a word. The air changes, crackling with turmoil, my breaths coming out choppy.

He jerks forward, like he's ready to launch at me, only to stop short. He's blazing with intensity, with lust, with love, I think. But beneath all that, lurks the questions. The threat of potential heartache. I stumble back a step, colliding with the wall behind me. I'm not sure what I was expecting, but this level of standoff wasn't it.

No turning back.

"Carter," I start, licking my lips. "I—"

In a second, he's in front of me, his dark eyes consuming my vision as his fingers ghost over my lips. He doesn't say anything. Just shakes his head, but the meaning is unmistakable.

Not yet. Not tonight.

I worked myself up, created the perfect script in my head, but he doesn't want to hear it. My face burns, scorching my eyes and the tip of my nose as I do everything I can not to cry.

Tremors overtake my knees and just as I'm about to shove him away and run, he whispers, "Come with me." Fingers grasp mine, gently squeezing. His voice is low and smooth, but it hits me so deep it compels me to allow him to lead us through the kitchen, down the hall, and into his bedroom.

I glance around, finding my robe hanging on the back of the open closet door and I'm positive I didn't leave it there the last time I wore it. Upon entering the bathroom, a gasp flees my lips. All of my things are in here. My toiletries, hairdryer, all of it.

Did he move me into his room?

Something about that alleviates some of the unease from my chest.

Carter wants me.

He knew I'd come back. He was giving me space and time. Precisely what I asked for. And as he starts the shower, it seems he's giving us a little more. No words tonight. Just simple, straightforward movements and actions that feel anything but.

He undresses me, taking care to remove my jeans and underwear, kissing and caressing my lower belly as he goes. My stomach quivers at that, those tears threatening once more. My shirt and bra are next and once I'm completely naked before him, he strips down too, starts the shower, and guides me in under the warm spray.

My eyes fall closed as his hands rake through the tresses of my hair, wetting them and massaging in shampoo. His shampoo, though mine is now directly beside his. My caveman is staking his claim, branding me in his scent, and I have no complaints about it. His brand of possession swarms my chest until I have to gulp for air. It's consuming. Raw. Passion-filled and without mercy.

It makes my bones ache and now I can't stop the tears.

They fall, some silent, others not.

Carter doesn't stop. He washes out the shampoo and starts in on the conditioner. His body wash is next, touching, caressing me with scented suds without lingering. There is nothing sexual about this. It's purposeful and that hits me on a different level.

Carter and I have been ravenous for each other from the start.

He moves me in here, to his room, but he hasn't kissed me. His heated eyes have sought, but they've not explored. Is this him proving he wants to take care of me—that he wants me for more than just sex and fun—or is he done with that side of us because I got angry and ran out and now he's just playing the role of the baby daddy?

I shudder and shake, wanting answers to my questions, but refusing to put sound to them. He's not speaking. Not a word or a sound. Only the water slapping against the marble and my tears breach the silence.

I came home tonight, ready to fight for him, to tell him I was ready and that I want this. Him. And now here we are, and I don't... I'm doing everything he said I do. Overthinking and allowing my thoughts to stray to bad places. But he knows I do this. He knows! And he's still staying silent, not allowing me to speak.

The water abruptly shuts off, the kiss of the cool air-conditioned air hits my skin, making me explode in goose bumps. Carter swathes me in a fluffy white towel, another for my hair, and then he's gone, a towel around his waist.

When he returns, he's dressed in boxer briefs and nothing else, but he has one of his T-shirts and a pair of my panties. Nothing special. Just a plain satin thong, since those are all I generally wear.

I can't meet his eyes.

I can't meet my own in the mirror as I brush my hair and teeth.

This is not how I saw any of this going. I expected quick words and sharp tongues. I expected heat and passion and love. Carter is achingly tender and it's throwing me off completely. On any other night, I would welcome this, but not tonight.

"Carter?" I finally manage as the lights are off and we're in his bed, his arms around me, his chest to my back.

"Shhh," he shushes. "Not tonight, sweetheart. Tonight we're just going to get some rest. We need rest."

He drops a kiss to the crook of my neck and then settles in, holding me, forcing my mentally and physically exhausted body to eventually succumb to sleep. Leaving me bereft. Reeling. Grappling with more questions and no answers.

Scared that it's too late to fix this.

Especially when I wake up alone and realize he's already gone.

Stepping out of the OR, my last patient of the day needing a C-section, I scrub out, taking a quiet moment to do my breathing exercises. I haven't felt dizzy all day and I think it's because I've been hydrating like a madwoman and eating more snacks than I typically would have.

But now that my day is done, I'm not sure where I should go. What bedroom to sleep in if I do go back to Carter's. One thing I know for sure, we have a lot of talking ahead of us. I don't know what happened last night. What that was. Why he wasn't there this morning.

We saw each other at work today, playing cat and mouse, him doing his thing and me doing mine. He never sought me out. His only words to me today were asking if I was feeling alright when I was gobbling down a protein bar and chasing it with water.

I gave him a nod, and he gave me one in return, and that was that.

He's given me the space I requested. Too much space. No more calls. No more texts. No more seeking me out or kissing me into oblivion in a hidden corner during a stolen moment. The first time he's ever done as I asked, and I can't stand it.

I want to chase him down in the hall, corner him, and beat him up while kissing him crazy. I want the man and I'm angry with him and scared and confused and just fuck. I feel like a broken goddamn record. Scared and confused is all I've been since I ran out on Tony.

Screw this. I'm going home. Back to his place. I'm making dinner and then we're talking. We're figuring this out before this Cold War turns into something else. Estrangement.

Just as I turn to leave, a hand clasps my arm, dragging me along the hall in the direction of the locker rooms. Carter releases me, pointing harshly in the direction of the door. "Go shower. Get Changed. Do it now."

Okay. This stops here.

I step into him, staring up into his savagely handsome face and intense dark brown eyes that never fail to make my body shudder in the best possible way.

"Carter, you and I need to talk. Not fight. Not stay silent. Please listen to me."

He glares, grabbing the back of my head and dropping his lips to my ear where he breathes out harshly. "Go shower and put on whatever is in your locker." With that, he storms off and I have to admit, he is pretty damn hot when he's all worked up.

Still, if this is how he's going to be, we're going to have a long night ahead of us.

That is until I peer in my locker and discover the slinky red dress and matching heels with matching soles. No bra. No panties. Though I know I had a set in my locker. Hell, I had a whole slew of other clothes in here.

Carter Fritz apparently wants to play dirty tonight and I'm all for it.

I shower, taking care to shave my legs and then blow out my long blonde hair. Makeup is next and I'm still in my towel. I may put on that dress sans undergarments. I might even be wet the entire night because of it regardless of whether he touches me or not. But I'll never let him know I'm anxious for it by rushing through.

No. The domineering and prickly bastard deserves to wait.

But the moment the luxuriously silky fabric slides down my body, I know I won't be able to play it cool the way I hope. The dress is designer, expensive, contouring every curve of my body to perfection. The material hits my mid-thigh, my lower back, and the dip between my breasts with absolute precision. The sexy-as-sin heels adding height as they make my legs appear miles long. I don't even care that I was on my feet for twelve hours today and that these bad boys pinch my toes.

Now I have to walk out of here looking like this. I feel like I should put on my lab coat over this so no one sees, but Carter must have taken that too.

I paint my lips red, giving them a smack before I wink at myself in the mirror.

What is it about a hot dress and a killer pair of heels that undeniably makes you feel beyond sexy? Or is it the man who bought them for me, giving me no choice but to wear them since every other stitch of clothing was missing from my locker.

Carter is waiting for me, standing against the opposite wall and when I get a good look at him, all the air leaves my lungs. He's showered too, wearing a dark suit, a white button-down and no tie. And let me tell you, the man can *wear* a suit. It's like the thing was custom made for his body—which it likely was.

His dark hair is still damp, brushed back off his smooth face, his sharply angled jaw locked tight as his heated gaze sweep over me. He pushes off the wall, stalking toward me with a predatory gleam to his eyes. His hand drags around my waist, sliding up and catching the line of bare flesh of my back.

"Carter," I hiss, glancing frantically around, only to find the hall empty. "You're going to get us caught."

His mouth hovers over my lips, breathing into me without touching. "You look good enough to eat. And knowing you have nothing on under this dress is going to have me hard all night." His hips thrust into me, proving just how hard he is, and I whimper in response. Soft lips fall to the crook of my neck and then he takes my hand, intertwining our fingers. "Ready for dinner?"

Dinner? Is he kidding?

"Are we talking actual food?"

"You said we need to talk." A wicked smirk quirks up his lips. "Besides, I thought we'd play a little first."

I have no idea what that means, but I quickly learn when we reach the new casino at the Boston Harbor. I also learn Carter has a plan for me. A plan to torture me. I'm starting to understand why he left me without undergarments. Why he didn't speak to me last night and vanished this morning.

Punishment.

From the moment we step out of his car, Carter's hands are all over me. His touch, seemingly innocuous to everyone we pass—on my lower back, across my shoulder, skimming down my spine—sets off every pleasure sensor in my body. He knows it too. There is no fooling him when it comes to the way I react to him.

Every tremble and quickened breath he feels and hears.

His hand sweeps across my shoulder, along the nape of my neck, taking my hair with it and setting it on my opposite shoulder. His lips trail up my now exposed neck. "Should we gamble a little before dinner?"

I'm ready to kill him.

"Whatever you want." My voice is embarrassingly unsteady.

He grins against me, his tongue coming out for a swipe and

my nipples tighten painfully. I glance down, noticing how they went from barely noticeable to the turkey is done.

"It's torture, isn't it? Wanting something you can't have," he murmurs against me.

A shiver runs up my spine as his eyes rove up and down my body with so much heat I practically ignite into a ball of flames right here in the casino.

"I knew you were punishing me," I accuse.

"No sweetheart. This is just foreplay. The punishment comes later."

Oh boy.

"What's your game?" he asks, morphing back into a carefree version of himself, his arm panned out before us. He's serious with this.

I narrow my eyes. "I think that's my question right now. What are you doing?"

"Enjoying the evening with you. Are you not having a *pleasurable* time?" Rough knuckles swipe down my arm, his thumb coming out to graze the side of my breast.

"I hate you."

He chuckles, guiding me over to the main casino floor that is teaming with action. The lighting is muted, soft almost, aiming for luxury instead of gaudy. Even the slots aren't the typically loud, clanging ones.

"Craps? Blackjack? Roulette?"

"Carter?"

"Hmmm. Not much of a gambler, then? Too afraid to take a chance and lose? Here." He slides his wallet out of his back pocket and removes a stack of bills, all hundreds. "Go pick one. Place a bet. Then we'll have dinner and talk."

I stare at the wad of cash in his hand. He has to be joking.

"I can't... no. I can't do that."

"Sure, you can. It's just money."

I stare into his eyes and then around the room.

"I've never done this before."

"What's your favorite number?"

I lick my lips, my heart rate jumping even higher as he stands before me, staring down into my eyes. "Eight."

"Eight," he parrots. "Eight it is." Taking my hand, he walks me toward a roulette table, just as the dealer is getting ready to drop the white ball onto the moving wheel. Players are sliding different colored chips around, stacking them on various numbers.

"Carter. We can't do this. This is crazy. No one ever wins these things. The odds are like..."

"Thirty-seven to one," Carter supplies. "I know. But sometimes it's worth playing even if the odds seem stacked against you. Would you rather go with black or red instead of a number? Feels like playing it safe to me, but it's your call."

"I..."

Carter takes my hand and thrusts the money into it. "It's yours, Grace, and I don't care if we win more or lose it all. Take a risk."

Take a risk. Not something I'm particularly good at.

"Okay." With the money crunched in my hand, I place it down on the green felt.

The dealer splays it out, counting the bills. "Changing out twelve hundred dollars." *Twelve hundred dollars?!*

Suddenly a pile of chips are dropped before me, and I move quickly as the ball spins around the wheel a mile a minute, placing half the stack on eight and the other on red, hoping this will improve our odds and we'll win something.

"No more bets," the dealer calls out and my heart thunders in my chest. Never in my life have I been this reckless. Not with money or anything else. My parents had plenty of money, but I never felt like any of it was mine. I was always their burden. The second I hit eighteen, they were done with me, never looking back.

I know what Carter is worth. I mean, at least what their family is worth—they're twelfth on Forbes' list of wealthiest people in the world. The Abbot-Fritzes are insanely wealthy. Mega billionaires. But I never think of them that way. Oliver has always been Oliver and, well, Carter has always been his older brother or my attending or now my...

He steps in behind me, pressing my body back into his. Into his still hard dick that lines up so perfectly with the crease of my ass I'd moan right here if I wasn't so goddamn nervous.

"I can't watch."

"Open your eyes and watch," Carter demands, his cheek resting beside mine. "This is how I feel every time I'm with you. Heart racing, palms sweaty. You're a bet I never know if I'll win or lose. You push me well past my comfort zone, nearly to the point of pain. You drive me mad. Terrify me to no end. And no matter what, I always say and do the wrong thing with you. But you're a high, Grace. A fucking high. A risk worth taking over and over again."

Jesus. This man. "Carter."

"I want you. I want our baby. I want it all. None of this life is worth anything to me if I don't have you. Take the risk with me, Grace. Stay. No more running. Let's stack the odds in our favor. I promise it'll be worth the gamble."

Just then the ball bounces, clicking and clacking along the numbers, jumping from one to the next. I tense up, my teeth clenching down on my bottom lip. A zing of excitement catapults through me just as the ball lands.

"Red thirty-six," the dealer calls out and I jump up and down with a squeal, spinning around in his arms and throwing mine around his neck.

"We won. Thank God." I laugh into him. "I was scared out of my mind."

"But you did it anyway and look how it turned out. You won."

I blink up at him, my heart growing so full. "I won." I won with him.

He smirks like Satan himself. "You got lucky with that, Doctor. Don't think that's how the rest of the night will go for you."

L ast night I reached my boiling point with Grace. I couldn't talk to her when she walked through that door. I saw it in her eyes. The fight she was ready to throw down but after spending too much time with her ignoring me, pushing me away, maintaining a distance that should never be between us in the first place. Yeah. I was done.

She fights her feelings for me—so goddamn terrified I'll be another mistake, another heartache she has to survive when at this point, I think it's pretty damn clear I won't be.

She took me by surprise coming home last night, but it was too soon and too late. I couldn't stay up all night talking and fighting with her. She needed rest, and truth be told, so did I. Words aren't going to do it with her. I could tell her I love her. Tell her I'm in this with her. But a woman who has heard all of those things before only for them to turn out to be a lie, needs to be shown that this time, it's real and it's forever.

No more dancing around. No more playing games. No more pretending.

"Your table is right this way, Dr. Fritz," the hostess says, her eyes blatantly eating me up as she shows us to the back of the restaurant.

"Thank you."

Grace's hand in mine tightens and I give her a squeeze before helping her into her chair.

"Will there be anything else I can get for you or your friend?" the hostess continues, handing us our menus.

Grace snorts at the word friend. "No, I think we're all set, thanks."

The hostess skulks off and I can't fight my smirk, hiding it with the menu I pretend to peruse. Grace knows I'm up to something, I haven't exactly been very cagy about that. I know she's mad at me. I know she thinks I've been pushing her out of her work in favor of another. I think she believes what I said to her the other night was more of that. But she doesn't know that's not the case. That I haven't been able to talk about it because some things are beyond my control.

Tomorrow will be a busy day.

"What looks good to you?" I ask as my hand glides under the table and finds her knee. Her breath audibly catches, her skin warmer than usual. She's completely naked under her dress and only she and I know it. "I was thinking maybe the filet?"

My palm drifts higher up her thigh until I'm resting my hand just under the hem of her dress. Her legs are crossed, and I push her leg off her knee, forcing them open the perfect amount.

"Carter?" she hisses. "What are you thinking?"

Always so goddamn afraid of getting caught. Of taking the leap and reaping the reward.

"No?" I ask, lowering my menu and my voice, tilting my head as if I'm genuinely giving this some consideration. "Bad idea? You think I should go with the lobster tails instead?"

Her cheeks are stained the most beautiful shade of rose, her lips slightly parted as she sucks in a breath when she feels my thumb glide back and forth along her inner thigh.

"I think—"

"Good evening," our waiter greets us with a pleasant smile. "Is this your first time dining with us?"

"It is," I answer, inching my hand higher. She tries to push me off and I squeeze her thigh, letting her know that's not gonna happen.

"Welcome," he continues, completely oblivious. "Can I start you both off with something to drink? A bottle of wine or perhaps a cocktail?"

"Grace?"

"Just some ice water for me," she rasps, having to clear her throat as she tries to squirm out of my touch, but oh no sweetheart, not tonight. Tonight I have the upper hand. Tonight I'm the one who is going to throw her off-balance. Out of her comfort zone. She's had my head and my heart all twisted up for nearly two months now. Hell, for over a year.

She's held my heart in the palm of her hand because I gave it to her oh so willingly.

I need her to feel that in return. For me.

I want her to burn and rage and die and live the way I have been for her.

I have to know I'm not fighting this never-ending battle alone.

I need her to trust me and be with me. Fuck, I just need her to *be* with me.

But for right now, I'm too fucking fired up not to do this. I want to torture her and pleasure her in the same breath. I want to have fun and be naughty and spontaneous.

"I'll have the same," I state. "Thank you."

In a flash, he's back, filling our glasses with ice water, all the while my eyes are locked on hers. Blue fire. She's both incredibly turned on and nervous as hell. Heart-stoppingly, breath stiflingly exquisite.

Once he's done with that, he asks if we'd like him to go over the specials and I tell him we need a minute. He moves on to the next table while I reach with my other hand, lifting my glass and taking a sip, sucking an ice cube into my mouth before removing it with my hand.

"First, I should tell you I'm sorry for what I said about your work. It's my natural instinct to run like a bull into a china shop and not think twice about what I'm doing. Landon told me it's because I'm a middle child. Whatever. I would still like to discuss this with you. Come up with a plan in case you do need to slow down a bit. But I will support you one hundred percent in your career. Always. I will never hold you back and I will always help you reach the highest potential for your talent. I got scared. That's all that was. But I've realized the error of my ways and I hope you feel you can talk to me about this. About anything. I trust your judgement when it comes to your body and your work. Please trust me in return with being open and honest about both."

She swallows, her face streaked with surprise.

That only grows when I place the melting ice cube on her inner thigh. A yelp springs free from her lips and she jolts back, tipping the high back of her chair. I slide the cube higher, the heat of her skin melting it faster and faster, dripping water all down her leg.

"You're getting me all wet," she squeals, and I can't fight my smirk. Hers comes on strong when she realizes what she just said.

"That's my goal, sweetheart. To get you so worked up and needy and desperate for me that you never run from me again. To show—*prove*—to you over and over again that you're mine. That I take care of what's mine."

"I hadn't meant to run. You said the wrong thing at the absolute worst time, and I freaked. I just needed time to think. Some space. You were being such an asshole about my job and the things I had to do, and ah!" she cries out as the cube goes higher, gliding up and down her bare pussy. She sucks in a shuddered breath through her teeth, her eyes wild as they cling to mine. Her hand launches out, gripping the edge of the table, tugging on the white cloth, and shifting our place settings around. "You're going to get us caught."

"So what? I don't care. No one will see anything I don't want them to see. You're mine, Grace. You're only for me and I want the world to know it. No more hiding. Learn to let go. Trust me enough to do that with me."

Up and down, I glide the ice, knowing it's cold, but also able to tell by her body's reaction just how good it feels on her swollen clit. In her hot opening. Before the cube completely melts, I remove it from between her legs, popping it back into my mouth and sucking on it.

Her breath catches, her eyes twin blue saucers of desire.

"Do you think you're ready to order?" the fucking waiter asks, and I can't do this here. I can't tell her all that I have to tell her, touch her the way I have to touch her when we're surrounded by this guy.

I stare at Grace, smiling. She smiles in return, a million things passing between us. "You know what?" I say to the waiter. "I think we're actually going to pass on dinner. Sorry for any issues this caused." I stand, tossing two one-hundred-dollar bills on the table and then I reach out for her. Grace instantly places her hand in mine and then we're running out, hand in hand, laughing and breathless.

I grab us food on the way home, and we take turns feeding each other chicken sandwiches and fries.

But the moment we enter the apartment, bathed in darkness, all that humor dies instantly. Tense air crackles between us as she takes a step forward and then another, her hands landing on my chest, palms flat and eyes on mine.

"I moved you into my bedroom," I tell her, though I know she already knows that. That was step one. "I want it to be our bedroom. And the small office next to it, if we decide to stay in this condo, I want to convert it into a nursery for the baby—once we know things are where they should be with the pregnancy. I want us to be a real us and I want us to be a family."

"I want that too," she says, and the words absolutely sideswipe me. Never in a million years did I ever think she felt that way back. I was gearing up for the fight of my life. "I know I've made it hard for you. I know I've been resistant at every turn. But it's only because I was afraid of how right everything between us felt from the start and I didn't trust my judgment. I've been walked out on, left behind, and disregarded so many times. All by people I loved who were meant to love me back. I couldn't handle that from you too."

With that, I scoop her up into my arms and carry her down the hall to my bedroom. Our bedroom now. I set her down by the window, kissing her neck before taking a step back. "Strip for me."

Her hands meet the thin straps of her dress, lowering one over her narrow shoulders and then the other. The material falls away, catching on her hips until she does a little shimmy and then it falls away completely, pooling on the floor.

I stare at her, drinking up every inch. So inconceivably beautiful it hurts to look at her. *Mine.* Then I'm on her, my mouth covering hers in a stolen kiss before I kneel to the ground, kissing up her thighs, over her mound, to her belly.

I look up into her eyes. "I hadn't seen you in years. I was doing my residency in Virginia, and you were either in New York or here. In truth, I hadn't thought about you much prior to that. You were Oliver's best friend and three years younger than me. But when I saw you on my first day as an attending, it was like the breath had been knocked out of me while someone simultaneously smashed me over the head. I was screwed and I knew it. Day by day, no matter how hard I tried to fight it, I fell harder and harder in love with you. It was miserable. You weren't mine to have."

Her hands thread through my hair, brushing back the strands from my face.

I swallow thickly and add, "But now you are. Now you're mine and I'm never letting go. I love you. I've loved you for so long, even when I had no right to. Grace Hammond, I've fallen so hard in love with you."

A tear glides down her cheek. "I used to pick fights with you just to get you to react to me. To talk to me and notice me. Janet has been starving for you, and I hate her for it. But you never looked at her. Never noticed or cared about her advances. You watched me and I loved watching the heat in your eyes as you did. The way you'd look at me in those few, rare moments, I was able to crack through your shell. I had no right to love you either. But I think part of me always has. I certainly do now. Carter Fritz, I've fallen so hard in love with you too."

Grasping her hips, my lips plant into her belly. The belly that's growing our baby. She told me in the car on the way home that her labs looked good. She told me all about her appointment with her neurologist yesterday morning. Fingers crossed things continue to stay on course. This is a time when being a doctor, a fucking OB-GYN at that, sucks.

I know every potential thing that can go wrong.

But wow. Fatherhood. I'm going to be a father.

There is a tiny life that is half Grace and half me. She and I are total opposites, features-wise. I'm dark hair and dark eyes and she's blonde with blue eyes. Who will this baby favor? Her, I hope.

Then I trail lower, kissing her where she wants me to, parting her thighs, my tongue sneaking out to lick her clit. We've been worked up all night—for days—for each other and now, after knowing for sure she's mine...

Two fingers slide into her as I ravenously eat her pussy. I can't get enough. I'm greedy for her. Insatiable. She moans, grinding herself deeper into my face. Rocking forward, her hand pulls on my hair as she works to keep herself upright. I move her backward, pressing her back and ass against the glass of the window and then I take her legs and swing them over my shoulders so I can deepen the angle.

"Jesus, Carter," she cries out, but I don't stop. I keep going, increasing the pressure of my tongue, fucking her with it over and over again. One of her heels slips from her foot, dropping to the floor with a clunk. Her other digs into my back, spurring me on. When I bought this pretty dress for her and those shoes, this is exactly what I envisioned doing to her.

"You taste so good."

"Inside me," she begs on a choppy breath. "Carter, please. I need you inside me."

With a growl, I suck her clit between my lips before I release it with a wet pop, lowering her feet to the ground and standing up to take her mouth as I undress. I hold her against the window and in one motion, I have her legs back around me and I'm inside of her.

Forehead to forehead. Eyes open and holding. Breathless gasps tumble from us both, my lips layered with hers. I set a sensual pace, swiveling my hips, stroking every inch and nerve ending inside her.

Soft hands grip my hard shoulders, her nails burrowing into my muscled flesh as I gradually increase our pace, our passion building, no longer able to be contained. Her legs clamp fiercely to my hips as she holds on, unable to do much else other than get fucked. The windows rattle and shake as I drive into her harder, deeper. Grunts and groans of pleasure escaping me as I build us up, bring us higher.

My hands are everywhere, gripping her ass, rubbing her clit, pinching her nipples, squeezing her tits. She moans, writhing against me, her head tilted back against the window as I plow into her like a man on the edge of his sanity. So tight. So warm. So wet.

So fucking made for me.

Her body clamps to mine, begging me to take her harder, deeper.

Our skin is slick with sweat, our bodies entangled, and I give her exactly what she wants, wrenching a cry from her throat. Sinking her teeth into her lip, she grinds against me, getting the friction she needs on her clit, and I stare down in awe, watching as my cock slides in and out of her tight pussy that grips me like a fist. As she starts to come all over me, convulsing with tattered screams.

Violent tremors shake through us, twisting her body and arching it into me as she loses herself completely. My lips claim hers, wild and messy, losing precision as I nibble at her while her moans grow louder and louder.

"Fuck," she cries. "Carter!"

"Yes! I'm there with you."

Losing my breath and my sanity, I fall apart. A throaty groan my only sound as I clench my teeth and fuck her through her orgasm that seems to go on and on, prolonging mine with it.

Just as she sags against me, I walk us over to the bed, collapsing us both while staying inside her. My hands roam her body. Her face. My eyes following each movement. I can't stop.

Forever, that's all we do with each other. Kiss and touch and caress and make love. Over and over, our bodies stay coiled. One.

"You're the only one who has me, Grace. Now. Always."

And just as Grace falls asleep in my arms, a sweet,

contented smile on her lips, I send up a silent prayer asking for this to last forever. Begging whoever or whatever this is where we start, never to end. All I know is one thing for sure, no matter what, I can't lose this. Not now that I've finally gotten her.

35

"I have to deal with a few things this morning," Carter says as the elevator car slows. "Will I see you for lunch?"

I shrug. "Who knows?"

"Let me amend that, sweetheart. I will see you for lunch. In the cafeteria. With Oliver and Rina."

"No," I gasp.

"Yes." He smirks in return.

"But it's too soon, Carter," I cry out just as the doors open. "We can't. People will see. They'll know."

"Things have changed. Leap of faith, Grace. Remember?"

That's all he says before planting a kiss on the corner of my lips, right here in broad fucking daylight I might add, and then sauntering off like he has zero fucks to give, and cares are only meant for the weak.

Still, I'm smiling in a way I'm positive I never have before as I step off the elevator, store my stuff in my locker and hit the floor.

But the moment I round the corner, going for the nurses' station to find who my patient is, Janet is standing there waiting for me with a self-satisfied gleam that is not to be ignored.

"You're done here."

I roll my eyes, plowing past her, leaning against the counter of the nurses' station while scrutinizing the board. Except my name is nowhere to be found on it. Not with Westerfield. Not with Carter. Not anywhere. *What the fuck?* Then again, neither is Janet's.

What the fuck is going on?

"I saw you. With Carter. Last night. I finally caught you." She's the cat who ate the canary, bones and all. "I was leaving the building and saw you kissing in the parking lot before he helped you into his car. Did you honestly think you could hide your illicit doings?"

I nearly snort at that. Where has she been? I walked out of here wearing red—sans undergarments—with the man in question by my side and no one so much as batted an eye. Likely because everyone has suspected for months without directly asking. Teasing. Poking. Prodding.

I never let them go anywhere with their teasing.

Because what he and I were doing was unethical.

I forced Carter to keep our secret, positive we wouldn't last and then I'd be attendingless and called one of the many stupid, archaic, female bashing terms. My career, respect from other physicians, all of it would have suffered greatly. No one just gets involved with a Fritz without repercussions, not even me. Especially when said Fritz is your boss.

Now everything is different. I'm living with him. He's my boyfriend. I'm carrying our child.

But by withholding our relationship, both of Carter's and my reputations are in jeopardy—mine more than his. Let's face it, I'm not only a woman, but I'm also a resident.

I rest my hand on the counter, trying to steady my breathing and rapidly beating heart.

"I'd say it was nice knowing you, but it wasn't," she continues, sidling up beside me and dropping an elbow onto the blue

Formica while enjoying her front row seat to my horror show. All she needs is some popcorn and candy. "I've told the head of the department about your affair. They're meeting now about it. Carter, I'm positive won't lose his job but you will."

No. Likely not. Carter and I aren't the first of our kind. When you spend sixty to eighty hours a week with someone, stuff happens. The problem comes from us hiding it. From me not switching supervising attendings when I had the opportunity. Still, likely nothing more than a slap on the wrist and a review of my work?

I don't know. There might be wishful thinking in that?

Especially when the smug grin on Janet's face has me rethinking everything.

I'm in my third year. I'm pregnant with my attending's kid. No other program in this city or even the surrounding areas will take me on as a transfer resident. Especially not with a tarnished reputation. The only thing I can do now is come clean about my relationship with Carter and let the pieces fall where they may. Leap of faith, he said. It's time I learn how to trust again. How to be the woman, the doctor, I want to be.

"You know what's sad?" I ask rhetorically, staring into her dark eyes. "You getting off on hurting others. You think what you're doing means you won? The truth is, Carter and I are very much together. That secret hasn't been much of a secret because he and I weren't very good at hiding our feelings for each other. Whether I'm here or not, that won't change. No matter what, you're still a less-than-mediocre doctor, requiring your parents' money to get you places, undercutting fellow residents when you could have been a friend and colleague, learning to be a top-rated doctor on your own merit. You set women back too many centuries for me to count."

"Grace, Janet." Carter pops out from the corner. *Speak of the devil.* "Can you both come with me?"

"Sure," I tell him with a confident smile I don't quite feel.

I'm scared. I love my job. I love this hospital. I love working with Carter. But at the end of the day, I know I'll be okay.

Janet's self-satisfied smile is still there, but her eyes show a different story than the one she initially tried to sell me. What an ugly world when women try to destroy each other.

"Of course, Carter."

Carter. His first name when he's only ever been Dr. Fritz to his face before.

"Can you please make a note that both Dr. Johnson and Dr. Hammond will be unavailable for the remainder of the morning?" he asks one of the nurses as she walks back to the station. She agrees and then he spins back around without checking to see if we're there.

He doesn't say anything as we walk. Offers nothing in the way of an explanation for this... I have no idea where we're going. It doesn't matter. I have no defense. I love my career, but I love Carter too. More. I love him more.

So I guess that means I'm willing to fight for this. For him. For us. For my career.

I take his hand in mine, not even caring anymore. I'm claiming him, right here for him to see and feel, and for everyone else to acknowledge. No more hiding. No more playing it safe.

He's worth the risk.

His surprised eyes find mine, his eyebrows at his hairline, but there's a smile there too he's trying to hide beneath his serious countenance. I give him a squeeze and he squeezes back, lifting my hand to his lips and kissing my knuckles before releasing me.

Janet hisses something under her breath but doesn't comment further. Her footfalls slap hollowly against the harsh floors, soulless and dejected as she now ambles behind Carter. Her confidence has waivered and whatever scheme she's playing at won't end how she wants. I open my mouth no less than ten times on our short journey, only for no sound comes out. I can only hope Carter won't be affected, but with Janet here, I can't ask.

"Right this way," he instructs, pointing down the hall when I go toward his office. "We're in one of the conference rooms."

"We?"

He doesn't reply.

"In here." Carter opens the door, waving Janet in.

It's the room where we hold M&M's (morbidity and mortalities), resident meetings, small conferences, and occasional pharmaceutical peeps trying to sell us their wares. Today is a different matter.

"Not you, Grace. You need to wait out here until we ask for you. They want to speak with Janet first."

I blink rapidly, sucking in a choppy breath. I can't see who is at the table inside. Both Carter and Janet are blocking my view. "Carter?"

"It shouldn't be too long," is all he says, but he's in total business mode. His expression is shuttered. All he does is point to the wall behind me indicating where I should wait, and shuts the door behind him and Janet. That's it. I'm forced to stand out here while there is a meeting on the other side of that door deciding my fate. And if Carter's wooden features are anything to go by, none of this is good.

My heart hammers in my chest, my legs jelly as I slowly coast to the wall before dropping against it with a heavy thud. Racing thoughts swarm through me, my stomach churning as fear grips my insides.

I have no idea how long I stand out here, sweating and freaking out to the point of physical pain. All I know is, it feels like forever before the door opens and Janet goes storming out, her face a painted warship of rage.

Her eye catches mine and for a second I think she's going to charge me when Carter steps out into the hall and points for her to go. A shrill sound flees her lungs, her lips form a pompous snarl before she beats a path down the hall, forcing anyone in her way to scatter to the walls for safety.

What the hell just happened?

A glimmer of hope swarms through me as my gaze casts back, finding Carter standing there, ever the stoic bastard. "Grace? You ready?"

Do I have a choice? I want to ask.

And just like that, that glimmer of hope is gone.

Especially when I step foot into the room doing everything in my power to contain my gasp. The CEO of the hospital, Dr. Smart, the head of the surgical department, Dr. Rohrs, the head of OB-GYN and Carter's boss, Dr. Westerfield, all lined up at the table. Carter takes his seat beside Dr. Westerfield on the opposite side of the table, leaving me stranded and alone.

This is absolutely *not* how I saw this morning going.

"Dr. Hammond," Dr. Smart greets me. "Please, come and have a seat." He waves to the empty seat across from all of them, and all I can do is nod dutifully.

Dread pools low in my belly and I can't look at Carter though I feel his eyes. Imploring and impenetrable, they're making me nervous instead of filling me with reassurance.

"Dr. Hammond, do you know why we called you in here today?"

Are we back in grade school or are you a cop, I want to ask him. Who asks bullshit questions like that?

"Not exactly, sir," I reply, taking my offered seat and settling in, pushing myself in my rolling chair up to the oval-shaped table. Ready, but not even close to ready at all.

"Alright. Well, there are a few departmental matters we'd like to discuss," he continues. "They are of a very sensitive nature and everything we discuss here this morning must remain confidential. Even after a formal announcement is made."

"Of course."

Dr. Smart nods, seemingly mollified before turning to his right. "Dr. Westerfield, would you like to take over?"

"Sure." Dr. Westerfield smiles warmly at me, placing her hands on the table in front of her. "Grace, first, let me begin by saying that your work here during your residency has been exemplary. Your patient care has been top-notch as has your work with the residents, fellows, and other attendings."

"Thank you," I manage, my voice caught high in my throat.

"It has been on our radar for some time now that there has been animosity between Dr. Johnson and yourself. Complaints were registered by her in the months she's been here, yet we haven't received any from you."

I swallow hard and nod, my fingers knotting in my lap.

"Complaining about my fellow residents isn't exactly how I like to conduct myself," I state simply. "I'm here to work, to do my job to the best of my ability, not to be disparaging about the work of others."

"Are you aware she's made multiple disquieting allegations about you?" Dr. Rohrs jumps in. "Both personally and professionally."

I lift my chin. "I'm not aware of anything specific she's claimed. Only that she's made them as she already informed me of that."

A look passes between Dr. Rohrs and Dr. Westerfield before they return their focus to me.

"After Dr. Johnson's accident, we did a formal investigation at the request of Dr. Fritz. We interviewed everyone from the nurses to the patient and her spouse to other residents who were in the room when the event took place. You see, she had stated in her incident report that she was spread thin with her patient load. That the reason she 'fell'"—Dr. Rohrs puts air quotes around the word—"is because she was rushing, trying to keep up. She claimed you weren't picking up enough patients and she was carrying the burden."

"That's absolutely false," flies out of my mouth before I can stop it, my hands now gripping the underside of the table so I don't shoot out of my seat.

"That is precisely what Dr. Fritz told us as well," Dr. Westerfield cuts in. "A matter we'll discuss in further detail in a moment. However, the difficulty with this situation only began there. Especially with the most recent allegations Dr. Johnson has made against you."

I shake my head. "I don't understand."

"When Dr. Fritz first came on, we were aware of your relationship with his family and the potential conflict of interest with him as your supervising attending. We overlooked it as a potential concern at the time because Dr. Fritz assured us any personal relationship you had with him, or his family would not impact your work here."

My gaze flickers briefly to Carter before rebounding back to Dr. Westerfield. I lick my lips nervously, unsure how to respond.

"I would say this has remained true," Dr. Westerfield goes on. "Wouldn't you agree?" She twists her neck to Dr. Rohrs.

"Absolutely," she states emphatically, tucking her brown hair behind her ears and shifting in her seat. "Even when Dr. Fritz informed us of the change in your relationship status. Which is why we were so surprised by the concerns Dr. Johnson has raised."

Flattening a hand across my stomach, I attempt to brace myself for what I know is next to come. Wait... "I'm sorry, what?" My head snaps in Carter's direction though he is a perfect mask of indifference. He told them about us? When?

"Dr. Johnson's incident occurred prior to Dr. Fritz informing us of your personal relationship," Dr. Westerfield maintains, leaning forward and placing her forearms on the table between us. "But her report was filed after."

"I still don't follow," I admit.

"We had already conducted a review of your work, Grace," she informs me. "Of your evaluations, of your schedule, of your time with patients, of your work with your residents. All of it. So the allegations Dr. Johnson had made about you not taking on an adequate patient load didn't quite add up with our own report on your work. By the time her incident report came in, you had already been moved onto my team for evaluation while still receiving instruction from Dr. Fritz. This had been done since Dr. Fritz was no longer able to analyze your work objectively."

"Alright." I'm so confused.

"After we reviewed her incident report, and the interviews of others," Dr. Rohrs picks up where Dr. Westerfield left off, "we were concerned to say the least with what we discovered. As a matter of protection for the hospital, we shifted Dr. Johnson's schedule to allow for more one-on-one time with Dr. Fritz as we felt she needed more direct tutelage. As you can imagine, for legal purposes this was kept entirely confidential."

I fall back in my seat, rubbing at my mouth while staring at each of these doctors in turn.

No wonder I worked mostly with Dr. Westerfield and not Carter. No wonder Janet worked so many hours side by side with him. It wasn't because Carter was pushing me out or had lost confidence in me after my seizure. It was because he had told them we were together, and I could no longer be evaluated by him because our relationship posed a conflict of interest for him.

That and they knew Janet was a subpar doctor and needed to protect their asses. It makes sense now why Carter always blew me off about it whenever I tried to question why he was working with Janet and not me. He wasn't legally allowed to tell me anything.

Only Janet didn't know he had told anyone about our relationship. Hell, neither did I.

Which is why I automatically assumed the worst—especially with Janet filling my head with that.

Why didn't Carter tell me he told them? Oh right, because I asked him not to tell anyone and he knew I'd freak the fuck out. Yeesh.

"So when she came to us overnight with claims of you engaging in unscrupulous and scandalous behavior with Dr. Fritz, to use her words, we were, well, shocked."

I sit up straighter. "I can explain. Dr. Fritz and I have always tried to keep our personal relationship separate from work. What she saw was after our shifts ended beyond the walls of this hospital. When it comes to our work here, Dr. Fritz has always placed that first. Never once showing favoritism or treating me as anything other than his resident, equal with all others. I don't know specifically what Dr. Johnson claimed, but if any of it involves Dr. Fritz engaging in anything unscrupulous or scandalous, it's an absolute lie."

Janet can say what she wants about me, but us hiding our relationship was on my terms. Terms Carter clearly didn't abide by. I'm the one at fault. Not him. I won't let her take him down with me. If that's my fate, so be it, but I will not let it be Carter's too.

I suck in a breath, holding it tight in my lungs.

"Yes." Dr. Westerfield agrees emphatically, glancing first at Carter and then over to Dr. Rohrs. "Now you understand why we're meeting today. This situation is troubling indeed. Dr. Fritz has been transparent about your personal relationship from the beginning, even going so far as to continue your education while passing your evaluations over to me so as to remove any form of misconduct. Which is why we know everything she's claiming to be false."

I shake my head, totally, completely, utterly flabbergasted. "I'm sorry, I think I'm missing something."

"Dr. Johnson informed everyone in this room in the wee hours of the morning, I might add, that you're holding sex over my head in exchange for stellar evaluations and good recommendations for after your residency has ended," Carter states flatly. "She claims that you used my infatuation with you against me."

"Um." Yep. I might be impersonating a goldfish.

"She was obviously unaware that I had already removed myself from a position of power over you. Months ago. Our number one priority—as you stated on my behalf though that pact came from both of us—has always been and will always be patient care and we vowed from the start of our relationship that anything you and I engage in beyond the walls of this hospital would never interfere with that. There was no way you could demand stellar evaluations from me when I was no longer evaluating your work."

I think I blink about a thousand times.

"No." That's as good as I've got at the moment.

When the hell did Carter go and do all of this? Have my evaluations transferred? It makes sense with everything that's transpired. I've worked more with Dr. Westerfield since Janet's accident. I just didn't think much of it as she's the head of the department and makes rounds through all the residents, benchmarking our training. I was more consumed with the notion that Carter was freezing me out while taking Janet in.

"These latest accusations are the tipping point for us with Dr. Johnson," Dr. Smart states. "She claimed her initial incident happened because she was spread too thin with you not picking up the slack when we know not only is that false but that she had actually been changing the board herself to remove your name and place hers on there instead. You understand how dangerous that is for our patients and other providers. It's why we have protocols surrounding that sort of thing. Protocols she breeched which ultimately led to her mistreating her patient. We had been giving her a second chance to work on improving her behavior and performance, but after last night we can no longer do that."

My head is spinning like a top.

"I..." I have no idea what to say. I shake my head, sinking back into my chair and rubbing my hands up and down my face. "What's her future position in this program?"

"She has none," he informs me. "After the notes of this meeting are registered, we will be terminating her contract as a resident. She was made aware of this just prior to your interview. We gave her the option to switch to a lesser role within the department. She declined."

So Janet is gone. Not me.

"Grace?" Dr. Westerfield says softly, drawing my attention back to her. "We want to thank you for your continued dedication, professionalism, and discretion. We hope that in putting this situation behind us, we can all move forward in a more positive direction.

I meet their steadfast gazes and say, "Thank you. That is my hope as well." Then I expel a heavy breath.

How the hell did this turn out this way?

36

"I don't understand what just happened," Grace says to me as we make our way back toward my office.

I shut the door behind us, feeling yet another weight off my chest. I wrap her up in my arms, holding her supple body against mine. Her eyes, so pretty, so blue, gaze wondrously back at me like I'm a hero she never saw coming or knew she needed. But it was her taking my hand the way she did right in front of Janet and anyone else in the hospital who happened to walk by that stole my breath.

She's mine, is what she was telling me. She chose us. There are no more obstacles between us now. Everything is out in the open just as it should be.

And here we are, together on the other side of it.

"It's like I told you last night. There is no one else for me but you. That means I slay all who attempt to fuck with you. I destroy any who want to hurt you. You are who I kill, maim, and die for, sweetheart. And I will fight ruthlessly toward that death if it means you come out standing on the other side."

Doesn't she understand? Her body. Her love. Her soul. I'm crazed with her, well beyond the point of madness or obsession. And now that she's carrying my child in her, I am a man to be feared by, how I will fight to protect her.

"I love you," she whispers into me, pressing her mouth against mine, those words on her lips never failing to ruin me all over again. "My fierce caveman."

"You wouldn't have me any other way."

"Not for a second. But... how did you know what she was up to? And when the hell did you tell everyone you and I were together?"

"This was never temporary." I flick a finger back and forth between us. "I had always planned on more. And I couldn't be your teacher with you and I being more. So I told all of our supervisors and explained that I would continue on as your secondary attending since there was no one else available who could teach you as much or as well as I could but that I would no longer evaluate your work as your boss. Dr. Westerfield doesn't do as much teaching as she used to now that she runs the department, but she agreed to take on your evaluations. Once Janet got hurt and we realized what she had done with the board and how lacking her skills were, I didn't have a choice but to up her training."

"You said nothing to me."

I shrug. "I wasn't allowed. Plus, I really didn't want to hear about it. I swear, sometimes I think you pick fights just so you can hear yourself yell at me."

"It's like listening to an aria or a sonnet. Beautiful as it enriches and fills the soul."

I snort out a laugh, kissing the corner of her lips.

"What happens to Janet now? They said she was gone. What does that mean? I didn't think it was right to ask for all the details."

"She gets expelled from program number two."

"Number two?" Grace gasps incredulously. "I thought she transferred. I thought her parents bought her way in here."

"Oh, they did. But it wasn't the first thing her parents bought."

Her eyebrows scrunch together. "What do you mean?"

"There was something off about her from the start. Her lack of ability in the OR. Her not teaching her residents. Her never actually delivering a baby or if she did, there always being a complication. Then that woman who was hemorrhaging when Janet broke her wrist. That was the final straw. It never should have happened. After that, I did my research. She barely graduated medical school, much of her grades and reports were purchased by her family. In her last program, they only kept her on because of her parents' money until she had a poor patient outcome there. She left to come here before they could do much about it."

"Jesus," Grace sighs.

Grace's arms encircle my neck. "What a nightmare. But why isn't my name on the board?"

"That's because I knew this was going to happen this morning, but I wasn't allowed to say anything to anyone until they spoke with Janet and then you. Plus, there's something else we have to do. Something that if we don't do now, could have dire consequences in the end."

"What?" Her face dances with concern.

That's when the *knock, knock* comes on the door. "Carter?"

Grace's eyes instantly widen. "Oliver," she hisses under her breath. "You had Oliver come up here. Why? You said at lunch!"

The wary tilt of her head tells me she already knows why.

"Are they in there?" comes another voice from the other side of the door.

"Rina too?" she squawks.

I grin. "Do you want to face the consequences of *not* telling them? Especially Oliver? And if you tell him in the cafeteria, anyone could hear."

"Ugh. I wouldn't have minded waiting a couple of weeks."

She sags in my arms before retreating a step like she needs the space and the moment to get her head in the game. She flicks out her hands, pops her neck and then says, "Alright. Let them in."

The second I unlock the door, the two of them come toppling in, almost like they had their ears pressed to the door. "Dude," Oliver starts, shutting the door behind him. "Your floor is like a beehive with all this swarm and buzz. What the hell happened this morning?"

I launch into a whole account of the events of this morning. Well, the things I can talk about anyway. The hospital hiring on a resident like that, seeing potential dollar signs can be embarrassing and discrediting for a program and hospital if the word got out.

"But Dr. Johnson is not why we called you in here this morning."

Rina and Oliver exchange glances and then look between the two of us skeptically. "You're not getting engaged, right?" Oliver questions, a harshness to his tone. I don't think he wants me to beat him on that. I think he's dying to make it real between him and Amelia.

"No," Grace tells him, jumping right in with that when what I'm really thinking is, *not yet.*

"Then what's up?" Rina asks, sitting on the corner of my desk and staring at us expectantly with her big green eyes.

Grace gives me a quick, nervous side-eye before she marches over to Oliver who is leaning against the wall beside my hanging diplomas. She stands before him and takes his hand but fails to say anything. Instead, she looks like she might pass out.

"Honey, you're scaring the Jesus out of me. Whatever it is, just say it."

She goes to open her mouth when Rina cuts her off with, "Oh my god, you're pregnant."

"How the hell did you know?" Grace hisses at Rina.

"I didn't. I was kind of kidding. But what the hell else could it be?" Rina blinks, tilting her head. "Wait. I was right? You're actually pregnant with Carter's kid?!"

"Shhh," Grace snaps. "Christ, Rina, say it a little louder, would ya? I don't think *everyone* in the hospital heard you the first time."

"You're serious?" An incredulous Oliver pushes off the wall, standing tall over her. "You're pregnant? With my brother's kid?"

Grace swallows thickly and nods. "Yes. We. Um. It was certainly not planned, and still very early, but we wanted to tell you both. You know. So you know." She shakes her head at that last part, but still manages to hold firm.

Oliver, meanwhile, is a statue. A stone casting of my brother. I don't even think he's breathing.

"Wow." Rina hops off the corner of my desk and comes straight for me. "Wow," she repeats. "That's absolutely incredible. Congratulations. Are you happy?" she asks me. "You look happy."

"Zip it, Rina," Oliver clips out, still waging some sort of silent war with Grace.

"You zip it, Oliver. This is good stuff." Rina twists back to me. "You are happy, right?"

"The happiest."

"Grace?" Oliver pushes.

She places her hands on his shoulders, staring straight up into his eyes. "It's crazy. Unexpected as hell. But we're excited about it, and I hope you can be too."

He blinks at her, stunned. "What about your epilepsy?"

"I saw my neurologist already and we have a plan in place."

"So you're pregnant. And you're with my brother. Not just living together but together *together* and that means I'm going to be the uncle to your kid—not just in title, but for real—and once Carter mans the fuck up and marries you, you'll be my sister, again for real."

Grace gnaws on the corner of her lip, trying to hide her amused smile. "Yes. That about sums it all up."

"I wasn't asking. I was telling you. That's what's happening here, Grace."

Now she laughs. "Slow your roll, Uncle Oliver. That's what happening. Minus the whole marrying me thing. It's far too soon for that and truly, a woman does not need to be married to a man in order to have his child. It's a patriarchal, archaic notion, not to mention misogynistic."

"Agreed," Rina chimes in.

"And yet you all cry like fucking babies when we get down on one knee and put a ring on it."

"You'd know," Grace snorts at him. "Is that what Amelia did?"

"Damn straight. And I haven't even done it for real yet. Admit it," Oliver says, undeterred. "You love us. You need us. You just don't want to."

"I think that goes both ways, don't you?"

"Definitely both ways," I add, coming over to stand beside Grace, resting my hand on her hip and making sure Oliver sees my possessive gesture. Understands what I'm nonverbally saying. It's a guy thing that only he would get. It means I've got this. It means he doesn't have to worry because I'll always take care of her.

He stares into my eyes as I give him that promise.

So he knows, for me, there is no going back now. Only forward.

EPILOGUE

S ix weeks later

MY CROSSED KNEE bounces uncontrollably as I stare around the waiting room, glaring at the pea-green walls that remind me of the color of baby poop and the fish in the tank with the Nemo and Dori lookalikes, judging me for being this nervous.

"Dr. Hammond?" Dr. Rodriguez, the maternal-fetal medicine specialist, calls my name and I rise. "Are you ready to see your baby?" he asks as I approach him.

I glance up at the clock on the wall and sigh. "I guess."

He guides me down the hall, instructing me to hop up on the table, lift my shirt up to just under my bra and scooch down my leggings. "You know the drill," he says. "I doubt I have to tell you anything." He goes about tucking in drapes for modesty and to prevent me from getting gel all over my clothes.

Just then the door to the ultrasound room flies open and a harried Carter comes running in, wheezing. "I'm late. I'm sorry.

It took me forever to get over here. Then I had to sprint from the parking garage all the way across the damn hospital and the stupid elevator took forever. Did I miss it?"

"No. They were running late too."

He sags in relief, stumbling the five steps over to the gurney I'm now sprawled out on and falling into the chair up by my head. He kisses my forehead, his arm wrapping around my head and holding the hand I have resting on my chest.

"I'm sorry," he whispers in my ear. "It's not easy getting over here from our hospital when there's traffic."

I know it, but I'm not going through this with him again. I can't have this baby at our hospital. I know every doctor. Every nurse. Not only will my vagina be on display for my work colleagues, and I'll have to labor in front of them, but I won't get a moment's rest because they'll be all over us and wanting to see the baby after it's born.

No thanks.

Right now, I'm just relieved he made it. I know he is too. Carter has been nothing if not overly attentive to me and this pregnancy. If I end up staying late at the hospital, he either waits with me or I come home to find that he's made us dinner —something obscenely healthy of course. Then he proceeds to rip my clothes off, fuck me to the point of exhaustion, and then ensure I'm getting as much sleep as I can.

On nights I have to be in the hospital, he demands I take twenty-minute naps the way union workers get fifteen-minute breaks. Twice a day, plus lunch.

I know I told him I loved him, and I meant it, but with each passing day, it's like I had no clue what love was the day before. This man beside me obliterates it each and every day, not just telling me, but showing me over and over again.

I kiss the corner of his lips. "I know it's a pain but thank you for not fighting me on it."

Dr. Rodriguez squirts warmed lubricant onto my belly and

with a flick of his wrist, sets the ultrasound probe down on my tiny bump. "Here we go. Are we learning the sex of the baby?"

Carter snickers. "I have no idea how we won't see it if you're on that part of the anatomy."

"Probably true, but if you'd rather not know, you can look away during that part of the exam. I'll warn you in advance."

I look up at Carter whose face is hovering over mine. "Surprise?" I ask.

He grins down at me. "Hasn't everything so far been just that with us? I think we should keep the streak alive."

We both turn back to Dr. Rodriguez. "Warn us," we say in unison, smiling stupidly because that's how we seem to be lately. Stupidly in love. My first trimester has gone along shockingly well. Other than a few episodes of dizziness and nausea, I haven't been too bad off. I've been able to maintain my regular work schedule, delivering babies and doing surgeries.

Plus, well, there is the small fact that no one knows yet.

They know we're together. There's been no hiding it and no longer a reason to. But we've been holding off on telling anyone other than Oliver, Rina, and Landon, who Carter told that night I ran out that I'm pregnant until, well, this ultrasound.

The image on the screen comes into focus and there's my uterus, the walls thick with blood and tissue—a protective barrier for the baby that's chilling right in the middle.

Carter squeezes my hand as Dr. Rodriguez takes measurements of my uterus and blah, who cares. Finally the image zooms in and there it is, our tiny little thing that looks very much like an alien with a large belly and head.

Two arms. Two legs. Oh my god. "That's our baby."

Carter's eyes are glued to the screen, same as mine, but the side of his head drops to my forehead as we watch in awe as our little surprise moves around inside me. I only wish I could feel it.

"It's playing peekaboo," Dr. Rodriguez says. "Moving a lot.

Doesn't want to behave for... oh wait. Here we go." Then he zeros in on the heart and four valves moving just as the whoosh of its heartbeat echoes through the room.

We've heard it plenty of times—a sound that never gets old. My OB has done it in office, but Carter and I have done it many times just the two of us at home. Occupational bonus, we call it.

But this is the first we're seeing it. In all its glory.

"I should show Kaplan this."

I laugh under my breath. "No. He'll find fault and want to operate."

"It looks perfect," Dr. Rodriguez informs us. "Heart rate is one forty-five and everything is good so far. As you know, we don't do a full analysis until your twenty-week fetal survey, but for now, I'm happy."

"And what about nuchal translucency? How is that measuring?"

Dr. Rodriguez chuckles. "This is why I hate treating health-care professionals."

"Us too," I agree. "But I'm with Carter on this one."

He zooms away from the heart and goes about locating the baby's head and spine. He clicks some buttons on the keyboard, taking his measurement. "Looks to be about 1.8mm. Within normal range for this gestational age."

I blow out a breath I didn't realize I was holding. "Holy toast, this is stressful. I don't think I'll make it through the twenty-week fetal survey."

"You can relax. Everything appears the way it should so far," Dr. Rodriguez assures us. "But now's the time when you need to close your eyes because I'm going to check out the rest of your baby."

Ugh. I don't want to. I want to keep looking. I had no plans on having a baby for several years, and I'm still worried about what it will mean for the end of my residency or potential future fellowships should I want one, but I can't help but be excited, too.

I close my eyes, leaning back and not even two seconds later, Carter tenses.

"Shit," he says. "I looked."

My eyes fly open and I pull away from him, glaring. "You looked?"

He gives me a sheepish nod. "I looked. I couldn't help it. My curiosity took over and I thought I'd only open for a quick peek just to see its legs or something, but that's not what I saw."

Dr. Rodriguez clears his throat—to hide a laugh, I think—but otherwise stays quiet.

"So you know?" I snap.

"I know."

"Carter! Dammit." I smack his shoulder. "Now I have to know too."

He shakes his head, fighting a smile and failing miserably. "You don't. I don't have to tell you."

I roll my eyes at him. "Yeah. You do. You'll slip at some point. I know you." *Ugh!* "You know what? Don't tell me. If you got to see it, so do I." I turn back to Dr. Rodriguez. "Can you show me?"

He grins warmly. "Of course. It's right here."

I blink, staring at the blurry ultrasound image and then smile, my heart fluttering in my chest. "I had a feeling."

Carter laughs. "Me too. I would have been happy either way."

Dr. Rodriguez finishes his exam and then gives me some cloths to get cleaned up before excusing himself, asking us to meet him out front before we leave. The moment the door clicks behind him, I sag back, staring aimlessly up at the drop ceiling.

It's real now.

I mean, I had been taking my prenatal vitamins. Eating

well. Sleeping whenever I can because lawd, the exhaustion is something else. I saw my neurologist who said we're going to monitor me closely, but since we're not putting me back on any anticonvulsants—they're not the best for the baby—then I'll just have to keep on doing what I've been doing.

I've been following everything I should while simultaneously trying not to think too closely about it. I was waiting for today. For this moment, I think. My life from here on out will never be the same. I'm going to be a mother. Carter is going to be the father and while we want to do this together, we've only been together such a short while and—

"You're doing it again," Carter accuses. "Overthinking and allowing your brain to go to the dark side."

"I'm scared." Of so much.

Carter shoves me over on the tiny gurney that is definitely not built for two. Somehow he manages to climb on, twist to his side, and then lift me up, dropping me on top of him so my face rests over his steady heart. He kisses my head, running his fingers up and down my back.

"I was thinking you'd take six weeks off for maternity leave," he says. "I was thinking I'd take the six weeks after that off. Then, when the baby is a few months old, we'd put it in the daycare in the hospital. That way we can both go down and see the baby during the day. You'll likely even be able to take a break to nurse it. That would put you right at the start of your fourth year. But I'm attending, Grace. I have nothing left to prove."

"Carter."

"Just hear me out, okay? I've been thinking about this a lot. I want to buy a place in Beacon Hill or Cambridge, close to Rina and close to the hospital. I want it to be our home, not just a condo we live in. I want it to have a backyard where I can eventually put a playscape and the kid can run around. Where its siblings can eventually run around. I want to be what my father was to me. A dad. So my plan is this: after the baby is born, I intend to cut back my hours to two days in clinic and two days on the floor for surgeries and deliveries. That's it."

"What about me?"

"Your fourth year is your time to shine, Grace. And me and the baby will be with you the whole way. After that, we'll figure it out. Together."

Tears stain Carter's shirt but he doesn't seem to care, and I can't seem to stop them. Damn hormones. "I don't deserve you, but I love you so much."

"I love you too, sweetheart. My heart doesn't beat without yours beside it."

I plant a kiss on his chest. Right over his heart. Where mine will always beat beside his. "We're having a baby, Carter. You and me."

"You know what this means, don't you?"

My head pops up. "No. What?"

"We have to go and tell my family we're pregnant. And that includes Octavia."

Oh shit.

EPILOGUE CONTINUED

"She's going to be so mad at me," I say as we pull up in front of the Fritz compound.

"Yep. Both of us likely."

"You don't think she'll understand that you're not supposed to tell people until you hit the twelve-week mark?"

"No. We're talking about my mom here. She's going to be hurt, but she'll get over it and be crazy excited."

Lord, I hope so. After all, Carter and I are unmarried and don't exactly have plans to become so. I mean, Fritzes don't behave this way. Even Oliver is keeping his ring on Amelia's hand as a placeholder, though they're not technically engaged.

Which makes me wonder.

"You don't think Oliver spilled it already, do you?"

"If he did, I'll kill him, so he better not have."

Carter's parents returned from The Vineyard house back in early September. Some of Octavia's tests came back troublesome and her doctor wanted to start her another round of chemo even though the PET scan was inconclusive.

No one is really talking about it. I don't think any of us know what to say. There is so much fear swimming under the surface right now and every member of this family is on edge with it. If we lose Octavia Fritz, no one will be okay.

But knowing we're about to deliver baby news will hopefully be a bright spot for her. The woman's greatest wish is for her children to be happy in love and settled. Now here we are, and I can't wait to tell her, but I'm also scared because yeah, she'll be upset we held it back for so long.

Telling her feels better than telling my own mother. Octavia's reaction matters so much more to me. The woman who never failed to embrace me as one of her own and keep me in her home and her family.

Carter puts the car in park and comes around to help me out, not releasing my hand as we walk up to the house. "I have to tell Oliver myself. First."

Carter glances over, meeting my eyes. "You don't want to do it together? He is my little brother. If he doesn't like me there, I can just noogie him until he cries for mom like he used to when he was a kid."

"You're cute when you threaten violence, but I don't think that's the key to winning him over."

Carter tugs on my hand, yanking me into his chest. "Hey," he says, all big, dopey smiles. "Can you believe it? We're having a—"

"Are you just going to stand out here all day making googly eyes at each other?" Oliver comes out from the doorway.

"You mean the way you did with Amelia before you were even actually together?" Carter retorts.

"Exactly like that. It's gross. Grace can do better." He shifts his focus to me. "Honestly, you have the worst taste in men."

"Oh yeah, well, guess who's having my son?"

"You absolute motherfucker!" I yell, shoving Carter off me. "What is with you today? First the ultrasound and now this? You can't just yell that at him? That is not what we talked about."

"No. You said you had to tell him first. So I did. Now he knows it's a boy."

"Ugh. Carter, can you control yourself at all today?"

He's still grinning like a kid on Christmas morning. "Nope. Too damn excited, sweetheart." He grabs me by the waist and hauls back me into him for an epic, Hollywood-style kiss. If this were a movie, my foot would pop.

Except Oliver is standing on the massive front porch, his jaw unhinged and his eyes comically wide. I don't even think he's breathing. "He... a boy? Grace?"

"Now you've done it," I grumbled to Carter under my breath, as I pull away, addressing Oliver now. "Yup. We weren't going to find out and then Carter looked and yes. A boy."

Oliver blinks at me in rapid succession. "Who you're naming Oliver."

I roll my eyes at his statement. "Whose name is undecided. I'm only twelve weeks, Oliver. Give a woman a break."

He stumbles down the stairs of the porch, wrapping his arms around us both and hugging us fiercely. Oliver took the news about the pregnancy as well as he took the news of me and Carter being together. I never realized how overprotective Oliver is, but I'd be lying if I said I hated it.

Since then, Oliver and Carter have worked it out. You can't keep the two of them apart for long. Any of them really.

"Are you happy?" Oliver asks, his voice hoarse.

"Very. Another Fritz boy. Are you kidding?"

Oliver laughs, squeezing us both.

"Can I tell mom now?" Oliver asks, and I pinch his side, making him grunt and jump back.

"Absolutely not," I reply indignantly. "Carter told you the sex before I could, so now it's my turn. Dammit, you're both like a pack of wild puppies. Rein it in, boys."

Carter beams at Oliver. "She's going to be a great mom."

My heart swells at that, but there is no way I'm letting him know.

The Fritzes typically do Sunday dinners when they can all manage it—crazy healthcare worker schedules and all. But today is Friday and we requested everyone be here. No one other than Oliver, Rina, and Landon know I'm pregnant.

Carter made me promise the moment the ultrasound was over; we'd tell the rest all at once. So now, here we are.

Everyone is sitting out in the solarium, laughing and enjoying a bottle of wine when the three of us enter. Light classical music plays from built-in speakers in the corners, invisibly encased in the small strips of white wood that support the room. Other than that, it's all windows in here. Windows that hide nothing of the beautiful grounds of the compound.

Kaplan, Landon, Stella, Luca, Amelia, Layla, Rina, Brecken, Dr. and Mrs. Fritz. The gang's all here and suddenly, for the first time since this whole pregnancy began, I feel like I'm about to throw up. For the first time, I'm seeing them all with new eyes. My adoptive family feels like a term of the past. Now I'm meeting them as a woman not only dating their son, brother, uncle or friend, but pregnant with his child.

I survived so much heartache because of the people in this room. They assuaged the blows my parents' intolerance and eventual indifference left in me.

Carter takes my hand, bringing my knuckles up to his lips, his eyes staring deeply into mine. "Ready?"

I nod. My ability to speak is gone. Nausea swirls in my stomach as my nerves frazzle, my heart in my throat.

"There you are," Octavia says as she catches us entering the room, her smile so reminiscent of Oliver's, I can't help but return it. We greet everyone, hugs all around, as is customary with this crew. Even Dr. Fritz gives me a hug and a knowing wink as he looks at Carter, who hasn't released my hand. Carter is his father's younger doppelgänger. The only Fritz to get both the dark hair and dark eyes.

Finally we reach Octavia, who I note didn't rise off the chaise she's resting on to hug us. I bend down to hug her, only to have her drag me onto the cushioned seat beside her. "What about me?" Carter gripes, feigning indignation. "I don't get a hug?"

"I like Grace more than I like you," his mother teases, winking at him.

"Well that's good because she's pregnant. With my kid."

"Oh my freaking god, Carter." I glare at him. "What is wrong with you today? Have you no filter?"

He laughs, but the room is damn silent now.

"Carter? Grace?" That's Dr. Fritz who is now the spitting image of a man who looks like he just stumbled upon Medusa. We had told Carter's parents we were dating. They were still at The Vineyard then, but since they returned, we've been here together a few times as a couple. But this is different. So different.

Octavia takes my hand, hers bone-thin and ice cold. I squeeze it gently, turning to meet her eyes. I feel like a teenager telling my mom I got accidentally knocked-up as words start spewing from my mouth. "Well, you know I had a seizure about ten weeks back now and they gave me some medication that interacted with my Depo and..." My face falls to my hands. That was a total TMI if ever there was one.

"And you're pregnant," Stella cuts in, breaking the painful silence we seem to be creating all over the place. "Cool. I get a baby cousin. Can Layla and I babysit?"

"Yes," Layla agrees with a squeal of delight. "We'd be awesome babysitters."

Leave it to the teenagers to help things along.

"Wait. So this is true?" Octavia presses, touching the side of my face and forcing my gaze back to hers. "How far along are you?"

"Twelve weeks," Carter tells her, saving me for once today. "We wanted to wait to tell everyone until after the ultrasound today. Grace is superstitious like that."

"Twelve weeks?" Emotion clogs her voice as her other hand covers her lips, her eyes welling up. "You're twelve weeks pregnant with my grandchild?"

"Grandson, to be exact."

She sucks in a breath, her hand now trembling in mine. She looks over to Dr. Fritz who has come to stand beside us, hovering over us like a tall, dark shadow though the delighted expression now transforming his features softens him tremendously.

Suddenly I'm swathed in a hug, Octavia surrounding me with her arms as she starts to cry on my shoulder. "Thank you," she whispers to me. "You have no idea how badly I wanted this."

"You're not mad?" I check.

"Oh sweetie, I'm furious. I can't believe you waited so long to tell us. To tell us all of this."

"I'm sorry."

She laughs, pulling away and wiping at her face. "No, you're not, and just because you're giving me another grandchild, don't think I'm letting you get off easy. I'm in charge of decorating the nursery with you. Oh, and Amelia, Rina, and I will plan a baby shower. Here, at the house."

I can only shake my head. "Whatever you want." Because there is no way I could say no to her. Not now. Not ever.

Carter is surrounded by his brothers and sister, all giving him congratulatory hugs and asking a million questions. "Wait," she snaps out of nowhere. "When are you getting married?"

I choke on my tongue while Carter appears completely unfazed. She turns her glare on him.

"Carter James Fritz, you are going to propose to her, right? She's going to be the mother of your child."

"When would you like me to do that, Mom?" he asks in total seriousness. "Now? Here?"

"If you're asking my opinion, the answer is yes."

My lungs empty. "Um. We. I. I don't think. I'm not..."

"See, she's not ready yet," Carter cuts off my bumbling, taking my hand and kissing my knuckles. "But don't worry, Mom. I won't let that go for too long. Whether Grace likes it or not, one day, she'll be my wife." He winks at me. "I'll make sure of it. You're mine, Grace. Forever. There is no separating us now."

The End.

END OF BOOK NOTE

Thank you love readers for taking the time to read Doctor Mistake. I hope you enjoyed Carter and Grace's story. It was an emotional one for sure!

Carter, if you do not already know, was first seen in my book, Surrender which is written in Corrine Michaels' Salvation Society world. Carter is a side character in that and that's where his first love Alanna comes into play.

I cannot tell you how excited I was to finally get his voice on paper and I love how he and Grace were with each other. This book has a lot of tropes to it, but at its heart, it was a forbidden unrequited love. At least for Carter.

As a nurse practitioner myself, I wanted to make Grace's epilepsy as authentic as possible. I hope I did it justice. Their love while being somewhat easy between the two of them, had a lot of external complications. Plus a bitchy work colleague to deal with.

But one of my favorite things about this family is that no matter what, they always have each other's backs. They love their people and they love them fiercely.

Next up is Landon's book and let me tell you, that one is an emotional punch. You'll love him, I promise!

A special thanks to Danielle and Patricia for helping Carter and Grace's story be all that it turned out to be and to Joy for giving it the final look over. I don't know what I would do without you very special ladies!!

To my girls and my husband who are endlessly supportive, I love you. And to you my lovely reader for sticking with me on this amazing journey! I am so eternally grateful for you.

XO,

J. Saman

THE EDGE OF CHAOS

Prologue
RINA

The guy I've been staring at for the last hour doesn't even know I exist.

"Either go up to him or let it go," Savannah says, drinking her virgin martini with tiny, dainty sips as if the nonalcoholic drink will leave her hungover tomorrow when she's back to work and saving lives. I don't have the same issue. Tonight is my last night in this city. "He's seriously not worth your time. Hot, but not New Year's hookup worthy."

"Now it's become more of a game than anything else," I explain. "I'm tempted to chuck something across the room just to see how close I can get to hitting him."

"No. You're looking at him because he's easy pickings. If you stood in front of him he'd see cute boobs and blonde hair and do anything you asked of him. Bo-ring," she singsongs. "Besides, his dude-bro behavior suggests his blood alcohol level is likely higher than his IQ."

She's not wrong with that. On both accounts. Cute,

malleable, not-so-smart guys are the only ones I go near lately. The other ones... the smart, cocky, gorgeous, masters of the universe ones? Yeah, they're dangerous.

And I no longer have space or time for dangerous. With good reason.

"He's a douchemonger," my brother Carter states flatly. "If you're that determined to find a midnight kiss, keep looking. I'm giving that guy a hard no."

I snort. A midnight kiss? So cute. So brotherly.

What I'm looking for is my last night in New York to leave me with something other than what my previous three years have been.

Terror. Pain. Chaos. Torment. Nightmares.

I made it through when no one thought I would. When everyone told me there was no shame in transferring schools and coming back home. I stayed and I don't regret that. If anything, staying made me stronger. But tonight, I don't want to think about the past. Tonight, I want to have some fun and let loose in a way I haven't been able to before.

Having two of my five older brothers as well as Savannah and her husband here helps.

When your fortress is still in disrepair after someone smashed it down, you surround yourself with those who will keep you strong.

"Or maybe you should stop looking," my brother Oliver chimes in. "That guy is surrounded by easy pussy, Rina. He is the last dude in this bar you should be going for. Besides, you're leaving in the morning. It's not like anything can come of it."

Now I laugh under my breath because that's the only reason I'd even entertain going up to him. It's why he's perfect. I raise a pointed eyebrow at my brothers, speaking to such, and watch as Oliver frowns and Carter scowls, both attempting to hide it while they gulp whatever the hell they're drinking these days. Gimlets? Who cares?

"Tonight's the night for some fun," I announce, slamming my hand on the table with a bit too much gusto. It's an easy one to call. I have protection in the form of two older brothers. I have the anonymity of leaving this city in the morning. It's also been too long. Like seriously too long since anyone other than myself, my vibrator, and my gynecologist have seen my vagina.

I might also be rocking a slight buzz, but that's a different matter.

"How about you switch places with me," I suggest. "I've been stuck in this corner all night and I think that's been my downfall with the guy."

"I'll switch with you," Carter says, a warning in his eyes and in the grandmotherly finger he's directing at me. "But let it be known, I'm cockblocking you all night with that guy. I can't let my baby sister go home with a douchebag like that." Carter grabs me, practically by the scruff, and hoists me up and over his lap, scooting under me at the same time. My ass lands firmly on the edge of the booth, and suddenly it's like freedom is at my fingertips. "There, but I'm fucking serious about that guy."

"Yes," Oliver agrees wholeheartedly. "I'm with Carter on this one. Anyone but him."

Anyone but him. I can work with those terms. Still...

I open my mouth to explain to my lovely brothers that I'm twenty-two and more than capable of captaining my own romantic entanglements—okay, that's kinda a lie—when the game announcer cuts me off.

"Alright," he booms in a husky baritone that has been the delicious soundtrack of my night.

My previous seat left me at a disadvantage booth-wise, rendering it impossible for me to see his face, but his voice is like an erotic audiobook dream. As if proving my point, Savannah simpers, fanning her face that has instantly gone all flush.

"God, he's hot," she crows. "You should go for *him* instead. If only I weren't married and pregnant, I sure as hell would."

She gets a pinch to the ribs for that from her husband Royce, making her squeal and laugh. He leans in and kisses her lips, followed by her large round belly.

"This is the last round of the night since we're nearing midnight," the announcer continues. "Get your game cards ready and remember, phones face down on the table. No cheating allowed. First question: Do blondes really have more fun?"

My head flies up at that ridiculous, non-trivia question and instantly I lock eyes with our host, almost as if he were waiting for me to do just that. Deep and dark, but obviously blue, his eyes are like rare sapphires, equally as beautiful and alluring. They're also sparkling with mirth at my expense.

His gaze says *gotcha*. Mine says *I'm not amused.*

He quirks an eyebrow and I return the gesture, which for some reason makes him laugh and has me smiling. A tickling flutter fills up my belly at the sound. At the way he's looking at me.

"Oh my gosh." Savannah gasps, reaching over as best she can and smacking my arm hard before shaking it. "That was for you. He's totally flirting with you. Look at him. Like a cat chasing a mouse. Do you think he heard me?"

"No idea," I mumble, still unable to peel myself away. "If he did, he doesn't seem bothered by it."

"Just kidding everyone." He speaks into the microphone, his eyes gleaming with challenge. "That's not the real question. I was just trying to get someone's attention... *finally*." He smirks arrogantly, winking at me. "The real question is, who did Madonna kiss at the 2003 VMAs?"

"Easy as hell, guy," Savannah chirps. "I can go Britney and Christina all night long and I bet Royce would like to watch." She snickers at her own joke, writing her answer on her sheet and then glancing up at me with a tilt of her head. "And since we're talking about all night long and steamy, scandalous midnight kisses, Mister Sexy Voice up there should be the one you go for. If London were here and not suddenly in love with her long-lost wilds of Vermont guy, I'd push her all over him. Did you see that smile? And those eyes?" She fans her face again. "Add to that, he's making come fuck me eyes all over you. You should come fuck him—or come while he fucks you—and report back. It's like doing a service to all hitched-up, knocked-up womankind."

London is my BFF from college, Savannah's younger sister. But that's completely beside the point. Savannah is spewing all this at a decibel, I have no doubt the entire bar hears. Including Mister Sexy Voice himself.

"I think you've had enough of your faux-tini," her husband admonishes, sliding it away from her grabby hands.

"But I've only had that one."

"Which is already more sugar than you ever typically drink."

She starts pouting but quickly gets over it, overtly pointing at Mr. Sexy Voice's crotch and then over toward my vagina, in case I wasn't getting it before.

"Jesus, Sav, do you really have to?" Carter groans as he peeks over at her trivia paper, copying her answer onto his own sheet, because obviously he has no idea who Britney and Christina are. Sad, really.

Me? I haven't even been able to write down my answer yet because I haven't been able to tear myself away. Savannah is right. It is those eyes. And that confident smirk. And everything Savannah just said... the whole coming on his cock while he's fucking me thing?

I could go for something like that. No, scratch that, I *need* something like that.

As if reading my mind, he does this whole once-over thing,

his eyes lingering and slow, lazy yet scrupulous in their investigation. He's devouring. Hungry. Staring at me with such focused attention I can hardly breathe.

A large hand runs roughly through his dark-brown hair, brushing back some of the sweat-dampened strands that fell onto his forehead. It's a hot move. But then again, he's pretty damn hot. His face is a lesson in perfection with a straight nose and a stubbled, chiseled jaw cut with sharp, sloping angles that beg for my hand. Not to run along his delicious stubble. Not to feel the indents of his twin dimples. But to smack and redden for staring at me like he's got me all figured out while making my panties just the slightest bit wet with his cocky grin and surefire stare.

It's tempting and unsettling all at once.

His tall, muscular body clothed in dark-wash jeans and a black button-up that hugs shamelessly to his cut chest and abs moves in my direction. Suddenly, I'm less than two feet from him. I sit up straight, quirking my head in question as he approaches me. A waft of his scent hits me at this very moment and I take a deep inhale of spicy cologne, musky body wash, and sweat. Dear Lord, it's a scent that should be illegal.

"Don't know the answer, Angel?" His voice is a coarse rasp.

Angel? I inwardly smirk. I'm Persephone, lured into the darkness of Hades. My spring stolen from me with just one glance from him.

"Everyone knows it's Christina Aguilera and Britney Spears."

He grins, his eyes flashing about my face as if he's trying to memorize it. "But you haven't written your answer yet."

"I was getting there. Someone distracted me. Besides, isn't it considered unethical to help players out?"

"Who says I'm helping? All I asked was if you knew the answer."

"Which obviously I do. Besides, if you're not here to help then what are you doing?"

"Talking to the pretty woman I've been trying to catch the attention of all night."

"In the middle of a game?"

He shrugs an indifferent shoulder. "Couldn't care less. This isn't my real gig. I'm just filling in for a friend who has the flu, so I can be as unethical as I want." He dips down, getting a little closer. And suddenly it's like there is no one else here but us. All I see are the blue of his irises. All I feel is the weight and power of his smile that makes my heart flutter and my belly swoop with anticipation.

That is until cockblocking Oliver sets his elbows firmly on the table, jostling everyone's drinks, ready to go all big brother on his ass.

"Are we going to get our next question or are you going to flirt with her all night?"

The guy laughs without removing his eyes from me.

"Boyfriend?" he questions.

"Brother," I reply.

"And this guy?" He juts his chin in Carter's direction.

"Brother," Carter answers for me. "And just as protective as the other. So maybe it's best to get back to your job now?"

Mister Sexy Voice is undeterred as he gives me another slow perusal. "Wanna help me do the next question?"

I go to say no when Savannah practically launches herself across the table, her belly nearly toppling over half the drinks, and shoves me out of the booth. "Yes," she screams. "She'd love to."

I stumble a step only for the guy to catch me before I face-plant on the nasty bar floor. I swivel back to her with a pointed glare. "What the hell are you doing? I'm about to win this game and take all you suckers down."

She shakes her head dismissively, her eyes wide like she's trying to tell me something only to come off looking constipated. I frown, pinching my eyebrows in at her and she huffs out an exasperated breath. "Whatever. Who cares? He's hot. Forget winning and ignore your brothers. Here..." She slides my drink across the scratched-up table. "Finish this and go call some trivia."

I turn back to the guy, staring into his eyes. Around us the anxiously waiting crowd is starting to grow impatient, more demanding as time ticks by. He's even getting a few nasty comments slung his way in slurred tongues. The charming stranger is unruffled. He looks like he has all the time in the world.

"About to win, huh?" he questions.

"I'm a trivia master."

He grins at that, making those dimples pop. "What do you get if you win?"

"Bragging rights and free drinks."

"I'll buy you drinks."

"But you can't give me bragging rights."

He considers this. "Tell you what then. I've got a better idea." With that, he turns, and I sit back down, furiously writing my answer to the last question, and then wait for the next. "Alright, last question of the night. If the beautiful blonde sitting over there" —he points directly at me— "gets it correct, she's going to be my midnight kiss. If she wins the entire game, she's going to give me her name and number."

My jaw unhinges itself as my eyes pop open wide. A flush creeps up my face, but I quickly wrangle myself in check. Bold. I'll give him that.

"Wow." I think Savannah is for once stunned speechless.

"What about me?" another girl calls out with a flirty tweet to her voice. "What do I get if I win?"

The guy chuckles, running his hand through his hair and

mussing it all up in that sexy, disheveled way. "Sorry, she's the only one I want."

"Damn." Carter whistles through his teeth. "He's good. I'll give him that. He's really fucking good."

"Yeah," Oliver agrees. "Should we kill him now or wait?"

"Wait," we all say in unison. I take a sip of my drink, gearing up some of my courage.

"What if I don't agree to the terms?" I yell, sitting back in my seat and folding my arms, lifting a defiant eyebrow in his direction.

"You will," he assures me, having this conversation with a microphone in front of his lips and a crowded bar as his backdrop. He is pure confidence. Not even an inch of doubt in him. "You're a trivia master, right? Determined to win? That means you don't back down from a challenge. You won't throw the game with the risk of losing."

Damn him. He's right.

"But I tell you what, I'll give you an out after the game if you really want it." And just like that, the discussion is over as he lifts the card, scanning it. His eyes meet mine again, that grin making my insides flip. "Hg is the chemical symbol for which element?"

A loud cackle flees my lungs as I peek over at my brothers and friends, each of them with matching smug grins as we write our answer. "Like shooting fish in a barrel," Savannah exclaims.

"That's because we're a table full of nerdy doctors and nurses."

I nudge my shoulder into Carter. "Should I throw it?" I ask, already writing mercury down as the correct answer. It isn't in me. I couldn't do it if I wanted to. I'm way too competitive and anal-retentive for those kinds of shenanigans. It's annoying that Mr. Sexy Voice was able to pick up on that within seconds of talking to me. Clearly, I'm more of an open book than I like.

"Alright. Are you ready to go over the answers?"

A loud whooping cheer fills the bar as he goes over the answers to all the questions he's asked tonight. And when he's done, he saunters across the room once more, lifting my card out of my hand. He reads over all my answers one by one.

"You got them all right."

I nod. I already knew that. I know where the highest waterfall in the world is. I know the third sign in the Zodiac. I absolutely know who discovered Penicillin. I know what name Sean Combs is better known by. None of the questions he asked were much of a challenge. I am Wikipedia and an encyclopedia's cooler love child. My fascination with all things factual has only grown over the last three years but we don't talk about why that is.

Without a word, he takes my hand, hauling me up out of my seat and resting a hand on my hip as if to steady me. "So what do you say to my offer?"

I push his microphone down to his side. "What the hell are you doing?"

"Trying to get you to agree to that midnight kiss. I figure if I get everyone in the bar in on my plan you won't say no."

"You went to all this trouble just for a midnight kiss from me?"

"No. The kiss is just the start. I'm hoping you'll give me your name and number. If I'm really lucky, you'll go home with me and then allow me to make you breakfast in the morning."

I stare at him, utterly dumbfounded.

"What do you say?"

I gnaw on my lip. Who asks something like that of a complete stranger?

"I watched you come in tonight. You started dancing with your friend. Then eagerly dove into this game. I watched you the whole time because I couldn't take my eyes off you. I don't even care if your brothers are glaring at me. I think you're worth the risk."

I shake my head. His honesty is a bit too powerful. I'm not accustomed to it from men like him. "You don't even know me."

"So let me get to know you."

"I think I should go home instead."

"I think you should stay here with me." His head dips ever so slightly, his eyes bouncing down to my lips where they linger for a hellishly long minute before they find mine again. "I never approach women. Ever. Yet I came over to talk to you and now here you are." He grins, finding my lips once more. "It's like it's fate or something."

His long fingers splay along my hips, inching upward until they're practically wrapped around my waist. A shiver unexpectedly engulfs my body. He grins, his lips now hovering over mine. I taste the whiskey on his breath. The hint of cinnamon that's nearly lost beneath it.

I have no idea what I'm doing right now.

But I don't think I want to stop either. There is something about him drawing me in. Something exciting and daring. Tomorrow my life is going to be so very different than it is now. It's New Year's Eve. A night to throw caution to the wind. Possibly literally in this case.

What the fuck do I have to lose? It's not like I'll ever see him again.

"Don't leave," he whispers, his nose brushing against mine. "You'll always wonder about me if you do." It's like he's reading my mind. I will always wonder if by saying no to tonight I made a mistake. He shuts off the microphone and sets it down on our table. Then his now free hand dives into my hair. "Come on, Angel. Say yes to me."

I stare up into his oh-so-blue eyes and contemplate my next move. "It's only tonight."

He watches me closely. "Can I ask why?"

"You're insane. I mean, who does something like this? Who walks up to a total stranger and says those things? Who announces to a crowded bar you want to kiss me and get my name and number?"

"Me. But I'll prove you wrong and you'll stay." He says it so simply. Like that's just really how it is. I start to tell him that it truly has to be one night, crazy aside, when people begin to shout, *ten, nine, eight...* he cuts me off with, "It's a new year."

"Just about."

"I want to go into it kissing you."

Two, one. Happy New Year!

"Then do it. And after you can take me home."

A smile lights up his face right before his lips crash into mine. Now both hands are framing my face, holding me impossibly close as he consumes my mouth in a soul-splitting kiss I don't want to end. His tongue invades my mouth, tangling with mine, and my knees nearly give out beneath me. Holy Christ, Mister Sexy Voice can *kiss*. He groans into me, angling his head and deepening the connection, his hands slipping from my face back into my hair where he holds me tight.

Pulling back, he nips at my bottom lip. "Fuck." He licks his lips, tasting me on them. "I can already guarantee one night with you won't be nearly enough."

Except I already know one night is all we can ever have.

Want more of Brecken and Rina? Pick up The Edge of Chaos now!